LAST SARDANA

Book I

Ray Harwood

Matador
9 Priory Business Park,
Wistow Road, Kibworth Beauchamp,
Leicestershire. LE8 0RX
Tel: (+44) 116 279 2299
Fax: (+44) 116 279 2277
Email: books@troubador.co.uk
Web: www.troubador.co.uk/matador

ISBN 978-1784623-302

British Library Cataloguing in Publication Data.
A catalogue record for this book is available from the British Library.

Printed and bound in the UK by TJ International, Padstow, Cornwall

Matador is an imprint of Troubador Publishing Ltd

Followed by others in the series:
Sardana Encore
Sardana Renaissance
Letters to Peter
…and the Sun did Blush

To follow:
Sardana Shadows

Also by the same author:
Blokes, Jokes and Forty Stags
On the Left Hand Side of the Axis

Cover Design: Jacqueline Abromeit
at www.goodcoverdesign.co.uk

THE SARDANA 'INTROIT'

There must be something to be learned from the time when, sometime in the 16th century, the natural instincts of first one couple, then others, all entered into the fun and celebrations of a village festival, linking hands and forming a circle in which to express themselves in dance.

The Sardana, as it came to be called in the Catalan region of Spain, meant unity to those who were party to following the music with such certainty and daring, in response to the rhythm and interpretation of a travelling Cobla band.

Family units were often the village foundations from which to set up the circular team line and to begin, in unison, their small, concise, fairly simple formal steps. The Sardana has point and bounce, just as many families do (we hope), and the pace of the dance quickens and slows to allow emotions to spill out.

The "introit" is played by a flaviol and the dance starts with a tap on a small tambori drum. The circles then flow in traditional patterns, which it is customary for those participating to follow in a disciplined but fun way.

The Martinez family, at the beginning of the development of the Costa Brava region on the Catalan coast, were to follow that set tradition.

It was also evident that, to pen a story against such a backdrop, I too would need my chain if I were to try and follow, on my terms, uncharted and imaginary beginnings.

The support and encouragement of my wife Dean, who has been on hand to help with the spellings or to fill in the odd memory out of which to develop an original idea, have been beyond the call of any matrimonial vows. OK, so as I tend to write on vacation, which takes us worldwide, that has been some consolation. So hopefully chatting through breakfast in Jolly Harbour, Antigua, after dinner at Pelangi Beach in Langkawi, Malaysia, or over lunch in the Hotel Arts, Barcelona, has been something of a thank you and an apology for this intruding hobby.

Frequent accompaniment on rounds of golf at the Hotel Golf in Santa Ponsa, Majorca, the undisturbed peace and quiet at the poolside and the help on hand from Emma de Reus, with permission from her husband Peter, the proprietors, for the occasional Spanish translation have surely been a plus, to add more authenticity to the storyline. Busy writing days usually terminated with dinner on the terrace or superb steaks at El Ciebo or fish at Rheno, which in a different era could well have been caught by Paco, a major influence on the creation of this storyline.

None of this, though, would have been possible without the dedication of Alison Clarke (additional help with the Spanish), and Kristina Tang (with her Malaysian homeland knowledge and UK keyboard skills), and their assistance is gratefully acknowledged. Despite the fact that they are already acquainted with him, they are all keen to once again meet Peter Martinez.

I would have been completely lost without Linda Lloyd's hugely helpful criticisms and polishing, which show up her immense editing talent.

INTRODUCTION

Who can really tell what influence there is on an unborn child by the activity of the mother prior to releasing her offspring into the hard, tough world? But there is, undoubtedly, a relationship – usually built for life.

In Rosas, on the north-eastern coast of Spain, Pedro "Peter" Martinez's lifestyle certainly replicated the passion, creativity, bonding and fun generated by his greatest fan and most severe critic, his mother Maria. Through her hereditary love of joining the swirling circles of the Sardana with her fellow Catalans at the Saints' Day celebrations in her Spanish village, Peter's roots were permanently implanted.

The reality of the life Peter was born into was taught to him not only by his mother and father, but also by all those around him as he passed through adolescence. The discovery of his manhood and natural compassion for his fellow inhabitants of the planet, and the freeing and nurturing of his super-creative talents, were part of a pedigree for success.

Peter's architectural ability removed him from his Spanish homeland and its gypsy influences, spiriting him off to career success and wealth in London and Malaysia; yet he was always magnetised back to the biggest love in his life, Maria, his doting mother… and the early promise of a young gypsy girl, and all the love and hatred she embraced.

And thereby hangs this tale.

CHAPTER 1

Perhaps it was a hangover from his parents' choice of first birthday present to him, but Pedro Martinez seemed always to have thought in shapes and dimensions. He possessed that sense to a far greater extent than those to whom he had to explain his own interpretation of design or his appreciation of music and art, or even the personal pleasure he derived from an attractive female body.

Maria and Paco Martinez had not been able to afford to buy Pedro the toys imported into Spain's various "Bravas" in the 50s and 60s. (These were seemingly just for the consumption of kids on family holidays with a bounty of grandparental pocket-money to spend.)

Their first gift to him had been a kaleidoscope, followed by a simple jigsaw, then more complex ones once he displayed a natural ability for matching shapes, not to mention pelmanism. The larger, grander puzzles helped to pass away the winter evenings while his father was at sea, as he and his mother had never been exposed to the temptation of becoming slaves to that tyrant, Television, in its early days, principally because the little family in their fisherman's cottage had no money for such new-fangled luxuries.

They had a supply of hot water that fed the kitchen, into which they had installed a sparkling new stainless steel sink. A priority on Maria's intense saving programme – into which she religiously put some of her earnings from the couple of cleaning jobs she did to supplement Paco's income from his fishing boat – was to build an extension to the cottage big enough to house a shower. Perhaps also a bath, which she always hinted would be an added bonus.

Maria and Paco's first source of joy in married life had in fact been the use of the shower on their wedding night in Paco's brother's small guest-house further south on the Costa Brava, as it was then being commonly called.

Their second joy was the birth of their son and heir Pedro in 1937, 40 weeks to the day after they had worked out there was just about room in the mosaic faced cubicle in the corner of the bedroom in the little cottage Marco had built in the grounds of his property for the two of them to shower together.

Maria's attention to the cleanliness of her young husband's body was in itself fun, and a revelation, after the solemnity of the wedding service, which Maria had meticulously planned, despite a fairly passive bridegroom. To be fair, Paco was mainly charged with organising the festive side of the event. The pride and excitement of taking his beautiful bride into the open courtyard, which was part of the original Martinez family house, was the centrepiece of the Catalan celebrations, from which to launch the young couple's future together.

The overture to the fiesta had started in a dignified manner: Maria in her white silk dress and simple veil and Paco in his pristine white shirt, black trousers and slim black tie. The young couple first invited their respective parents, then bridesmaid attendants, the groom's close friends, the aunts and uncles, cousins, friends, neighbours and the other villagers interested in the free-flowing availability of sangria, to join their Sardana circle in the traditional Catalan formation.

With linked hands, the human circle perambulated, moving to the left in the precise step sequences that had been the format through centuries of performance. In time, the call of the flute and the faster beat of the drum encouraged more frenzied leaping and stepping in time with the small but specialist orchestra. That was the downside, where Paco was concerned, as the heat generated and the sweat expelled flushed out the smell of his years at sea and the handling and cleaning of fish.

In the overall gathering, Paco's body odour was not conspicuous; but later, alone with his young bride, it certainly was. Hence the shower had been most essential to their first Catholic coupling, and through that experience Maria developed a strong enthusiasm for cleanliness, to complement the passion she'd had for her husband since their teenage years.

The beauty of those moments was to stay with Maria for a lifetime. Cleanliness became her fetish. She washed and re-washed Pedro as a baby, initially using a plastic container that was one of a number Paco had bought to put his catch of sardines and ice into, for daily presentation at the fish market. Of course, it had never been used for fish and it was to be many years later that Pedro, as a maturing young man, learnt the origins of his very first bath. It had been a better alternative than the original ceramic sink which she had ruled not to be good enough as the daily font for her joyous child.

Maria's voice was very much the foundation of Pedro's early years, and that was to stick through a lifetime. Paco was not the disciplinarian in the family. In some respects, his teachings to his son from a young age were restricted to the university of life. True, he taught Pedro rules and conventions to train him for a later life based on inheriting his father's trade of fishing and hunting.

But it was to his mother's commands that Pedro most reacted. It was clear that it was her clamouring for knowledge that had entered Peter's genes, and her inner instinct that a healthy body would produce a healthy mind backed up her demands that she firmly implanted for his personal hygiene.

It was only later in life, when Peter was near to death, that the gentle hands of Gina Faro were to remind him that the daubing of a soft sponge worked the same wonders his mother had promised him at the age of three. As the enforced sedation wore off, his awakening brain opened the memory bank of his mother supervising his ablutions: prior to going to school for the first time, getting muddy playing football at the age of seven.

By eight and nine he had been left more to his own devices.

"Lavate bien," was the repetitive maternal command.

"Si, mama," was the least contentious response.

However, Pedro's developing analytical mind could not reason why the hell she would not let go for just one morning. A growing kid, even one of just nine years old, could tell that if he didn't break the mould soon, he was under the thumb for life.

Why was washing his neck more important to his mother's day than making sure the sun would rise and warm the air, and bring healthy fruit to the vines and olive trees, which supplemented Papa's fishing livelihood?

Why re-visit that same neck before going to his extremely firm bed, which consisted of a cut-down barn door and a couple of blankets handed down from relatives who had saved up for a modern replacement? (They had bought a divan base with spring mattress, which, with a headboard carved out in the original joiner's shop in downtown Gerona, was an early sign of becoming middle class in any village in northeast Spain, long before the desire to replace the larder and its fly-deterrent netting with a fridge.)

Why the obsession with cleaning up part of his body which, in any event, didn't get that dirty during the day and which certainly was unlikely to be scrutinised by the school inspector in the middle of the night?

His mother always seemed to want to quash Pedro's natural desire to rebel. If he didn't finish the plate of food put in front of him, the threat was that the school inspector would be called and he would get a thorough ticking off. If his school shoes were dirty, that same ogre would have something to say about that. He was bright enough to wonder how the priest had got away with his lack of attention to his own foot attire. Pedro was not to know his mother was sowing foundations from which he would reap rewards in the future, if God and luck happened to come together on a sufficient number of days.

He had to be tough to deal with the new routine his mother had now dreamt up to wash below his armpits.

For God's sake, was nothing to be private from now on? He knew he was growing hair under his arms, but how would that get dirty? The only time it would be exposed was when he went swimming. The seawater was always clear and fresh on the little beach just outside Rosas, at the end of the track that dissected the grapevines and the olive trees, and which flooded in winter when the storms over-spilled from up in the backcloth of mountains.

His mother would never give up on finding a new fetish, or so it seemed.

"Y usas jabon en tus axilas… si… non…"

"Si, mama."

That was his easy way out; if he didn't confirm he had, he was definitely under threat of the penalty of not being allowed to go to the jetty to welcome back the boats and, in particular, the one captained by his wonderful father.

Papa never seemed the slightest bit concerned about Pedro's washing ability or state of cleanliness. He oozed love and affection for his growing son and the grubbier the boy got, the more pleased Paco seemed to be.

Pedro never, ever forgot the day his father had taken him into the hills to shoot a boar for the Santa Maria Fiesta. They'd had a lean day until about 3.30pm, when suddenly they'd come across a suitable prospect for the intended communal table – two boars and their offspring.

Pedro's father put a finger to his mouth: not a sound, he indicated, or the boars would flee and there would be no festive meal.

Pedro's natural instinct was to hope that his father would have spared the animal threesome by firing into the air and scaring them back up into the hills; then, perhaps, explaining that there is sometimes greater joy to be experienced in saving a life and losing the hunt. Pedro felt he personally would glean more joy from that result than from being on the winning end of a killing.

The sounds of the shots from both barrels of the family shotgun rang out. One was aimed at the father, another at the mother. Hopefully the time delay for reloading would allow the piglet to get the hell out of there, Pedro thought. But like a lamb, or a child in need of parental guidance so as to not miss washing his neck, the instinct of the dependent boar was to just sit and stare at the blood flowing from its parents' bodies. It was not conscious of the threat in the bushes from Pedro's father and the lethal weapon he had now recharged.

Pedro thought the echoes of the third shot would never stop reverberating in his ears. Transfixed by a sudden deafness, he watched as the piglet's legs buckled, as if in silent slow motion in one of his grandfather's films, which before his death he had proudly shown on the day of the birth of Christ each year. The young boar's eyes had glazed over. Its body was no longer nubile as it joined its parents, who by then were each transformed by an instant rigor mortis.

"I'll carry the two," came his father's voice. "I'll lift the piglet onto your shoulders, my son. This will be a feast beyond the expectations of our family. The village will celebrate with us on our lucky day."

As they made their way back through what must have been ten or 12 kilometres of rough terrain, Pedro felt the first sense of moisture running down his back. His own sweat he would comfortably have tolerated, but it was mixed with the weeping blood from the young boar.

It was Maria who greeted the hunters on their return, scolding her husband for allowing their son to be tainted by the trickles of blood that had effused from the piglet's wounds on the victory march home. Despite a kiss on each of her husband's cheeks for the joy he would bring to the village fiesta, she stepped back and said, "It is too early for our son to learn."

"Now go and fill the galvanized zinc bath in the garden and ensure you scrub your whole body, dear little Pedro," she ruled. "If you're not clean, you won't go to the fiesta."

It was from that day on that Pedro's father encouraged time to be put into the boy's education beyond his learning about history at school. Being taught to count fascinated the young lad particularly, and whilst the other boys in his class seemed content to live with the relativity of mathematics – that given three baskets of grapes, one may contain more by visual arrangement than the other two, which appeared to be the same – Pedro was only satisfied when able to assess positively the weight of each basket so that, at the age of nine, he was able to make a scientifically based analysis of the situation.

His father's approach went beyond that. He taught Pedro logic, and about natural phenomena. They practised reading cloud formations and interpreting the winds over the terrain. He explained that if the wind blew from the sea, his return from the essential fishing trips would be faster than if the wind held the fleet off the land.

"When your mother allows you to meet me at the jetty, be sure to study the way the pines are leaning. If they arch to the hills, run to the quay – we may be home early. If they bow to the waves, walk while we toil to get home. When we hunt boar, as we did on the day of Santa Maria, be sure always to have the wind blowing into your face. That way, you'll smell the boar, rather than the prey discovering your presence and avoiding capture."

Pedro learnt that his father was receptive to his desire to learn and welcomed his son's questions.

"Papa," Pedro plucked up courage to ask one day, "you remember the day you shot the two parent boars and you had no more cartridges loaded? You re-loaded and killed the young boar. Why didn't you satisfy yourself with the two and let the baby go free?"

"If the baby had gone free, it would have had no protection and would have fallen prey to other animals in the great food chain. Kill the whale when you can, as long as you follow behind with a net to gather the small fish, of which the whale would have deprived you. So the sacrifice of that one extra shot served a dual purpose: ensuring that it was we who killed that boar, rather than the animals lurking in the shadows; and our friends in the village gained respect for our hunting skills and, in their turn, will owe our family a favour."

Pedro couldn't help but think that if they had not shot the third defenceless animal, he would have had an easier journey home and would have been saved the discomfort of a cold bath in the back yard. But maybe his father was right.

His loving mother's voice was the first thing he heard that day after the fiesta in 1949. A day to change his life.

"You're dreaming, Pedro!" his mother shrieked. "If you're going to meet your father's boat, you'd best hurry. You need breakfast."

The sun was rising as Pedro sat down at the kitchen table, which was covered by an oil cloth. His mother had prepared a plate of fresh figs from the tree in the yard and a stick of bread she had collected from the patisserie before Pedro woke up.

"Did you hear the storm last night?" she asked Pedro. "The rain was torrential and the sheet lightning lit up the whole sky. The animals were screeching."

Pedro had been too exhausted to have been disturbed. The night before had been the celebration of Thanksgiving to God for the harvest – the one night of the year when the whole village, children as well, ate communally in the village square and then danced in ever-entwining circles of linked arms and flailing feet in non-stop celebratory Sardanas.

The lecture continued.

"The cobbles will be slippery. Mind how you go. Help Papa with the fish, but be sure you're back to school for nine o'clock. Otherwise I'll have the school inspector here asking why I've kept you away."

Pedro hugged his mother's waist. Said thank you for breakfast. Slipped on his flip-flops and ran off down the cobblestone pathway to the jetty.

The wind was still blowing hard across the groves. Some of the trees bent inland, others out to sea. It was all confused. Pedro knew his Papa would have some real sailing to do. He'd be tacking all the way back to harbour. Pedro settled on the rocks beneath the beacon where he always squatted to get first sight of the fleet coming round the promontory. With the wind blowing in the direction it was that day, he'd probably hear the sound of the deep throbbing piston engines even before the three or four fishing boats came into sight.

The sun was higher than usual and the boats had still not come into view.

Pedro thought for a while about the God his parents so fervently believed in and upon whom their life was so modelled. As the gulls hovered above the choppy sea in anticipation of the scraps they would be thrown as the nets were emptied and cleaned, Pedro questioned why God would have created such a storm after the celebrations of the night before. It had, after all, been a Sunday of Thanksgiving. The priest certainly seemed to have acknowledged that by the fact he had cleaned his shoes and joined the village in drinking sangria after evening mass. He had even joined in the Sardanas and surprised Pedro with his nimbleness of foot, which he noticed as their respective circular chains passed.

After one gyrating carousel, where Pedro had to reach up high to link his hands with his mother on the one side and her lazy cousin on the other, as the Catalan pipes and flutes reached a crescendo and brought that set to a halt, the circle he was in stopped immediately behind the one the priest had linked into.

Father Amadis had turned and, recognising Pedro, and probably due to the fact that he'd had a jug of sangria too many, said, "Now there is another great judgement of our God. He has halted me into the arms of his disciple, Peter." He leant forward and pulled Pedro's head into his own chest. He kissed the thick black hair and said, "So bless you, Peter."

Pedro looked up and said, "But Father, I am Pedro."

The priest roared with laughter and, pulling the boy's ear, said that Jesus's disciples had only covered a limited area of the earth, and numerically they had remained as the twelve. But it was he, Pedro, and others who were now the generation of disciples and when in Rome they would take an Italian name, in France, his Pedro would be a Pierre, in the English-speaking nations he would be Peter. "So, young man, be ready to spread your wings and answer your calls. Be Pedro for as long as you can, because that will mean you are within our shores. But never shirk the opportunity to travel. It will always be your good self you'll see in the mirror, but as I see you as a traveller, I'll call you Peter. Just at the fiesta, anyway."

Pedro wasn't sure he had understood that and was still puzzling as to why God had whipped up such an angry storm after such a night of celebration. Especially as Pedro had rarely seen his parents happier together.

His mother and father made a majestic pair. Maria had made herself a new black dress. She had apparently seen a photograph of Audrey Hepburn in a newspaper left in the local bar she cleaned on a Thursday night for her cousin's husband. Pedro thought that the skirt was rather short, but who was he to judge? It just looked short compared with all the other women's skirts and

Sunday best frocks. There were no sleeves to the dress, allowing her shapely arms to be seen. She had pinned her hair high, showing her angular cheeks, high forehead and long neck to the full. Pedro always liked her hair that way. She had worn her one pair of high heels, so Pedro knew it was a real celebration.

His father wore black, crisply creased trousers and a white shirt. To be fair, so did all the other men, but somehow Paco Martinez stood statuesque among them. There was not a ripple of fat on his body. Where he had rolled up his cuffs, his arms were chestnut coloured and his hands were huge and rough to the touch. He was clean shaven and more than Pedro's eyes followed his bouncy Sardana steps with his strong arms and hands held aloft.

They had eaten well. The fish, which Pedro was sure could only have been caught by his father, was fresh and grilled on the open-topped, cleaned-out oil barrels, once used to carry fuel for the fishing boats, now cut virtually into two. There was lamb and pork and beef with salads and vegetables. The flans and apple tarts seemed to just keep coming. Pedro was sneaked a glass of white wine and was told not to let anybody know it was other than apple juice.

In between Sardanas, his parents sat holding hands. His father occasionally brushed the back of his mother's neck. Although Pedro hated to see it, he knew that they touched lips from time to time and he did hope that nobody else had seen them.

"Do you have to fish?" he heard his mother say.

"My darling, how will we buy food and renovate the house, provide Pedro with school clothes if we have no fish to sell?"

"I'll do some more cleaning for my cousin's husband. Don't go to work, we're having such fun. The tide will take you away from me before midnight. It'll be like the fairytale of Cinderella, except I won't lose my shoe at midnight, I'll temporarily lose my love."

"But like a princely frog, I'll be hopping at your door in the morning with a few peseta notes in my hip pocket."

They pushed Pedro into a children's Sardana ring and as he whirled around in the image of his father, he glimpsed his mother and father holding hands, silhouetted by the full moon as they knelt amidst the pines at the edge of the vineyard.

Pedro had kissed his father fondly and watched him walking down the cobble path towards the harbour at about 11.30pm, which was late for him to be allowed up. Paco turned and waved once, but did not look back again and so missed the second sweeping movement of his son's hand, as if it was a flag at the end of his outstretched arm. Maria put her arm around Pedro's shoulder, which she noticed was considerably higher now since a youthful growth spurt, and ushered him into the house. She reassured Pedro that his father would have received his second wave in spirit, if not in fact.

"Lavate bien, Pedro. No te olvides tu cuello, y usas jabon…"

Before she could finish, Pedro pleaded, "Not tonight." His mother looked up at the clouds racing across the moon and said, "OK, chiquito."

CHAPTER 2

He wasn't very good at judging time. He knew roughly how long a class was at school, but he could tell the fleet was getting very late. From where he was sitting on the rocks he could see that a number of people from the village were gathering on the harbour wall. The gulls seemed impatient. Pedro's lips were getting a bit sore. It wouldn't be long before he needed to spend a penny.

At first he thought it was a gull squawking. Then he was sure he heard his name. That is, Pedro, he thought to himself, not that stupid foreign name the priest was going on about. "Pedro, come here quickly."

He heard his mother's voice, turned and saw her part-walking quickly and part-running towards him. Gone was her pinned up hair and new dress. She was wearing denims and a thick cream knitted sweater she had made through last winter.

She hugged Pedro as they met. There was a desperation about her breathing. "No sign of papa, eh?" she said, trying to be reassuring.

"Papa's very late, isn't he?"

"Don't worry, dear, there are the four boats together. They've all got radios so they can talk to each other. Cousin Pablito has been to the coastguards and they haven't received any contact, which is a good sign. I expect they sheltered from the storm in one of the bays. But listen, you should be at school. We'll have the…" She saw the look of anguish on his face. "OK, we'll give it half an hour. We'll go and wait on the harbour wall together."

Paco Martinez had his own boat. He was the second most experienced of the five captains who made up their little fleet, intending to trawl as many sardines out of the local waters as possible. Their bonus would be the odd catch of John Dory, which always got a good price from the hotel industry developing on the coast of Spain, north of Barcelona and up to the foothills of the Pyrenees. In the season they used to drop a few lobster nets as well, to pick up on the way back in the shallower water when they hugged the coastline nearer their home harbour.

They were not rich, but it was a living.

Paco was the younger of the two Martinez brothers who originated from down the coast just outside Palafrugell. Elder brothers always seemed to have the perks and Marco had been left the family land in his parents' will with an additional note, by way of an expression of a wish, that Marco should do all necessary to support his younger brother in making a living either on the land or in another way.

Paco had met Maria at school, sparking something of a family feud, as Marco too had declared a soft spot for her. The young stags had almost come to blows until Maria made her choice. She and Paco thought it best to distance themselves from the family silver and exited up the coast to Rosas.

Marco abided by his father's wishes and gave his brother sufficient to buy the fishing boat so he could make a living and support his bride.

Paco was certainly the better sailor, although the Martinez family had taken to the sea for years. Originally, they had a couple of two-man rowing boats which they took out two or three kilometres or so around the headland, where the fish used to be fooled by the shaft of light emitted from the large oil hurricane lamps mounted on the stern, believing it to be the moon's rays.

The Martinez patriarch then graduated to a long boat with a 250 cc diesel outboard with an investment in nets. Paco sold that and now had a naval destroyer by comparison. It was a tug to the uneducated observer, part of a fleet of a dozen or so believed to have been "acquired" by a fairly dodgy German entrepreneur who had managed to finesse a deal with the original owners in Singapore. Doubtless, they had originally been painstakingly constructed in the manner passed down by generation to generation by local Malaysian labour on the Malaccan coast. They were made from trees logged and crafted into seaworthy, deep-water hulls.

Paco always sailed in the same fleet of five, sometimes four if sickness struck one of the other captains, or in the more likely event that, just as he was ready to leave home to sail, his wife, or the infamous village hooker, had enticed him into bed for a bit of trawling of a more intimate nature, and made him miss the tide.

José G, for Gonzales, had not shown up. Paco, Miguel, Juan and Manuel laughed about that as they met with their customary hugs of camaraderie on the quayside. "The randy bastard was OK at the fiesta, certainly well enough to visit our table and drink most of a jug of sangria," Miguel mused.

"I'd bet a hundred pesetas he's in the sack with his missus. You'd think she'd be satisfied with four kids and wouldn't let him miss the income it looks like we might get tonight, boys!" Paco added.

Two hours out and the radios crackled away.

"What a headwind, eh!"

"I've known this before at the full moon."

"There they are. Can you see the reflection on the surface between the rollers?"

"By the life of Mary, those stupid fish are a field of silver!"

Paco took control. They knew from experience the radios were not now for idle chat, but were the point of command and income.

"Miguel, you lay up on my port side. Juan, Manuel, go starboard. We'll line out on them."

"Lay good, full-sized nets. Throttle back onto my stern."

The radios crackled into superfluous silence.

They all knew the procedures from there on in. They would all dress in military fashion against Paco's boat as a marker and move slowly forward in a straightish line, or as straight as possible into a strong headwind with two metre high waves. Their nets would cover a good 520 metres of water. Hardly a single sardine would escape that trawl.

They would advance a couple of kilometres and would by then instinctively know their nets were brimming. They would ease off the throttle and with each of their young deckhands, apprenticed to take over when their captain had had enough, would set the deck hoist running and haul in the catch.

A second trawl was rare. Occasionally, if they felt lucky, they would roll open the nets, dumping the fish onto the deck imprisoned within the high solid surrounds and, as the catch gasped their last breaths and flipped their final triple salcos, they would clean up the nets for a second foray.

The background crackling noise of the radio gave way to a lone voice. Paco's. "Who's for another run?"

Miguel was the first to respond. "It's a hell of a force of wind. We're fairly loaded. Do you really want to?"

"Come on! We don't see fish like this every night. It's God's message for Santa Maria."

"I'm on!" Juan crackled. "Last night cost me a week's wages anyway."

"I'll go along with the crowd," came an indifferent response from Manuel.

"So three say yes. What do you think, Miguel?"

There was far too much esprit de corps for Miguel to duck out. "OK," he piped through to the others, "but we'll be loaded high going into the headwind. Let's turn about and then we'll have the wind behind us to sail back. Jesus Christ Paco, have you seen the speed of the clouds against the moon? I'd still question the need for more."

"We take when we can, my friend. I'll buy you paella for breakfast."

"You're on," Miguel replied, not for a moment wanting to think about food.

The fleet was still in close formation from the previous trawl. They had a second rehearsed routine to follow to turn about.

The port anchor boat would break left in a fairly wide 180-degree turn. Paco would do a tight turn. Number three position would wide sweep and come between the previous one and two positions. Starboard number four would tight turn. It was a 30-minute manoeuvre. The waves were undoubtedly higher and there was no sign of a cloak of silver floating around the surface.

It seemed from the silence that it was Paco's call. "OK friends," the others heard him say above mega radio interference. Heading back with a tail wind made the fleet rise and dip to a greater extent. The extra tonnage of fish already on board was there to be felt. The sky was livening up like the backcloth to an old Charlie Chaplin film. Flash lightning flickered some three miles away.

Paco had no greater idea than the others where the sheen of sardines was within the swelling water. He relied on his instinct as he used his narrow shaft of hunter's vision to pick out the spot and to choose the moment. He shuddered and momentarily felt the warmth and comfort of his marital bed.

"Nets out!" he commanded.

The captains, as one, wedged their various makeshift devices into the capstan wheels that controlled the rudders, which would enable them to go onto an effective auto-pilot, freeing them to make their way from the wheelhouse at the aft to lend an experienced hand to their one-man crews as they lay out the nets.

The quartet formation had Manuel on Paco's port side, then Juan and Miguel to his left.

The nets were hard to lay as the waves whipped up by the tail wind stopped them from trailing out behind the heaving tugs like graceful bridal veils. But soon they were all out.

In the darkness of the storm, Paco, still up front and out of radio contact, could be seen indicating with both arms aloft to push forward. The captains scurried across the lethal decks, semi-glazed with the contrasting shimmer and dullness of the previous catch, now without life. From experience, Paco had in mind to draw away from the nets, releasing them and dragging them into a more useful purpose than their current restricted position, which was being forced by the turbulent swell against the aft of each boat.

The various captains, back in their wheel houses as if released by some imaginary starting pistol at the start of an Olympic relay race, together accelerated in a combined forward move within seconds of each other. The effect was to create a balloon of nets, rather like a train behind a wedding gown, but below the surface of the sea, as they spread behind their respective brides as if held there by a ghostly throng of page boys and maids.

Paco's eyes pierced the darkness ahead. Momentarily, he thought the flash lightning must almost be directly over Rosas and his little family tucked up in their beds. At least he had his son to take over the family boat when his own strong torso gave way to the hard life he led. He had always been sorry Maria had not been able to face a second child after the tough experience she'd endured giving birth to Pedro.

The reality of the night was suddenly upon him. He was sure the last flash of lightning had reflected off the scaly backs of their unsuspecting prey. The moon broke through the racing clouds. There was a perceptible drag on the nets.

The back of his tug dipped, raising the boat's nose as though to sniff the potential success. The wind acknowledged momentarily by abating. All captains suddenly felt their stomachs churn. If they hadn't experienced that moment before, they had heard their fathers, uncles and cousins tell them about it.

"When the wind blows wildly at force from the north into Africa and the eye of the storm is south, south-west, there is some sort of demon force that holds the breath as if to turn its own head out of the force of the gale. When it looks due east, the storm changes direction and, having had its moment of respite, it turns and blows with great vengeance from the east to the west, crashing its roller coasters ahead into the rocks and the coves and the inlets in its path. You must brace yourself, stand firm, and to pray would not be a disadvantage."

The line abreast of captains knew this was one such moment.

Manuel's boat was on the exposed flank and suddenly, it was like being rammed by some torpedo on the surface of the sea. The wedge of his lucky olive branch auto-pilot device, which he had used to free him to spread out his nets, was stunned out of position, clattering onto the deck of the wheelhouse. The wheel spun freely and out of control. The rudder reacted accordingly and went into freestyle too.

Moments before, in the split seconds of the lull in the wind, Paco screeched out above the roar of the waves, "Cut the nets!" Miguel and Juan had known that was the right thing to do before Paco's command had reached them.

Manuel was stunned by the sudden broadside he had suffered, and although even he had known instinctively what to do, or had heard Paco's command, he was too out of control to react.

As if his boat was the last skater to join the spinning line at the Christmas ice show, he knew the wind was blowing his vessel through an arc too close for comfort in the configuration they had set up. He dived across the wheelhouse to take control of the rudder, but could not reach the wheel and lay helpless on the deck as his tug continued in free rein.

Paco thought his young deck hand, the son of his good friend in the boatyard, had done really well to cut the nets free. Lamentably, in a split moment, he realised not only had his second opportunity to create a record haul slipped through his fingers, but now he had the worry of affording replacement nets.

Sensing more happening than was apparent to the aft, he turned sharply to look to his left. There, approaching at what he knew was an alarming rate, was Manuel's ghost ship, which conjured up the sight of a chariot at the end of an octopus's limb at the local touring August fair, whip-lashing towards him and his boat.

There was no momentary remedy. He prayed to God to soften the impact. The nose of his tug was still high and the bow of Manuel's boat was approaching below the waterline of Paco's floating prison. There was a dull lasting thud as the two vessels collided. Paco and his mate were thrown to the decks, sliding amongst the first successful catch.

The hull of Paco's boat was opened to the wild sea through a hole punched into the ageing Malaysian timbers, crafted to withhold the force of many a turbulent sea, but incapable of any real resistance to the force generated between the like-for-like materials.

Miguel had had perhaps 20 seconds' advance warning of the dangers passing down the line abreast. He instinctively steered to the starboard and picked up the changed direction of the tail wind. He had no time to look back, but sensed drama.

Juan had about 15 seconds to react. He too spun the wheel hard down to the right, praying as he did that the links and connections to the rudder worked positively. Paco's boat lurched down to the left as water entered the open hull. The nose started to dip as the catch of sardines all slid to the bow.

The otherwise faithful tug rolled to the left, tipping fish, captain and crew towards the protective deck's solid side rails. None of those at sea were counting but within those seconds, during which they hailed their God in prayer and mentally submitted their requests for help, the boat was sucked down into the depths.

Manuel, although still horizontal on the deck, saw this disaster in slow motion without realising his vessel too was getting lower in the water. There was a sudden sound, like water draining out of a bath. Simultaneously, the chasm, caused by the sub-oceanic vacuum when the depths dragged Paco's boat towards the seabed, caused a huge wave to wash over Manuel's vessel and the sea entered into the hatches left open to receive the catch. The nose of the boat dipped and within a minute the whole vessel dived into the cold ocean. It sank too.

The radio crackled. "Shit, Miguel," Juan almost confided and then sobbed.

"Miguel, oh my God! Have you looked back? Paco and Manuel have been sucked into the sea!"

"Oh my God, Juan! Oh my God!"

Young Carlos, Paco's deck hand's father from the boatyard, was there by now. Manuel's wife was busily chatting away to Juan's father and Miguel's other half, with their two-year-old.

Maria and Pedro were as tense as the others. There was still a stiff breeze blowing, although the tempest of a few hours earlier had died down.

A couple of local dogs started barking. The younger villagers who had gathered, with their keener senses, thought they could pick up on the *thud, thud, thud* of diesel engines, just around the headland.

"Look!" shrieked Juan's father, himself an ex-fisherman who had passed the family boat on to his son. He knew the feeling well from the reverse incoming perspective of rounding the headland to bring the harbour into view. There were always some people waiting with a welcome Thermos of coffee on a cool winter's morning, iced water in the summer.

The fellows who ran the fish market always set up at about 5.30am, ready to display the catch. They would service about ten boats these days. A far cry from only a decade or so before when the demands were mainly for the private family plate. Now they made additional money meeting the requirements of the hotel industry. Even the growing population of Barcelona needed more fish and was prepared to pay for the extra haulage down the coast.

Today, the managers had left their static positions behind the desks on which they would normally be preparing to deal with the sale proceeds from anxious buyers. The air all around was filled with an uneasy expectancy.

Those with a more practised ear chatted secretly between themselves. "That's not the throb of four or five boats," one said knowingly to another.

"Only four went out. José Gonzales is over there. He must have been sick."

"Well, it's still not four. Maybe three or even two."

There were gasps as the lead boat came into sight. They always returned in a follow-my-leader straight convoy. It helped with the berthing. They would usually tie up alongside each other and ferry the catch from boat to boat onto the quayside. At that distance, nobody could tell whose boat it was. So the tension mounted.

"There's another," the boatyard expectant father shouted. All heads and eyes focused on the distant vessel. Some minutes passed. The specks became blobs. The thuds became a rhythm, a mechanical sequence of pistons.

"Shit!" said one of the managers. "They wouldn't normally be that far apart. Their rule of the sea has always been to stick together. This looks bad news."

Maria had a sinking feeling in the pit of her stomach. Why had Paco gone? She had suggested he continue their family evening entwined in the matrimonial bed as so many others did. Of course, she understood Paco was the breadwinner. He'd had the misfortune of being his parents' second child. His brother never left his bed, although it was a family secret that Virginia, his wife, gave up sharing it with him when she found out he had been sleeping with one of the chambermaids from the guest-house they ran.

Pedro was gripping her hand hard and peering between the larger bodies towards the two boats now well within range. Nobody speculated which boats they were. The men had their own views. One of the managers leant across to his brother-in-law and whispered, "Miguel and Manuel."

"What, missing?"

"No, returning."

"Miguel yes. But maybe Paco or Juan."

"Shit," the manager said again, but this time with more remorse. "Either way it's bad. There are only two."

Miguel's stature became recognisable at about 200 metres out. He was half inside his wheelhouse and half out. His deckhand was standing just behind his captain. Puffs of smoke from his cigarette blew away from the boat at almost 180 degrees. There was still a steady wind coming off the sea.

All eyes were set on the second boat. Those who understood those things recognised the red painted band around the hull which Juan had painted on.

"It's Juan," the fishmonger confirmed to his brother-in-law.

Heads turned to look towards Maria. They sought out Manuel's wife too.

Miguel's deckhand threw a line onto the quay. It seemed almost a hundred hands reached out in concerted sympathy. Nobody wanted not to help. Sobbing could be heard. Some were tears of relief, while the others were of compassion as Paco's and Manuel's wives awakened to the reality of the moment.

Juan tied up alongside Miguel and stepped into the adjoining berthed boat. Miguel held his arms out to hold Juan to him. They were grown men; hard weather-beaten sailors, yet they were both crying openly. Not in pain. They were stricken by grief.

With an arm over Juan's shoulder, they walked the few metres down the gang plank. There was almost total silence, pierced only by the squawking gulls swooping down onto the decks and stealing whole fish from the catch. Nobody minded their feast on this occasion. Miguel's wife could not hold back. She ran into her husband's arms.

Juan's father stood firm. Emotionless, so it would seem, but those close enough saw the tears running down his face. Juan put his arms around his father's shoulders and sobbed into the crook of his neck.

The two loyal deckhands, both having now experienced a side to their apprenticeship they would have wanted not to, linked up with those waiting for them.

Gradually, without direction or command, the quayside was emptying, like some dramatic scene in an opera. But this was a single performance, not nightly with a couple of matinees during the season. This was a one-off, never, hopefully, to be replayed. Exits from stage left and right were being made.

Maria found herself face to face with Manuel's wife. They were two lonely women suddenly, and traumatically, confronted by the dark shadow of widowhood.

Miguel and Juan braced themselves and walked in determined military steps, almost as though they were carrying an imaginary wreath to lay on the steps of the village church on the anniversary of the Spanish Revolution. They approached Paco's and Manuel's wives.

Suddenly there was a cry of anguish. The experiencing of real pain.

Pedro screamed, "No, not my papa," and turned and ran. He was running anywhere. Running away. He needed an escape. The cobbles were like an ice-rink and the rubber soles of his flip-flops had no grip. They were like slicks on a wet day. His left ankle gave way and he fell to the ground, sliding forward.

His mother gave chase with Manuel's wife not far behind.

"Chiquito!" Maria cried. "Chiquito!"

She glanced over her left shoulder at the surviving captains, who had followed in pursuit, their mission having been interrupted by Pedro's flight of panic.

"Was there any pain?" she asked calmly.

"No," Miguel replied.

"You are both very brave, kind men, and friends too. Later I want to know. Now, I have a young man who needs me."

CHAPTER 3

There had been times when Maria had felt she would never laugh again. Paco's 'accident', the term she always used to Pedro when referring to his father's death in 1949, had seemed like somebody switching off a life-support machine. She felt bereft and hollow and the grieving never seemed to lessen. She still had her secret moments of tears.

There was anger in her, too. Typically, as she now totally recognised, the Martinez family were all a little short on self-guidance. The family called it a hunger but she thought there was a greed motivating them all. To be fair, Paco's drive to go for a second catch, as Miguel and Juan had subsequently explained, had Maria and Pedro's best interests at heart. How, though, could that be supported when the risks were so great, on that wildest of wild nights, and when a far better place would have been tucked up in the family bed. Who knows, if the compassion and tenderness Paco had shown Maria at the fiesta, the gentle squeeze of her hand waiting for the flaviol flautist to send out the call for the partners to join hands and form the initial circle for the Sardana dance set to begin, had continued into the night, Maria may have given in to his desire to father a second child. At least she had often pondered how he should not have gone to sea.

Paco was never to know that the usual excuse to not, as he put it, "make love", was not in fact the bad time she had experienced with Pedro's birth. That had been a mask for the fact that Paco's advances had always been – put bluntly, as Maria did in her mind – animal. As they had moved into the future of their marital status, it seemed Paco's initial tenderness had been an exception rather than the norm.

The girls in the village joked about how their husbands performed, usually followed by each collapsing in their partner's arms and waking in the early hours dishevelled, to be reminded that they should look orderly by the time the kids came in to their bed the following morning. That seemed to have rarely happened to Maria, although she felt the other girls were likely to be exaggerating anyway. But then again, it might have been true.

She did not know the comparative intimate matrimonial details of Miguel,

Juan, Manuel and all those others whose nights of conjugal harmony were put on one side, as hers with Paco had been, to be replaced by the need to earn a living and the camaraderie out at sea.

Maria often thanked God for the influences on her life, and certainly for helping her to convince Paco not to go to sea on the night of their wedding.

Maria reasoned that nobody, surely, would go fishing on their wedding night and that became part of the matrimonial deal, representing Maria's first successful attempt at putting her foot down.

She had determined they'd marry on the Saturday. The family would party into the night. Maria and Paco would then slip away to the cottage in the grounds of the Martinez family home, now part of brother Marco's inheritance.

It had been Paco's and Marco's father who had set out the stall for family ambition: to not merely replicate the living standards of their forefathers but make the most of the well in the middle of the courtyard. His friend the blacksmith in Palafrugell had made a pump and brought in an electric motor. They pumped water into a header tank, installed high in the disused windmill tower abutting the inner quadrangle, and they were supplied with running water. Running water, enough to supply more than just the original kitchen, washroom and outside toilets, but sufficient to feed hand basins in a number of bedrooms. It was Marco's idea to take in paying guests to benefit from the freely available sand and sea naturally abutting their large plot of land. The idea had overspilled into the building of quarters for him and his wife Virginia, and the cottage which he thought families would enjoy for a holiday.

Paco took some convincing that his body needed cleansing after the heat of the wedding day, and their dancing, but said he would if she would join him. At first, Maria had been shy, giggling her way into the shower with Paco. If there was a likelihood of a conception, if that were to be God's intention, then she resolved their child should be clean in body as well as spirit. So it was necessary to flush the perspiration from her body, and definitely his.

The shower water was cool and invigorating. The soap was made from pine, lavender and the perfume was calming. At first she had insisted she shower in her cotton petticoat. The practical side of her said she wouldn't be wearing that again if it did lose the shape in the drying out process.

The tenderness of Paco's touch and the roughness of his hands allowed her inhibitions to dissolve away, with the water running to waste. Paco had carried her from the shower swathed in his grandmother's special high day and holiday towels. He had laid her down and kissed her body gently. She had no awareness of him uniting their bodies, no screams of pain and anguish needed to be let out, which all the young married girls in the village had talked about. Their act of consummation had been calm, in compliance with the requirements of the Catholic Church.

The sickness and the deformity of her girlish shape two months after were made acceptable by thoughts of God's great blessing.

Oh, how she had needed Paco to repeat that act as the years passed. His coming home from the sea after Maria had washed and cleansed herself at the start of her day and the end of his night and pulling her onto the bed before his body gave into the exhaustion of the catch was not a platform from which to launch an extended family.

Fear of another caesarean seemed a convincing antidote too.

It was for the love of both Paco and Maria, and the immediate concerns for his nephew, Pedro, that when the phone call she had made from the local bar where she worked had come in from his cousin in Rosas, Marco had dropped everything and driven at breakneck speed along the coast road from Palafrugell to Rosas. Virginia, his wife, had seen his face age some 20 years. *Why's that?* she was thinking. *I suppose the wretched builder is going to let us down again and won't sort the plumbing out so that the paying guests will continue to moan, like they do.* How she hated the challenge of making bookings for customers for their bed and breakfast accommodation and then putting up with them when they came. Or putting up with Marco's temper when they cancelled or just did not show up.

"Oh, my God!" she heard him say. "Are you sure? Do you have him then? How can you be sure? Miguel witnessed it. And Juan? My God, Manuel too? So it must be right. Oh my God! And Pedro? God bless him. Does he know? I'll come immediately."

"When?" his cousin-in-law Maria asked.

"Depending on traffic, by midday."

He replaced the receiver. He was suddenly an ashen old man.

"What's all that about?" Virginia asked.

"Paco's been lost at sea."

"Oh, my God!" she said, with little originality. "And Maria and the boy? How have they taken it?"

"For God's sake, woman, do you have no feeling? No imagination? How would you take it if it was me and we had a kid? Don't bother to answer that question. Loving and grieving has never been in your nature."

He went to the wall safe and lifted out a bundle of notes. He took out the keys to the Citroen shooting brake. Marco thought momentarily.

"Watch out for the builders. They're due at eight. I'll be back as soon as I can."

"Will you stay overnight?"

"If I'm needed, yes."

"Don't you need a change of clothes?"

"Hell, yes, I suppose so."

He packed six clean shirts. His razor, some soap, some spare trousers. He thought again. He took his black suit, white shirt, black tie and black shoes and threw them into one of the heavy leather cases his parents had used on their honeymoon to Gibraltar.

"I'll be back as soon as I feel I'm not needed."

He kissed her forehead. She heard the car's slowly moving tyres crush the gravel of the drive.

Virginia sat down, still troubled by her breathing these days. She sobbed. She tried to love him, but she reminded herself he had betrayed that love with the village tart.

Marco went straight to the fisherman's bar. There was Miguel with a row of empty brandy glasses in front of him. Juan was staring blankly at the wall.

Marco knew them well. The fishing world was a small community and occasionally Marco would sail with the fleet. He got a buzz from fishing, but did not share his brother's love of shotgun hunting. Marco didn't like the sight of blood, yet his younger brother had always revelled in it. "If your body hasn't been washed with the blood of the vanquished prey, then you can have no knowledge of the animal's fear and suffering. It makes a man out of a child!" Paco would say, sure he was near to lighting the touchpaper of Marco's emotional cauldron.

"Shit, Paco! Piss off and shower off that blood. One day there'll be an animal that learns to turn a gun on you."

Marco broke the ice.

"Miguel, my friend, you've had an experience." Miguel looked up and was suddenly stone cold sober.

"Marco! I am so, so sorry about Paco. He didn't stand a chance."

"I don't know what happened yet. Can you bear to tell me?"

Miguel recounted the tale. They'd had the one good trawl and Paco suggested they go for another. He explained how Manuel hadn't been keen, but Marco would understand that when Paco was in a mood to drive on, he took others with him. That was Paco; Marco agreed. Miguel still did not fully understand how Manuel had lost control. Perhaps a linkage between the wheel and the rudder had sheered, but certainly the tug had no steering. It was out of control. He explained how the angle of impact must have been so critical that Paco's boat must have gone down in the first couple of minutes, whereas Miguel and Juan had had those few extra seconds and had broken free and steered windward. Suddenly though, when Paco's boat sank, Manuel's was sucked in behind it.

"So there was nothing more or nothing less than an act of God and the vengeance of the sea?"

Miguel said, "Yes," and a tear ran down his unshaven face.

"Did Paco suffer pain?"

"Only the pain of the realisation of inevitability, I'd guess."

"And Maria?"

"She doesn't know any detail. The boy was distraught."

Marco walked to his brother's fisherman's cottage. All was quiet. He knocked with the wrought iron letter plate. Maria opened the heavy timber door.

A shaft of sunlight hit her face. *My God, she's aged,* Marco thought. They stared at each other for barely a moment. Marco held out two heavily muscled arms. Maria stepped into them. He felt her whole body trembling. Never before had he felt such an urge to be protective to a being in such need of support. Another full minute passed which felt like an eternity. The one body was signalling to its brain to speak. The other was saying: words are not required. Marco released his hold, stepped a short distance backwards and looked down into her open face, seemingly dreading his words of predictable compassion.

"We've both lost the one we love. We must be brave."

Maria found that so adequate she just nodded.

"And Pedro? What about young Pedro?"

"He's 12, 13 next month. He knows the reality of love, but in his adolescent way he's shirking the facts he so well understands. He says his tears are because he's sprained his ankle and is in great pain. I've given him some broth laced with a little brandy. He's sleeping. When he wakes, I hope he can be brave about the loss of his dear father."

"And how would you describe your own feelings?"

"As though a major possession's been stolen, one that's irreplaceable."

"Well, I'm devastated too."

Marco stayed on, sleeping on a sofa in the small living room. There was not much talk between the three of them. Marco had not needed to say anything too complex to Pedro. On the first day, Pedro woke and went into the living room, and found his uncle gazing out of the window down the path to the sea, almost as though expecting Paco to walk into his gaze.

"Uncle, I knew you would be here," he said simply. "Papa would have known too."

"Of course! Now, let's have a look at that ankle of yours."

Marco knelt down as the boy lifted his foot. He held the back of the calf in his left hand with his right under the arch of Pedro's foot.

"My, that's a big sprain, Pedro."

"Yes it is!" He turned his head, but there were no tears.

Perhaps that was the day Pedro became a real Martinez.

Two days later the local gendarmerie found four bodies on the rocks below Cadaques. Marco and Manuel's brother identified their respective kin. The fathers of the crew members completed the identification.

The coroner reported death by misadventure.

The village church was full for each of the four individual funerals.

The only serious item on the agenda between Marco and Maria, which Marco had anticipated, was where Paco should be buried. Maria suggested with his parents. Marco was very relieved, he could not have asked for more.

So after the church service in Rosas, the three led a cortege down the coast to Palafrugell and there Paco was laid to rest. Marco touched base with Virginia and checked the builders were performing and then returned to Rosas with Maria and Pedro.

Marco stayed on in Rosas for a few extra days, his clean shirts representing the days crossed off on the calendar. He was desperate for Maria and Pedro to be taken under his wing back to the family home, but it was too early to mention the idea.

"Right now Paco/Papa would want you to continue with your normal life. You, Pedro, must get back to school. Your foot seems better now too. We've got Easter coming up and I would love to have you down. We could show you the plans we've had drawn up for a small hotel. We had an approach for two acres of land we have in that old barren olive grove on the main road from an agent for Total, the petroleum company. You know your old uncle, though, a Martinez through and through – I've contacted Esso and asked if they're interested, and if four men visiting from London is anything to go by, I reckon they are interested. There's talk of a sale of that land for nearly twenty million pesetas. That would build about thirty rooms."

"And a pool?" Pedro enquired.

Marco looked quizzically. He thought, what's a boy of nearly 13 asking questions like that for?

"Yes, son, and a pool."

Maria thought for a few moments. "There seems a big following in England, Germany, France and Europe generally for tennis. Would a court be very expensive?"

"I really don't know," Marco replied. "But that seems a good idea. Although none of us are likely to play, we ought to be thinking about the tourists' needs." He thought to himself that Maria really did think about things too.

Pedro was quiet for a few moments. "I think Papa would have wanted me to learn tennis. He taught me about winning."

Maria choked back a tear. *His ankle's better,* she thought.

The Easter seemed ages coming. Maria and Pedro limped through the weeks after Paco's death. The mornings were the most difficult time of day. It just seemed they got up, washed and dressed without a purpose. Pedro had to be forced out of the house to go to school.

"What about you, Mama? What will you do?"

She had some extra cleaning jobs, which helped her make ends meet.

One week, Miguel might drop round some fish and a brown envelope with a few pesetas in it, explaining they had had a good catch. Juan did the same. When Maria went into some shops, she would find they often had a cancelled order of meat or vegetables "going cheap".

So she survived. Deep down, though, she knew she was the focus of charity. Paco would have hated that. When he'd had a bad week of fishing he would always say that if God did not want him to rob the sea of its life, he would take his guns to the hills and see if God wanted to balance up the land's flora and fauna with the needs of the Mediterranean. When he came back with a couple of wild pigs to trade with the butcher, or a few brace of partridge or hares, he'd say God did work in wondrous ways and was pretty good at getting his message over as well.

Pedro had left for school. Maria was tidying the house when there was a knock at the door. A young man in a city suit was standing there. "Señora Martinez?" he enquired.

"Si," she replied with slight puzzlement.

"My name is José Romanez. I'm from Iberia Co-operative Insurance Company. We have received your claim for the loss of, am I right in believing, your late husband's boat?"

Maria gasped inwardly. She had found this legal-looking document in Paco's dresser drawer, and put together a short but direct undated letter to the company as the terms of the contract were not clear. She had written:

Dear Sir,

I am the beneficiary of my late husband's estate and I have a copy of the Insurance Policy under which my husband's effects are covered.

I wish to make full claim in accordance with your policy terms.
Yours faithfully,
Señora M. Martinez.

Maria's education had been basic. She'd been to the village primary school, then to the convent, and at 15 her father had died, making it essential for her to go out to work. She had got a job in Palafrugell public library, a relatively small building, dependent more on its books being distributed village to village in the two converted coaches the local mayor had provided than on people being there to scan the shelves of its very good stock of literature.

As she restocked the various shelves, she would take every opportunity (if the librarian was out, say) to flick through the pages of any book she found attractive, before poking it into its alphabetical place, no doubt to gather the dusts of time. Each time she read a word, or a line or paragraph she felt it taught her something.

"Would you like to come in?" Maria suggested. She sat the young man down in one of the easy chairs in the living area. He looked kind. "Would you like some coffee?"

"No, thank you. I'm here in a business capacity."

"It doesn't matter what sort of capacity you're here in, I'm offering the hospitality of a Martinez home."

Hell, thought José Romanez, *I've offended her.* "I really would love one. My Head Office would fire me if they knew I'd accepted hospitality while dealing with a claim, but may I have a black coffee, please."

"Of course," Maria said as she moved into the kitchen.

He could still see her as she filled the kettle and placed it on the stove. He would guess she was about a year younger than himself. About 29. He'd expected to meet a 60-year-old widow in traditional mourning. The records showed Mr Martinez had been dead less than six months, and here was his widow, in denim with a soft feminine blouse. *Shit,* he thought, *I bet her husband kicks himself for passing on and leaving such an attractive young widow behind.*

Maria returned with two cups of coffee on a tray. Milk was on the side and sugar in a separate bowl. That's how the Martinez family would do it. "I've put a couple of biscuits out and I promise that won't get back to Head Office either."

They sipped their coffee.

"Firstly," said José Romanez somewhat courageously, "the company wishes me to express our condolences at your sad bereavement…" He would have expected the claimant to soften at such an expression of condolence.

"You surprise me by saying that because, as you explained, your company has sent you here in a business capacity and, if I might help to put you at your ease, I expect they've instructed you to pay out the minimum possible on my claim."

He inwardly winced. Wow, this was some woman. He had never ever been pushed back so firmly in his tracks before, or so quickly. Even the staff training college had not tried that one to knock the trainees off-balance.

Maria, in turn, told herself this was not her speaking. It was Paco Martinez at his hungry worst, speaking through her at this pleasant young man. Maybe he was two or three years her senior but there was something about him that reminded her of Pedro. Perhaps an air of naivety, innocence, even subservience to a matriarchal figure.

"You've obviously studied my claim."

"Yes, we have, and as you know, your late husband's boat was insured this year for a total write-off figure of five million pesetas."

Her stomach churned. She must keep calm. *Hell! The boat was never worth anything like that!*

"Please could I stress – and this is *not* on my company's instructions – I really don't wish to cause you any more grief than you must have already suffered. There's the delicate matter of the life policy, which attached in the event of your husband's demise being at sea and, as it were, with the vessel at the time of its loss."

Maria paled. She visualised what Miguel and Juan presumed had happened at sea. She saw Paco standing proud at the helm as the hull was punctured. Forgiving Manuel for his short-term ineptness. A tear rolled down her cheek.

José Romanez lifted himself from the easy chair. "This is not a company handkerchief... there, please," he soothed, offering her the comfort of a crisply ironed cotton square.

She looked exposed. He hated himself for finding the light perfume from her morning shower appealing. He was here to save his company as much on their obligation to pay out as he could. He had a good record for not paying to the limit. But his mind was wandering. *Shit,* he thought. *This is no way to look at a widow when you're trying to agree a claim.* But she was so young.

"As you know," he continued, sensing she had pulled herself together, as had he. He resolved not to see her as a portrait hung to satisfy his inner male instincts. He must do the job he had been sent to perform.

"The life policy element would not have applied had your husband's unfortunate death been disconnected from the fishing fleet policy. So, the delicate question I have to ask is whether you have a record of your husband's last three years' earnings from his fishing activity?"

Maria had found a little notebook with the policy in Paco's dresser drawer. She stood and went to the outer hall to where she had moved Paco's much-loved piece of furniture and then on into the bedroom, he guessed. "Let me see what I can find."

José Romanez glanced around him. He got up and walked to the china cupboard to have a closer look at the photographs.

The young bride was Maria Martinez. So the swarthy young man was the deceased. Ten years or so, he presumed, had not changed her greatly. She was then an immensely attractive young, happy girl. Remove the layer of grief now lying over her and the vibrancy was still there, he thought. He didn't know if they had children. But then he didn't need to know that for the purpose of the claim. Still, the boy in one of those photos had Maria's eyes and the makings of the husband's physique.

José had his own son, who was only eight and just becoming interesting. His wife was going on about a little brother or sister, but he really wanted to upgrade their living status first. They had a two-bedroom apartment in the same block as his mother-in-law. His aim was to buy one of the houses being built on the outskirts of Barcelona, but all the wretched Germans and Italians, and a few French people, were leaping in and buying as though there were no tomorrows. He could get a subsidised mortgage through the company, but his salary only went up by inflation, and the Krauts were running prices by demand at an uplift of about 15 per cent per annum.

He was startled by Maria coming back into the room and catching him nosing around her pictures.

"Is this a picture of your late husband?" he asked, kicking himself for stating the obvious.

She didn't affirm or otherwise, which made him feel clumsy.

"I think these represent my husband's accounts," she said, holding up a small spiral-bound notepad. She moved quite close to him and opened the book. It started with a heading of 1945. Then, there were 52 lines over four or five pages, each line with a figure: 500, 1100, 1400, 3000. Then came a heading of 1946, followed by similar data for the next successive years.

"It looks as though this represents my husband's average weekly cash take, which he then totals to give a yearly wage."

"Good, that's four years' income."

"How does the computation work then?"

"In fact, we take the average of the last three years."

Oh Paco, she said inwardly, although you're not here in person to protect Pedro and me, you're doing it from within God's house.

José Romanez switched to business mode. After all, if he saved the company money on this claim he would be first in mind for promotion again. He'd been moving up in seniority at quite a rate.

He had scribbled down the figures for the last three years and divided it by three.

"So if we take the average year at say 1,250,000… Sadly we can't forecast what 1949 was going to be."

Maria was thinking hard. "Mr Romanez. That seems to suit the company too much. The actual figures were…" And as she said that, she leant across the dining table and picked up a biro. Oh boy, here was suddenly a tigress roused! Ready for a fight!

"But that's the way we do it," José Romanez said in a very controlled manner.

Maria appeared not to be listening.

"…the actual figures were 1,005,000, 1,255,000 and 1,505,000. That's…" – she scribbled her arithmetic with a more determined alertness– "3,765,000. Averaged is 1,255,000. That 5,000, Mr Romanez, is a lot of money to a hardworking fisherman."

"OK, I was just trying to make the calculations easier. So, let's say, subject to my office accepting the book as a record of your late husband's earnings, 1,255,000 at a compensation level of the three years' income attaching to the policy would be 3,765,000 pesetas."

Maria seemed confused. "You mean the policy was based on three years' earnings?" She had been typically quick on the uptake.

"Sorry, I thought you knew."

Maria said could she have the book back. She scratched away again on a loose piece of paper.

"I think you should look at this another way."

"Which other way?" the young man, who was learning the lesson of a lifetime, responded quizzically.

"If you look at my husband's figures for January and February already this year, they were running at a monthly average of 150,000. So, if you take the years on a March to February basis, they would be 1,150,000, 1,350,000 and 1,550,000. Now that does make it easier to work out." She scribbled down a column of figures. "That's, say 1,352,000 for three years, making 4,056,000."

Christ! José thought. Maria Martinez was the most intelligent of any female client he had dealt with; in fact, more switched on than most artisan males.

He appeared to be calm, which Maria wasn't sure was a reaction she knew how to combat.

"So," he began, "the company is being asked to settle at five million plus 4,056,000, which makes, say, 9.05 million." Which was fine, because any minute now he could become the magnanimous benefactor, as he was able to settle within his level of authority up to ten million.

Maria took a deep breath. "You've been very kind. Very gentle and understanding and I wouldn't wish to push my luck. But all my husband's nets were lost… could we say they would make up a consequential additional loss" – words she had once seen in a manual on insurance at the library – "of 150,000, and settle at a figure of 9.2 million?"

José would have to report that figure back to the parent company in the UK at about £46,000, which seemed a huge return on the annual premium of only 200,000 pesetas. But that had been hard some years for Paco to find, especially with Pedro growing out of his clothes with such regularity.

José Romanez stood up. He felt drained, yet exhilarated. He was below his limit, so he'd get a pat on the back from his line manager; and he had been in the company of a truly remarkable woman, and a beautiful one at that.

He held out his hand to shake hers. Here was one of the strongest women he had met, yet her hand was limp in his. She said, "Thank you."

"The payment will be cleared in two weeks."

"I don't have a bank account."

"Mrs Martinez, if you're about to come into possession of nearly ten million pesetas, you really must open one. I'll send a cheque. Or would you prefer I deliver it?"

How nice it would be to see this young man again…

"Would you be so kind as to post it? And do you have time for another coffee without the company knowing?"

He smiled broadly. "Actually, thank you but I must move on. May I very sincerely offer you my condolences again, but may I also say your husband would be proud of the way you represented his interests. That's not to mention the coffee too. Thank you."

He left and as he trampled the gravel into the path, he hesitated for a moment, as if to turn, but did not. He didn't want to see Maria's tears of relief, or sense the certain churn in her stomach. She was too soft and pleasant to have been able to conduct herself as she had without some elements of fear. He would respect her right to privacy.

Now he was out of sight. Maria fell to her knees, then rolled sideways, pulling her bent legs hard into her stomach. "Oh Paco! Oh Paco! Oh Paco! My darling, you made me a Martinez. We won't let you down. Was I greedy? Oh Paco. Why did you go back for more? I've just seen the same habit in myself."

She sobbed for what seemed like hours, but by the time Pedro had returned from school she'd pulled herself together. Pedro thought his mother looked younger than of late. Her hair was smarter. She was wearing a skirt and heeled shoes again.

"Mama, how's your day been?"

"Pedro, my son, it's been a good day. And how about you?"

"Yes, Mama. Good too. And it's only three weeks to Easter. I'm looking forward to seeing Uncle Marco and Aunt Virginia again. It'll do you good, too."

How my child is maturing, she thought.

"Go and have a wash and I'll get your tea."

"OK, Mama!"

"Go on. You've been playing football. I can tell. You smell like a young man."

The weeks after José Romanez's visit dragged. Waiting to hear, waiting for the visit to Marco's.

Pedro arrived home on the Wednesday before Easter, his school bag brimming with books. He was coming up to take his entrance exam into either the local secondary school, just a short bus ride away, or the mixed convent, a little more akin to an English grammar school, which would mean a 30-minute bus ride there and back each day.

Maria said he must try for the convent, and what was 30 minutes in a coach if you could become a doctor or a lawyer one day? He threw his bag onto his bed and went into his mother's bedroom. She was putting a few more clothes into a case to take on their two-week break.

"Mama, you look sad."

"I'm not really, Pedro. Well, really I am always a little sad these days. We're missing your father."

She stepped forward and took him into her outstretched arms, then let go and took a retreating pace backwards. "You've grown. You've really grown this term. You're getting a really big boy. Now go and pack some of your school books. It's not going to be all holiday, young man."

Marco had insisted on coming to pick them up. He was writing to them most weeks. Virginia, so he said, was really looking forward to their visit. Maria knew better. The sisters-in-law didn't really get on, they had nothing in common, even though they each had or, in Maria's case, had once had, a Martinez to love, honour and obey.

In Virginia's case, once she found out that Marco had strayed with his honour, she had apparently, so Paco said, given up on the loving and obeying bit. Virginia would show off her social graces, but doubtless would, when alone with Marco, find fault either with Maria or Pedro.

Packing was the order of the day, so Maria kept silent that she had taken the bus into Gerona that same day. She had worked out that it was best to open a bank account away from the village, from the confines of the local bank, to gain anonymity.

She had worked that out a couple of days earlier, after José Romanez's promised letter arrived.

The formal looking envelope had duly popped through the letter box, on time. Initially she was disappointed, as the letter was very formal on typewritten headed notepaper. It asked for a response by signing the attached further letter, which signified that Maria would be acknowledging the enclosed payment cheque in full and final settlement of the cover the company had provided.

Then came the chilling experience of seeing the cheque itself. It directed the Bank of Iberia to pay to Mrs Maria Martinez the princely sum of 9,200,000 pesetas and as if Maria was not expected to believe that numerical statement, it reconfirmed "nine million two hundred thousand pesetas only" in written form.

Momentarily, she thought: *Should I have pressed for more?*

There was then a small envelope paper-clipped to all the formal documentation. She opened that slowly, thinking that José Romanez would have attached some personal note and the envelope probably contained that, as indeed it did.

Dear Señora Martinez, it started. (He had pondered the desire to address her as "Dear Maria," but she was in mourning and he'd get fired if ever his bosses found out anyway.)

I am pleased to be able to enclose all the attached confirmatory paperwork in line with my recommendation to settle the matter I came to see you about at the figure we agreed. I regret that my words when we met might have appeared shallow, but I am not very good at expressing myself when I know I am appearing on someone's scene at probably the lowest ebb of their life. Such is the downside of my job.

May I say I remain filled with admiration for the way you handled the delicate matter.

The coffee and biscuits will remain our secret.

If you find yourself in need of insurance advice, feel free to contact me. There is a rumour I may be transferred to dealing with general commercial matters soon. They also now say they think I may have had enough experience in Marine and Life.

Please look after yourself and your son.

Yours very sincerely, José Romanez

That's a kind note from a nice person, she thought. She stared at the cheque for ages. What a replacement boat that money would have bought Paco! Or maybe he might have purchased a little shop and spent nights at home. Who could tell?

Then something dawned on her. José Romanez had referred to her "son". Yet she was sure she hadn't mentioned Pedro… *What a nice touch,* she thought. José Romanez had noticed the family photograph.

CHAPTER 4
1949

Marco was proving to be a Mr Stabilizing Influence. He had said he would let Maria know when he would be arriving to pick them up for Easter. He had duly done that and was expected around ten or 11, subject to traffic conditions. That reliability was a Martinez trait and Maria was conscious of reciprocating that.

Marco had left home for the two-hour journey at 7.30am, on a clear bright spring morning. He had his car radio tuned into a local station, which kept going in and out of signal range. He wasn't really listening anyway; he was deep in thought. Virginia was still going on alarmingly about Marco's hotel idea. More so since his last meeting with the petroleum real estate people. They had stuck at their offer of 28 million pesetas, so Marco had said he would only sell an acre and a half for that and they had gone away to think about it.

When the Esso team made their return visit unannounced, he threw his arms into the air in despair. "If you'd said you intended to come back with an offer, I wouldn't have got to the point of closing the deal with Total."

"Have you closed the deal with them?" the Esso Spanish agent enquired.

"In the style of a Martinez, I almost have. We've shaken hands at 30 million, but I'm talking about selling less land as part of that deal."

"Marco, I've known your family years. You know we would like to do the deal with you. What will it take?"

"With two acres or less?"

"It has to be two."

"OK, if you hit 32 million, I'd take it off the market for a month while the lawyers fart around."

"I'll be back tomorrow."

True to his word, the agent appeared the day before Marco went down to pick Maria and Pedro up for their break. He had a formal offer on Esso headed notepaper at 32 million.

Marco held his hand out to Sanelez Sargo, the agent. "That's a fair deal," he said, and as he said it, he felt happy. *So that's Pedro's pool and Maria's tennis court.* He wished he could come up with something for Virginia, but then she had lost all her sense of adventure.

"Marco, you're as mad as your younger brother. If you banked 32 million, we'd live like royals on the interest alone. You could restock the vines and that would give you a nice little hobby. I'd be happy to keep the guest house going for, say, eight months of the year and then we could put our feet up for the winter." She looked at Marco's impassive face.

"Marco, listen to me."

"I have, Virginia."

"Then will you do it?"

"No. My waters tell me not to."

"So, you have more faith in your bloody smelly water than you have in the words of a wife who's trying to put your best interests first?"

Best interests, he thought. The best interests would be for Maria and Pedro to be taken back under the family's wing. For them to have the shelter of the family home. Paco would have approved of that. Now, if there was a hotel, Maria could work alongside him. Pedro could go to the new grammar school in Palufrugell and be educated to establish a new, wiser, more intelligent next generation. And Virginia. What of her? Maybe she would come round.

He was ahead of time, he thought. Maybe he would grab a quick espresso in the village before going to pick Maria up. She would be bound to offer him a refreshment when he arrived, but he would prefer not to create the bother.

He made better time on the last third of the journey and certainly had time for the coffee. He parked the car alongside the church and walked across towards the bar in the middle of the square. The church doors were open, to act as a vacuum to those drawn in by their faith and their special need to express it in God's House and probably not their own.

Marco stopped. Looked at his watch and turned back. The incense was heavy from the early morning mass, which was always well attended during Easter week. He stood in the doorway, allowing his eyes to adjust, as one never seems to have time for when driving into a road tunnel. The light was playing hard on the stained glass windows. He remembered this was the fisherman's church and the jigsaw of ruby red and deep sea blue irregular shapes of glass made up a pattern of a sea scene, with a beach and fishing boats carelessly scattered amidst the complex design. The fishermen were depicted as disciples and there were baskets of fish at their feet.

Marco thought about Paco. Was he now a disciple, doing God's work for him? Paco the hungry. Oh shit, Paco, why Paco?

Marco walked across to the third row of pews, and slotted into the end of the thick oak carcass that had supported some of the most religious bottoms in the 400 years of worship the church had seen. Taking out the hassock to genuflect, he reverently knelt and bowed his head in prayer.

His message was to Paco. The Paco with whom he now wished he had spent more time. Perhaps he should have interpreted his father's wishes in a different way. Maybe they should have fished together; at least Marco, the elder, could have called time on a good catch when the elements cut up rough. Perhaps they should have been hoteliers. The Martinez Brothers, Restaurateurs had a certain ring about it.

"Oh God. Please look after Paco now that you've called him and his good friend Manuel too, mother and father and all the former generations of Martinez. Please bless Maria and Pedro. Please direct them into the safe haven we wish to provide for them. And Virginia. Please help her to forgive my indiscretions. Confirm to her it was a physical, not spiritual encounter out of selfish animal hunger. A passing careless moment. In the name of the Father, the Son and the Holy Ghost. Amen."

He opened his eyes. Blinked at the spotlight created by the shaft of morning sun bouncing its rays off the old stone flags beneath his feet. *I'll run out of time for that coffee if I don't hurry,* he thought.

With all the packing done, and 15 minutes until Uncle Marco would be there to pick them up, Maria told Pedro she was just popping down to the church.

Pedro gave her her space. He had noticed she spent quite a lot of time in the church these days. "If Uncle Marco arrives, offer him coffee. You know where it is… and the milk…"

"Mama, I know where the coffee is. The milk's in the larder. The water's in the tap. The kettle's on the range…" He smiled. "And the church is down the path. Please go. I'll look after Uncle Marco if he's early."

She'd decided to wear a skirt, blouse, little knitted jacket, stockings and low heels, so as to make the right conservative impression on Virginia. She had never quite forgiven her sister-in-law for her bitchy comments when Maria once turned up in Levis. "So, are you going on to a barn dance?" Virginia had sniffed.

"Do you mind me wearing denim?" asked Maria.

"A Spanish girl should try to be proud of her heritage. If you think God would welcome you to pray in his church wearing jeans, then go ahead. If you think he might turn you away from his church, then you should dress more appropriately. After all, don't you think Paco might have been offended if you'd turned up to get married in denim, not satin and lace?" Maria told Virginia she was being unreasonable – fashions had changed.

Virginia, to be fair, had taken that comment to heart and looked at some of the fashion books you sometimes see in the bookshops of Gerona. "It's true, everybody does wear jeans," she wanted to say, but her pride failed her.

Maria hurried along the street leading to the church.

There's Marco, she said to herself. *Coming out of the church, now that does surprise me. I thought he only went to weddings and funerals. Surely it is Marco, or is it somebody who looks very like him?*

Marco walked on towards the bar. Maria continued to look on in surprise. She raised her hand to her mouth and clenched her teeth. Or is it Paco? How alike they looked, silhouetted against the ten o'clock sun. Their walk. Their shoulders. "Oh Paco!" she whispered.

She went into the church and straight to the front of the altar. She touched her forehead with the forefinger and middle one of her right hand. Touched both breasts and drew an imaginary vertical line, addressed to the stained glass window.

Oh God, she said in her mind, *please teach me to pray alone. To pray for my love to be sent to Paco. Teach me to protect Pedro. Show me the way ahead.* She nodded. Stood. Did a little curtsey. Crossed herself again. Turned and hurried up the aisle.

Back home, Pedro looked up as she walked in.

"He's not arrived yet."

"No, I know. He'll be here on time though."

Marco entered the bar, which had its front shutters wide open to the spring elements. The cigarette and pipe smoke from the previous evening was clearing. There were the usual retired mariners with nothing to do, nowhere to go, and some were those with wives who knew they had to get out from under their spouse's feet. There was the odd clink of a domino laid in excitement by an arthritic hand that could no longer tend the nets.

Marco went up to the bar. "A large espresso, please."

The proprietor was not known as Mr Personality Costa Brava. He was dull and unwelcoming but because it was the only bar in the village, it was the social epicentre of Rosas. Marco put down a 50-peseta piece, which the patron gobbled up as though it might be the only take of the day.

"Gracias," he muttered.

Marco lifted the small cup, and saw a suitable table quite close to where the sun was now beginning to stream down. He took two spoons of sugar and started slowly stirring his morning treat. Virginia had banned him from smoking and drinking espressos. "I don't want you dying on me with a massive heart attack," she would say.

Suddenly there was a shadow cast across Marco's table. It was Manuel's brother, whom Marco had met a couple of times before. He stood staring down at Marco.

"You're Paco's brother, aren't you?"

Marco went to stand up, but was held back by a firm downward pressure on his left shoulder. "Yes, that's right. I'm Marco Martinez." He saw menace in the eyes looking down at him. "You're Manuel's brother, aren't you?" he added politely.

"Manuel has no brothers. He has no parents, he is friendless, childless, Manuel no longer breathes, no longer lives. All who were around Manuel are now in a time zone of emptiness."

"Look, I'm sorry, I don't remember your name."

"I'm Carlos," the man replied.

There was a silence between them. Suddenly Carlos placed both his large hands around Marco's broad neck. With enormous force, he lifted Marco to his feet, and Marco was no light weight. In a flash, Marco realised this Carlos was demented. He drew back his right arm, clenched his fist and with all the power generated by the air he was able to expel from his lungs through his ever restricting trachea, he forced his ungloved right hand into Carlos's solar plexus.

Carlos's eyes rolled, and he released the grip on Marco's throat like a pair of hands dropping a sack of potatoes off the back of a lorry. The bar's owner was upon them both. Two younger men who had been taking in early beers were standing over the one groaning man and Marco, who was breathing deeply, letting out the occasional wince.

Carlos was fully conscious after his sudden wounding. He was helped to his feet. He stared into Marco's face, his lips curled. He rolled his tongue and spat full into Marco's face. "You, brother of a murdering swine!" he yelled.

Marco was completely taken aback. The patron said, "Are you Paco Martinez's brother then?"

"Yes I am," Marco replied emphatically.

"Well, you ought to know that folk around here know the story that it was Paco's greed that could have taken eight men to their deaths. Carlos has taken it all very badly. He was very close to Manuel. When their parents died, Manuel became an entire family to Carlos. Carlos was retarded, you see, and needed Manuel to do his thinking for him. Now he has no-one. He came in one morning with Manuel's wife when Paco's widow was here cleaning. A bit like today, he spat full in her face and said she was the bastard widow of a man who had killed his brother."

"You mean Maria?" Marco enquired.

"Yes."

"How did she take that?"

"Like a man really. She stood her ground and said that Carlos should know Paco was a man of love and would never – other than as a result of a misjudgement – do harm to anybody or anything. Carlos spat at her again, but she stood firm. Manuel's widow took Carlos by the arm and led him away as if he was blind, deaf to her words and a little sobbing boy of no more than ten years old."

"And Maria now?" said Marco.

"I'm afraid I had to ask her to leave."

"So what does she do for money?"

"She cleans the church and gives reading lessons to a few children in the village. She's not really welcome now in the village. You know what folk are like, I'm sure. Will you have a brandy on the house?"

"No thanks. I'm 30 minutes late for an appointment with the future."

Marco did indeed eventually arrive 30 minutes late. Pedro was beside himself with excitement and delighted to see his uncle. He was waiting at the gate and as soon as he saw Marco, he ran to greet him, forcing his uncle's arms to open wide in welcome and provide a wrap around his nephew, as if to protect him from some wild herd of charging beasts.

Marco looked up to see his sister-in-law framed in the porchway of the little cottage. Everything about her was natural beauty. Her jet black hair was a discreet shoulder length, though still long enough, he didn't doubt, to be piled high on top as she'd worn it on her wedding day. Her skin was still a light olive colour and she had a hint of perhaps a light cherry-coloured lipstick. It could have been she had no makeup on at all. Her neck was long and slim and she still wore the locket Paco had bought her for her 21st birthday. She was wearing a crisp white blouse with a tiny stand up collar. Whoever designed the exact location at which the V-neck ceased to form a "V" and changed to the neat little front pearl button shirt arrangement must have been female. A man would have the slashed "V" all the way down to the wide waistband on her skirt. The female designer certainly had no idea what a tempting effect she was to have in dressing the bust, which had always caused Marco's mind to wander. In Virginia's younger, more possessive days, she used to tell Marco that he was gawping at his sister-in-law.

The black skirt was probably one Maria had made for herself. She was an accomplished seamstress, a talent she got from her mother, whose Singer electric sewing machine was now hers – a present to her mother from her father when he received a bonus on finishing his teaching career at the local grammar school.

The backlighting created by the whiteness of the painted cottage, bathed in young spring sun, accentuated the fact that every intricate thread in the weave of the material seemed to have been formed to follow the exact curve of the body it enveloped. Marco thought Maria had lost weight since Paco's death. God! How he must miss his beautiful wife!

The shoes were neat and Virginia would be pleased Maria was wearing stockings. "She looks so underdressed with those bare legs of hers," she used to confide.

Marco released one of his arms from the bear hug he had been giving Pedro. He held his left arm out and said, "I've got room for another small one." Maria smiled. Goodness, she hadn't done that for an age, it seemed. She walked her natural walk, which to Marco would have done justice to a Hartnell gown on a catwalk, though it was not a strut; it was a simple movement to the shelter of her brother-in-law's comforting arm.

He gathered them in together, as if they were a football team taking on board their captain's game plan. "Look, I'm sorry I was late. We need to get a move on. Are you going to tell me you're not packed yet?"

The three of them had to break rank to get through the cottage door. Pedro got in first and gathered the two cases together, almost knocking his mother and uncle over in his rush to get them to the car. Marco looked around the living room. It was almost clinically clean by comparison to Virginia's level of housekeeping, but then, to be fair, she had asthma and the worst thing to exacerbate that was disturbing house dust – and allowing the dog into the house, she was always quick to point out.

"I'll check the windows and doors," Marco volunteered. "We'd best leave the place like a fortress while you're away." The locking up took about 15 minutes, ten of which consisted of Pedro saying, "Come on, you two," and "Auntie Virginia'll be wondering where we are."

The three finally stood on the front step with all gazes fixed on Maria's pretty little hands as she turned the large key in the mortice lock. They took a couple of steps down the path. Maria halted like a horse in gallop that comes to an unassailable fence.

She put down her small 'emergency' case. Said she was sorry but she'd left something behind. Both men sighed, as men do. It would take two minutes, she assured them. She reversed the custodian locking up process, opened the door and rushed into the living room. Grabbed the framed picture of her wedding day, backed out of the house, and locked the door under the watchful eyes of Marco and Pedro. Then, like a young girl sneaking a pin-up of her favourite pop-star into her home and being caught red-handed by her parents, she brought the photo in her hand from behind her back.

"I want us all to be together," she said, slipping it into her bag.

It was time. They climbed into the car, Marco and Maria in the front, Pedro sitting forward on the back seat with his head between the two front seats.

Maria shot round to Pedro as if he was about to be accused of some serious misdemeanour, then raised her hand to her mouth – the usual pre-cursor to announcing she had forgotten something.

"Oh Marco," she said, with apology in her voice, "we didn't even offer you a coffee or a glass of water!"

Marco laughed. "I sneaked a quick one at the bar. I actually arrived early but I thought you wouldn't be ready."

"Mama wouldn't have been there anyway," Pedro said, in the typically over-informative way of children, sufficient to receive a glare from his mother.

"Oh, where would you have been then?" Marco enquired.

"Church," Pedro continued, spilling the beans.

"Really?"

"I wanted to pray for a safe journey," Maria said, "and if you, my dear brother-in-law, don't concentrate on the road, my prayers for us all really will need to be answered!"

They travelled in silence, all their brains racing. *What if I'd met Maria in church?* Marco thought. *We couldn't have missed each other by much.*

I wonder when Uncle Marco will tell us how his hotel plans are going, thought Pedro. *I wonder if he's got any drawings of the pool.*

Maria was in an agony of anxiety. Marco hasn't said if he met anyone in the bar. Oh God, I wonder if he asked if I still worked there?

Maria turned to Marco after a while. "Did you see anybody you knew in the bar?" she enquired.

"Not really. I think it was Manuel's brother who was there."

She went cold. Some ten minutes passed. Marco, his gaze fixed on the road ahead, said, "I didn't find the locals too friendly in the bar." Maria squirmed. "I tell you what, it looked pretty grubby. The patron says he lost his cleaner." Marco turned and looked at Maria. He smiled and patted her knee.

She stared ahead, then shrieked, "Pig!" Marco took immediate offence and turned away, in time to see a pig double back on itself in its run for freedom from a farm where the gate had been inadvertently left open.

"You nearly hit that pig! Please keep your eyes on the road," she said, establishing that at least for a while she was right and in control. She leant across and patted his knee. "Brother-in-law," she smiled.

Virginia heard the car pull up outside the family home. Marco beeped the horn a couple of times. She took off her apron, patted her hair into place and adjusted the comb at the back of her head. She still looked like something out of the 1930s. Virginia suddenly realised she was quite pleased to have some visitors who were not expected to pay for their board and therefore on whom she would not be expected to dance attendance.

Pedro ran round to the boot and took a case in each hand. They were heavy, but when Marco offered his assistance, Pedro resisted, indicating he could manage.

Virginia almost broke into a trot three or four metres away from Maria. A quick snapshot burned into the cornea of her eyes: Maria was still respecting Paco's death by being in mourning. Well, at least there was some black about her and she was suitably dressed with heels and stockings. *Thank God she's not showing off her bare legs for all and sundry to admire,* she thought, and, apart from that, the nice little blouse meant Marco wouldn't have had the joy of a two-hour car journey looking down her cleavage. No, she sensed this was alright. She and Maria engulfed each other in one of those female hugs where the emotion of the moment speaks silent words between two people who have a mutual understanding, if not affection.

Virginia stepped back, still holding each of Maria's young hands. "How's it been?" she asked.

"Oh, OK. Pedro and I are slowly coming to terms with it all. We're missing Paco enormously."

"And Marco too," said Virginia. "He's been worried for you and about you both. But we'll talk about that sometime over your stay. Now, where's the heir to the Martinez throne?"

Maria had never contemplated the fact that, as Marco and Virginia had no children, Pedro could be in line to pick up the family silver. Paco would not have wanted that. He had often stressed that the difference between Marco and himself was that his elder brother had it made and would never need to work. He had the family home, no mortgage and plenty of land to live off. As for Paco, he doubted he'd ever be rich, but used to contemplate Pedro's education as being the foundation of a new Martinez dynasty, where wealth of knowledge was key. With that and a bit of luck and good health, this branch of the family tree would sprout new boughs.

Pedro appeared from the back of the car a little laden. "Pedro, put the cases down and come and give your aunt a kiss," Maria called.

Did he have to? He really didn't want to. He didn't like all this sissy hugging and kissing. All the girls at school were beginning to develop into premature aunts as they used to spend their break time deciding who they wanted to kiss the most.

He had gone home upset one day in particular. Maria was prepared to give him space nowadays which Paco would have filled, having slept his way through the day and risen just as Pedro returned home from school. "Change quickly," his father would say, "we've got three hours of daylight left. What do you want, a bit of hunting or some fishing? A game of football or shall I explain what the clouds mean?"

This one particular day, Pedro went to his room to change and had been gone ages. Maria knocked on the door. In earlier days she would have gone straight in but now that Pedro was developing and maturing, he needed space. As indeed did she in their close-knit mother-and-son duo.

Pedro's voice was quiet. "Yes, Mama."

"Can I come in?"

"Yes, of course."

He'd been crying.

"What's up, chiquito?"

"Mother, could you not call me chiquito?" It was second nature to Maria. He was and always would be her hijo, but this was probably a call for space, a cry for help in some sort of early adolescent crisis.

"What's wrong, son?"

"Well, the boys at school have given me a nickname."

"What's that?" she said, knowing it couldn't be complimentary.

"They're calling me pretty lips."

He did have pretty lips. Paco's had been pretty too. They were lips that spread wide open when they were happy. They were wild when they embraced her neck and kissed her breast. They were soft when he talked tenderly. And taut and scaly when he was angry.

"Who's calling you pretty lips?"

"The boys. Apparently Juan's sister has told him that all the girls want to kiss me because they've voted that I've got the best lips in the Junior School."

"So, let's look at the logic in that," Maria had said. "Young men use their lips to woo young girls. It's the first touch of intimacy at the beginning of a lasting relationship."

"But Mama, I don't want a girlfriend. I don't want relationships."

"Pedro," Maria said with a broad smile, "the day you're offered a young girl's lips and decide you still don't want to be kissed, or want to have a relationship, and you turn away from her, tell me, phone me, write to me and confirm

43

again what you've just said."

Pedro listened. His mother was usually full of good advice.

"There's another thing," he continued in a slightly more confidential tone.
This boy is only 12, she told herself.

"There's some writing on the wall of the school toilet."

"What's that say?" Maria asked.

"There's a drawing of a fish with very large lips and the writing says, 'and now Pedro's father kisses his own'."

"Oh chiquito… tough little man. I'm so sorry… here…" She cuddled him to her.

The next day she was at the school at 8am, when she knew the headmaster arrived. She stormed into his office unannounced. "You can't see me without an appointment," he said.

"You come with me," she demanded, nostrils flaring and beckoning with a confidently menacing forefinger. "I'm taking you to the toilet. Then tell me if I need an appointment to see you!"

The head realised he'd best follow this tigress on her charge. She burst into the empty cubicle and looked around. "Look! Are you all blind?" she said, pointing at the outline of the pursed-lipped fish.

"Oh my God! The teachers are all saying Pedro isn't his normal self. Poor child," he said with a great degree of understanding. "We'll find out who did this and expel them."

"Don't you dare! That would be too easy for all of you. Just get it removed. The Martinez family can get through this patch. We're the family of a brave, proud man."

"We know that," said the head.

"So, give your aunt a kiss," Maria instructed. Pedro closed his eyes and did what he was told.

Virginia stepped back and said, "My, you're taller than I am now! What are you, 160 or 170 cms tall? You're built like a bull! I can see you're a Martinez. Let's get you a drink. You must all be parched after the journey. There, I haven't even asked if you had a good journey."

"We nearly didn't make it," Pedro confessed.

"Really!"

"Yes, Uncle Marco almost ran over a pig."

Marco appeared. "Did I hear my name being taken in vain?"

"Pedro was just saying you nearly ran over a pig." They all laughed. "Come on, let's get you freshened up."

Marco took one of the cases and paired up with Maria as they went into the house.

"Maria," Marco said earnestly, "it made it easier for me when you went back into the house for your wedding photo. There always will be the three of you, but there'll be times when your memories will be too hard to bear. Virginia and I have argued endlessly which room you should have. I've been saying you'd probably like to share. Virginia thinks you should be in the guest rooms in the house. How would you feel about the cottage?"

Maria's stomach heaved with fear. "Our honeymoon cottage?"

"Yes, the one you did stay in when you got married, but also, we remembered every other time you and Paco stayed with us after your wedding."

That's true, she thought.

"You see, I believe if you don't consider that as your heritage, your corner of the family home when you come here in the future, you may look on it as a shrine to something in a previous life. Take the plunge now and it'll continue to form part of your new life with your own growing young man."

"You're are absolutely right, Marco. I'll do as you suggest. Forgive me if I don't look too bright, but I probably won't sleep for a night or two!"

"You'll look just fine, I'm sure. Let's get the cases dumped and we'll have some refreshment."

They enjoyed a light lunch and took the dogs out in the afternoon. Virginia chatted endlessly while Marco and Pedro bonded over boys' topics like inspecting the vines and checking out the olive groves.

"We're going to fish," Marco announced. "You women put your feet up. Tonight before dinner I'll show you some sketches of the hotel."

Maria and Virginia talked, sitting on a sheltered part of the terrace. "You see," Virginia said, "I really have a problem dealing with the guests we have at the moment. They're all foreign these days and Marco and I don't speak English or German, perhaps a little French. So really it's most un-relaxing. I suppose I'm OK once they go out visiting."

Maria thought about that. She had done a short conversational English course when she was at the library. She really ought to pop in and see them there while she was in Callella. Palafrugell was only just up the road by bike.

She was lulled off by Virginia's constant chatter. Her eyes closed and she slipped into a 40-wink time zone.

Pedro and Marco sat on the rocks together round the little bay. The local fishermen were preparing their long boats during the daylight hours for their late night foray to lure the unsuspecting fish into their snaring nets behind the oil-filled hurricane lamps.

Pedro was full of questions. Marco realised that whenever he had been in the boy's company before, Paco had been there. If the lad asked a question of Marco, Paco answered.

As brothers, they had got on famously until women came into their lives. There were four years between them and, although it was never a subject for discussion, there was a hint that there'd been a daughter born between them. Their parents had never elaborated on the circumstances, but it seemed the little girl had been stillborn, and that their mother had been at risk of losing Paco too during her pregnancy.

When Maria came on the scene, it was Paco who brought her to the family home. The boys' father and Marco both developed a soft spot for her, for the fun she generated and the excitement her blossoming young womanhood brought into their strict Catholic surroundings.

So, Marco felt great envy for Paco and then when he and Maria produced a honeymoon child, he over-reacted and sought Virginia's hand in marriage within a year. During the first five years of their marriage, every attempt to procreate failed.

In frustration one month, as Virginia moaned and sobbed in bed with a hot water bottle laid across her distended stomach to counteract her usual stomach cramps, she had accused Marco of being a reproductive failure.

In one of Marco's less controlled moments the next day, he had purposely sought out "that girl" all the men talked about in the village. The rest was family history, which Virginia had resolved never to let go. He'd been found out. That was going to be for life.

Marco would never knowingly have let his jealousy show. Now, however, he heard Pedro asking question after question and himself giving direct answer after answer.

"Were those like the family's original fishing boats?" Pedro asked. "Those, my son, are the family's original fishing boats. Your father and I sold them to part finance the one in which your father was lost." Pedro went quiet. "Uncle, do you think Papa was hurt in the storm?"

"Now I'm not going to answer that. You must. So tell me how many times you saw your father not in control?"

"Never," Pedro replied.

"And did you ever see him in pain?"

"Yes!"

"You surprise me. When?"

"When his father died."

"Look Pedro, I'm going to treat you like the man I think you are. I spoke to your father's fellow sailors from that dreadful night, Miguel and Juan. They both said that the sinking was so quick. Your father would have been thinking, scheming, trying to get out of trouble. Only at the very last minute would he have realised the inevitability of the situation."

"What do you mean, the inevitability of the situation?"

"Pedro, tell me the truth. Did you know your father couldn't swim?"

Pedro thought long and hard. "No! But now that I think about it, he was always standing on the breakwater in case I needed help. It was Mother who came in the water with me. If we were in the water together, it was when he was fooling around, or ducking me. He could swim under water. I'm sure."

"Pedro, your father would have known nothing about the accident."

"Uncle, another question."

"I'll try."

"Which boat sank the other? Was it my father's or Manuel's?"

"Both Miguel and Juan are agreed the steering on Manuel's boat failed. His tug sank your father's. But is that important to you?"

"No. But it seems very important to Manuel's relations because at school…"

"Pedro, my dear friend. Can you not see why? It was Manuel who inadvertently caused your father's and his deckhand's deaths. It could be our family blaming Manuel's. But we are Martinez. We know how to forgive. That is, apart from your aunt," he said with a grin, "but don't tell her I said so."

The smile and the one it produced from the boy took the heat out of the moment. "I think I understand now," Pedro said.

They fished on in silence. Both had their thoughts. Pedro reeled his empty hook in, pointing at it. "Look, the little buggers have taken the bait!" Those were words Paco would have used.

Marco copied the boy's example. Was he going to be a better fisherman too? "Look," Marco exclaimed, "mine too!"

Pedro started to laugh. "Which one of us did the baiting?"

"You did," said Marco.

"No, it was you."

"You know something. Neither of us put any bait on." They both roared with laughter.

"Let's walk back. I'll show you how the hotel fits into the bay."

They clambered back over the rocks at the foot of the small escarpment dividing the higher plateau of the olive groves from the rocks and sand leading to the sea.

"So, we'll climb the cliff and at the top level I'll show you where the pool goes, and then the hotel."

The cliff was only about 20 or 30 metres of gently sloping face. They were both a bit breathless when they got to the top. "So, when I show you the drawings this will be where the pool is." Marco paced out about 50 metres. "And the hotel will start here and finish there. Then there'll be a garden area at the front of the hotel."

"Can you build right back into the groves?"

"No, the authorities will only allow you to build within 150 metres of the tidal line of the sea."

"Do you own the rocks down to the sand?"

"Yes."

"And the cliff?"

"Yes, unfortunately. Now, if that was flat that would be a different matter."

"Where would you put the tennis court?"

"Now, that's a problem. Your mother has a good idea there, but I don't think we can get it in."

"I think you'll have to break that news to her. She keeps talking about it."

"There's a way of explaining things to women. Leave that to me," Marco said.

"I can't wait to see the drawings."

Maria changed her skirt for a tailored pair of black trousers, which meant she could un-pop her suspenders and go barelegged without offending Virginia, or turning Marco on.

Pedro was made to wash. "You smell of sea salt," Maria had said accusingly. "What did you catch?"

"Well, Uncle Marco and I got a bit carried away with our conversation and each of us thought that the other had done the baiting. By the time we realised what had happened, it was a bit late so we headed back and looked at the hotel site."

"What was the conversation you had?"

"Oh, Mama, this and that. Men's chat, I suppose you'd call it."

She had noticed Pedro was developing a secret side, which she didn't much like. She was comfortable when she knew his thoughts.

"Well, it's a lovely location, as you must know, but I just think Uncle Marco may have it wrong."

Maria's eyes widened. "How on earth can you say that? You're 13 in a week or so. You mustn't begin to think like that. Marco's bound to have it right. He knows buildings. Now you remember, we're guests here. It would be rude to criticise and it could jeopardise our stay."

"What's jeopardise mean, Mama?"

"Put at risk."

"Oh, I see. OK, I'll check on Uncle Marco's good mood then, before I say a word."

He was getting so much like Paco and it was barely six months since that dreadful storm. Paco, as a matter of principle, would always start off by not accepting what Marco said or advised. They'd argue it out for days and then come to a compromise and push off to the bar for a few beers and some brandy before they swaggered home to announce what had been resolved and how the compromise was so much better than what had previously been mooted.

As Maria and Pedro entered the living room from the terrace after the short walk from the cottage, Marco was reading a paper and Virginia was crocheting.

Marco put the paper down. "I see the French are proposing to run the SNCF straight down to Narbonne from Calais. Bloody French are still mad. They think they'll transport all those tourists down to stay in the Narbonne region. There's talk, though, that they'll have train decks for cars on two tiers. I reckon what'll happen is that the canny English will sleep on the trains overnight and be relaxed enough then to drive over the Pyrenees and come down into Spain."

Virginia said, "But what good will that do us? They'll all go down to Barcelona and those places like Tossa and Sitges."

"No, I think they'll stop at the nearest string of resorts to the Pyrenees."

Virginia laughed. "And you, Mr President, rule that will be Callella and Tamariu."

"Yes, I do."

"It'll be a bit like the Romans then. They marched until Ampurias, camped down there and decided to build a small stronghold." Those were Pedro's words.

All the adults turned in silence to look at him. He looked puzzled. "Did I say something wrong?" he said, erring on the side of caution and fixing his gaze on his mother.

"No, I think you just made your uncle's case, but backed by a very strong historical reference point, whereas he relies on his water to form a judgement."

Maria felt twitches of excitement start in her toes, then run through her legs and burst like a collection of Red Admirals in her stomach, sending warmth and excitement chasing through her body. Marco noticed her proud moment. "Hey! I think it's time to have the plans unveiled."

Virginia packed her crochet materials away and stood up, brushing her skirt to free the little pieces of raw cotton that had collected in her lap.

"Well, that's a sign for me to go and prepare the meal."

Maria stood too. "Let me come and give you a hand."

Marco commanded, "Not on your life. I really want you to see what we've got in mind. You'll have some useful comments, without a doubt. Right, Pedro, you can be my right hand man. You sit here," he said, patting the leather seat of his parents' original dining suite, pulled up to the table on his right-hand side. "You, sister-in-law, come and sit here." He patted the seat of the left hand chair. If he was slow, she might sit on his hand even. Maria deftly lifted his trailing hand and sat down.

That first night the plans were unveiled, Marco was careful to start with some sketches of the pilasters of the gates. He'd had them drawn by his local square-minded friendly architect, who knew about the design of a local village house but had a long way to go to originate a commercial structure. But he drew what he was told and got excited too about something he didn't even understand.

Pedro showed great charm even in the way he questioned the first image of the neat square gate piers, with no gate swinging from either side. "Uncle! Do you intend a gate?"

"No. What perhaps you need to understand is that if you have a gate then somebody has to be there to open it for each visitor. You can't expect a couple of tired tourists to happily jump out of the car to open the gate, drive in and then get out of the car again to close it every time they come in and out."

"Does it cost a lot to build those piers?"

"I'd say 200,000 pesetas. But it's worth it. It's the first impression." Maria glared at Pedro as if to burn the word *jeopardise* onto his forehead with a branding iron.

"... and so the entrance off the road has an access driveway about four metres wide leading to the front entrance to the hotel, which is here," Marco explained, pointing to what looked like a large circle set into the plan.

"And what's the roadway made of?"

"Oh, I'd say crushed gravel. They usually are."

"Uncle, what did the Romans use for roads?"

"Cobbles. But you'll notice they're taking those up now in Palafrugell because with all the heavy traffic they're going shiny and are like iced water in the wet."

"Are they OK laid flat?"

"Well, yes. Pedro, I'm beginning to understand that behind every question, you're testing some sort of thought in your mind. Why the questions about the gravel?"

"I'm just thinking things through."

"Maria, how do you force out what's in your son's mind?"

"Marco, I think you'll have to say to him that you're happy to hear his view and that you won't send him to bed for being a precocious 12-year-old!"

"Pedro, if you think that might be the case, then you don't yet understand the Martinez mentality. We will *always* listen. Then, perhaps three or four days later, we'll consider what we've heard. Then we're likely to say those were the ideas of an out-of-work bull in the bullring, if the ideas weren't good. Or, on a good day, we'll quietly accept what's been suggested and steal the idea like a North African carpet salesman in the market. So, let's go back to the gates and start again."

"Well, Father used to say we Martinez represent years of establishment. So, I just wonder why a Martinez hotel has contemporary gate piers without a gate. Can't we get hold of some old columns that are meant to indicate an entrance in themselves, yet make a statement of age and ancestry? Supposing we picked up some Roman pillars near Ampurias for 10,000 pesetas in some builder's yard. Perhaps ones that came from a demolished building. Then we'd have 190,000 to buy some of the cobbles they're lifting in Palafrugell, cart them here and get some locals to lay them. It's a level approach drive, so they won't be dangerous when they're wet... everyone approaching the hotel would then get a feeling of it being established." He went on in full flood. Aunt Virginia listened, spellbound. Everything she heard made such sense.

"Will there be a lift?" Pedro asked.

"Lifts are renowned for going wrong, besides, we get so many power cuts and we'll only be building three storeys."

"OK, so we'll have to rule out people staying here with a bad heart."

"Why, in the name of Santa Maria, should that be?"

"Because we had a master at school with a bad heart and he couldn't ever go to the first floor to teach as we didn't have a lift."

Maria remembered that first induction day some weeks later when they were discussing what they should do now that the three religious days of Easter were behind them. Neither she, Virginia, nor Pedro had dared to mention the plans, spread out in the garden room, that Marco was brooding over. In the meantime, Pedro decided to keep out of the way.

They'd had a communal breakfast. Virginia asked what the programme was, and Marco said the boys had got plans for the day.

"We thought we'd drive the pick-up to the builder just this side of Ampurias to see if he's got any bits of columns they don't want to salvage in their rebuilding of the old Roman town they've been excavating."

Pedro looked shocked.

"Then we need to call in on the road works in Palafrugell. We need to find out if they'd let us cart their unwanted cobbles away free of charge."

As the two women looked on in surprise, Pedro grinned at his uncle across the table. "Who'd know it wasn't an original Martinez entrance anyway?" He walked across to Marco and dropped an arm around his shoulder.

"So what are you girls up to?" asked Marco.

Virginia said, "You go gallivanting. I've got to go to market."

"Maria?" Marco enquired.

"Perhaps I could hitch into Palafrugell on the bus with Virginia. I'd like to go and see how the library seems nowadays. Maybe I'll go and see who's around who remembers my father up at the school."

There was no mistaking the library. Maria was in a happy but reflective mood and as she pushed the horizontal bar on the glazed timber entrance door into the building, she closed her eyes. The smell of the old leather bindings laced with mildewed pages from years gone by was sucked into her nostrils. It was almost a feeling of being back in a previous home. She opened her eyes.

God, she thought, *it hasn't changed! It has stood still in time.*

Am I seeing things? the man wondered. The hair was longer, darker, shinier, yes, translucent. Her skin was a richer tone of olive. He'd heard she'd had a baby but there was no sign of that in the flat-fronted tummy contained by her slim denim jeans. Surely it was Maria.

"Is it Maria, or a wild dream I'm experiencing?"

"Señor Carlos Sanchez," she said, almost in shock. But why? She had expected to see him. He was the librarian. She ran the eight or nine paces towards him. Threw her arms around his neck and, realising that was not the most professional greeting she should give to her former employer, stepped back and offered a soft cheek, reciprocating his left against her right, and then his right against her left.

"So, how are you?" she said.

"Fine, absolutely fine. More than 12 years older, I have no doubt. But what about you?" He offered her a steely gaze. One of his intelligent gazes, right to the rear of both eyeballs. The gaze you could never cheat, or lie to, or mistrust.

She hadn't answered.

"I know about Paco. I know you have a son. How about you?"

"It's been bad. Sad and unhappy. Yet for all God has borrowed, he's has given me a wonderful child. Well, a young man really. Effectively now 13 going on 18."

"That sounds like Paco to me," Carlos said with one of his wry smiles. "So, what are you doing here?"

"We're staying for a couple of weeks with Marco and Virginia."

"Stay for a couple of years," he said. "Oh Maria, I'm sorry, I shouldn't have said that. You just referred to home being Rosas, but, seeing you here, like some ghost in the library, has lifted my heart. The place seems to be alive again. It could learn to laugh through the silence it's become used to over all its decades."

"Stay for a couple of years," he had said. What a wonderful thought. A new life. She could continue with her English.

"Look, let's have a coffee in the office. Then I'll let each one of the books know you've popped in. They'll be remorseful when I tell them it's a fleeting visit."

They sipped coffee. Yes, his family was fine. He was a grandfather, did she know that he might be made mayor in a couple of years? He'd invite her to the ceremony if he made the election by the Parish councillors.

"Must you really leave?" he said as she looked at her watch and wondered where their reunion time had gone... it had flown.

"Yes, I'm hoping to look in on the school."

"Where your father was?"

"Yes."

"They're having a bad time."

"Why?" she said in horror.

"Well, people are moving south. There are jobs in Barcelona and anybody who can look as though it's a pleasure to carry a plate and deliver a knife and fork and serve food to a sunburnt tourist is finding jobs galore further south as a waiter or waitress. That means there are fewer children in the school."

"Are there places then?"

"Oh yes, plenty. They're still very selective, but if a child has the capability and the grades, there's certainly no queue to get in.

"Maria, come and see me again. Give me time to think through my strategy to win you back. Emile, you remember, Emile Lomas, has given up the assistant librarian job. She's having to move to Barcelona with her husband who has a job in the government. The times I've thought, and I should add, offered up a little prayer of you coming back. Help make my prayers be answered."

She went on to the school and all that Carlos Sanchez had said was true. *Well, it wouldn't not be,* she thought. But things were different there. They had built a sports field where they had football pitches and archery. They had a large indoor pool that had been built for the region's Youth Championships. Her father would have been thrilled. They now had a language laboratory where pupils could speak onto tape and listen to their accents.

They still had a mixture of boys and girls, of course, which would be good for Pedro. What on earth was possessing her? She had visualised Pedro actually at that school. She had seen him playing football, swimming length after length in the Olympic-sized pool. Laughing with the girls and amusing them with his tales of Rosas and the heroics of his father.

She returned on the bus alone, frozen with fear. She was silent when she got back. Feeling she could not face Virginia's constant chatter, she developed a diplomatic headache and went to the cottage. Pedro and Marco had yet to return. She lay on the bed staring up at the ceiling, as she had on the night of her wedding. Then, she remembered, she had been totally possessed, completely satisfied, humbled by the beauty of her husband's passion. She was at home.

Today was unsettling. She had not contemplated continuing her life anywhere other than Rosas. After all, that was their home, not a double bed with a view of a ceiling. But then Paco was here. On each of the days of Easter they had been to his grave, just round the corner. Pedro had said once when they were in Rosas, when he was particularly missing his beloved Papa, that it would be nice to be able to pop just down the gravel path to talk to him.

The door to the cottage was thrown open and Pedro hurled himself onto the double bed next to his mother. The bed bounced and the boy was like a virile young gymnast executing an excited routine on a trampoline.

He was full of *we've done this, done that, been there, bought these, arranged to buy some of those…* He was absolutely brimming with excitement, and the day's success, and the ecstasy of a future, as opposed to the horrors of a recent past.

"Mama, are you alright?" he said. "I'm sorry, I forgot, Aunt Virginia said you'd got a headache."

"Come here, chiquito." She gave him a huge hug.

"Mother, please don't call me chiquito."

"Chiquito!" she said tantalisingly. "I'll stop calling you that the day you play football for the first eleven."

Pedro looked at her as if she had gone mad. "But we don't play football at school. You know that."

The next day was a Wednesday. Maria was awake early, but then she had hardly slept again after waking at about 3am.

The first thing she was aware of was that she had come through another of those recurring dreams she now had to endure. The subject matter was always different but she always seemed to wake as her subconscious told her that, again, in this bad dream, there was something missing. Paco never featured, as such, but she was sure the missing component each time reflected the fact that he was lost, never to return.

But awakening in the early hours had been different this time. She had the usual sense of bereavement, but this time it was immediately replaced with a feeling of joy. The library at once came into her mind and then the school, the hotel and the kind young man from the insurance company. Some outer force was putting together a game plan for her to follow.

She wafted in and out of a light sleep until she sensed the sun was about to rise.

She left Pedro to sleep on, slipped into the bathroom and gingerly turned on the shower. She set the dial to a warmer temperature on this chilly spring morning. She always felt embarrassed in the shower as guilt swept over her for never putting the memories of that wedding night shower with Paco out of her mind. She dried herself off and slipped through to the bedroom with one of Virginia's large cotton and wool bath towels draped around her like a sarong.

As she let the towel drop to the floor, Pedro opened his eyes. He'd been dozing when the torrent of the shower against the glass screen had awakened him from the storm he was sailing through in his dream journey.

It was only a half-light that silhouetted Maria's body on the other side of the half-opened door.

In the confines of the close environment they found themselves in, Pedro was now noticing the female form, embodied by the odd glimpse he got of Maria changing, showering, brushing her hair… all those things a mother would find quite normal in front of her child. Pedro was maturing, though, and he was getting a pretty good idea that girls were on the planet to provide some pleasure or other to their opposite sex.

His mother looked fit, athletic and young. He watched her slide on a pair of black cotton pants, which he had thought looked so incomplete hanging empty on the washing line. Now her body was being poured into the gently stretching fabric. Those bra things, he thought, must be uncomfortable. Surely they weren't that necessary unless a girl was going swimming, of course.

Maria eased a black skirt over her hips, put her arms into a black silk blouse and slipped on a pair of low-heeled strapped sandals. She flicked her hair with both her hands, getting a quick glimpse of the effect in the mirror just within Pedro's vision. A touch of lipstick completed the Madonna.

She entered the area where Pedro slept on an extended put-you-up just as he raised his head.

"Hello darling," she said, "how did you sleep?"

"Fine," Pedro replied. "Where are you off to?"

"I woke up and felt I wanted to go to church. I'll slip down and when I get back I'll make you some breakfast. I have a feeling Virginia isn't herself today."

"Why, what's wrong with her?"

Maria laughed. "Oh Pedro, we've got so much to learn together. I'll explain to you sometime. There's so much to teach you in life's rich encyclopaedia. I'll see you shortly."

The doors of the church, which perched on the brow of the hill overlooking

55

the sea, were always unlocked. For how much longer, the priest had explained to this congregation on Easter Sunday, was a matter of conjecture. "We were once invaded by the Romans," he lectured, "and the Moors. The Crusaders used us as a refuelling post and now our freedom is being threatened again by the tourists who have little regard for our traditions and our faith."

A young couple had spent the night inside the church and if the priest was not mistaken they had indulged in the pleasures of the flesh. The majority of the congregation winced with sheep-like horror at such a dreadful insult to the Virgin Mary depicted in the stained glass window. A couple of young men chuckled, and two young choristers found it amusing too.

The door groaned as Maria gently pushed it open. She was usually alone in her visits at this early hour but today there was a hunched male body partly obscured by the backs of pews close to the altar. So she silently slid into one at the rear of the church, kneeling and crossing herself with due Catholic reverence.

"Oh God, please guide me." She had not stopped thinking about the library and Carlos's kindness in suggesting she take on the assistant librarian's job. Then the school. The slightly haunting memory of how Rosas had seemed to turn against their little duo of a family. Pedro's lips... Marco's kindness... Virginia's need of a sister figure to act as a sounding board for all her moans and confessions.

"Oh God! Could you please get together with Paco and guide me into the future."

She was kneeling in deep thought with her eyes closed and head down when she heard heavy footsteps rattling the loose grilles in the floor, which covered the single pipe heating system, turned on in December and January to warm and dry the church out. The loud thuds reverberated from the antique quarry tiles on the aisle, forcing her to look up.

"Marco," she whispered.

"Maria." Marco's voice echoed back as his large form kept walking, partly in embarrassment and partly out of respect for her privacy.

When Maria left the church, Marco was sitting on the stone bench by the gate to the path leading up to the church. It was just 30 or 40 metres from where his mother, father and Paco had been laid to rest, and from the little unmarked stone traditionally depicting the absence of a baptismal blessing for an unborn child.

Maria felt it was her prerogative to speak to Marco first. "What made you visit the church this early morning, brother-in-law?"

Marco smiled a Martinez smile. "I came to pray that Virginia's period doesn't strike her down for more than a couple of days."

Maria lowered her head to disguise the blush. "Marco," she said in a tone of disapproval.

"And you, sister-in-law, have you been to pray for forgiveness for not choosing me as your husband?"

"Marco," she said in a shocked tone, "what has got into you today? What is it with you – is it 'All Saints I hate women day' or something?"

Marco smiled an easy smile. "Oh dear sweet señora, let's get everything into perspective. No, it's not 'hate women day'. It's just the beginning of one more day in the calendar that, when it gets crossed off at the end, when the sun sets, it'll be 24 hours nearer to the day when you say you have to go back to Rosas and rob us of your fragrance around our table, and for me to lose my friend and nephew, Pedro.

"Maria, do you know I think that boy might just be some sort of Saint sent by God to teach me flexibility. To instruct me to understand that there have to be two opinions to resolve every question.

"Being with Pedro is a bit like having to discern between good and evil; and I'm sure it's no family secret that I haven't always been the best at achieving that. Maria, that boy walked through the intended site for the hotel. He asked this and that. About the layout, building lines, whether we owned the useless slopes down to and including the rocks. Then, when he'd got me to establish the facts, I listened to his previous advice that we would need a pool, and then he questioned me about where your tennis court would fit in. Maria, I'm am so sorry, I tried hard to fit the court in, but I couldn't.

"Then yesterday, question 5,061 from young Gaudi was 'Uncle, is it cheaper to build a stone wall than dig a hole in the ground?' Now, this wasn't a question I could answer, and I told Pedro so, and said that he should think out a more comparative situation and explain what was puzzling him in greater depth.

"And did he rise to the challenge! 'Well, uncle,' he said, 'I've been thinking, where you intend to build the pool you'll have to excavate quite a crater and that'll be in rock and I would think very expensive.' I told him it would be at least two million. 'OK, so if you were to build a wall an average of two metres high in local stone on the edge of the rock line where the rocks meet the sand, and then two further end walls back into the slope from the top terraced level down to the rocks, you would have created the same effect as if you'd spent two million on excavation and even then you would've had to tip the dug material somewhere.' I said I'd think about it.

"And you know what he said? 'Well, uncle, you better had because if we do that we'll save valuable space at the terrace level that we've reserved at the moment for the pool, we could move the hotel around a bit and there'd be room for mother's tennis court, and you know how we have to keep these women happy.'"

Marco sighed. "Maria, how I'll miss you both. So, I'm going to be honest with you, hopefully for Paco's sake too, I've been to church and asked God to force you to stay. Keep Rosas by all means as an escape route, if you ever need one."

"And did God advise that if he answered your prayer, Pedro and I could rent the cottage in the garden to give us a feeling of independence?"

"What!" Marco said.

"And do you think God would give you a hand to build a small one-room addition so that Pedro had his own area to sleep and study?"

"Maria, listen, I've got one woman in my life I can't understand at the moment. Please don't make it two."

"Marco, I think, subject to asking Pedro how he feels about not going back to Rosas, God has answered two prayers in the same church this morning."

Marco grinned his biggest version of the Martinez grin and said impulsively, "Want to know a secret? It's one of those ideas Pedro and I are absolutely at one over. Let's go and tell Paco about it then we'll choose the moment to tell Virginia."

They knelt in silence at the graves and then on the walk back, Maria didn't stop. She told Marco about the library and then the school and about Pedro's unhappiness about his nickname. Then, when Marco could get a word in, he confessed he knew Maria had lost her cleaning job and about how he had floored Manuel's brother...

Neither had realised the sun was just above the height of the shorter pine trees. There was a hint of early summer warmth on their faces as they hurried back.

"I'm back," Maria called out to wherever Pedro was. "I'll be making breakfast. How do you feel about an omelette?"

All she could hear in the distance was, she thought, Pedro kicking a ball against a wall. It sounded a bit stranger than his usual antics, though.

Virginia was usually so meticulous in her kitchen. The spice jars were always pristine with their various names clearly showing. Saucepans were hung in diminishing size, their copper bottoms polished weekly. Frying pans were of the same order. "Where's the omelette pan?" Maria said to the glittering, newly installed stainless steel sink unit. "Virginia, love, what have you done with the omelette pan?" she asked the butane-fired range.

About the only thing Virginia had expressed any interest in, on the subject of Marco's 'project', was how he reckoned the gas supply company in Palafrugell would feel about running a pipeline out to the bay for the project to collect the limited revenue from potential commercial usage.

"I'll have to boil the eggs. Pedro likes them cooked that way just as much," Maria then told the fridge.

Not everybody had a fridge in these parts, not by a long way. They had only had electricity for about 20 years and it still went down whenever there was a storm in the hills. You could scatter a few candles around the living room, but you couldn't run a fridge on candles. Virginia still put faith in her walk-in larder.

Maria boiled the eggs for about four minutes. Laid the table and then followed the sound of the bouncing ball to let Pedro know breakfast was ready.

Pedro saw his mother, now fully dressed, he noted with a hint of embarrassment in his mind. He stopped hitting the tennis ball against the flat rendered surface of one of the outhouses. Somewhat gingerly, he put the racket behind his back and greeted her with a free left arm round her shoulders.

"Did the priest forgive you for all your deadly sins and let me off on the Hail Marys for not working enough?" he jibed.

"What's that behind your back?" Maria asked searchingly.

"You mean my arm?"

Maria pushed free from his half bear hug and reached behind him. "No, I mean this. You rogue, you've got Virginia's omelette pan and what's more you've been using it as a tennis racket!"

"And watch how good it is, Mama." He threw the ball high and served it hard into the wall from the middle of the pan.

"Who taught you to serve like that?" his mother asked, with some good reason because it really did look most effective.

"Mother, let me just say it appears to be God's wish that we do build a tennis court within the hotel perimeters and it would be pretty poor if the family who own it can't play the game. So far I've taught myself. I'm available to get you into some tennis shorts and give you some lessons."

"Look, my dearest son, if you don't polish up Aunt Virginia's omelette pan and put it back where it belongs, we'll be on the next coach back to Rosas. We'll go into town and see if we can buy a couple of cheap racquets later. We could play on the municipal courts behind the library."

In fact, that wasn't a bad idea, she realised; she could have the odd game in her lunch break and after work. Deep down, she had a yearning to play tennis. Quite where that came from she wasn't sure, but she was happy moving along just doing what God had planned for her. She'd been close to losing her faith when she was robbed of Paco, but God was now directing her life in a way that made her feel He was on her side.

59

When his mother told him that if he could pass the exam into the Palafrugell school he'd have no trouble getting a place, and if his education was certain they perhaps wouldn't go back to Rosas for a couple of years, Pedro was absolutely delighted.

"Mama, you know dreams do come true," he said, to her delight.

A couple of months later he had passed the entrance exam with flying colours and impressed the headmaster at an interview to be offered the place he longed for.

In his first week at the new school, a person from the year above would be assigned to show him the ropes and explain the inner workings of the institution. Although he was confident for a boy of his years, it seemed that to have a guide was a very good idea.

His uniform was clean, a white shirt and navy blue trousers with obligatory black shoes that had to be cleaned daily.

Laura thought from a distance that he looked quite naval with his dark mop of curly hair and lightly tanned skin with a hint of five o'clock shadow. Surely he was too old to be in the entrance year? If not too old, he was certainly big enough to be in the year above. She had so hated the idea of showing some new wimp the ropes for the first week of his or her school term, but suddenly the chore was taking on a new perspective.

"I'm Laura," she had said in a confident, if not commanding manner. "Laura Orlandez. I'm in Form 2A and it will give me the greatest pleasure to answer all of your questions and your requirements in your induction week at the school." Exactly the words said to her a year earlier by her own mentor.

Pedro shook her hand and stepped back. He guessed she was about 14 and noticeably developing at a rate to be appreciated. Last year's blouse was a bit close-fitting against her chest, and was tucked in to the waistband of her regulation navy-blue knee-length skirt. She must have enormously long legs, he worked out, because he was about 1.6m tall and she was only a few centimetres below that, yet her waist seemed high off the ground.

"I'm Pedro Martinez," he said.

"I know, I've got a whole CV on you. You're from Rosas. You like tennis and football. Academically, you like history, geography and art and want to be an architect."

She had pretty blonde hair cut fairly short. Her skin tone was Mediterranean bronze, enhanced by being outdoors a lot. "Do I get to know your CV?" he asked.

"Well, I'm hoping to be a notary, so I'll need history and maybe classics.

My mother's French so I'm bilingual. I play tennis, not football, and I swim, of course."

"Why of course?"

"Well, everybody swims if you live near the sea, surely."

"Not everybody. I don't, for one."

"Then I'll make it my job to teach you to swim if you'll teach me at least the rules of football, then I can see if I can kick a ball within the laws."

"That's a deal."

"I'd expected to be inducting another girl, you know."

"Actually, I thought you'd be a boy."

"At what stage were you disappointed?"

"When I realised I wouldn't get to find out where the boys' toilet is for a whole week."

"Don't worry, Pedders. Oh, can I call you Pedders? You can use the girls' one until you've got your bearings. By the way, when the bell goes you go into that classroom there. I'll see you at morning break."

"Thanks for your welcome," Pedro said sincerely.

She replied, "You're welcome," which made them both laugh. "You've been a very pleasant surprise."

Laura spent the week networking him into pleasant, almost handpicked cliques of both boys and girls. They all found things in common – particularly, they all declared, that they were at school to learn and do well for themselves, and to be a credit to their families.

CHAPTER 5

Four years on, the days, weeks, months and the years themselves had flown by. Pedro saw a lot of Laura both in and out of school but, as though following some outdated history of needing a chaperone, she would always say whenever they planned to go out, can I bring Miguel and Tammy along, or Carlos and Elizabeth, or some cousin. She seemed to want to ensure they were rarely alone.

Pedro was fine with that, though he did have increasing urges to touch Laura's truly magnificent developing body. Sadly, one of the teachers had advised Laura to ask her parents to buy her some new blouses. "It would be preferable for you to wear white bras instead of black," Laura reported to Pedro, mimicking the haughty voice of the deputy headmistress.

"What do you think Pedders," she asked, "can you see anything wrong with black?"

"That's the problem," Pedro opined, "all the boys find there's nothing wrong with wearing black."

Laura's French mother had once been a catwalk model of some repute, and Laura had many press cuttings of her on boats in Monte Carlo and adverts in Vogue. Pedro thought that Laura was in fact far more beautiful than her mother, and she had a brain to go with the body. If Laura made it as a lawyer, even went to England and became a barrister, she would really be something quite magical.

In fact, that's what really troubled Pedro. Laura was first and foremost a friend. She was his first independent sounding board. If he asked his mother if he should wear his hair longer or shorter, she would give a typical, "Well, dear, if you want your hair shorter I'm sure I'll like it. If you wish to have it longer, I'm sure I'll get used to it."

If he asked Laura, she'd say "yes", "no" or occasionally she'd throw her head back and shriek, "Don't be silly, my beautiful Pedders, the world loves you as you are!"

They kissed. Well, that is, they kissed formally cheek to cheek. Laura ensured their relationship was controlled. It was almost as though she was afraid to show great emotion and, while their mutual friends recounted tales of nights of great passion with kisses that "must have gone on for at least half an hour", their relationship brought no such issues onto the agenda.

His tennis improved. Laura was really quite a good player. She learned the rules of football and supported his every game. He was turning into quite a useful player.

Then there was swimming. Of necessity that was not in a pool in controlled surroundings. It had to be in the sea. He could now swim but, without Laura knowing the reason why, he always panicked if he was under the surface of the water, as it conjured up the perceived last moments his father had endured.

She found that funny, or, in more legal terminology, very strange to understand. For Laura there always had to be logic, but she needed to be told about Paco.

Once, when Pedro asked her why their friendship did not include any of the fooling around and experimentation that their other friends enjoyed, she had said, "If ours is to be a deep, long-standing relationship, then we'll have years ahead when we can 'experiment', as you put it. But why run the risk of building a life based on an immature few moments of trial, however enjoyable they might be? Such moments might seal our fate for too many years to come and make us change our ambitions."

He'd asked Marco what that meant, as Marco understood womanly things. His uncle had laughed and said, "What she's trying to say is she's scared of losing her virginity with you and, if she did, and got pregnant in the process, she'd have your balls forever. She'll want to understand exactly what she's committing to, before compromising herself. Pedro, old buddy, she's scared. I'd bet her mother made a single error of judgement in an early relationship and has implanted seeds of déjà vu into her daughter."

Marco's words had encouraged Pedro to ferret and, piece by piece, he compiled a jigsaw from Laura's various answers to his relentless questions – "How long has your mother known your father for?"; "When did they marry, did you say?" – until he finally had the full picture. Laura was her parents' lovechild, born when her mother was just 18. There was little doubt in Pedro's mind that the club, or the pickle, Laura's mother had been put into had put an end to her modelling days, sufficient to make her want to ensure her daughter did not suffer the same fate.

It was a summer morning in June during the Whit break when Marco called Pedro from preparing the now newly-built pool for the onslaught of the summer bed and breakfast season, to say Laura was on the phone.

She was crying. "Oh Pedro, sweetest, we've just heard my mother's father has died. Yes, quite unexpectedly. No, not immediate, today that is, my father has to finish a case he's on, which should be tomorrow, and the plan is we'll go to France to be with my grandmother."

Pedro consoled her as much as he could. "Would a game of tennis get your mind off things? And we could swim. The sea's getting warmer."

They decided she'd cycle over and they would play on the hotel court, which had now been open since Easter after hours of deliberation. Marco and Pedro had decided to build it on the road side of the development, although they had taken up Pedro's original ideas of building the pool further out to sea. They had built a crazy golf course alongside the dining terrace. Pedro thought it would add another dimension, allowing parents to have a quiet drink while the kids played crazy golf and kept out of trouble.

In fact, in the previous season, with such paying bed and breakfast guests as there were, it had not worked out like that and it was the parents who played as the kids sat down and had an ice-cream and kept out of trouble.

Laura looked as beautiful as ever. She turned up in a vibrant scarlet pair of hot pants with a simple white halter-neck tennis top. She purposely wore a black soft-fronted bra, partially nowadays to annoy Pedro, who was bound to say at some point that he wished she would listen to the sports mistress's advice that when she wore a white top she should wear a white or flesh coloured bra. The teacher obviously knew how young men felt in the complicated process of growing up.

The last time Pedro had made such a suggestion, Laura had hooked a forefinger round one of the black straps and pulled it down to rest sexily on her upper arm. "No, Pedders, I wear black bras for you, because I know they turn you on." Laura knew how to tease.

"I don't think that's at all fair," he responded, "one day I'll find something that turns you on and I'll give you a taste of forbidden fruit. Anyway, you haven't apparently noticed: the really communicative girls these days don't wear bras at all and they can't be doing that without it being an open invitation to a more physical relationship."

Laura rose to the bait. "Look, my dearest friend in the world, you can go for a cheap fondle if you want, but get yourself and your plaything over-excited and unprepared and that can impact on lives forever."

Pedro's frustration was at boiling point. "If you both know there's a distance to run, you train for that distance and when you've covered it you stop, wind down and analyse how good the race was."

"Yes, sweetheart, I suggest you get yourself one of those little bra-less tarts to run your big races with you. But be careful they're not better at it than you are, and if they're faster, you're going to finish up frustrated anyway."

Pedro reckoned she was just going through what Marco described as her "sensitive time". He would get cross with her when she was like that.

"OK," he said, "here's an idea. You give me 15 points every game today."

"Why the hell should I do that?"

"Because I'm down 15 each game psychologically because when you're serving, my concentration goes when I look at your boobs. When I serve, you bob up and down as you get ready to receive the serve, and that's equally distracting."

"So, what about poor me? When you're serving I have the rippling body of a muscular stud to contemplate, and when you're receiving serve, you seem to have a lot to bounce with too."

Wow, so it was a sparky day. Pedro thought the underlying reason was probably the unhappiness brought on by her grandfather's death. They reached an awkward silence. It was all meant to be fun. But then she went into a reflective mood, which he had now learnt to read. He broke the ice. "I'm sorry about your grandfather."

Laura knew herself and all her emotions very well. Of course she was upset by the bereavement, but her greater fear was that her mother might want to stay on with her grandmother for a while, insisting Laura stay with her under her wing.

She knew her mother had often thought about such a proposition. It would serve a number of purposes. Laura's mother had had to flee to the security of her then-lover's arms when she'd first discovered she was pregnant. Her parents certainly were not prepared to provide shelter in that storm. Yet having lived in Spain for some 16 or 17 years, she'd had several summons back to her homeland, where it was promised all was forgiven. But her lawyer husband was not prepared to go to France. "Our bed has been made here in Spain. Here we should continue to lie in it."

However, Laura now knew that, from an original suspicion that her parents were only just about lying in the same bed now, all was not well in that relationship.

Her mother was permanently edgy and with that had lost the spark and fun she used to generate. She seemed miserable and introverted. When Laura put her arm around her mother's shoulder and asked why she was grumpy, she invariably replied, "Oh, it's just one of those moods. It'll pass. Just excuse me for a while. Now tell me what your arduous young man is up to. He's so nice and handsome and polite. Do give him a touch of affection – all growing young men need that. But remember I've explained how you can and should control such a situation."

She had lectured on the subject before. "The difference between a man and a woman is that once the wooing and the courting is behind him, a man becomes selfishly interested in his own satisfaction. Rarely does he give his partner much of a thought as he goes about extracting his own pleasure. Once he's achieved it, the male instinct is often to then cycle home, while the female one is to cuddle for hours afterwards. Darling, you've got a lot to learn about men."

"Oh mother, you're generalising too much, and maybe reflecting on your own circumstances and the nuisance I was." Laura had once before challenged on that exact basis.

"Laura, my beautiful child, you'll have to learn these things from your own experience."

Laura had once sought her father's involvement in showing his kinder, less selfish side to her mother. But he wasn't interested, saying that her mother's original insistence that they should marry for Laura's sake was in fact the real selfish act.

Laura had an old head on a young beautiful body and deep down she knew her parents' romance was over.

So, if her grandmother made a strong enough play for her daughter's companionship, even for a short while, and won that loyalty, Laura would be sucked in too. If only she could pluck up courage to explain. *Oh beautiful Pedders, who I'm sure I love for all the right reasons, what I need to tell you, to show you, is that I'm really scared that if our physical relationship was as compatible as our existing one, you and I would replicate my parents' mistakes... and then we'd face our own disaster, so please help me to wait.*

Laura came out of her reflective mode and rose to his challenge, which helped to ease her grief. "Then God help you, Pedders, I'll swing my boobs at you at a penalty of 15 points a game. Your payback will be we swim on my terms." She blew him a kiss.

As she went to the baseline, her back to Pedro as she collected a couple of balls, a tear rolled down her beautiful cheeks. As she bounced the ball she whispered, "Oh Pedro, make this easy on us. I think I must say au revoir for a while."

Those 15 points a game took Pedro's mind off Laura's attributes, at least for a while. At two sets each a truce was called as the evening sun said its own au revoirs, and they took to their bikes, cycling to the cove around the bay where, in seclusion, Laura had first got Pedro swimming. They followed their usual habit of waiting until they got to the rocks to change into their swimming gear, out of sight of each other.

This early evening it was different. She was playful.

"You can turn your back on the beach. Come on." She ran ahead. She sat on the sand, wriggling out of her hotpants into the bottom half of a bikini. "No looking!" she shrieked and, with her back to Pedro, slipped out of the much criticised bra and into a black bikini top matching her bottom half.

"Last one in is a chicken!" she shouted as she set off down the beach. Pedro struggled with his swimming shorts, leaving his abandoned T-shirt, shorts, socks, shoes and pants in a neat pile by the rocks.

This was the part he hated, entering the sea, although today he did not have the normal fear he had when confronted with high waves. Laura was already halfway across the sea to Africa, or so it seemed. She turned and swam back to him with a steady firm crawl. Pedro swam a contrived side stroke, as he often did, until he had the confidence to put his face in the water.

Laura laughed. "Now listen, you big fish, if I'm in France for a couple of weeks, how can I rest knowing you'll have nobody to make you get your face wet? Come here. Can you stand?"

"Yes," came his uncertain reply.

"Then here's your reward for all the fears you've overcome to get this far in beating your swimming phobia."

She put both hands behind her back and unclipped the bikini bra. She held it high out of the water.

He gawped in utter amazement.

"Look," she said, "I'd like you to see me."

He stood transfixed, not by her piercing Madonna's eyes, but by the sheer ecstasy he knew was waiting beneath the gently swirling waters. "You want to look. Here, give me your hands."

She pulled his outstretched arms in a gently downward motion and, like a submarine instructed to dive slowly by its captain, Pedro's head was gently and calmly and slowly submerged.

Laura stood tall as his knees buckled. She gazed down at his face, magnified and beautified even as it was distorted through the salt water. Raising his outstretched arms, she drew his head above the water like a periscope being lifted into the failing light. She took a step and a half towards him, leant forward and kissed him fully and beautifully and tenderly and lovingly and confidently on both his beautiful lips.

"Next time, keep your beautiful eyes open." She stepped back a pace. "Dive, dive, dive," she gently commanded her submariner as she tugged his arms downward. As his head broke downwards through the surface of the water, his eyes were wide open in utter bewilderment. He was controlled, yet out of control.

Her breasts were exposed specifically and definitely for his pleasure. He felt his trunks were going to explode, unable to contain the bulge. He suddenly realised that his head would also explode if he didn't surface. It shot out of the water, and although his eyes were smarting, he could see her, now a metre or so away again. She laughed as he caught his breath. Impulsively, she did a dolphin dive towards him. He felt her hands on each of his hips and then the shock of her pulling down his trunks.

Of course she'd had baths with her father, and been on school tours to capital cities where all the girls giggled together at the sight of stone-carved genitals. His, though, were not cast in stone or bronze. Below the water, where he couldn't see her face, she grabbed his private parts. Quite how or why she subsequently never had understood, but her animal instinct told her what was required.

She held her body well away from his, and as her head resurfaced, and her lips covered his, Pedro could take no more and released his submarine depth charge. Laura screamed as she felt the texture of the salty sea change in her hand. She performed an almost full backward dive upwards and out of the water and within ten seconds she was 20 metres out to sea.

She screeched from where she was for Pedro to pull his trunks up. "It's still dangerous," she shouted, "that stuff can swim, you know! I'll see you on the beach."

She swam a circuitous route back to the shore, by which time Pedro was waiting.

"Laura, can I thank you?"

"Of course, Pedders darling. But you can show me your gratitude by buying me a new bikini. I've lost my top in the sea. Now listen, if you've just fertilised every angel fish in the sea, that's your problem, OK?"

"Laura, *you* are my only angel fish in the sea and if that's the only moment I remember the day I die, my life will have been worthwhile."

"Darling Pedders, the day you die I doubt you'll get through all the memories you've yet to come. That will pall into insignificance. Hey! We'd better go. I have to leave with mother in the morning. How will I explain losing my bikini top?"

The first five years plus a few months into 1955, since Maria's uprooting, had flown by. She'd watched Pedro mature and had made it her priority to see him educated and happy, but the construction of the hotel was her other obsession. She unselfishly put the emotions in her own life onto a back burner. They'd occasionally more than simmered, of course, but keeping

Pedro's head down so he could get to Madrid to study architecture took up most of her emotional energy.

Not allowing Virginia's indifference to the hotel to affect her was another major task. Marco had long ago given up on drumming up any wifely interest or support for the project. But what was not forthcoming from his other half was well supplemented by the encouragement of his sister-in-law and his now very good friend, Pedro.

The three now almost prayed for Virginia's post-supper words of, "I've had a hard day, I think I'll turn in." In the early days, Maria would urge her to sit and chat about the project. To be fair, Virginia had on a few occasions sat in, but had added nothing. Her indifference depressed the otherwise enthusiastic trio.

Marco was always the catalyst for lengthy discussions, which was just as well. If left to his own devices, his very ordinary tastes, embellished with touches of glitz, would have no doubt produced an edifice that was old-fashioned at birth. He wasn't much good at financial control either.

Pedro would add youth and an innovative style of design quite ahead of anything else made of concrete that the Germans and Swiss were throwing up with such abandon all along the adjoining coast. Design, balance and taste were in his blood. He got his practical side from his mother.

Marco would start a post-supper discussion by perhaps saying, "What about the staircase?"

By way of an answer, Pedro would seek reconfirmation that, even though they were arranging to build only three floors, "so that we stay below the height of the pines," the inclusion of a lift was still on. Marco had hesitated.

"Then OK," Pedro said, in due deference to this uncle who was, after all, the money behind the brains, "what's your idea?"

"Terrazzo."

"What, all the way?"

"Well, of course. Come on, Pedro, you don't have a ladder with different rungs."

"No, uncle. But the whole of a ladder leant against a wall is seen at once. There's an opportunity to see the staircase in two parts. Firstly, the flight from ground to first. Excellent. Terrazzo or marble seen as you come in to the entrance would be great. Affluent. Clean. Expensive. But if you've got a lift, then the lazy bastards are bound to hitch a ride up to the first and second floors. When they get out, they'll step onto carpet. So if they were hot stepping it up to see a girlfriend on the second floor from their own position on the first floor without using the lift, they'd not notice if the staircase was carpeted. Carpet is what, 25 per cent of the cost of terrazzo? So! Let's say the cost of ground to first is four million pesetas as 100 per cent terrazzo. Then continued first to second would also be four million. That's 200 per cent. Take my option…"

Cheeky young nephew, thought Marco, *he doesn't really have an option, but I'd best hear him out.*

"So, the cost would be 125 per cent, compared to the total terrazzo idea… and remember the whole staircase is never seen all at once…"

"I'll think that through," Marco would typically say at the end of such conversations, while Maria listened and inwardly smiled with pride.

When she felt they had all moved forward with their thinking, she too would typically say, "I think I ought to turn in. I've got to be at the library first thing. I'll leave you boys to resolve these manly things. And when should we girls decide about the curtains and colours?" Well, OK, she knew the "we" would ultimately be just herself, but Maria felt for Virginia and would try and include her if she could.

As Maria brushed her teeth, she'd think of Paco, and talk to him. It was now almost a nightly ritual. She'd whisper, "God, that boy of ours is bright. He's so logical. Thank you for those genes you've passed on."

As she put her head on the pillow, her mind spun with the content of each full day. Sleep was her haven.

The boys would talk on, and Marco would now relax with Pedro. "Some wine?" he'd say, or sometimes venture: "Let's have a real brandy."

He'd been saying that for the past five years to a young man whose brain was focused on school work and his evening job as a hotel planner.

Pedro was Marco's replacement brother. He'd had to advise his nephew at 13 that he needed to shave every day. He was the one who said to Pedro that by the time Virginia served supper, Pedro was a bit "high" and either needed to wash or go to the chemist and enquire about the new deodorants. Pedro and Marco had an affinity, except where alcohol was concerned. Pedro's tipple was water or very occasionally Coca-Cola.

Gradually, spurred on by the fact that the foundations had been cast, the trio jointly made decisions about the final look and name of the hotel.

"We're thinking of calling it Hotel Playa," Marco told Virginia.

"I think Metro Centro would be better," she replied, "on account of all the people we're going to have to put up with."

That made Marco so sad. The way he had needed to fund the hotel building was by getting together local labour without appointing a main contractor. It had been a slow process, but they had predicted about four years to completion. In that time, he had hoped Virginia's views would change.

Looking back, 1950 had heralded a critical point in Maria's life. Paco's death remained a painful memory, but time was becoming something of a healer and her new pattern of life in Palafrugell seemed to be almost predetermined, as if she was being magnetised by some external force.

She was so proud of Pedro, whether he remained as the Pedro she and Paco had conceived or not. He seemed destined. Destined for what, exactly, she didn't know but it seemed unlikely that his various talents, his youthful beauty, creativity and humour would send him out to sea to earn a living.

Marco continued to adore her presence and her aura. She was not just a beloved sister-in-law, but also a friend and ally.

As for Virginia, she saw Maria as a sister. She would never be lifted from the isolation she'd cultivated, but at least she was able to sound off to Maria, whereas Marco, and all the others in her life, had developed a certain deafness founded on disinterest and resistance to her own emotional insecurities.

Then there were the inner thoughts of a healthy young woman, in her 30s, cruelly deprived of her conjugal entitlements. Maria was not living in an era of the liberated press, particularly in Catholic Spain. In the available magazines there were no gurus prepared to express publicly the emotions and desires of their readers. Maria would not have been able to read that the cure for all those feelings would be a trip to a sex shop, or a sheepish mail order purchase of a deaf-mute vibrator from the personal column of the local newspaper.

Although she would not mention it in her prayers, and certainly skipped past it in her thoughts, Maria needed physical attention, just like any other 30-something-year-old outside the Victorian era. Paco's love had been abruptly terminated and, just as an osteopath treats major physical damage by applying a similar force to the injury to the one that caused it, so Maria would doubtless need another turbulent emotional intrusion into her life, to replace what she had lost on that stormy night.

She had revived her allegiance to the library and the enormous affection she had for Carlos Sanchez, who had given her the lease of life she needed to return to Palafrugell, beyond the needs of her family. She knew the place inside out, the shelves, the books, and could answer the constant requests as to where a particular volume could be located.

At work, she used to apportion her day into administrative and housekeeping duties. Mornings tended to be spent dealing with fines for late returns and dealing with requisitions for particular publications when they were returned damaged by previous borrowers.

Afternoons were spent on book-keeping in its most literal sense: tidying the shelves and slotting back recently read books into their alphabetical niches, to once again sit shoulder to shoulder with their less popular neighbours.

One dull Thursday afternoon, she had been reaching perhaps a little too high from the fourth rung of the mobile ladder stack she was so used to manoeuvring between the aisles. It was a skirt day, as opposed to the trousers she sometimes chose if she thought she would be climbing a lot to replace the returns.

A strong, somewhat frustrated-sounding male voice suddenly boomed upwards in her direction.

He'd been looking around for assistance, somehow ignoring the young lady at the top of the ladder.

Now his gaze alighted on a beautiful pair of ankles, which led to equally wonderful calves that had been gently tanned by their daily exposure to the Mediterranean sun, up to the hem of a neat knee-length black skirt. Beyond this point, he was too much of a gentleman to intrude.

Hell, he thought, *what must the knees and thighs and hips supporting those legs be like?*

The waist above was neat, trim and accentuated by the wide leather belt that bound the waistline to a tailored blouse. Looking upwards, he saw the silhouette of a lovely young woman, topped by a shiny crop of black hair, hanging freely into the nape of an aristocratic neck.

An aura of calm came over him.

"Excuse me. Where would I find a copy of Romeo and Juliet? English version, please."

"Shakespeare," came a slightly disinterested reply from aloft.

"I'm clearly no scholar, am I?" came an apologetic response. "I've been looking under 'R' for ages. I hadn't realised you filed by author."

The voice, the apology, the sincerity were all so magnetic – and familiar. Maria stepped slowly backwards down the ladder. On landing, she looked upwards into a face that was as open and sincere as his confession.

"Mrs Martinez!" the voice announced in shocked recognition. "Mr Romanez!" was her equally stunned reply.

She smiled. He grinned. "So, who else could I possibly hope would guide me to Romeo and Juliet, filed under 'S'?"

"It's the balcony scene re-enacted," came her response. He held out both hands. She accepted the gesture. Neither needed reminding of their one and only previous meeting.

"How long is it?" he asked.

She made out she was calculating. "I'd say six years."

"Could I be so bold as to say it's my turn to offer the coffee? That's on a personal front. I'm on a day off so company rules don't apply."

"How could I refuse? The problem is, this time *I'm* working and not a free agent."

"What time do you finish?"

It was eight, but if she spoke nicely, as she could, to Carlos Sanchez, she was sure she could get off at six.

"Probably six," she replied.

"So you're still the negotiator. Are you saying I can buy you a drink at six, or probably I can?"

"You definitely can," she said with a giggle. "Does that give you enough time to brush up on your Romeo and Juliet?" Hell, why on earth had she said that? He paused. *I've messed it up,* she thought.

"All I need to check is that it's a happy ending… and that Juliet succumbed to a glass of chilled white wine and not boring old coffee."

"So she did," Maria replied, covering the earlier faux pas she thought she'd made. "Outside the library at ten seconds to six, to show you I really will be looking forward to seeing you again."

"Till then," he said.

She watched him leave. Empty-handed. She reached across for the translated Romeo and Juliet. *I'll bring it with me,* she whispered to herself.

Carlos Sanchez had been mayor of Palafrugell since the autumn of 1954, for a three-year term. That, in its wake, had brought a further dimension into Maria's life. She had agreed to work full-time at the library, which was fine for Marco. Somehow her brain was still fresh enough most evenings to go through the planning sessions for the Playa. Their job seemed to be prompting Virginia for any flicker of an opinion or thought on a subject, mainly housekeeping issues like crockery, or colours of cloths and serviettes. The design of duvet covers almost brought about the Martinez divorce.

"Duvets!" Virginia let forth with all the force her asthmatic lungs would allow. "We'll have eiderdown and sheets, surely!"

Marco, Maria and Pedro met the outburst with a sort of stunned silence, then Marco broke the ice. "Well, Virginia, our likely guests will be mid- and northern-European types. They'll expect duvets…"

"…and sauerkraut, frogs' legs, roast beef and I suppose a hole in the ground for a toilet! If they want their home comforts, they should stay at home!"

"Darling," Marco replied, "if they stay at home, we'll go broke."

"Well, first remember I've always been happy with what you've provided me with. You've no need to import all those foreign ideas just to make a bit more money… and a lot more hassle. You'll have to excuse me, I've had a hard day. I'm off to bed – my eiderdown's calling." Exit Virginia stage left.

Once she was out of earshot, the trio burst into laughter.

"Poor Virginia," said Maria.

Carlos, capitalising on the daytime job, had sprung an even newer idea on Maria. One day he'd called her into the library office for what he called a "coffee conference".

"I've got a problem. You know my wife of old. She's never enjoyed the best of health and now arthritis is taking over her body. She says she can't get out with me any more for the canvassing, let alone the formal functions I'm expected to attend with a partner. It's her idea that I ask you if you'd be prepared, with no strings attached, of course, to fill the gap for the more important functions."

Maria looked on with hesitation.

"Now hang on," Carlos interjected, "there's more to be said before you say yes or no. Firstly, I'd give you a dress allowance because I appreciate your wardrobe might not have the appropriate clothes. More importantly, if I become mayor, I'd recognise the importance of your support. And, my becoming mayor would coincide with the opening of your brother-in-law's hotel.

"The mayoral calendar includes a three-day visit to Germany, hosting the mayors of a number of other European regions because Spain's been chosen as the epicentre of European Co-operation. What's more, there's an option to host Europe Travel 1956, which will be attended by most of the big European tour companies, and I'd reckon I was a pretty poor friend if I didn't fill your hotel with conferences. Now, what do you think?"

Maria said that she was overcome and much complimented by the thought. However, she didn't have the confidence to do it. She'd never met dignitaries, she wouldn't know what to talk about… she'd be lost.

Carlos looked amazed. "Maria. My sweet, beautiful olive-skinned Maria. The men will melt in your presence and their wives will go out of their way to hold your attention for themselves, to keep you away from their drooling other halves. Besides, it'll be very good experience for you in the lead up to your beautiful Pedro's sparkling career-to-be. You've said, in this very room, that he's developing a real charisma and if, and when, Juan Carlos of Spain is looking to marry off his daughter, he'd be a fool not to extend his sights towards Pedro!" As he said it, Carlos threw back his head with laughter.

"How long have I got to make up my mind?"

"As long as it takes. But you ought to read this." And he produced a large gilt invitation from his top left drawer. "The Mayor and Ancient Wardens of the City of Barcelona, invite Cllr C Sanchez and Mrs Maria Martinez to attend the…"

Her eyes filled with tears. Nobody had ever shown such faith in her before. She felt 100 metres tall.

"Of course," she said, and leant across the desk and pecked him on the forehead. "You're a lovely friend. Your wife is generosity itself for lending me her role."

A decade is merely a moment in time. It's just that much longer than a second, minute, day, week, month or year. It is often a yardstick to occasion change, as one does on New Year's Eve by electing to give something up.

So a change of a single digit in Maria's calendar marked a new ten-year lease in her life. The past year had been a happy, hard-working one. Pushing Pedro, forcing her grief for Paco another year back. Keeping Marco enthusiastic about the project. Trying to stimulate Virginia into all the planned changes 'for the better', as the trio put it.

So, yet another dimension – or two. The proposal to act as first lady of Palafrugell Province. And now, out of the blue, in had ridden her Prince Charming. As she contemplated six o'clock, Maria pinched herself. Was it possible that she could ride away into the sunset with this re-visiting prince?

She'd actually momentarily panicked when she saw José Romanez, and now she was remembering that he was seriously spoken for. They had only met once but in that short space of time, he had talked of his wife and son.

Should she stand him up? Was she encouraging him to flirt or cheat, even for one evening? Not that anything was going to happen to them over a drink for old times' sake.

On the other hand, if she had caught Paco sipping a drink with a female acquaintance in the early evening, after she had toiled at home all day, he would have had hell to pay.

She would stand him up, she resolved. She would meet him outside at six, give him the book, say she had a migraine and rush back home.

She still wanted to look her best though. At 5.40pm, she popped into the ladies'. Stripped out of her skirt and slightly crumpled blouse. Splashed cold water over her thighs and stomach and slipped her blouse on again while her skin was still damp. She shook her skirt to shake away the creases of the day and slid that back over her hips, zipping it up the side. Her look was completed by high-heeled black sandals, which she preferred to keep at the library than at home, thus avoiding Virginia's inevitable jibes.

Would she seem boring to José, with her hair still the same as when they'd first met? She flicked it away from her shoulders with the tail comb she always carried in her black patent leather bag.

The mirror wasn't good, but what she could see didn't look too bad for the end of the day. *Pity about the migraine,* she thought.

Something compelled her to walk out of the front library doors at exactly one minute to six. She knew because Carlos had bought her a little Bulova watch to mark his election as mayor, and that never lied.

A voice came from the side of the footpath.

"You'd best slow down. You're running about 45 seconds too keen!"

Taken aback, she blushed very slightly. José had such an endearing smile. He was so in control.

"Actually, I needed to be early. I didn't want you to be hanging around. You left the book," she added, and handed it to him. "I'm really sorry, I'll have to duck out of the drink. I've got a migraine."

"Looking as beautiful as that?" he countered. "Look, there are three things, well, four actually I'd like to get out of the way."

Why on earth did he have her rapt attention? She was acting like a 16-year-old. Before she could say a word, he continued.

"I want you to know, I'm not cheating on my wife. That's explanation number one, which I'll go into over a drink. Secondly, I just want you to know how very, very pleased I was to happen to stop alongside your ladder. Then there's my magic cure for a migraine. Sparkling wine with a hint of grenadine… and, of course, I need to know whether Romeo had a better ending with Juliet than you seem to be proposing for me. I had in mind that drink, out in the air on the terrace of La Tortuga, and you'll be home by eight… and there's a fifth reason for that."

Maria felt swept off her feet, a feeling that lasted a number of weeks thereafter. José's assertiveness in that situation mirrored what her own role had been since Paco's accident. She had become a dominant personality in almost all her encounters.

With Pedro, she was forcing him to keep his head down and not be distracted by all the hotel planning. In a different way, she was holding Marco's hand and keeping him on a straight and narrow economic path… and embellishing some of his more mundane proposals. Virginia, she had worked out, was not only insecure and isolated, but was suffering menopausal depression at quite a young age. At the library, Carlos needed her leadership too. So as they moved off in José's red Alfa Sprint, doing what she had been told to do, she had a pleasant feeling of calm about her.

"Have you been to La Tortuga?"

She wished she could say yes. She was getting used to bluffing with those worldly types she had to mingle with as Carlos's leading lady, wanting them to think she was not some upstart from the local village, so it was strange for her to feel honesty would be appreciated.

After due deliberation she said, "No. It will be nice there, I know." She gave him a broad smile, which took his eye off the road.

Good God, she was more beautiful than he ever remembered. She oozed a serenity and calmness that blended perfectly with his James Last classical tape.

"It's 10 kilometres, or so, towards Palamos," José informed her.

They sped on with just the music for sound. Who needed to speak? Then it dawned on Maria that José didn't live in Callella; she would have remembered if he had.

"So, what brings you to these parts?" she enquired, realising as she said it that she really didn't want to know.

"If I said it was to find you, would you believe me?" He hadn't lost that smile.

"No."

"OK, let me try another one. My parents have moved out to Llanfranc. We've got a boat in the harbour there and we try and get out most weekends. There's no library in Llanfranc and José junior needs a copy of Shakespeare for his pre-secondary exam. So I came to the library.

"To be absolutely honest, I'd heard you worked there, but my son really does need the book, so my visit was two-fold. I just took a chance on you being there. You probably won't remember, but you came to the mayoral dinner in Girona. It was something to do with the region's forthcoming elections, and my company took a table there to promote our Municipal Indemnity Scheme. You floated in on the arm of your new man. I couldn't bring myself to come and speak to you.

"OK, do you want me to be honest? I was jealous. Why a man so much older? I asked myself. Then I plucked up courage and asked one of our guests if they knew who he was. They said they thought he was the mayor of Palafrugell. Then I asked who you were, and they said they presumed you were either his mistress or, as a long shot, his wife. So, I was more cross than jealous. OK, maybe envious."

Maria let forth a screech of laughter. "Oh my God! You really thought that! That's Carlos. Yes, he's the mayor. Yes, he does have a wife. No, I'm not his wife, or his mistress. His wife can't get around and I'm her nomination, her stand in. I'm also Carlos's assistant librarian and I go up and down ladders finding books for men like you."

She continued to laugh, then became conscious that he was pulling over into a lay-by. The car came to a halt. He reached forward and turned the music down. Unwound his window slightly to let in the cool spring evening air.

"I'm truly sorry," said José, "I felt like biffing the man on the nose who told me. He did sound convincing though." He took a deep breath. "My wife can't mind me buying you this drink." He caught his breath. "She died two years ago."

Any hint of laughter still lingering around Maria evaporated in a frozen haze. "So, I misjudged you too," she said quite calmly. "Would you like to tell me about it?"

"Well… yes. But *you* know how it hurts. We thought she was pregnant. Quite unplanned, as it happens, because she wanted us to get settled into a family house a bit nearer to Barcelona… she was worried about my daily commute. In the middle of the night she developed what she thought were cramps. I don't know, it's all irrelevant now but she had some name for them."

"Yes, I expect so," Maria interjected.

"She didn't want to call a doctor, said she'd be alright. Then she got up to walk around. She was crying in agony for two or three hours until I wrapped her in a blanket and drove her to the hospital. We had to drop José off at her mother's on the way. To cut a long, traumatic story short, some fool of a house doctor agreed it was pregnancy-related. It was appendicitis. Her appendix burst before a surgeon could get there and I left the hospital at six in the morning a widower. The hardest part was waking our ten-year-old and saying mummy wouldn't be coming home."

Maria could see José's anguish in his transformation from fun-generating person to sad raconteur. The whole time he had been telling the story, she'd noticed his tense grip on the highly polished gear change lever, as if to say, "That's out. Thank God."

She reached her left hand towards his right one, still resting on the gear change, then stretched her right arm across her lap and placed that hand on top of the gear lever. His left hand came across to build the fourth layer of a hand-castle, as they might once have done as kids. They remained perfectly still.

"How quickly can you get us that drink?" she said. "Cut out the grenadine, my migraine's gone…"

He threw her a piercing, doubting glance. "OK," she said, "I made it up." They laughed as he turned the ignition key, raised the volume on the music and took off at speed.

"One cool wine coming up."

The terrace at La Tortuga was indeed spectacular. There was a north-south view from the high point on which it had been built, and for miles in each direction. They were shown to the cliff face of the terrace, and José took charge, ordering a bottle of local sparkling wine. Maria chuckled as he stipulated the brand, and told him she'd get squiffy if she was expected to drink half a bottle.

She realised later that it must have looked rude when, as the waiter put down a dish of mixed olives and almonds, she looked at her watch. But José had rationed their time together, as if she was Cinderella, and she was already dreading the end of the evening.

It was 6.40pm.

José said, "Shall we get the eight o'clock deadline out of the way too?"

"I wasn't checking how much time we had left," Maria lied. "I'm sorry, José… I was just… it's been… well… it's just that I'm happy for the first time in… no, that's not actually true either. I've been extremely happy in all but one direction. What I meant was, I hadn't realised how really happy I could be."

"Here's to you, babe," José joked as they lifted their glasses. "The eight o'clock bit is a ritual – I always promise José junior, unless I know I'm going to be away, that I'll kiss him goodnight and tuck him up. I'd never willingly let him down. I'm his security. The car is to give us a toy to bond over, and the boat, although not intentionally, is a sort of haven where we're forced into a close environment together, where we talk about fishing and tides and winds… Oh hell! Maria, I really wasn't thinking…"

She patted his hand affectionately. "I can feel the wine and somehow or other I can share thoughts of Paco with you. What's your wife's name?"

"What is, you say. Everybody else says what was!"

"José, remember I'm a year ahead of you. Paco still 'is'. So, what's your wife's name?"

"Anna."

"Then Anna and Paco shall remain as 'are'." They both chuckled.

They chatted and giggled their way through the wine, Maria telling José how she and Pedro had come for a short sojourn with Marco and Virginia, and had stayed. How she had let the cottage in Rosas and got involved in the hotel project. She confided that soon she would have to reach an agreement with Carlos. "What, to give up being his mistress?" José interjected.

"No, I'll need some flexi-time through the summer to help Marco cope with the bookings. With any luck."

José reported his success with the insurance company. How he was now regional director of the north-east of Spain, which meant he had a direct line of communication back to head office in England. Yes, Maria thought, *maybe Pedro too would eventually benefit from at least a spell in the UK if he was to become an international architect.* Young José was likely to become a sportsman. He had kept pace with his father when they took up golf, as a further means of bonding without a mother's presence. José explained how his mother-in-law looked after the boy Monday to Friday while José senior trekked to Barcelona, but how he then would take over at the weekend.

Had Maria spent her insurance payout on perfume and fancy goods yet?

"No! That's as safe as houses in the bank."

"Is that the most advisable place for it to be? Interest rates are low and all the pundits say inflation is set to rise, so really you ought to consider investing where you'll keep pace. You worked hard to secure that payout!" He beamed his beaming smile. This time it was his hand that covered hers in a moment of great compassion. She pushed his hand away playfully.

"You were easy," she mocked. "If I'd cried I'd have got another ten per cent!" But once she'd said them, she wished she could catch her words back.

"Press me and I'll tell you what head office said I could go to."

"OK, José. Have I really known you for ever?"

Her hand moved back to cover his. They looked at each other in silence.

"My left shoe has just fallen off," she said. "I think you should look at your watch."

José did just that. "Hell," he said, "you're so right. Come on, Cinderella. Drink up."

"Suppose I say I won't," Maria asked.

"Then I'll never invite you out again. I'll leave you to the demands of the mayor."

She picked up her glass and swigged the contents. "Now there's a good obedient girl for you."

As they climbed the steps to the parking level, he put his hand behind her tender elbow. It was smooth and feminine as she pressed it firmly into his guiding grip.

He unlocked the passenger side of the car, opened the door and stood over her as she placed her rear onto the leather seat. With one deft movement of both beautiful knees in unison, she swung her legs into the well. Her skirt naturally just reached down to her knee, so, in that one sweeping gesture, it rose to expose a further four to six inches of those beautiful olive thighs. She tugged at the hem with both hands.

"I'm used to a mayoral limousine, I'm afraid."

"Poor old bloke doesn't know what he's missed," José retorted. As they drove away, James Last came into his own.

"I didn't tell you about the boat," he suddenly remembered. "I was involved in a big claim. It was probably the reason for me getting a directorship, because it went quite well for the company. A timber merchant's premises on the edge of Gerona was totally destroyed. The proprietor was a bit crook. You know, his timber yard was the most stocked it had ever been. All his lorries happened to be garaged there overnight. The claim was millions of pesetas, yet we knew the premises had been passed down a number of generations without incident.

The owner was a tough shit. I took a bit of a flyer, probably something I'd learnt from our own negotiation." He gave her hand a friendly little squeeze.

"I told him that a series of circumstances encouraged me to think of putting the matter into the hands of the police to investigate arson. He seemed to panic and… well… to cut a very long story short, we settled at 40 million pesetas. London thought I'd done a miraculous deal at £200,000 or thereabouts, they'd put at least 100 million pesetas on the reserve. The proprietor and I had concluded the transaction when he suddenly announced he'd forgotten about something the company owned in Llanfranc. I said, 'Too late amigo, the deal's closed.' 'It's a beautiful little boat,' he said.

"I told him the deal was done, we'd take all the company assets, the boat as well. He shrugged and called me a tough bastard. So I returned the complete inventory to head office. They flew a guy out to congratulate me on saving them almost 60 million pesetas. I was a blue-eyed boy. Then we sold the demolished premises for about twice the insurance payout, which pleased them even more.

"When I told them about the boat, they took a chance on it not being a gin palace and said it was mine as a bonus for all I'd done. So there, young lady, is how I have this boat."

"Can you sail it?" Maria asked, with a somewhat protective interest in José senior and junior's wellbeing.

"Of course I can. I did a mariner's course at night school in Barcelona. It helped pass the evenings instead of going to the discos every night."

"Go on," Maria encouraged.

They were within a kilometre of Callella. "Where would madam like to be dropped?"

"I'll show you. No favouritism. There's a point in the road where the mayor's chauffeur used to drop me because he could turn the car round there. Then you can take the fork back to where I imagine your parents are… Here!" Maria said in a firm raised voice.

José stopped the car, got out and walked round to open Maria's door. "You really are a gentleman," she said.

"Not at all," José replied. "It was fun seeing you get in. I can't wait to help you out."

He extended both hands. She tucked her handbag under her left armpit, which pushed her left breast firmly towards its sister, accentuating her still firm cleavage. She held onto his powerful hands and allowed him to pull her across and out, somehow finishing on tiptoe just below his head.

"The timber man was right. You *are* a bastard, but a lovely one." She pecked his cheek, broke free from his hands, stepped back and said, "Thank you, thank you, thank you." She turned and walked.

"Maria," he called, "no, it's thank *you,* gracias, gracias, gracias. Can I call you at the library?"

"Sure, but you'll have to get past the librarian."

CHAPTER 6

José phoned the next morning, with fresh things to talk about. Those morning calls became a habit; somebody, in fact the only person, regularly to enquire how she was. She was always "fine" but never bold enough to say she would be even more fine if she could have José's company all the time. But then, they were partially opening the hotel in the late June following Maria's reunion with José, so she had a lot to occupy her mind.

When she found prime time for just herself, she reflected back to José's third or fourth call the week after they'd been for their drink at La Tortuga. José had announced excitedly, "I've got this brilliant idea. José junior's got his Whitsun scout camp so he'll be away the weekend of the 16th, in about three weeks. Could you grab some time out of, say, the Sunday or even the Saturday, or both, and I'll sail you out for a picnic. Can you snorkel? OK, you could have a lazy day first and top up the tan…" It seemed he would have kept going with his enthusiastic commentary of things to do.

Maria interjected. "Hey, when's it my turn to talk?"

He stopped. "Now, providing you say yes."

"It's no to the picnic. It's yes to the trip. Sunday's fine." (She thought she'd be able to go to mass on Saturday evening, instead of Sunday morning.) "You'll have to teach me to snorkel, I'm afraid."

"Terrific! But why no to the picnic?"

"José, let *me* surprise *you* every now and again." She'd like to do the picnic. She could probably even borrow Carlos's Thermos boxes, which he sometimes turned up with when he knew there wouldn't be time to eat during electioneering.

"Can I pick you up from home?"

"Not just yet," she said, hesitating. "Can you remember where you dropped me the other night?"

"Vividly."

"Then you say the time and I'll wait there."

"Eight in the morning."

"Wow! That's early."

"I want it to be the longest day ever."

She blushed in response to the attention. "Well, I'll want you to be home by eight."

"José gets back on Monday."

"I'll need my beauty sleep, you know."

"You're doing well without."

"Lying toad. Romeo and Juliet was for you, wasn't it? All this charm."

José roared with laughter. "You're incredible, Maria!"

"Should I say thank you?"

"No, just stay incredible, that'll be recompense enough."

"Hey! I'm busy."

"Phone you soon."

"Cheers."

"Cheers." She felt she wanted to blow him a kiss down the line.

Three weeks, she thought. She'd diet a little. Maybe, just maybe, she would buy a new swimming costume. It was years since she'd been swimming.

What the hell would she tell Pedro and Marco? What on earth would she say to Virginia? To go missing for a whole day on a Sunday would take some arranging…

"Penny for your thoughts," Carlos said on his way through to his office.

"You've just answered a prayer," Maria said, as she looked up in surprise. "Could you support an excuse for stocktaking over the Whitsun weekend?"

"Surely you don't want to work over a holiday weekend?"

"Well, I don't. But I need some space and I'd like to tell Marco and Pedro I'm working."

"Is it the young man who met you last week?"

"OK, Carlos. You're a canny old friend. You got it in one."

"Of course, I'll support your outrageous lies on one condition."

"I hope it's not too hard to agree to."

"It's conditional that you come in on the Monday looking as radiant as you have for the last week."

"Hell, does it show?"

"All day long. Yes. He looked a nice young man from a distance. I hope I'll get to be one of the first to be introduced."

What a really nice friend Carlos is, Maria thought to herself. José and she might turn out to be some short-lived fantasy, but at least Carlos was showing his acceptance and support of the inevitable: that Maria would have a life. After all, she was still a young woman.

"Carlos, could I ask you another favour?"

"Maria, whatever it is will only be a small repayment for the support you've given me in the run up to the mayoral election and now this busy year of office. What's it to be?"

"Could I possibly borrow your Thermos boxes?"

"What, just for stocktaking day?" he mused.

"Yes, just for that."

"Of course, they're already here in the stationery store. Consider them there for whenever you need them."

She thanked him. Three weeks to go!

Both Pedro and Marco were of a like mind, that going in to work on a Sunday was too much, but if Maria had to then they knew nothing they could say would make a difference.

Marco turned to Pedro, beaming. "Well, if your mother's working then it would seem alright for you and me to slip down to Barcelona for the game."

Barcelona were at home to Benfica in the semi-final of the European Cup.

"We'd have to leave at the crack of dawn. The traffic'll be heavy," Marco advised.

"I'll tell you what I'll do, I'll make you a special breakfast to set you up for your journey," Maria offered.

So that would help; she didn't have to worry about leaving them behind. Virginia would probably sleep all day.

Time moved on and, fortuitously, one of the evening hotel planning meetings touched on the subject of tablecloths and all that went with them.

"There's a new store in San Feliu," said Maria. "I saw pictures of it in a magazine we have delivered to the library. The article said they're stocking the very latest in European designs and fabrics. Would you like me to look for some ideas?"

"That would be terrific," Marco said.

Maria had also read about a new ladies sportswear shop that had recently opened. She could combine the two retail investigations.

When she mentioned it to Marco, he said, "How would you feel about taking Virginia along too? You could make a girlie thing out of it." Maria's heart sank. "Fine by me," she said convincingly.

"Oh no." Marco suddenly changed his mind. "She'd probably be an absolute pain. You'd be better by yourself."

Maria's heart raced. "You're a bit cruel, brother-in-law."

"I know, but I bet I'm right. No, on second and final thoughts, don't mention it. Just go."

Maria did go the following Saturday and, like a young girl with a surprise inheritance, made straight for the sportswear shop. The window was crammed full of Adidas. Nothing fetching at all. It was all clearly aimed at the serious athlete.

Feeling a bit downhearted, she started to walk away and gave a casual glance to her left. There, with a discreet window display of two simple bikinis, was a shop with a sign saying "Mademoiselle Playa." She took a deep breath and walked in.

She felt she was going to sink into the carpet, it was so thick. As the door closed, a bell sounded and a pretty, slim young sales assistant appeared, her hair black and sleek.

"Hello, madam. Can I help you?" Experience had taught the girl that it was always best to let the customer think they knew what they wanted and to identify that with what they could then be tempted to buy.

"I'd like to treat myself to a new swimming costume."

"We've got a really good range of Jantzan's latest. Do you have a colour preference?"

Maria smiled nervously. "Look, if I'm honest, it's years since I bought beachwear. I'm a bit out of touch. I'd welcome some suggestions."

The assistant stepped back and took a long appraising look at Maria's body. "Can I level with you?" the assistant replied. "Let's start by me saying my name's Mercedes." She held out a soft, genuine hand.

Maria took it. "I'm Maria."

"OK, Maria, this is where I become frank. I'd say you're a 75B bra size and 90cm hips, but I'm guessing a 61cm – 65cm waist."

"You're being a bit flattering! I'm a good size 40 dress."

"OK. So why a costume and not a bikini?"

"Look, I'm the wrong side of 30 for a bikini."

"Never," Mercedes stated emphatically. "Second question, do you intend to go topless?"

"Goodness me, no!" Maria blushed.

"Maria, everybody's doing it. But let's just try and keep some options open. Pop in the changing room and I'll hand some things in for you to try. How do you feel about a stunning scarlet?"

"Ideally not, just something tasteful, I don't want to draw attention to myself."

"Then it's black or white. It depends whether you want to look virginal or in mourning." She wasn't to know how loaded that question was. Maria had to be brave about the fact that she didn't know which option either.

"I'll go for black and white," she replied with a smile.

Mercedes was quite taken aback. "Do you know, I might just have to

86

cheat and sell you a white bra and a black bottom by breaking a set." They both laughed.

"Slip your things off. I'll start with black."

As Maria undressed, she caught her breath as she glimpsed the caesarean scar. She'd forgotten about that. She was about to call out to Mercedes when the young woman put her hand in through the curtain. "You'll look really super in this."

Habitually, with hygiene always in her mind, Maria kept her briefs on and slipped the bikini bottoms over her ankles, up past her knees and then, with a wiggle of her bottom, over her hips. She gingerly looked in the mirror. Were her knickers covering the scar? She pushed them down so they were covered by the bikini briefs and turned again to face the mirror. No scar. She hurriedly slipped her bra off and put on the bikini top. It was strapless and fastened at the back. She tugged the front of the top up to make her breasts more comfortable, then stood back. The curtain parted and the assistant appeared.

Mercedes's voice broke the silence of Maria, shocked, seeing herself as a young woman again. She never spent time dressing at home and rarely appraised herself because, for one thing, she didn't need to give her body any attention, just for self-gratification. Secondly, she was always worried Pedro might walk in on her.

"Are you going to let me give you an opinion?" Mercedes offered.

"I'm cringing, looking at myself."

"Out you come, madam. Can I suggest you put your shoes back on. We'll get a bit more shape with those on."

Maria pulled the curtain wider and moved out of the cubicle. Mercedes looked her over again.

"Maria, I hope you'll come back and see us again in the future, so I'll only give you an honest opinion. You look absolutely stunning. The briefs are just a touch shy…" She stepped forward to smooth them around Maria's rear, then took a step back. "Well, Maria, there'll be a lot of young men's heads turning if they are allowed to see you in this get-up."

"I'm only interested in turning one head," Maria laughed, in an all-girls-together way. "I'll take this set."

She dressed and then carried the little outfit to the desk. She'd peeped at the price as she put the two-piece on. Well, she would spend some of the interest on the insurance money. She smiled broadly as she thought that the head she hoped to turn was the very one who'd put her in funds. She arrived at the tablecloth shop with little enthusiasm – that is, until she saw a sign pointing upstairs saying "Spring sale of dress fabrics". Perhaps she would just have a peep after she'd looked at the tableware. She gathered samples of a strong parchment coloured range of cloths, napkins and chair covers. Her visit was well worthwhile and, as the advert said, it was all undoubtedly the latest European style. Upstairs might be a different matter.

What do you wear for a picnic on a boat? she asked herself. The boat would be white, she supposed. What sort of boat would it be? Oh God, would it have a loo? Supposing it didn't? Well, she'd have to go for a subtle swim. She'd have to slip out of her newly acquired bikini bottoms though. No way could she soil those at that price!

So, if it was a white boat, she wouldn't want to wear a white outfit. Then she saw a beautiful material, described as "non-creasing", which had a black background and large sunflowers printed at random over it. The effect was a warm orange colour, and in the same display there was a blending fabric that might be suitable for a blouse. She could wear her high white wedding sandals but she wondered if the shoe menders in Palafrugell had an orange dye. That would look stunning, or even black would be OK.

She bought enough sunflower for a skirt and then went back for another couple of yards so that she could make an over-wrap for her bikini.

In the remaining days, she put together a simple menu for the picnic. She wondered what José ate. Would he like fussy food or simple male fodder like Paco?

Oh, Paco! She felt guilty about how she was looking forward to her date. "Look, Paco," she said, "if you hadn't done that silly thing and gone in for a second catch, then you'd be here now. If you'd come back in one piece, which I always prayed for, then I doubt I'd even have met José because there wouldn't have been a claim. And it was you who took out the insurance in the first place."

Then she went into one of her moods of remorse, which were noticeably less frequent nowadays. "Oh, Paco. It's nothing serious. It's a friendship. You're OK with Carlos. Well, it's exactly like that. Friends move on, I'm sure in a few weeks' time it will all be a silly memory. Show patience, my love." That helped her make her mind up. Definitely not male fodder like Paco had enjoyed.

Some smoked salmon, pre-prepared in those cigar-type rolls into which she could stuff some shrimps in mayonnaise. She could prepare some pâté on toasted French stick and chicken legs. It would all fit into the little plastic containers that came with Carlos's ice-box set. A few cheeses and a small apple flan would complement the main intention.

What about some wine? She wouldn't overdo it with champagne or anything too pretentious. She always felt terribly unpatriotic but she did like Mateus Rosé, even though it was Portuguese. So would José, she was sure.

Pedro was at his evening study class in advanced English on the Friday before picnic Sunday, as Maria thought of it. She would do her legs while he was out. Mercedes had whispered to her as she was leaving the shop that she didn't want to be too personal but, as a friend, as it were, it was *de rigueur* to shave one's legs these days. Especially in a designer bikini.

"How do you do that?" Maria had asked with a modicum of shock.

"You either borrow your husband's razor without him knowing" (Maria still wore Paco's ring, of course, so Mercedes thought she was on safe ground) "or you buy these new little throw-away razors. You can buy them in most markets, and if you really want to be the epitome of style, you slip your bikini bottoms on and draw a line around the waistband and around the crutch with an old eye pencil, take your briefs off and hop in the bath and shave away untidy hair showing outside the line."

"I'll not be wanting that much style," Maria had said as she shook hands with Mercedes and left.

But, in the end, she got a pack of razors and found an old eye pencil. She tried her bikini on for the first time since acquiring it and, whether it was that she'd been existing largely on fruit, or that she didn't have her knickers on underneath, she was happy with how she looked.

Out with the pencil. In to the bath and, hey presto, modern stylish lady. She just hoped José might notice… *Oh no,* she gasped, *supposing he brings his parents?* She made a note to ask him if anyone else was accompanying them.

Virginia had actually shown a rare interest in someone other than herself when Maria started making her sunflower outfit.

"I got the material in the shop in San Feliu when I went to look at tableware," Maria said. "Next time come with me. We've got bed linen to choose."

"Surely there's nothing to compete with white," Virginia proffered. Maria was in no mood to argue.

"I tend to agree," she said, well-knowing she intended to follow the table theme into the bedrooms as well.

Making the outfit went according to plan. It was quality material to work on, which always made a difference, as did the Sylko thread from England.

As she took her really early shower on the Sunday of the trip, Maria felt excited. She washed her hair with a mimosa shampoo, which she'd also bought in a trendy little beauty shop in San Feliu. She ran her hands under her arms and into the tops of her thighs, testing for stubble. Giggling as she thought back to the trepidation of her first tidy-up.

Her black bra and briefs wouldn't show under the orange blouse and always made her feel a bit more feminine. Marco had once made a jibe over the family evening meal that he'd seen some pretty grown-up underwear on the washing line. "Is it some secret you've been keeping from me, Virginia?" he asked with a smile.

"No it's not. It's some little secret Maria wants us to know about," Virginia parried a little bitterly. "But you'll have loads of that stuff to peep at when you ship in the waitresses and chambermaids."

Pedro joined in the banter. "Do you know, Aunt Virginia, I'm going to buy you some French underwear for Christmas. I really want to see you as one of the girls and not to be left out."

"Do that, young man, and you'll be out of my will."

He knew she meant it.

Maria was beginning to have second thoughts about volunteering to cook the boys their pre-match breakfast. Why had she suggested it? Guilt was the most obvious conclusion she came to. She slipped on her housecoat and went into the kitchen.

Pedro arrived first, clean-shaven and shower-fresh. Maria's stomach leapt. How he reminded her of Paco, particularly at this time in the morning, which symbolised the mariner's return from the sea. He kissed his mother softly on the cheek. "Hey! You smell good."

"Don't I always smell good?"

"Of course you do. You smell especially good. Is it lily of the valley or something?"

"Go on, chiquito, one day you'll learn how to charm some young lady. No! It's mimosa."

Maria seemed particularly relaxed. Now was his moment.

"Mother, it's likely I'll make the first eleven in the autumn. Is our promise still on? You won't ever call me chiquito if I make it?"

"Yes, darling. But you *will* always be my chiquito."

Marco arrived. He too kissed Maria lightly on the cheek.

"You smell good. What's this in aid of, your dirty Sunday?"

Maria hoped afterwards that she hadn't blushed or shown her instinctive reaction. "Dirty Sunday? What on earth do you mean?"

"Well, stocktaking a load of fourth-hand books must at least be dusty."

"Oh, I see." She oozed relief. "Well, maybe I didn't rinse my hair well enough."

"Your hair looks lovely to me."

"Marco! Is this some sort of chat-up line you're rehearsing for the girls at the match in Barcelona? Remember it's my son you might be teaching!"

"I don't want to tell tales out of school, but young Pedro doesn't need any lessons in that area."

"Uncle! Come on, we promised we wouldn't let on about our male reconnoîtres. If you're not careful I'll speak in a louder voice for Virginia to hear."

"OK, let's call it a draw. We don't want her losing out on her Sunday beauty sleep."

After they'd enjoyed her offering of eggs, mushrooms, toast and a plate of cheese, Maria waved the men in her life off into the early morning, put the finishing touches to the picnic she had smuggled into the kitchen the night before, took the wine from the back of the newly installed fridge, and popped back to the cottage.

The weather was dry and warm for the time of year. The sea would be cool, not at its most enticing but she liked it when the temperature was crisp. She looked at her Bulova – she only had 20 minutes if she was to be at the road junction on time. She slipped into her new skirt. Put on the blouse and carefully buttoned it up, allowing just a hint of cleavage. She had packed a weekend handbag with her neatly folded bikini and wrap, all very compact so it wouldn't look as though she was taking luggage with her for the trip. It was all to look very casual. "I've thrown a couple of bits in to change into," she would say if José caught her out on her pre-planning.

It was now almost five to eight. She would just make it. She made sure she had all her bits and pieces, and money in her purse should she need it. *Here, at last,* she thought. A final flick of the hair, a smoothing of her pale coral lipstick. On went her rope slip-on wedges and she put the cool-box down to free her hand to close the door behind her. She started up the rear garden path to cut out the main entrance where the new cobbles were being laid.

Suddenly Virginia's voice rang out. *She must be talking in her sleep,* Maria thought. Awake at four minutes to eight?

"The sunflowers look lovely!" she shouted.

Maria stopped and waved, shouted back, "Good morning!"

"Bit of a waste for stocktaking, isn't it?"

"Oh! Yes. That's right. No! I'll wear overalls. But you never know, Carlos might feel so guilty that he'll buy me supper. I've done him lunch," she said, pointing to the box. "Must fly. Have a good day."

"What, with nobody here, I bet I do!" Virginia shouted out sarcastically.

Maria set off at pace again. *Blast it!* she thought. *She's made me completely late.* She got to within 50 metres of the junction. Stopped. Put down the cool-box. Delved into her bag. Took out the heels, slipped them on, and popped the wedges back in to replace the sandals. Then she picked up the box again and changed pace from a hurried walk to a strut.

She rounded the hedge to find Mr Reliable waiting, leaning nonchalantly against the gleaming red Alfa. He was wearing smartly pressed blue trousers and a crisp white shirt with short sleeves. He cut a very dashing figure. His light brown hair didn't have a strand out of place.

José walked quickly towards her, stooping as they met to put his strong hand on the handle of the cool-box. As he rose, she realised he was holding her hand and the handle as one. They instinctively bent down in a single motion to put the box on the ground. When they stood back up, they were still holding hands.

"I thought you might just have had a migraine," he said with a smile. They touched cheeks; instinctively they blew a kiss to each other.

"Hello," she said, "no migraines today. I promise. I've just got a pain of a sister-in-law."

They turned to walk to the car, he with the picnic hamper, she at his side, ensuring her bare arm brushed the sleeve of his shirt and lightly haired forearm. He put the box in the boot and walked round to the passenger door where Maria was waiting. José stopped and took a step backwards. "Stay still. I'm taking a photograph." He didn't have a camera but held his hands together as if to frame his model.

"Smile please. Maria, you look fabulous."

"OK, go on. I bet you say that to all the ladies you take on your boat."

"If we're counting, then it's been only one other one. And that was my mother. So, unless you accept my compliments as they come, you won't even get to be the second."

She smiled and did a little curtsey. "Thank you, Captain."

"Now, that's better. Seriously Maria, you are beautiful." They touched hands. He unlocked the door and she swung herself in.

"And you've got better thighs than my mother."

"Now I'm beginning to think you're exaggerating."

He rounded the bonnet and climbed in beside her, and behind the steering wheel. "Llanfranc harbour, here we come."

"I don't know what to expect," Maria said, "is it a boat or a dinghy, does it have sails… how big is she?"

"You'll have to wait and see."

"Oh God, I've just remembered. Does it have a toilet?"

José laughed out loud. "We've got a his and hers bucket. Mrs Practical."

They swept down into the harbour. "I'll park up. It's not far to walk." They walked along the quayside. José stopped. "Well, there we are." Maria looked at the gleaming white boat with its deep blue coloured lower hull towering above them.

"Pull the other one!" she said.

"No. Really, here she is."

"José, you'll have to explain because I don't know about boats. But this seems huge!"

"Well, it's not huge. It's a good size, about thirty-six feet. I tell you, Mr Timberman had good taste, even if he was a crook. When I took ownership, it was called Contiki Two, with a 'c', which must have been a play on the Kontiki, but I saw the 'con' as a bit of a self-reference, so I changed the name."

Maria, tottering on one leg like an insecure stork, put a hand on José's shoulder.

"What are you doing?" he asked.

"Well, you won't want my stilettos piercing your deck, will you? I'm changing my shoes."

"Maria, you're great. When I saw them I did think to myself: how do I get her to take her shoes off and now I know, Mrs Reliable."

"Come on, show me the bucket, you con-man."

"All in good time," he laughed, flicking up the closed bar to the steel and plastic gangplank that linked the harbour wall to the spotlessly clean deck.

"I've been practising the conducted tour," José announced, putting the cooler in the shade on the deck. "Let's start at the top. You go up these steps first and then I can see you wiggle for attention."

"I'll follow you," Maria said sternly.

He led the way, explaining once they were up there that this was where all the sailing and navigation was done. In front of the safety glass sloping screen was an area designed exclusively for Maria to sunbathe on, or so he said. The view was magnificent. There was nothing in the harbour to obstruct it.

"Let's go down to the fancy bit."

José produced a key, one of a number on a key ring and chain secured inside his left trouser pocket. He unlocked a glass sliding door and they entered an air-conditioned galley.

"This is where we can prepare your picnic and there's a fridge. I'll leave you to do the housekeeping."

The tour was over. That was it, Maria thought, until José reached for a concealed handle in the front screen wall of the galley. The wall slid open into a small lobby, where three panelled hardwood doors provided a secure screen to wherever they lead.

"Here's your bucket room," he said as he opened the door on the left, exposing an ante-room with a flush toilet, a separate shower cubicle and drying/dressing area. "So, you'll remember where this is when you want it,"

José said mockingly. "This is actually José junior's berth, though we've not slept on the boat yet. We've never sailed overnight and I suppose we're not natural mariners. Remember this was forced on me," he said, chuckling again.

He turned as though to finish the tour, and Maria asked, "What secret lies behind that locked door? Is that where you keep your mistress?"

"Not that I've ever discovered…" He opened the door to expose an un-made up, double built-in divan berth, which looked as though it had come straight from the constructor's yard.

"Is this a bit unfinished?" Maria half-joked.

"Totally," José replied. "Unfinished, unstarted, uncomplicated. Actually, it's so unaccustomed to being seen, it's rather sad," he added, without his usual smile.

"Right, that's it, unless you want to see engines and boys' things. Let's get going. Are you any good at undoing ropes and making sure you've released the side of the boat that's secured to the capstans as I pull away? I'll tidy up in the wheel-house. You put your stuff in the fridge and in five minutes we'll be on our way."

He bounded to the upper deck. Maria took the cool-box into the galley. She put the wine in the fridge, but decided to keep the food out. She'd bunged some croissants into the box at the last moment, thinking that neither of them would have had breakfast before setting off.

She wondered how the boys' journey was going. Wow! They'd be impressed with this boat. She wondered when she might tell them about her adventure. She would also tell Paco about it in one of her conversations with him. How different it had been with him. He always saw his boat as a work-horse, and it was only very rarely that Maria had been on board. Even then, they were short visits, after which she felt she needed a shower because she was sure she reeked of fish, and probably did. This mini gin-palace was a different matter. It was clinically clean. José must have spent a lot of time keeping it in shape.

Maria suddenly realised she was daydreaming. She'd been given five minutes of housekeeping time. She wondered how she looked, and so found the secret sliding panel and then the door on the left hiding the loo. She used it more out of excitement than need, then shook her hair, touched up her lipstick and stood back, thinking how much she appeared to have pleased José.

Gingerly opening the door to the large cabin again, she stood in the doorway. It was bare and cold compared with the rest of the boat, a blank canvas, as though the artist had started a work, knowing where he wanted to finish but without the emotion to get there.

The berth was light and airy. It needed curtains and covers for the bed, and Maria remembered she had seen a really cheerful print in the tableware shop, which she'd loved. Pinks and lilacs and blues. That would be ideal, she thought, the room needed a bit of character, that's all. She pinched herself; she was daydreaming again.

Back on the rear deck, she looked up to the wheel-house and cupped her hands over her mouth.

"How are you doing, Captain?"

"All set, crew."

"Which ropes do you want me to cast off?"

"It's OK. Climb up here and see it happen."

She was confused. Even her little knowledge of sailing told her you had to be at the quayside level to cast off. However, she decided to do as she was told and found herself close to her Captain's side.

"I've radioed over to the harbour master. He's got a little man who pops across to help lone mariners set off. He'll be here in a minute or two."

"José. I could have done it."

"Maria. I couldn't have you spoil your beautiful skirt and blouse."

"OK, you spoilsport! I was going to take them off."

What on earth made her suddenly say these things? She supposed her defence mechanism was to counter-attack. She'd got so used to protecting her own domain.

"Besides," José said, "you smell too nice to be a sailor's mate. Is it mimosa?"

"You got that in one. All the men in my life thought it was lily of the valley."

"Well, there you go. We'll have to educate them. Right, here's the harbour master's lad."

José turned a key, pushed a couple of buttons and there was a roar of engines aft. The calm of the harbour water was suddenly disturbed as the twin props sent a near tidal wave shooting across to the other side of the bay. Little crafts rocked and rolled as they were hit by the shock. The lad busied himself unhitching ropes from the capstans built into the harbour roadside.

"Here," José beckoned, "press this button."

"Only if you tell me what I'll be doing," Maria retorted.

"You'll be weighing anchor electronically. Mr Timberman was a lazy bugger."

"I'm pleased he was. I'm very pleased he was a crook and I'm delighted your bosses aren't as bright as you are. Most of all, I love the boat."

"Now *you're* being the flatterer. That won't wash."

She lifted his hand and gently kissed the back of it. "Well, it's true," she said.

There was a shout from the quay indicating the lad was ready to let go. José waved his hand. Turned the wheel, pushed and pulled at a couple of levers and the boat slowly moved away from the quayside, expertly missing other boats fore and aft.

"OK, mate. It's your choice. North or south? In which direction would you like to cruise?"

"I'm no good at directions. Give me a clue."

"Left or right when we get through the harbour wall?"

"What if I go negative and say straight on?"

"We'd eventually hit Italy."

"We don't want to do that, do we? Is Barcelona left or right?"

"It's right."

"Then we don't want to do that, do we?"

"Why?"

"Because I don't want to bump into Marco and Pedro on their way to the football. This is our day out."

"So it's left, OK?"

"Wonderful. As long as you find some shallow water where you can teach me to snorkel."

"Listen. Get yourself off and go down to the deck and you'll find some things that look like big balloons hanging over the edge. Pull them on board and then we're away. But don't fall in." He paused and added, "If you would please, mate!"

"Aye, aye, Captain."

José laughed. "By the way, don't ruin your outfit and don't blame me. Don't be too long either, I want you to see the navigation channels on the way through the wall."

There was really nothing to the task she'd been set. But it was all about taking part and contributing. She was back at his side within minutes.

"Well, there you go," he said, "and back as fresh as a sunflower on your skirt." He had a chart laid out professionally in front of him.

"What's that?" Maria enquired, pointing to the monitor hanging from the bulkhead.

"That's the radar. It'll tell us if there are any boats likely to get in the way."

"And that?"

"That's a depth reader. That will tell us when we're going to run aground."

As they powered through the sea wall, José waved to the harbour master who was standing in front of his little stone built office.

José revved up to eight knots. "Is this the speed we'll be travelling at?" Maria asked.

"Yes and no. It's up to you. I'd normally cruise at 12 to 15 knots. But it's your cruise. You set the speed."

"Well, I was thinking it's quite calm at the moment and I was going to suggest I serve the Captain some croissants and coffee."

"Wow! That sounds a really good idea to me. I'll stick to this speed on an idea like that."

She squeezed his arm and descended to the galley, returning moments later with their light breakfast. José was grateful to be refuelled and turned the boat up to 15 knots, which pulled the nose appreciably out of the water in a proud prance ahead, cutting its way through the light waves. They sat on the fixed stools looking ahead, silent, so as not to compete against the roar of the engines from aft. Maria took a sly peep at her watch. Gosh, it was nearly 11 already. There was truth in the adage that time flew when you were having fun.

José beckoned for her to come over. "D'you reckon you could hold on to this thing for a minute or two?" indicating it was the wheel he wanted to entrust to her.

"As long as you won't want me to change direction. I reckon I can, but don't leave me too long."

"I need to go to see the bucket," he confided, and she took control. As José went into the lobby outside the toilet, he could smell her haunting fragrance, which was suddenly bringing life onto the boat.

He washed his hands, which he knew Maria would appreciate, slipped into José junior's berth and took a pair of swimming shorts from a cupboard. He slid his trousers off and instinctively put them on a hanger and into the otherwise empty wardrobe.

Subconsciously, he looked in the mirror and patted his hair into its neat place. As he turned to go back, he caught a glimpse of a photo frame and, in it, his favourite photograph of Anna with her arm around young José's shoulder, taken on their short holiday in Tossa a month or so before she died. He gulped back a pang of guilt.

"Look," he said inwardly, "we had our moments. We shared José junior. But the last couple of years were hard. Our ambitions were going separate ways. You would have hated the boat. You know that as well as I do. You didn't want adventure or change. Let's be happy with that book of life we shared. Anyway, for all I know, you're already with some bloke where you are by now." He kissed the glass covering the picture, opened a drawer in the built-in dresser and slipped the frame out of sight.

He re-appeared behind Maria, stretched each arm around her and took hold of the wheel, sandwiching her, yet without physical contact. "Now, that was very good. We haven't veered off course at all."

She reached back to push him away, ducking as though passing under the human arch while playing oranges and lemons at a kid's party, but on this occasion, to break free. Her hand reached his bare knee and, surprised, she let out a squeal. Instinctively, he moved his right hand from the wheel as though opening a gate through which she could escape.

"Wow, you shocked me! You might have warned me you'd come back having lost your trousers."

They both laughed.

"There's not much to see from here up the coast for an hour or so. The odd flying fish and hungry sea eagle. The coastline's pretty much the same. So, if you've got a costume, you could catch up on a bit of sun."

"Do I look as though I need to?" Maria said challengingly.

"No, of course not. You can't change the colour of an olive. I'd just like you to have some prime time relaxation. Make the most of being lazy. We've got snorkelling coming up in an hour or so."

"OK, Captain. I'll take your offer. I just happen to have something to slip into."

She didn't quite know where to change. The shower/wc wasn't quite suitable for preparing for her next on-stage appearance. The main berth area would be a bit presumptuous. Anyway, it wasn't exactly open for public use yet. José junior wouldn't mind, she was sure, so she slipped in there.

She laid her skirt on the bed. Put the shirt on the back of a chair, stuffed her bra and pants into the bag she took her bikini from and, suddenly realising she was nude, shot round to where she'd earlier seen the photo of, she presumed, Anna, and for sure José junior, from his striking likeness to José senior.

She was sure the photo had been there. Maybe José hadn't wanted Anna to see her undressing and had moved it. Obviously of a like mind. Free from critical gaze, she slipped into her bikini. At least the mirror seemed to approve. It advised her to lift the bottom half a little, it was always going to be a close call as to whether it covered her scar, which really only she noticed these days. She ran her hand inside the bra top, then, satisfied with the overall effect, covered it with her sleeveless sunflower top. She gave her hair that little flick, and set out to enter from rear stage.

José was checking the charts as she arrived behind him. How tempted she was to trap him in her outstretched arms and take the wheel from him. She decided not to though.

"Hi," he said, engrossed in a map. "Ampurias on the left. This is the view you'd have had if you'd been Roman all those years ago." He looked up and gasped. "Now, Madam Sunflower, that is something of a stunning second entrance of the day. Do I get to see what's under that?"

"Now listen, your job is to steer and read maps and stop us going aground. My next job is to chill out on your sundeck and I don't want some lovesick old mariner gawping at me." She beamed a beaming smile of satisfaction at her host for the day.

Maria plotted her course carefully round the wheelhouse, sensing José was watching every inch of the journey. So now came the difficult part. Mercedes would have had no trouble slipping out of the robe, tucking her tummy in flat and forcing her knees together as she sank to the deck.

Now she sensed the boat slowing. The throb of the engines had certainly stopped. Her back was to the wheelhouse, so she had no idea what was happening. She heard clapping and then José's cheerful voice call out, "Third entrance I rate the best. In fact, the whole crew did. Hang on, don't get comfortable."

She turned to find him inching his way around the wheelhouse, laden with thick, deep blue Dunlopillow mats. "There, put your beautiful body onto one of these. I'm afraid they don't colour co-ordinate with your outfit. They were bought for us boys."

He knelt beside her as he laid the loungers out. "Maria, the first time I saw you, I thought you were the most beautiful yet frail female creature on earth. When I saw you in the library, I was no less impressed. I never dreamt I'd be treated to such a view of your vibrant body, now so strong again. You're beautiful." He leant across and pecked her cheek. "And if you say 'go on you old charmer', I'll throw you overboard."

"I've given up on ducking compliments. Thank you. It gives me so much pleasure to be the focus of your attention. Now listen, even I can sense we're drifting. Get back to your job, Captain."

"Aye, aye, mate," he responded, "the next part of the smooth journey coming up. I'll cut the knots down a bit to allow you to rest."

His view of her from the wheel was spectacular. First her hair acting as a pillow for her head. Then her shoulders glistening in the spring sunshine. How he wished he could have applied the lotion she had rubbed into every pore of her skin. Then there were the mounds of her breasts, strong and pert as he had first seen them outlined, divided by a cleavage which, from his angle, seemed to plunge forever. He could barely see her tummy, but then he was focussing on the defining line created between the black bikini bottom and the light olive flesh above. She had one knee bent upwards. He was sure that was not done for effect, it was her natural repose. She'd slipped her shoes off, but what a star to know to wear shoes with a costume, a trick practised by any serious Miss World contender.

Twenty or 30 minutes later, her head turned onto its left side. She'd kept her neat little pearl earrings on, he noticed. She'd dropped off to sleep. He slowed the boat to a reliable seven or eight knots and decided to hug the coastline a little. He checked the charts. *How ironic,* he thought as he panned the distant hill of Rosas, looking out over the port side. He smiled. *So that is where it all started,* he thought.

At first it sounded like the screech of an injured gull or a blown bearing in one of the motors. But it went on longer than either of those. He panned round to where the noise was coming from and saw Maria sitting upright, ahead of the wheelhouse, but with shoulders hunched forwards. Her head was steady. She had a fixed view straight ahead of her. *Maybe she's been stung by a wasp,* he thought. He cut the engines and scampered out of the wheelhouse and along the guardrail, as fast as he could. He threw himself to his knees directly in front of her. Her eyes were glazed. Her face was perceptibly white. She had aged 20 years. "Oh God," he said to himself, "this is Anna all over again." He held both his arms out, inviting her to take comfort in them from whatever pain it was she was suffering.

Maria lifted herself to her knees by swivelling them under her body and knelt as she accepted the shelter he was offering. He thought it best not to speak. Her whole body was trembling.

Finally she broke the silence, "José." (At least she knew where she was, he thought.) "José, I think I must have dropped off to sleep. I awoke and sat up and there," she said, pointing 50 yards into the distance, "Paco rose out of the sea. He had his arms wide. He was a huge figure. He urged the boat not to go any further forward by crossing his hands frantically in front of him, like I've read the ground crew do to tell the captain of an aircraft that he's docked."

José let her shake in his arms. "You think I imagined it, don't you?" she said in a cracked voice.

"Let's just get through this, you're not alone. Then we'll work it out together."

"Paco was warning us not to go forward, José. He was telling us that there's a danger."

"Maria, my little one…" And she was to him, in her pitiful emotional state, almost childlike. "… let's first get through this and, as I've promised, we'll work it out."

He produced a crisp white handkerchief from the pocket of his shorts and blotted her eyes. The colour was flowing back into her cheeks. He stood up, making sure he was between Maria and the spot ahead to which she had alluded.

"Turn around," he instructed her in a firm but friendly manner. "Now take my hand and lead me to the wheelhouse." She did as directed. "Now I want you to look straight ahead. Here, put your hands each side of the wheel. You did that without help earlier."

He firmly placed his arms outside hers as he now stood close behind her. God, this was difficult for her, but it was not easy for him to have the fragrance of mimosa so close to his nostrils. He had a job to do, so he put out of his mind the thought of enveloping her whole body and gave sailing the priority.

Leaning across, he turned a key, pressed the starter button and eased the throttle open. "Now show me the spot again. You can point if it helps, but don't take your eyes off it. OK, right now, if Paco is there, he'll stop us both together."

They moved forward and, as the distance diminished, so Maria's pointing hand slowly lowered, like a royal standard. As they hit the point of focus, her body shook. She spun around, looking back at the spot.

"Now, what we'll do is wave to Paco, just in case he was there. Blow him a kiss and say 'false alarm, no danger but thanks' and you're allowed any terms of endearment you like to go with that."

She didn't quite do what she was told, but simply closed her eyes in prayer, for minutes it seemed, but in fact it was seconds. Suddenly, she was strong again. She looked younger than José had ever seen her. No longer shaking. Still locked between the strong barriers of his arms.

She slid both arms upwards within José's firm clinch until they were at shoulder level. She let them slide on until they were behind his neck. Her head raised and tilted slightly backwards, she lifted herself onto her bare toes and let her lips brush José's in a soft kiss. No fire, no fervour, no explicit clamouring between them for sexual encounter. They kissed as friends, as one in need of the other, a kiss of security.

Maria released herself and said, "Now, Captain, you've got an important job for two reasons."

"I've got an important job here for many reasons, but which have you got in mind?"

"I need you to mark your chart with a cross in exactly the position we're at, according to your moon and stars and clever night school books."

"Why?"

"Firstly, I'll always want to know, whatever happens between us, where we had our first embrace. Secondly, where I saw Paco."

"I understand fully," he replied.

He released her, and asked her to take the helm so that he could consult the charts. He did a couple of swift calculations and then lifted the binoculars and looked landward. He marked the chart. *Shit,* he thought to himself, *the Bay of Cadaqués.*

"So, where are we, sweet Captain?"

"Left out of Llanfranc, as instructed, Ma'am, and some way up the coast."

"Well, keep the cross on the chart. If it hasn't got a name, we'll have to think of where to call it."

"OK, but no cross on a chart is going to stop us if we're going up the coast for a bit of snorkelling, frankly, whether Paco likes it or not."

"How do you make such fun out of everything?" she laughed.

"Fun, that's right. We're on a fun day. Here's your next command. Your mascara's smudged, go sort that out and on your way back you'll find a bottle of champagne in the fridge. You'll need four glasses."

She looked at him quizzically. "Do you mean what I think you mean? On our day of fun, one of them's already gate-crashed. I'll bring just the two."

CHAPTER 7

So often Maria thought back to that day. She remembered it as one of the most wonderful days in her life.

When she'd brought the champagne, mascara duly replenished, they had chinked glasses. José moored in the shallow waters of the Capa de Creus and sent Maria back to top up her tan. Only if he did too, she'd insisted.

So they lay there side by side, with the bottle in an ice-bucket, and chatted naturally, as they always seemed to. They were first and foremost friends, but José had an almost now declared obsession with Maria's body too. Perhaps due to her conservative upbringing and not fully fulfilled married life, Maria kept telling herself that she was behaving like a teenager, more like she'd expect one of Pedro's girlfriends to react.

The more José either joked about her presence or complimented her physical attributes, the more she tingled with excitement. Paco always, always said thank you after sex (though he also did, she had begun to realise five years into their marriage, after she had cooked him his meal, found a sock or mended a shirt). When she did yield to his requests to make love, despite the being turned off by the permanent perfume of fresh fish, he always said how good she was after the event.

Now here was José, who seemed to be saying "you're as good as you are", even before the unpromised event. He simply seemed gratified by her presence, maybe a little infatuated.

They had, by their own admission, been squiffy after the bottle of champagne, greatly compounded by the Mateus Rosé they drank with the picnic.

When José saw the table of food laid out on the Perspex-topped table on the aft deck, he had crossed over to where Maria was standing, arms outstretched, as if to say, "Here, this is for you." He enveloped her in his arms, which now felt so natural between them.

"You, my sweet Maria, are a feast enough for me, but mainly for dessert. Hell, you've got all my favourites on the one table."

Then, as they sat, he looked down through the clear Perspex and continued, "…and two of my very favourites under the table."

It was those moments that had made her go all coquettish, and still did. She remembered he'd made coffee and they had sat out in the warm shade of the spring afternoon. Then he'd briefly disappeared into José junior's berth emerging with a large plastic bag.

"Here, this is yours," he announced with pride. He gave her a pink snorkel, complete with mask and a horrendous rubber type tube and mouthpiece.

"Oh José, I'm not sure about this. I've had too much to drink. I feel fat and the water looks cold."

"Look down here, over the edge. There's a paradise of fish down there."

Her body went into panic mode again.

Oh no, she thought, *I'll be swimming down there and I'll come face to face with Paco and he'll be very cross with me. He must know by now that I think I'm in love with José.*

José noted Maria's change of mood, the greyness that flashed across her face again.

"Now look, young lady. There are things that we're both afraid Anna and Paco wouldn't like to see. Us having fun, or the consolation of a loving kiss. Look, we took vows. If Paco's accident and Anna's appendicitis hadn't happened, no doubt you and I would still be making the most of our marriages. What we promised was that we'd fulfil those lives together. But there was a get-out clause. Did you know God was a lawyer? The vows were to last until death does us part, so, as I see it, our obligations have finished. No, finished isn't the right word because neither of us, I think, want to forget those relationships, which, let's face it, have given us our children.

"I expect you're thinking that Paco is going to reach out and tap you on the mask and advise you to stop having fun. You saw Paco earlier. Well, I saw Anna. There's a lovely photo of her and José, which he treasures. Anna saw me changing into these shorts which, OK, I think you ought to know, I bought especially for today. No, not to impress, just to look the part for you. Anyway, I shut her out, just temporarily, by popping her in a drawer. Of course, I know she's still there, but I'm comforted that she can't see me, us.

"Now, get your mask on and I'll lower you overboard for another of life's rich experiences."

"José, dearest José. I'm beginning to think all the owners of this boat are con-men. Promise if I get cold you'll warm me."

The snorkelling was fun. She saw for the first time that the deep was a beautiful place, full of colour and life and shadows and shapes. The sun warmed her back. After about half an hour, José signalled to her and they headed back to the boat. José held out a protective hand, which she took, and they swam as a pair, the one oaring with the left hand, the other with the right.

They reached the anchor chain and surfaced together, José linking one arm around the chain while he steadied Maria as she freed herself from the mouthpiece and tube.

"Oh my God!" she suddenly shrieked.

"What's up?" José said. Had she seen Paco again?

"The name of the boat!" Maria wailed, pointing at the lettering just above the anchor chain.

"Oh yes," José said. "Well, you changed the subject when I was about to tell you on our first date. As you're in the habit of doing."

"It's called Maria de Rosas!"

"Well, yes. I know. That's the name I changed it to."

"Who's this Maria de Rosas?"

"There's only the one."

"Tell me who this other woman is."

"It can only be you."

"But at the time, we'd only met once. We weren't even in contact."

"Maria, let's just say that if I'd only met you the once, I would have fallen in love with you for a lifetime. It's a beautiful boat, with a funny history. So I see it as Maria de Rosas. Now that you've graced it, it's been christened."

A tear ran down Maria's cheek. "I'm cold now," she said and swam slowly towards the steps. She helped José climb into the boat carrying the snorkel gear, then took him by the hand.

"We're going to a christening," she said, leading him through the hidden door into the main sleeping quarters. "My costume's wet and cold," she said, "could you undress me?" Mesmerised, he undid her bra. "Here," she said, "your shorts are wet, too."

They stood holding hands for a few seconds. Maria led him onto the uncovered mattress and a lifetime of missed passion erupted between them.

They lay silently together.

"Thank you, darling Maria de Rosas."

"Thank you, Captain."

They allowed time to waft over them. Maria broke the silence. "I see this cabin in pinks and mauves and blues. What do you think?"

"Whatever you say."

They giggled like a couple of teenagers. A shutter had suddenly been lifted, and they had walked through it into a place of intimacy and familiarity.

"You know your bosses would get far more business out of you if they didn't make you wear a suit and tie and let you go off to settle claims with your widows in your pants," she joked.

"Hey! I'd say the same about you. Give someone you're negotiating with a show of these and you'd double the settlement," he retaliated, brushing the back of his hand over her breasts.

"I think I'll take that advice. I've got to close the deal on the tableware next Saturday."

"Don't you dare even think of letting anybody but me see this magnificent body."

"Silly! I'm dealing with a couple of women anyway."

They laughed and chatted easily for a while.

"Come and shower me," Maria suddenly plucked up courage to suggest, or invite, as she supposed it was. Would this be difficult? Should she keep this particular ritual just for Paco? Yet it seemed such a natural part of sex, that it should continue through the freshening-up process, as a prelude to the shutter of respectability coming back down.

José broke back from a long lingering kiss and his secure hug under the warmth of the shower. "I've never done that before," he said.

"There are things we don't need not know about each other's previous lives. This is about us. We as a unit have never done this before."

She reached her hand behind his back and moved the thermostat valve to cold. It took a few seconds to react. Enough time for her to say, "There's a first time for everything, my darling."

"Shit!" he screeched. "That's freezing!"

"You need to watch your language, you're not among sailors now, and you need cooling down, you arduous Captain."

They were still laughing as he turned off the chill flow, and reached for the two blue towels hanging over the rail outside the shower screen.

He watched her towel her beautiful body down. "José won't mind me dressing in his room, will he?" she said, flashing her gleaming white teeth at her man, who momentarily took on a protective paternal air.

"Well, do it discreetly. Remember what I said about not letting anybody else enjoy looking at you."

"Not even family?" she said as she exited, centre stage, with a little wiggle of her bottom below the loosely draped towel.

José, now alone, reflected. "Christ, I so love that woman. Anna, please understand."

Enjoying hot coffee and flan on the aft deck, they'd discussed their relationship. It was Maria who put it into perspective.

"We must live for the day. Paco and Anna have learnt that the hard way. So, if today's our only day, then I'm thankful. If there's a tomorrow, or several tomorrows, then that'll be a bonus. But we mustn't let our own selfishness get in the way of José junior, for example. He's number one in your life and I don't want to demand love from you that's his, by right.

"And I have Pedro. He's almost a man and hopefully will be off to Madrid in the not too distant future. You're doing well in your career, and I don't want you feeling obligated to rush back and forth from Barcelona, or elsewhere, just to keep this little lady happy. We'll be a bonus to each other, not a burden. We'll speak… well, whenever. No daily rituals, because calls would be bound to get furtive.

"We're a pair of cheats really, just without vows, yet I think we both know what we discovered today is uncanny. I read a book from the library and in it this guy wrote that when infatuation turns to love, the flames of ardour are dampened. Darling José, I infatuate you."

"I infatuate you too, Maria."

They settled on the ground rules. Maria volunteered to have a little tidy up of the galley, the shower area and José junior's room. They screeched with laughter over the master cabin being left exactly as it was. Maria asked how much daylight was left and, when José told her about two hours, and that the journey back at 15 knots would be about an hour and a half, she slapped his backside and suggested he get his arse out of here and get them back home.

"Only if you're alongside me all the way," he ruled.

"All the way's fine with me."

They sat close together behind the wheel. José had not realised before that the captain's chair could have its arms let down to form a double bench seat. They linked arms, Maria bloused and skirted, José in trousers to keep out the cool evening air. He found a blanket and put it around Maria's shoulders.

A short while later, Maria suddenly stiffened and made gestures with her shoulders as though shuddering beneath another cold shower.

"Are you OK?" José asked.

"Yes," she said, "but I think somebody just walked over my grave."

She laughed nervously.

José looked at the chart. He glanced to the land on his right and recognised the Bay of Cadaqués in the late afternoon sunlight. *Shit,* he thought to himself, *maybe somebody did.*

A couple of minutes later, Maria put her free hand to her mouth. "José! Did you let Anna out of the drawer?"

"Yes, of course I did."

Half an hour passed before they spoke again.

"Do me a favour, Captain. Keep an eye on your charts and give me a shout when we're coming up to where I saw Paco, please."

"Do you want to know something?" he replied.

"What's that? I'm learning so much today, one more thing won't matter."

"We've passed it already."

"Shit, as you sailors say. And he didn't even wave!"

They both laughed with relief.

CHAPTER 8

Day one of year one of the Hotel Playa was getting closer. The evening planning sessions, three months short of the big day revealed that the hotel was on schedule. Plastering would begin by the end of the month. Decorating would follow close behind and, as Maria had convinced Marco that every wall surface should be the same oatmeal colour, to contrast with the darker mottled terrazzo and rust corridor carpets, the painters would whizz round with their rollers.

The lift they had ultimately decided on was being installed and, providing the electricity utility company performed, that would be up and running and tested in time.

Marco always seemed loath to discuss the pool surround and tennis court, and kept asking whether all the planned kitchen facilities were completely necessary. He did not naturally enjoy spending money.

One evening, Virginia had taken leave, which was now the custom. Pedro said he had some revision to do for his forthcoming May/June exams and would his mother and uncle excuse him. He'd actually had a letter from Laura, who was still with her mother in France, and he wanted to read it again quietly.

Typical of the lawyer-to-be, it was not a straightforward tome by any means, and, from his hurried reading when he first got back from school, it seemed full of innuendo and riddles he could not, at that time, get his head around.

Meanwhile, Maria and Marco were alone, an unusual occurrence. Marco seemed agitated about something; Maria had got used to recognising the signs. He would drum his fingers on the table. She was still really a guest in her brother-in-law's home, so she just had to accept it, annoying as it was: the slow motion of his little finger hitting an invisible keyboard, followed by the one on which Virginia made him wear a wedding ring. "Either on your finger or through your nose," she'd offered as options. The plonking down of the middle digit was always more determined; the forefinger and thumb seemed afterthoughts. And it was always the left hand. Perhaps, Maria thought, he couldn't coordinate the right hand.

No, it wasn't that. The reality was, these days she rarely saw Marco without a drink in his right hand when he was indoors. When he was walking around the site, or otherwise fully occupied, he didn't seem to need one, but on evenings such as this, Maria found it hard to recollect seeing him without.

"Maria, join me in a small glass of wine," he suggested.

"No, I'm fine, Marco, thank you. I'll be off to get my beauty sleep soon."

"Maria, if you slept for a year, you could never be more beautiful." Marco's response was quite natural, and she believed he meant every word.

She crossed the room and put her arm around his shoulder, leant across and pecked him on the forehead. "Marco, you seem worried. Or pre-occupied. Is there something troubling you?"

This was the moment he'd been dreading. The opportunity to break the news and offload his other concerns. "Would you have a glass of wine? It would help, I think."

"OK," she said quietly. Now *she* was worried. Perhaps he was ill, or maybe Virginia was. She hoped he wasn't going to proposition her again. She had made that position crystal clear once before.

He put a glass of white wine in front of her. She expected it would be his standard stock, Marquis de Riscal. They raised their glasses.

"I've run out of money," he said, going straight to the point.

"Oh, Marco. That's nothing to get all strung up over. But it isn't something to shoulder alone, and besides, I do the books for you and you're within budget. It should really be alright."

"Maria, dear sister-in-law, you're an amazing, calm person. You're a beautiful person and I never want to upset you. I agree, you've kept the books magnificently but I didn't involve you in the original budget. Then you started in-putting your excellent ideas and I could only agree. I really don't know how or from who I expected the funding to be provided.

"In the original budget there was no lift. That's a simple matter of four million pesetas. Then there's Pedro's pool idea. Of course it's right and I know it'll make the ambience of the hotel perfect, even though there's the beach. But the pool estimate is up two million, which in isolation wouldn't be critical.

"Then there's your tennis court. I really can't contemplate shelving that but overall it's another cool 1.5 million. Your ideas on tableware are wonderful, but at least another 400,000. So, overall, I'm short by, say eight million pesetas and we open in a few months. I've committed to the lift, but what I'm having to consider is putting the rest on hold until year two.

"Maria, I can't bear the look of disappointment that will be on your face when your fancy mayor comes to open the hotel, and finds it looking a bit like a building site. So there you have it. I think it's pride as much as anything that's getting to me."

"Marco, dearest brother-in-law, it's not pride that's getting to you. Can I speak freely?"

"Oh, Maria, need you ask?"

"OK, I think the drink is getting to you a bit. You've turned to the old vino for support. Tell me, do you realise that when you're sitting down, you're rarely without a drink. If I had a promise you would cut down, then I reckon I'd have some ideas to put things right.

"Now, I've been honest with you and you're to tell me if I'm overstepping the mark."

Marco looked stunned at her appraisal of his drinking. He was indeed a proud man and not one who easily accepted advice. That was probably where he and Virginia had reached an impasse. She lectured, never discussed or suggested. And, on more than one occasion in the last three years, she'd remarked how, when Maria put an idea to him, he was part way to accepting it before she'd even finished.

"When I suggest something, your starting point is to make up your mind it's a lousy idea. Maybe if you knew I'd got a black bra and knickers on, you'd be more receptive. Do you know she's shaving those wonderful legs of hers?"

Marco was still trying to work out a counter to Maria's observation. True, his brain wasn't working as fast as it used to and here was another numbing example. So, she was right yet again. He knew that deep down.

"Sleep with me and drink will never pass these lips again."

"Now listen, Marco. You may have been drinking, but that's completely out of line. D'you want me to tell Virginia you've made a pass at me? Then you *will* be in trouble.

"No deals, just a promise and I'll sit down and help you. Tomorrow's Saturday. We'll have a formal meeting in your office and set all the figures out. I reckon we'll open with the completed court, pool-paving, a lift and some pretty fancy tableware, plus a proprietor who's lost weight and can get into his ceremonial suit at the opening."

"I won't say yes. Well, not yet. There's a question."

"What's that? And by the way, I don't have to answer it."

"The day Pedro and I went to Barcelona, when we got back Virginia was beside herself. You won't remember it because you'd gone to bed early after your stocktaking day, but she was still up and about when Pedro and I got home. Actually, we could have done without that because we'd stopped in Palafrugell for a couple of drinks to celebrate the win.

"Anyway, she didn't even ask about the game, just pounced on me and said something about she thought you probably hadn't been stocktaking at all. If you were, she said you were all dolled up for it. That new skirt and blouse you ran up. Something about a cool-box. She reckons you were going on a picnic and not with an old school-friend. So the question's obvious: is there a man in your life?"

Maria looked at him unwaveringly. "The answer's no. There are five men I'm seeing at the moment. It's hard, but I'm dividing my time roughly equally between four of them and the fifth takes pot luck if I have any time left."

"Now listen!" Marco exploded. "I'm being expected to sort my life out. So hear this, Maria, we don't want you bringing disgrace on the Martinez household."

Maria threw her head back and shrieked with laughter. Her gleaming white teeth were bared, not in an angry snarl, which might have been justified, but in girlish fun.

"… and do you want the other fact?"

Marco hesitated. When Maria was like this it usually meant she was on a winning streak.

"What other fact?"

"Virginia is seeing two of them as well."

"What?" he said cautiously.

Maria got up and crossed to Marco's chair. She took his glass and held it up to the light.

"Right," she said. "The deal is never one of these before seven in the evening and then you're allowed two glasses. Ask me for a relaxation in the rules if the House of Martinez has a celebration, or Virginia buys some black undies."

"Oh hell! I give in. Yes, damn you. Now, who on earth is Virginia seeing and by the way, the question was about you, not her."

"OK, I'll explain. I'm seeing Paco daily, he's rarely out of my mind. That's number one. Then I'm very much in love with Pedro. I yearn for his success, so that the House of Martinez cherishes him as much as I do. The third, dear, confused, overweight brother-in-law, is you. I love you dearly too, but am loath to show you, or tell you, because you immediately want to sleep with me… Oh dear, this glass of wine is giving me Dutch courage, I think. Then there's my dear Carlos. Second to you and Virginia, he's opened up so much of a new life at a time when I most needed it. I don't love him exactly, but I'm enormously fond of him. So, there you are."

"You're a cheat, Maria Martinez. You really had me going then. Actually, I could have believed you have five suitors and the guile to keep them apart and play games with each of them."

He paused, drummed his fingers and fondled his empty glass. Then, like a spaniel with drooping eyes, he said, "Hey, that's only four."

"Oh, the fifth. Now he's the one who never has prime time with me. He's a very good, kind friend. I cheated. Yes, I wasn't stocktaking, I was taking stock. He invited me on a picnic, but we weren't alone." Oh dear, would she need to go to confession over that lie? Well, less of a lie, more a bending of the truth. Anna and Paco had been with them in spirit.

Perhaps she would go to confession on Saturday morning anyway. She needed to level with the priest about breaching Rome's edicts on birth control. Since that happy day, as she remembered it, she'd resolved to start taking the pill. The doctor she had seen was new to the village. Yes, he understood that as Maria had settled for just the one child, it would be a good idea for her to have a more reliable form of contraception and, not being of the Faith himself, he was happy to prescribe it. That was after checking her blood pressure and a synopsis of her family history, on the female side. She would take the pill just in case the opportunity arose to be back into José's arms again.

Maria had to wait a week after the picnic to be reassured that they would not have to pay for their compatibility in every physical and mental way with a pregnancy. Those moments had overcome them. Contraception was furthest from their minds when they had made love on the boat.

Oh, how that moment, or that day and all the hours of subsequent thought, would have changed if José had fumbled in a little drawer alongside the divan for a condom. "What a gentle gentleman he is," she reflected. Unlike Marco, who would be sufficiently worldly to carry one in his wallet, just in case. José had clearly, but perhaps with great risk, not pre-planned.

She came out of her daydream.

"Marco. If, and it is only a hypothetical if, my fifth man, or sixth or seventh, were to steal my heart alongside you other four, you, Paco and Pedro would have to accept that as a fact of life. Paco and I vowed to be true to each other under all circumstances, but you probably know anyway that God was a lawyer and he built in an escape clause to that contract, releasing one at the point of death."

"Maria, if ever there's a female dictator of Spain, or a prime minister, you'll be in the running. I find it hard not to be your sixth or seventh man, but the way you talk of loving me and still loving my lucky younger brother is some consolation.

"Incidentally, I said to Virginia when she told me all that on football Sunday to mind her own fucking business."

"Marco, go and wash your mouth out! Either you're reading too many American books or spending too much time with the builders. That's not the sort of language I'd expect from the Head of the House of Martinez."

"Then you'd better stop your son coming to football matches with his old uncle. He shouts words across the terraces I didn't even know existed!"

They laughed.

"Marco," she said seriously.

"Yes, my dear."

"I'm not ready to tell Pedro about the fifth man yet."

"Sleep with me and I'll keep your secret."

She smiled. "Not until you've lost weight. Now, it's bed for me, and before you say it, alone!"

Maria woke early, or earlier than usual for a Saturday morning when it was her turn, by rota, for a day off. Pedro hadn't surfaced and so she took the opportunity to take over the bathroom before it became too masculine.

She caught a glimpse of herself in the full-length mirror on the back of the door. She'd lost a bit of weight since the picnic. Certainly the attention José had paid to her body, putting every square centimetre under scrutiny and then declaring each to be picture perfect, had given her a new incentive to trim and slim the couple of places she knew were showing signs of the passing years.

She looked at the lighter skin where her bikini had been and thought: another time… *oh God, please let there be another time…* she would probably be comfortable about going top-less. That was, of course, if José did not object or think it a cheap habit of the brash tourists who were now invading the various Costas.

Maria was now in the habit of shaving on a regular basis. It made her feel better and cleaner, and although José had made no mention of it, she'd felt proud and relaxed when he included her navel on his circumnavigation of her body.

In the shower, she squirmed as she ran the tips of her fingers across the gentle curve of her belly, releasing her thumb in motions replicating his strong masculine tongue, before chastising herself for being so foolish.

Afterwards, she slipped into her summer robe and headed back to her room. Pedro was stirring as she passed by his open door. "Is that you, Mother?" he asked, through a haze of early awakening.

"No," she replied "I'm a blonde Benfica football supporter who stood in front of you at the match and, when Barcelona whooped us, you consoled me. I'm back to repay you."

"Bugger me!" Pedro whistled. "So come in and we'll screw."

"Pedro!"

"Yes, Mother?"

"Pedro, get out of bed and go and cleanse your filthy male mind and rinse your mouth in bleach. You're becoming a horrible young man!"

"Oh come on, Mother, you started it. Who told you about the little Italian blonde?"

"I made it up."

"Come on, Marco told you."

"He certainly did not."

"Then you're some sort of witch to know such things. Here, come and wake me up with a kiss." She did that willingly. "You smell nice. Is it that lily of the valley again?"

"Mimosa."

"Well, yes, that's what I meant. So who's on the receiving end of that today?"

"Marco."

"Marco? He'll not notice it. But why Marco?"

"We've got a meeting on the final financing of the hotel, and I want his nostrils tenderised before he flares them in temper."

"Oh Mother, please don't let's have a family upset."

"We won't, chiquito. I promise."

"Cut the chiquito, please. I'm in the training squad!"

"Would you like the treat of a cup of tea in bed?"

"Wouldn't I!"

"You rest your little footballers' legs then. I'll slip some clothes on and I'll bring you some tea."

After she'd put the kettle on, she scurried into her bedroom, where she dressed in a blouse, short black skirt, black leather mules, and went back to the kettle. *Have one yourself,* she said. One teabag for her, two for Pedro. A dash of milk for both and, hey presto, she was again sitting on the bed with Pedro propped up against the pillows.

"Is it a serious meeting with Marco?"

"Oh, we'll see. Tell me, what did Laura have to say?"

"Just this and that really."

"Oh, come on, a young couple who haven't seen each other for, how long is it?"

"About a year. Oh, Mother. Why is it whenever you come and sit on my bed there's a heavy inquisition?"

"Because that's the reason for mothers to sit on beds. But I'm not sitting here to pry. I was intending to make conversation, and to be truthful, to take the pressure off me and my meeting with Marco."

"OK, so you want to pry. Obviously Laura's always been special to me. But it could just be a young man's infatuation."

Her heart leapt; she knew how he felt. Uncanny that it was running in the family.

"Anyway, I thought we had a special relationship," he continued. "But she would always get to an emotional point and then run from it. She'd make an excuse. Anything so as to not get too deeply involved. By the way, that probably answers the other question in your mind. We never made love. Don't look shocked, Mother. You must have wondered.

"When she left for France, we had a very special time together. From my perspective, it was full of promise, yet it was strange too. As if she was scared of herself. We've been writing, as you know. It looks as though her mother's going to settle in France and she's insisting Laura stays too. She's done her first year at Montpelier, doing what she always said she would do, reading law."

Pedro confided a little to his mother about Laura's past, her fears of history repeating itself.

"But I actually thought time, and a touch of maturity, and a prescription from the doctor, would be a healer. But her letter yesterday put an end to all that," he said sadly.

"Tell me why, darling?" Maria said in a comforting tone.

"She's fallen in love and moved in with a new partner."

"Oh, I'm sorry, dear. What can I say? Perhaps he'll have the same problem with her too."

"He won't. *He's* apparently a she! Laura's discovered she's a lesbian."

"Oh God!" Maria said, putting her hand to her mouth.

"Mother! It's not the end of the world to be a lesbian. We're in an age of acknowledgement. And while we're about it, I'm queer."

Maria stared at him in dumbstruck horror.

"Christ, Mama! Of course I'm not. I'm pulling your leg. I just wanted to shock you."

"You little shit! That's not funny."

"Now who needs to wash their mouth out! Anyway, you'd still love me if I was, wouldn't you?"

"Only if you'd given me grandchildren first. You terror! Don't ever joke like that again. But you're right, whatever your orientation, your father and I would still love you."

"Then think. How could a balanced, strong, sexy couple breed a wimp?"

"You're right there. Now listen. I'm going to get on. I'm meeting Marco at nine."

"This meeting all sounds very set up to me," Peter said.

"Say a little prayer for me while you're working."

"Here we go, I suppose lecture two for the day."

"Too true, and do as I say and have a rinse with some mouthwash."

Virginia and Marco were growing further apart. Yet even though she felt no closeness with him, she was jealous of his relationship with Maria.

"You'll run out of excuses to talk when the hotel's finished. I heard you last night, talking into the night. What was that about? Her next shade of underwear or her boyfriend? I bet you didn't dare ask what she's up to. Well, if you're in a so-called meeting, I'm going into Palafrugell. I'll probably meet my sister for a companionable chat."

And that was that.

Marco wondered what Maria had up her sleeve. He would have to be patient and wait until nine o'clock.

"Good morning, Maria," he said, looking up from behind the table where they laid out their drawings and usually had their discussions when there were more than a couple of them present.

"Is Pedro joining us?" Marco enquired.

"No, I thought it best we had a one-to-one."

"Fine with me. Now, you called this meeting, so go ahead. "

"I'm hoping that the frankness of our chat last night means that we can cut out the bullshit," Maria said purposefully.

"Hell, Maria. Isn't that a bit blunt? When have I bullshitted you?"

"Oh Marco, many times. But don't let's fall out over a technicality. But I mean it. Straight, direct and truthful answers. What do the actual figures show? I know the costs to date and I did a projection of spend to complete. What's the total projected cost?"

"Well, to be honest, it's been surprisingly accurate. Do you remember my initial thoughts were that a complete spend of all the sale proceeds from the land to the petrol company would get us a 30-bedroom hotel? Which is what we're building. With your help, and not to underestimate Pedro's input, the figure remains as was, 32 million."

"OK, so what would you value the completed asset at?"

"Well, before we have a trading record, all I think it could be valued at is cost."

"What about the value of the land?"

"Well, now that we have death taxes, I'd be loath to give it much of a value at all. We argued, on Father's death, that the only inherited value was in the house and because not all the land's agricultural and producing a return, I had put on it a nominal value of 1,000 pesetas."

"But surely the land price paid by the oil company has an influence on the price of the land the hotel's on?"

"Well, no, again. That had a commercial frontage and development potential. It's not the same."

Maria thought on. "So, you're satisfied your worth in the hotel, as finished, will be 20 million. And you sold the land for 32 million too. So, your investment is 32 million."

"Give or take a few costs like legal expenses, yes."

"OK, so…"

But before Maria could finish Marco, who had been fiddling nervously with a pencil, interjected, "Maria, isn't this a little like the Spanish inquisition?"

"Marco, it has to be."

"OK. When you reach the point you want to make, if I don't realise, I'll rely on you telling me."

Maria laughed. "I hope that won't be necessary. Right, to continue. To complete the project with pool, tennis court, and lovely tableware," she said, with a smile, "is about eight million."

"Yes, that's about it."

"So you'd then have an asset worth 40 million."

"Come on Maria, we don't have to be Einstein to come to that conclusion, do we?"

"Marco, please don't play with me. Hear me through."

"I'm all ears."

"So, you need 25 per cent more money."

"Yes, that must be right."

Maria changed tack. "A hotel with just 30 rooms, which are very nice, a restaurant and a guests' dining room, bar and lift, we've always said would get a three-star rating. It's the pool and tennis court that would raise it to four stars."

"Well yes, put that way, it would."

"So to get our budgeted income, we've always assumed four stars."

"Maria, you're a lovely, clever lady. That's what's giving me the sleepless nights. I reckon we would get 25 per cent more on our tariff."

"So with the pool and court plus the unmentionables, we can add 25 per cent worth to the trading project which, if it's not down to you to fund, you could pass out as equity and be no worse off."

How she knew all this jargon was beyond Marco. She'd been a simple, beautiful child from almost peasant stock when the Martinez family first became embroiled with her. But, in truth, Maria's progress and motivation were now far outstripping her host family's.

"So, where you'll now be coming from," said Marco, afraid the meeting was a bit one-sided thus far, "is to suggest you know somebody who also knows someone who could introduce us to a 25 per cent mortgage, which would get the hotel finished. But the interest payments would soak up the potential extra tariff increase. The flip side, more to the point, is that a meeting like this between the two of us would become a wrangle then, as it would be, between three of us. Some chap in a fancy city suit would be sent down to keep an eye on us. So that's the point, eh? Well, no. I've thought about that but I don't want to upset the harmony we have."

"Wrong, Marco. That's not my point. Take in a partner. Get the eight million injected, although that's only 20 per cent of the overall cost, as the purchase of a 25 per cent share in the whole and you personally, and Virginia, are no worse off. You've got 75 per cent of a four-star asset so you'd be back effectively to enjoying 100 per cent of three stars. You would also get 75 per cent of income, which would equal the income you say you'd get from a three-star establishment."

"But Maria, a partner would be worse, he would be sitting down with the two of us plus Pedro and arguing with you about the colour of table napkins, and things like that. He'd probably never give Pedro the rope we've given him, and look at the great ideas he's come up with! Look at the entrance now. The marble, not terrazzo, up to the first floor. A partner would be impossible."

"Marco, I'd like to buy into the project."

"Maria, I'm sure you would but then you'd have to borrow the money and, again, we would have interference. With respect, what have you got to mortgage for eight million?"

Maria was furious. Marco and Paco were so alike. They both had moments of loving her, but had no idea that anybody other than a Martinez had ability beyond their own.

She remembered having been fired up earlier by the other Martinez in the family, and her moment of shock and disappointment that Pedro had pretended he was gay. So why not learn from that Martinez ploy?

"What the hell are you talking about, Marco? What do you mean, I don't have an asset to raise eight million?"

Marco paled visibly. "Look, the deal we did last night about the drink is off. I need a drink to get me through this charade."

"What charade?" she shouted.

"OK. Quietly, Maria. On what asset can you raise eight million?"

"No, Marco. On what asset *did* I raise eight million, in fact more." She was taking into account some interest earned.

"OK, what asset?"

"My body, Marco. The one you're always after, but it was the brain part of it which hooked a company to make an advance of more than eight million."

"You're a hooker?"

She stood up from her chair. Walked slowly round to Marco's, as he followed her move in slow motion. He lifted his head to look up, and leant it slightly backwards, looking at her.

"I, Marco, if I was a hooker, could have had that 30 million off you in one bed, in one night." She raised her right hand and slapped him hard across his left cheek. She turned. Her shoulders dropped and for the first time since Paco's accident, she sobbed hard.

"I'm sorry," Marco said, standing up and putting his arms around her quivering body. "We'll take a break and then you can proposition me again."

She blotted her eyes, smoothed her ruffled blouse and within minutes, they were on their respective sides of the table again.

"First and foremost, I'm sorry," Marco said. "But maybe you'd like to explain your apparent wealth and then we can talk about this partnership idea. If you're serious, Maria, I couldn't wish for a better partner, and there's a lot of common sense in what you've been saying."

"I accept your apology, but before I explain, I'll go and get a couple of ice-cubes for you to hold on your cheek. It's very, very red."

"Maybe I could have a martini on the ice?"

"You know the deal, Marco. No drink."

"Oh come on, it would only be for medicinal purposes."

Maria explained all about José's surprise visit after Paco's death, and the outcome. She amplified the bit about it only being her she'd actually had to use. She chuckled as the thought passed through her mind that, if she'd taken José to bed during their negotiations, she might have done better, even though she couldn't have loved such a man.

Marco listened intently. "Well, I'm surprised my baby brother had the foresight to insure, and insure so well. So, getting back to the principle of a partnership, are you really suggesting you'd risk eight million in this venture?"

"Subject to terms," she said, "yes, I would."

This really rankled. Here was his sister-in-law, clever enough, it was true, but telling him, her benefactor, that things were 'subject to terms'! "Subject to what terms?" he asked, choking back his anger.

"Let's get some paper," Maria said.

She put a few sheets and a biro in front of him and retained an equal amount for herself.

"OK!"

She wrote as he followed her example.

"One. The Partnership will be seen as an investment vehicle of 40 million pesetas, with each partner committed to the single objective of building a hotel."

Christ! Marco thought. She's not got a gram of legal training, yet she talks and thinks just like the family lawyer in Gerona.

"And two?" he said.

"The partners will be investors to the effect of 32 million and eight million. Three: the division of income after tax will be 75 per cent and 25 per cent.

"The partners will have equal voting rights and, in the case of disagreement, the matter will be settled either by a determination of the next of kin of the originating partners, or an independent financial advisor agreed upon by the partners.

"Five. Marco, got any ideas?"

"Yes. Five. The partners will sleep together on each anniversary of the signing of the partnership agreement. I think it should read 'on the first day thereof'," Marco threw in tantalisingly. "Seriously though, number five ought to legislate for how the partnership shares are dealt with in the event of the death of one of the originating partners."

"Then it should simply state that the partnership entitlements should, or can, whichever you prefer, be willed to the next of kin of the originating partners."

"OK." Marco said. "Look, Maria, I'm fine with that arrangement. I'll concede, I'll give up on the 'sleeping with you' proposal. "

"You've got a bloody cheek, Marco. That was never a proposal."

"Good, so we won't need our next of kin to arbitrate on the point."

"Christ, heaven forbid," Maria said. "Anyway, I haven't finished."

"I'm just realising how that insurance bloke must have felt!"

Maybe, she thought, *but ask him how he feels now!*

"What else?" Marco enquired.

"I think it ought to be stipulated that I dedicate 50 per cent of my time to the project between May and mid-October."

"And the winter months?" Marco enquired.

"Well, let's say 25 per cent unless you're on holiday."

Marco threw his head back and guffawed. "On holiday!"

"I said I haven't finished. This is all conditional on you leaving the site for four weeks in every year."

"I'll decide if I leave the place or not."

"Marco, you seemed to understand when I said about your drinking, and then the weight. Look at yourself, you've hardly moved away from the building work since it started, and the last time your car had a good run was when you came to Rosas to pick Pedro and me up. Virginia is bored stiff. She needs a break. Who knows, if you have some quality time together, the spark may come back."

Marco laughed again. "Spark! If there was a spark, who knows, we might just ignite and blow up!"

"It's up to you. It's part of the partnership deal. If I'm going to be investing, I want a partner who has a clear mind and a healthy body. I need him to be clear-thinking, and to get away from the shop to come back recharged. Marco, those are my terms. Take them, as they say, or leave them."

"How long have I got to decide?"

"If you haven't already decided, then I'd be surprised. One huge attribute you have is that you can conclude things quickly."

"So, how long have I got?"

She looked at her watch. "Three minutes."

"Then I'll take all of that," he said, looking at his watch in the same disdainful way Maria had.

He leant back in his chair, hands clasped behind his head and elbows protruding to the front alongside his temples. He looked younger already. In his mind, he took off Maria's blouse, drank in her perfume. He wasn't going to ask whether it was lily of the valley or mimosa. *Mimosa,* he thought. He'd known her over 25 years now, and she was still the Maria of those youthful beginnings.

Four weeks away from her would be a hard bargain, but he could see the sense in what she said. But with Virginia? He laughed at the notion of rekindling their spark. Well, of course there *had* been a spark. All the time Virginia thought she might get pregnant, she went at sex like there were no tomorrows, and that suited him. But once she had been to the Saint John Clinic in Barcelona and tested negative in the fertility stakes, her disappointment killed her drive completely. She found sex a chore. Marco still had his libido, and hence he had strayed.

So, he thought, there was more chance of getting the spark back by rubbing two sticks together than entwining both their bodies.

"Three minutes are up," he heard Maria say.

"How long is it till seven?" Marco enquired.

"Do you need a drink that much?"

"No, not at all. I just want to celebrate the deal."

"So, is it a yes?"

"Well, it's a qualified yes."

Oh hell, Maria thought. She was spent. She barely had the energy to lift her arms, indicating that he too had a right to qualification. With palms uplifted and arms outstretched, she suggested he just put it to her.

"You have to seal the deal with a drink and a kiss."

"You're a hard bastard, brother-in-law."

Maria leant forward, put her arms around Marco's neck and pulled him into a hug, touching his cheek lightly with hers.

He moved his hand onto her bottom and squeezed it. "Chuck this into the equation and you'd get a one per cent scrip issue…"

"…and you'd get the other side of your face slapped."

"So, let's decide how we tell Virginia and Pedro. He's got a football game. I think I'll go and watch and then buy him a coffee and gateau. Thank you, Marco," she said re-establishing the hug. This time his hand remained at his side.

Pedro had seen his mother's sprightly figure disappear around the bend in the garden path. There was, unusually, no building work going on, and no accompanying noise.

He was startled by a sound from the hallway. The postman… that was unusual. It then dawned on him that it was Saturday morning, which meant he was, unusually, at home when the post was delivered. *Hell,* he thought, *I've got football.* He leapt out of bed and went to take a cold shower.

He was all busy when his mother returned, cleaning his football boots and replacing a stud.

"How'd it go?" he asked, more nonchalantly than he intended. He sensed this had been an important discussion.

"Well," she said, "your uncle has agreed to cut down on booze and we've bought a 25 per cent stake in the hotel, which means it's all hell let loose to get the pool finished and the court built. On the girlie front, fancy tablecloths are back on the agenda… All in all, chiquito, I'd say it went pretty well."

Pedro's face was a picture. "Twenty-five per cent. Seems a reasonable morning to me."

Maria was inwardly a little disappointed. Pedro carried on with his boots. Minutes passed and he put down the second boot. He turned and walked to where Maria was busy washing up his discarded breakfast things.

Suddenly he screeched, "Wow!" and threw his arms around his mother. "How the fuck did you do that?"

"Pedro!"

"Oh, sorry, but it's a fair question."

"What time do you need to leave?"

"About 12.30pm. Kick off is at 2.30pm."

"OK my beautiful chiquito, let me tell you what a genius your father is."

And she explained, for the second time in 24 hours, all that she had kept secret over the years since Paco's accident.

"Mother, let's get the sentimental stuff out of the way, shall we. I want you to know I've always been proud of you. You were everything a growing boy needed. Discipline, love, pressure to do my homework, spurred on to do boys' things with Papa, when we both knew you didn't really approve… and now this mega-deal. I just want you to know, I'll never forget or underestimate my father's artisan qualities, but when I conquer my own corner of this globe, my inspiration will have been both of you."

A tear rolled down Maria's cheek. "You ought to be in films! Now, do you want me to drive you to the football?"

"No way, genius. I'm meeting the guys on the 12.35pm bus. We need to bond on the way."

"I'll come and watch."

"Oh, don't. Supposing I have a lousy game?"

"Well, it's up to you, chiquito, but I doubt you'll dare play badly with your father and me there. Besides, who wants you chiquitoed for the rest of your life."

"Do you think I'll ever be known as Peter? It's so much more modern than being named after a donkey or some ancient fisherman."

"Play in the eleven and I'll call you what you like," came Maria's happy response.

Before she set off on her way to the game, at about 1.45pm, she took pot luck and tried José's home number. Amazingly, fortuitously, José's cheerful voice answered the phone.

"José, it's me. Are you alone?"

"I'm never alone, darling Maria, when you're in my thoughts."

"Listen, creep, I'd so love to see you."

"Me too. Let's think. Are you around at 4pm, on Sunday?"

"I can be."

"Do you reckon you'd find the boat?"

"What, with a name like that? Yes, of course."

"OK, I'll be giving her a jolly good clean just before you arrive."

"Don't wear yourself out on my account."

"Oh, that's a pity. I hoped I would."

"José…" Now he was the third male in 24 hours she'd chastised.

"Maria, I so much look forward to seeing you and hearing all the news you have for me."

"How do you know?"

"My darling, I can tell."

"I'll see you at 4pm. Love you."

"You too."

What a day, she thought as she sat on the rolled beach towel she always took to the school's football matches in Palafrugell Stadium. Well, stadium was a kind word. The pitch was mainly dusty clay, and grass planted over the years had only grown on those parts of the pitch, by the corner posts, which seemed hardly used. There was a part-covered stand on one side of the ground with concrete backless seats, which Maria swore were designed to break your bones during the match. After that, rigor mortis would set in.

The teams ran out. Pedro was now the tallest in the second eleven. She was utterly biased, of course, but had she been 16 or 17, she was sure she would have found him the most handsome, definitely the most macho. He now had a really well developed physique, he certainly had the best legs and it was only she who knew that the little terror had been gay for about two minutes earlier that day.

Maria didn't really understand football and spent the game thinking of the more important things in life. José tomorrow. Only just over 24 hours to wait. She'd forgive him, she thought, if he turned up with a pack of condoms. They were a declared item and had broken the ice, as it were, so it would be natural for part of their reunion to be spent in union. She'd have to see. She'd certainly take her pill tomorrow morning with a great deal more gusto than on other days.

Her boy scored his second goal and received brotherly hugs from the rest of the team. He got another in the second half. Maria basked in the glory as the other parents turned to look at her, clapping with deep appreciation.

The referee blew the final whistle: four-one seemed a good result, given there was such tension as to the overhanging importance of the final squad selection for the coming season.

The sports coach was a rather dishy 30-something. He made his way up the steps of the stand, stepping onto and over the row of concrete benches in front of Maria.

"Mrs Martinez," he said, holding an outstretched hand. "If Pedro is selected, would it mean you would grace our team of supporters at every game?"

"What would a young man want his mother around for?" she said, with one of her challenging smiles.

"You obviously haven't noticed all the team lifts itself when you're around. Most of the guys want to be the centre of your attention!"

"Well, now I'd be embarrassed to come!"

"With or without your promise to follow us, I can say Pedro was a cert for selection before the game. His hat-trick seals his position, but please don't tell him ahead of the team posting on the school board on Monday."

"Oh, I'm delighted! I tell you what, with that secret. I'll try to resolve my embarrassment and I'll come if you promise they'll always win for us."

"Now, there's a challenge. We'll do what we can." He held out his hand, nodded as though receiving an audience with the Pope, and took her right elbow, which he shook with firm yet gentle intent.

Wow, she thought, *he's a nice bloke.* Maria eased her trousered frame down to the touchline, where Pedro was the centre of attention. Who were the two girls, she wondered, who had jumped around with joy at all the masculinity charging around, and seemed particularly ecstatic when Pedro scored?

Her boy, with number nine on his back, saw his mother and beamed. "Well played, Peter!" she said.

One of his team-mates overheard. "What's with the name change, Pedders?" he shouted excitedly.

"Oh, you know what mothers are. It's just a family nickname."

"It suits you, Peter."

The two girls giggled.

If Pedro had flicked a finger, Maria thought, he could probably have had both girls for the taking. *This is when I miss Paco's fatherly influence,* she thought. But then again, he was the last one to think about protection. No, she would have to speak to Pedro herself.

Maria left the match without Pedro, leaving him to the glory of the day and the journey home with the lads. Perhaps it wasn't their company he wanted on the bus… *Oh hell,* she thought, *I hope I'll be in time.*

She resolved to give him his further sex education in a practical form. It was going to be harder than she'd imagined. She had never been into the smart new pharmacy just off the main shopping street of Palafrugell. And what if she knew one of the assistants through the library? Then she'd just get some cough stuff. The condoms were, unusually, near the service counter. She took a canister of deodorant from the shelf and went to the counter. There had been a young female assistant there when she first went in. Now there was a man.

At first glance, she put him at 40. He was possibly the owner but, to her total embarrassment, he was also unnervingly handsome and virile. "Just the deodorant, madam?" he said in a distinguished voice. "Yes, thank you," she said shyly, feeling herself blush. "For my son," she added, just for something to say.

"Is there anything else, madam?"

She was sure he was teasing her. Surely not. He was, after all, a professional pharmacist.

"Oh, yes, you've reminded me." Now she was playing with him.

"What can I help you with?" he enquired.

"Do you have Bic razors?"

"Yes, of course. They're on the lower shelf, just to your left."

"Oh, I hadn't seen them," she said as she turned and bent, straight-legged in that practised way Carlos was always saying would hurt her back if she didn't bend her knees.

What a delightful bottom, the chemist observed to himself. She put the razors on the counter. He fed the prices into his till and looked up with a piercing glance. "Will there be anything else?"

She hesitated. "No, that's all, thank you."

"How old is your son?" He surprised her with the question.

"He's nearly 18."

"I hope you won't think I'm rude," he said. "You seem to want to protect his armpits, but he's at the age…" he hesitated, "…well, we're in the 50s, rock and roll, liberation and all that. I'm on a Barcelona Pharmacists' Committee and we're on a mission. I hope, for as long as it takes, to provide birth control to adolescents. Without embarrassment!

"Studies of youngsters of your son's age show that they don't use contraceptives because they can't bring themselves to walk into a crowded shop and ask for them over the counter. So, we've banded together and resolved to have what, in fun, we've called a happy hour. For the last hour on each Saturday, we send our pretty female shop assistants off home and we then ensure an all-male service. In fact, I'm a bit surprised you're not heading the queue. We actually get quite busy. The benefit to the medical profession is that if we can teach early enough, we'll help to stamp out sexually transmitted disease and unwanted pregnancies."

He smiled. "Anyway, you've been a great audience, I'd be obliged if you could pass the word on. It could save you becoming a grandmother before time and, to be perfectly frank, I'm not ashamed of making a profit as well."

Maria was charmed. "Thank you. It's actually a good pitch. My son's not likely to be around on a Saturday evening, he's got a Saturday job in a hotel. But I tell you what, let me surprise him. What should I buy? I'll drop the hint along with the deodorant. I might as well have a really bad day, I bet he'll swear he doesn't need that either."

"Now you've made me feel guilty. I had no intention of expecting you to do his personal shopping. Well, they come in packs of three. The older men buy them by the gross. But then we men always exaggerate… and live in hope."

They both laughed.

Here she was, a good Catholic mother, laughing with a strange man about things her own mother wouldn't have discussed with her best friend.

"I tell you what, I'll take two packs. One for him and one for his best friend, so as not to make him too embarrassed."

"Let's do it another way. That'll be 1000 pesetas for one pack. The other pack for the friend is on me."

"You're kind. And may I say I agree with all that your committee's doing. I'd rather deal with an honest professional male than a young girl assistant wrongly thinking the purchase is for me, and that I don't deserve sex anyway!"

They both roared with laughter again.

"I told you it was happy hour! Take care."

What a day, Maria thought as she stood outside the pharmacy. She'd become a partner in a hotel. She'd arranged some quality time with José. Her boy was a star in the making and was developing a fan club, albeit with only two members other than herself, and she'd almost got herself picked up, not only by the sports coach, but by a rather dishy pharmacist.

That evening, all was revealed to Virginia, though Marco had kept quiet about the enforced holiday deal.

It was just gone seven. "Who'd like a drink?" Marco said.

Maria agreed she'd like one. Virginia declined.

"Oh come on, Virginia. Join me in a glass of white wine. I've got a toast to make." She reluctantly agreed.

"Then here's to your holiday and our shopping trip, Virginia," Maria proposed.

"What holiday? What shopping trip?" said Virginia.

"Well," explained Maria, "Marco stitched me up at the end of our discussion by asking if I'd take full responsibility for the hotel twice a year for two weeks at a time. He's been feeling worn out by the constant teething problems and says you and he need a break. He wants us to help him cut down on his drinking too, and he's not going to drink before seven every day, even on holiday. I've forgotten what else. What was it, Marco?"

Marco stayed silent, outwardly calm but feeling out-manoeuvred. "I expect you've got the minutes."

Virginia turned to Marco and said softly, "Is it all true?"

"Yes."

"When?"

"How about the first two weeks in June?"

"Do you remember our holiday in Majorca?"

128

Oh, how Virginia remembered it! They had decided to try seriously for a family – "morning, noon and night," as Virginia put it – which they'd very much stuck to, although the noon attempt was skipped towards the latter part of the break, as they were frankly running out of energy.

Virginia smiled. She didn't know what made her say it, but she did. "Same terms, Marco?"

"Almost," he replied, "allowing for age."

"Hey! What's all that about? It sounds very secretive," Maria piped in.

"It is," Virginia said, squeezing Marco's hand.

There was more natural laughter that night than Maria could remember for some long time.

CHAPTER 9

Day one, year one in the annals of the history of the Playa loomed. The tennis court was as good as finished. The pool and surround was completed. The tablecloths were made and the seat covers in place for the à la carte restaurant.

As for the divan in the main cabin of the Maria de Rosas, it was now very homely. Maria's final negotiation was for the textile shop to throw in five metres of the vivid pink, purple and blue print exported from England. She had quietly run up a duvet cover and valance on the premise that she was making them for a colleague at the library, without Virginia questioning it too much.

José had taken a more than expected interest in the furnishing of his love nest. He had come down in favour of pink sheets, out of the options Maria put before him.

They met as frequently as they could on the boat. He was still busy in Barcelona, but he seized every opportunity, especially young José's regular Sunday afternoon golf sessions with his grandfather, to spend quality free time with Maria.

Once she had said it would be nice for them to stay the night together. To fall naturally asleep in each other's arms after lovemaking, rather than showering and going their separate ways. Maria was now dividing her time between the pristine marble reception desk in the hotel foyer, and the library.

Carlos had agreed to open the hotel officially on 7 July. They would be half-full at that time. August was, amazingly, fully booked. Lunn Poly and Kuoni had taken allocations, which for a first season was brilliant. As a bonus, Thomas Cook was recommending the new venture and taking space on an ad hoc basis. Marco and Maria were happy with that because they got a better tariff.

Direct bookings were coming in, particularly from the UK, where Maria had convinced Marco that it would pay them to advertise in *Harpers and Queen* and the *Sunday Times*. They then had a conference Carlos had arranged for the best part of ten days, so the start looked promising.

Poor old Marco, Maria thought after they'd had their final marketing meeting in May, before his Majorcan trip with Virginia. Maria was now so fed up with hearing about it, she'd begun to wish she hadn't come up with the idea. Yet Virginia really was excited and, as a result, a somewhat changed character. She seemed to have been fired up from the moment Maria announced that it was all Marco's idea.

A few evenings after that special one, when Virginia and Maria found themselves without Marco, Virginia asked if Maria had been serious about a shopping trip together.

"Sure," Maria confirmed, with a sinking feeling. "How about Saturday? San Feliu's very modern. I can show you the linen shop and I know a good swimwear shop. You could get some bikinis." Maria then thought, *Oh no! I'll walk in and Mercedes will say, "Did the bikini work for you?"* She'd have to ring through and tip her off to be a little secretive. Mercedes would be used to that, she was sure.

In the end, Mercedes had a very flattering two-piece costume, which they all agreed did a lot for Virginia's maturing figure – not that Maria, Mercedes or her assistant brought age, shape or anything other than style into the discussion.

It was hard going for Maria now that they were away. She had a lot to accomplish. The good news was that they had managed to persuade Antonio Martin, a burly retired languages master, to come out of early retirement and work for five months.

He had no great personality but, heading up reception, at least he could reply to potential guests if they were English, French, German and, unlikely but possible, Spanish. He was fairly conversant in Italian too, so Marco and Maria really thought they had the edge on any of the other hotels in the region. Sñr Martin was joining a week before the grand opening. Between them all, they had cobbled together some systems they would work to. They had to be manual ones originally, as the budget wouldn't stretch to one of the newfangled computers.

Maria reviewed the list of expected guests for July. They were mainly couples. Presumably without kids, because the schools were not breaking up until later.

It was a pity Marco was away when the Minister of Tourism man telexed about Maria's request that the hotel urgently needed a star rating. He fixed a date within three days. It was more important, Maria reasoned, to have them come as opposed to having Marco there. She arranged that Sñr Martin would be on duty the day the appraisal team came.

If challenged, she would have admitted she was scared stiff. There was a lot riding on the rating, not least whether the pool and court would have the desired effect of securing the fourth star.

Maria was becoming a real pro. She even thought to arrange for the lift to be serviced the day before the inspection. José was always most supportive, and it was he who put the idea into her mind.

'Star day' arrived, and a team of three from the Tourist Department turned up, one officious older man, another male of about 30, and a young woman in her early 20s. It was clear Maria was not just a makeweight but had a lot of clout.

Pedro had stayed off school. He accepted Maria's advice to wear a crisp white pressed shirt with a tie and blue, nicely creased, smart-casual trousers. His skin, as he matured, was taking on the olive texture of his mother's. He had beautiful thick black hair, trimmed neatly. Long hair was, of course, the fashion but Pedro favoured the athletic look.

The introductions were quite formal. The elder statesman said the routine would be for Maria, or any other nominee, to take the three of them around the parts of the hotel the owners thought relevant to the star rating.

They were instructed simply to say, "This is a bedroom, this is the pool," etc. They were not to elaborate or try a marketing approach. Maria was convincing. Sñr Martin had once gone through the evaluation process before and so was able to give some tips.

Maria's tour went as follows:

"These are the entrance doors. This is reception. I'd like you to meet our receptionist, Sñr Martin, who's fluent in four languages."

"How do we know you speak four languages, Sñr Martin?"

"Actually," he said, "it's five. My native Spanish, English, German, French and Italian. And all those I taught to matric level at Palafrugell Secondary Grammar School for the best part of 26 years."

"I see," exclaimed the main man.

Maria continued. "This is the lift. Would you ride or prefer to walk?"

"We'll ride," said the main man, but not without first crossing himself.

At the first floor, Maria tried a new tactic. "These are all bedrooms. Would you tell me if there's one you'd like to see?"

They chose number 27 and it was there, as they stood surveying the pool area from the open balcony door, that Pedro joined them. Maria didn't rush them. When they'd had enough of chatting quietly between themselves, and turned back inwards to the room, Maria said, "Oh, this is my son, Peter."

Pedro stepped forward and shook their hands in turn. The males kept anonymity. The young woman in the team announced, "I'm Anna. Anna Gonzales."

Maria confided later to Pedro that if he ever found himself in a bedroom again with an older woman, he'd best be careful.

"Clearly," she said, "that young lady had the hots for you."

"Oh, Mother, you're reading far too many books. She wasn't interested in me, I expect she has a whole queue of suitors."

"Mark my words, your mates would have said you'd scored. It was just as well the three of us were there to save your virginity."

"What part do you play in the hotel?" Anna had enquired.

"I'm the general factotum, really. I do what I'm asked to do." Pedro thought he noticed a little quiver, a sort of shuffle, as though Anna might have a job or two in mind for him. "I also teach kids tennis and coach adults who need it, and a bit of swimming, and lead out the staff football team when we play the guests in what we're going to make an annual event. Oh, and by the way, I do the commercials," he said with a broad smile.

Anna seemed intrigued by all that he had to say. "Commercials?" she repeated.

"Yes, I say outrageous things to bend the rules. Like these duvet covers were made by my mother."

"Oh, I see," Anna said. "You should have actually only said 'these are the duvet covers'."

"I know," he said cheekily, "but I'm so proud of my mother I couldn't resist."

Maria could see the rapport developing between the two.

Back downstairs, Pedro announced, "This is the guests' dining room. And this is the Playa Restaurant and I can't resist saying all the tablecloths are hand sewn by my mother. This is the guests' bar area."

The elder statesman seemed about to come into his own. "May I see the bar stock room?"

Pedro stepped back and waved his hand, as if waving through a vehicle pressing to overtake. He was beckoning for his mother to come back into the feature.

"Can't you show us the bar stock room?" the man enquired.

"No, it'll have to be my mother."

"Why's that?"

"I'm under 21 and mustn't have anything to do with the dispensing or control of alcohol," Pedro replied.

The three muttered between themselves, each scribbling another note to what looked in danger of becoming an essay.

"What about the pool and tennis court? Can you control and dispense those, Peter?" Anna asked with more than a half smile. "You'd best come with us, Señora Martinez, we don't want Peter getting loose in the ladies' changing facilities, do we?" she added, keeping matters firmly under her control.

Anna was extremely impressed with the pool and the way it had been sunk into the rocks, and she allowed Pedro to describe how that had come about, and how it was constructed.

He thought the men would be particularly interested in the water purification treatment, as indeed they were, making copious notes as they went.

They were likewise very interested in the fact that the tennis court surface, unlike others, would not need watering.

"We're very interested in the conservation principle. In fact, it's one of my hobby horses. I'm doing a thesis on the subject for my matric geography," Peter informed them.

Anna said how come he was still at school. "I'm leaving in two weeks. Then I work here until October, when I'm hoping to get a place at Madrid University."

"It's got nothing to do with your star rating, Peter, but what will you study?"

"I feel architecture is in my blood, so that's my aim."

Maria broke up the conversation. Pedro had, she thought, done well to secure one of the four stars they hoped for all by himself. And she was sure he could have got a rosette from Anna on top. Certainly she seemed quite captivated, and Maria recognised that interest in a fellow female fairly readily, as she was able to recognise it in herself.

"Would you all like some coffee?" she asked.

The senior inspector said it was not customarily allowed. Where had Maria heard that before?

"Look, I'm quite sure a coffee or a cold glass of water won't influence your decisions. I suspect that with all the experience the three of you have, you've already come to a conclusion. Please, if we're to get a star rating, we'll have to show this kind of hospitality to our guests. Seriously, we understand, no strings attached."

The team accepted. To be fair, it did influence their findings, which was Maria and Pedro's opinion when they later had the post-mortem. Gone, as the inspectors left, was their earlier cool approach. In Anna particularly, melting her way through her farewells with Pedro, could be felt a warmth and a hint that the management could expect a very satisfactory outcome to their visit.

Just over a week later, they received a formal notification, informing them that the Playa was a four-star rated hotel and that it had just missed qualifying for a rosette as well.

Maria was over the moon. She was now adept at pulling her young man's leg.

"Pedro, sooner or later you'll have to face up to where your duties lie to the partners who run and own this place. Nothing would have given me greater pleasure than you being the first to christen the duvets and sheets I've put so much loving care into. The rosette would have meant so much to us."

"But Mother, if I can't have anything to do with stocking alcohol, I'm blowed if I'm going to put my attributes to work without at least the reward of a glass of champagne!"

They laughed together.

The office phone was now installed. When all was quiet and Señor Martin had finished his shift, Maria phoned José.

José's secretary was now used to her calls, always discreetly announcing, "It's Mrs Martinez for you," and once he had spoken, offering a cheeky little smile as she asked, "And how is Señora Martinez?"

He would never rate her status as greater than 'fine'.

In this call, Maria was full of fun. "Have you ever made love with a partner of a four-star rated hotel?" she teased.

"Not four star," he responded.

"What the hell's that mean? Are you saying you have done with a partner of a three- or five-star one?"

"No, merely that I've made love to a partner in a hotel, whom I am speaking to now, but at the time she had no stars in the hostelry world, but deserved more than five in bed."

"No more than five? How about ten?"

"Well, she may be better now we've got some fancy sheets."

"Well, you listen here. I'll be on the boat at four on Sunday and if I don't show you ten stars and a certificate for four stars as an hotelier, you can pass on the event and finish polishing the chrome on the boat."

"That's a deal. See you then." And he hung up.

Maria placed the phone back in its cradle. *Gosh,* she thought, *that man's coolness turns me on,* but that would remain her secret.

Still, she was quite pleased when the phone rang. "Hotel Playa," she said professionally.

"I hear congratulations are in place, you've got our four-star status and you're due to get screwed on Sunday."

"You're a sod, José Romanez. By the way, it's not me getting screwed, it's you baby!" And she hung up.

She rested her head on her arms, folded on the desk, as she'd done as a child at school after lunch. *Well, it's nice knowing your fate,* she supposed.

Not knowing their fortunes, apart from the promise shown by the brochure and the correspondence of those who'd directly booked with the hotel, the ten or so families booked for various parts of August was an encouraging foundation for their first season, when added to the tour operator's bookings. They had an average of 60 per cent occupancy through July and then 100 per cent through August. 60 per cent back through October and, together with another of Carlos's conferences, a stronger than would be expected November.

After much practice at the library, Maria had established an alphabetic filing system, and then had made her own sort of diarised note on each potential visitor's card.

"Mr & Mrs Geoffrey Brown, Westerham, Kent, England. Two rooms. Son and daughter sharing aged 11 and 13. *Mrs Brown seemed nice on the phone. Probably bankers.*

"Mr & Mrs Graham Cook, Guildford, Surrey, England. Three rooms. Mrs Manning, Mrs Cook's mother. Two daughters 16 and 14. *He is diabetic, needs special sugar free diet.*

"Monsieur et Madame Duval. Rheims, France. No children accompanying them. *Sounded very organised and professional. Taking three weeks.*

"Mr & Mrs John French, Epsom, Surrey, England. Two sons, 5 and 3. *Require special evening meal at their tea-time.*

"Dr and Dr Guibaud, Montpellier, France and son Laurent, aged 6. *Dr Guibaud's secretary made the booking. Sounded very efficient and was very particular to enquire about the tennis court and whether bookings were essential.*

"Mr & Mrs Bob Hunt, Dulwich, South London, England. Very particular. *Mr Hunt made call. Insisted he should have the best room. Asked if there was a fridge in the room. When told there wasn't said he wanted to rent one. When told they could not rent refrigerators, said for management to buy one and put it on the bill. He confirmed by telex: management is to spend £500. Hotel confirmed back: this would be arranged."* Maria added a special note: *"Could be difficult.*

"Mr & Mrs John Jones, Bromley, Kent, England. Recommended by Mr Bob Hunt (no mention of a fridge requirement). *Correspondence required to his office, John Jones, Turf Accountant, Herne Hill, London. Note on file possibility his daughter and her family may join him. Would confirm during June. No confirmation received.*

"Mr & Mrs John Fletcher, Reigate, Surrey, England. Son and son's girlfriend. Two single rooms plus a double for Mr and Mrs Martin *(sounded very nice on phone and wanted to know if there was nightlife for his son and girlfriend).*

"Mr & Mrs Charles Parmentier, Paris, France. *Made a point of saying he ran some sports shops in and around Paris. Here for whole month. Said he would expect it wouldn't be long into their holiday that he would get landed with running the sports events. Of course, as it was his business, he wouldn't mind and would bring some things with him to make sure it all ran smoothly."* Seems a pain, Maria had thought. She wondered what his three children would be like.

Maria had discussed that with her Director of Sport, in the shape of Pedro. Neither he nor Marco had any idea how booked the tennis court would get so, on balance, they had decided to draw up a chart on an hourly basis for pre-bookings. It was Pedro's old head on young shoulders which worked out that there would be some distinctly better times to play than others and if they weren't careful, somebody could unfairly book the prime times for the whole month. So they wrote a rule, along with many other rules made during their evening planning sessions. 'Bookings for tennis could be made three days ahead. No jumping in the pool. Diving only off the five metre board by experienced divers. No ball games in the pool.'

They had bought some second-hand swings they had seen advertised in a home break-up sale. So, 'No adults on the swings.' 'No swimming costumes in the restaurant.' 'No food to be brought into the hotel.' 'No glass by the pool.' They added ideas as they came to mind.

Marco and Virginia's break in Majorca brought back some further ideas. The hotel they had stayed in was apparently full of rules. Marco had remarked as such to Virginia over his first drink of the day on their third night.

Virginia had squeezed his left knee, which she was sure had lost weight, and leant across in the bar of the Hotel Puerto Pollensa, where they were staying, and whispered that she knew there were loads of rules in the hotel, but they hadn't made one yet to control rampant lovemaking, which they'd been practising for the first two nights and one of the mornings of their stay thus far.

To be fair, Marco thought after the first night's antics, Virginia hadn't lost her expertise. Immediately after his affair was exposed, she had shipped out the double bed and replaced it with two singles. "Wear the carpet out as much as you want," she had ruled, "but you'll never grace my bed again."

Marco had booked two single beds for this break, and Virginia had seen the hotel confirmation on his office desk, which she dusted with regularity. She was always on her guard, always on the look-out for furtively scribbled phone numbers, though she'd never actually found one.

Reviewing his bedding arrangements, she'd decided, just this once, to interfere and phone to say he had made a mistake. The reservations clerk said she fully understood and changed the booking.

They had an en-suite bathroom. After their first dinner, and Marco's regulation two glasses of wine, Virginia softened and allowed him a brandy with a King Edward cigar for a treat. They actually chatted for the first time in years and when they decided to turn in, Marco was conducted into the bathroom first. He was always fairly quick to wash and turn in. He invariably read a little before dropping off.

Now it was Virginia's turn to use the bathroom. Although it may have looked like a typical feminine ploy to get her other half's attention, it was, in fact, a genuine oversight that Virginia had forgotten to take her nightie into the en-suite. She tip-toed out and slipped her hands under the pillow on her side of the bed.

Marco looked up and did what could only be described as a double take.

"I've left my nightie."

Marco stared at her newly acquired black underwear, courtesy of Mercedes. The bra gave her a deep cleavage, and the pants were not bikini. ("With respect, they really are for the younger girls," Mercedes had told her.) These were called French knickers, and Mercedes had advised, "I warn you now, don't be caught in them by your other half. Men do seem to love them."

Virginia was suddenly reminded of that fact when, about a metre from the bathroom door, Marco's voice resounded, yet somehow quietly, across the bedroom. "Hey! For a moment, I thought I was in the wrong room."

Virginia turned back towards him, a hint of accusation in her eyes. His stare made her feel shy. She crossed her arms over her breasts, so they were out of his view.

"Come here," Marco beckoned. She hesitated slightly, crossing one knee across the other. "Please... come here." He held out his hand in a welcoming manner, an emotion she hadn't experienced from him in years.

She walked slowly round the bed and along his side as he reached out and extinguished the bedside light. Light was coming in through the slats in the wooden Venetian blinds. He turned back the duvet as she got nearer, swung both legs as one out of the bed and stood blocking her path. She felt a pang of excitement she'd thought she would never feel again. He put a hand onto each of her shoulders. "Lovely," he said. "Is this for me?"

He crossed to the pull strings on the blind and swung the slats through 90 degrees. More light was cast into the bedroom and the shafts hit where he had been lying. He gently but commandingly took her hand again and indicated she should lie on the bed. He slipped to his knees, surveying her body as she lay on her back, her contours exaggerated by the intermittent rays of light. He rubbed his hand gently over her breasts, down her lower ribs and paused playfully around her tummy button, then moved on, letting the little finger on his right hand stray into the elasticated top of her knickers.

There began a rejuvenation process, which they both agreed became strong enough to take back to the Playa.

Thumbing through her cards, Maria came across the Hausmans, Herr und Frau, from Munich. They had two daughters who, at 16 and 14, were very keen to play tennis. Frau Hausman didn't speak particularly good English, and even less Spanish, so Sñr Martin had had to close the booking with her for Maria.

Sñr Martin was a distant, strange sort of academic. Marco joked that he was on drugs because of some of the things he said. For example, he once said that Heaven to him was being in England in the late autumn, early winter, and walking in the fog. Marco thought that was really weird for an overweight asthmatic who could sometimes hardly breathe and needed to carry a ventilator with him.

Maria was a little more philosophical in her summing up of the man. "All I want is for him to speak fluently with the guests, and if there's the threat of a world war over the use of sun-loungers, so long as he sorts it out, I'll be happy."

The Sylvano family were the only ones from Italy. Mr and Mrs apparently had a teenage son of 18, and Sñr Sylvano's secretary had said her boss would fly to Gerona and have a car laid on from there. What she hadn't said was that he owned the company which made the planes, and that they would have a chauffeur drive his favourite Maserati around the South of France and down through the Pyrenees for the boss to drive from Gerona to Callella when he arrived. A hired courtesy car was to be there for his wife or son, as the Maserati only held two.

The secretary hadn't mentioned either that the reason the Sylvanos left Italy for their holidays was that the husband and his attractive blonde wife got so much attention from the paparazzi that a holiday in their home country was a nightmare. Georgio snr, not to be confused with his spoilt but beautiful son and heir, Georgio jnr, had a track record of having his business commitments interfered with by a series of rumoured affairs, all apparently with wealthy blondes.

The secretary had said her boss and his family had chosen the Playa as it was unknown and as yet unfashionable, and they just wanted to spend some quality time together.

The Browns in Westerham had typically planned their break around their son and daughter's school holidays. They'd seen the hotel advertised in the Sunday Times and it gave them an edge when Sonya, the wife, was able to announce at the coffee mornings she attended: "No, we aren't going to the Algarve, no, we won't be seeing you in Majorca, or Sitges," or all those other places their contemporaries haunted. "We're going to this new, I have to say, rather exclusive new hotel on the Costa Brava."

"Oh no! Not Tossa, darling, surely?" one of her best friends said. "No, it's a new resort."

"Then darling, do let us know what it's like, we'd love to try it."

139

Geoffrey Brown was a banker. "You know, in the City…" was one of Sonya's stock phrases. He was, as he knew only too well, fighting life on all fronts.

Sonya's father had been one of those lucky chaps, lucky in the sense that, when an Austrian with a Charlie Chaplin moustache had taken the world's armies to war, he had been commissioned ahead of war breaking out.

So, from '39 to '45, he had a regular desk job at the Ministry, which had given Sonya and her brother a great feeling of security, a good education and a sense of superiority.

Geoffrey had seemed a jolly good bet to fit in with her social climbing aspirations. Once he had moved from the Tunbridge Wells branch of the National Westminster Bank where, to be fair, he was much liked and very successful, which was why he was moved in the first place, he found he was up against the banking class structure. He hadn't been to the right school, he was a grammar lad, his father had not gone before him in the bank to lay a path, he had played football – "positively the wrong-shaped ball," he was told – and he had not been to university.

All that apart, he'd co-produced two children (one of each), drove a Hillman Minx, funded by a 1 per cent loan from the bank, and had a mortgage of £7,500 to fund their four-bedroom family house in Westerham.

Basically, Geoffrey needed a holiday, and Sonya needed one to talk to her friends about. It would also give her an excuse to buy a couple of new outfits and perhaps a new costume, as she was a pretty good swimmer.

Bed attire was not on her agenda. She and Geoffrey wouldn't be setting the Playa duvets on fire. Sex was occasional. Tension got the better of Geoffrey and the harder he tried to satisfy Sonya's simple, rather unimaginative desires, the more stressed he became.

"There'll be things for the children to do," Sonya had confirmed to Geoffrey. "It wouldn't do you any harm to get a tennis racket and have a game or two with them. Peter is so much better than Anne that they'll need some more compatible opponents." She'd suggested writing ahead to the hotel to ask them to look out for suitable opponents. Geoffrey thought that was a silly idea. Why not just wait and see who was around when they got there? "That's your problem," she had said over supper a few weeks before the holiday, "you always leave things to the last moment and you never know what opportunities you may be missing. These are their lives. So I'll write."

Unlike the Browns, the Cooks still enjoyed their conjugal rights with regularity. They had met at university where he was studying for a BSc in the hope of doing quantity surveying. She was on a BA with teaching in mind. They had met at the Freshman's Ball and, although neither admitted it to the other for the first year of their relationship, they both knew they had found their true love. It stayed that way, and they'd make love in whoever's digs were more available, usually to the sound of Ella Fitzgerald's "Foggy Day in London Town" or Nat King Cole's "Mona Lisa". They became known as the "Cook items", rarely seen apart other than during lectures.

They stuck together, each hungry to achieve their academic goals, and they did.

Kathryn taught at the Convent School right up to the birth of their first daughter, Natasha, and was due to go back to work a year later when she found herself pregnant again with Joanne.

Graham Cook had read about the Playa in the Sunday Times too. His preference was to take the SNCF train out of Calais down to Narbonne with the car on board. He reckoned it would only be a four-hour drive down to Callella, subject to the warning one of his colleagues had given him about the traffic queues, which could develop at the Franco-Spanish border up in the Pyrenees at La Jonquera.

Natasha – 'Tasha' to the Cook household – was a fidgety 16-year-old, the same age as Peter Brown, but a much more mature and worldly person than Peter. She had finished taking her eight 'O' levels to which, she had given an almost monastic dedication, trying her hardest to get the passes she needed to take languages in the lower and upper sixth years.

Her job aspirations varied from teaching to United Nations work and, more recently, air-hostessing, much to her parents' dismay.

"You'll not need a degree to serve tea and coffee in an aeroplane," her father had said.

"Oh Daddy! You're so old-fashioned. That would just be a tool to allow me to travel. I could be in an office making tea and not learn anything about other people's cultures," she had argued.

Then there was the evening, with the exams behind her, when she asked her father what the ground rules would be regarding evening entertainment when they got to Spain.

That had put him into quite a quandary.

"Tell me what you have in mind and we'll negotiate," he had said.

"Well, there'll be discos, so a pass until midnight should do."

"Your mother will never agree to that," he said, a bit panic-stricken, realising that the danger zone would be from ten on, when doubtless the young Spanish waiters would be free from their evening stints and would be out on the prowl for virginal young English tourists. "Let's start at ten," he had suggested. Tasha went spare.

"Ten! Come on, Dad, discos are only just open by then. It's got to be midnight. And if you and Mum are worried that I might get seduced by some

Spanish oik of a waiter, remember they have afternoons free when they have a lot more energy for a romp!"

Graham had to admit he was a little proud of the way his adolescent daughter was rationalising her prospects of getting laid, or electing not to.

Although Graham and Kathryn were not themselves the slightest abstemious in the bedroom, they had waited until they were 21 and wished for their daughter to do the same.

In the end, they ruled that Tasha could stay out till ten, which led a very sulky adolescent to run up her parents' phone bill discussing the unreasonableness of mothers and fathers with all her like-minded girlfriends.

Maria supposed that the Browns and Cooks, both being English, with apparently similarly aged children, were likely to get on and become a small social unit on which others might build through the coming month of August.

Whether it would become stratified on a nationality basis, who could tell? The Parmentiers also, of course, had three mature teenage children, but whether the offspring would be such pains in the neck as their father seemed remained to be seen.

On the other hand, Maria thought, did it matter to her who got on with whom? She and Marco merely had to lay the foundations for a good holiday; the rest was up to their guests.

Maria did have some qualms about Bob Hunt. From the way the booking was conducted, and although she had to say his phone calls were always quietly charming, he seemed a man who knew what he wanted.

He had casually mentioned Mrs Hunt and how he wanted flowers in what had effectively changed from two adjoining family rooms to a suite of one bedroom and a living area, just for the two of them. That was the only way they could get the two bathrooms he liked to have for his wife. He was also the only prospective guest who had enquired about the colour of the rooms. Parchment he approved of, as Mrs Hunt was a colourful person who would not want to clash with the hotel's colour scheme.

"Extraordinary!" Maria had mumbled to herself after he announced that in one of their phone conversations.

Maria had almost jumped for joy when he'd asked if she could hire him a boat with a small crew for an occasional sea trip. She had rung José to see if he would be interested in a small charter, and he agreed, but only if Maria were to crew with him. They'd had rib-stretching laughter over what the demands of the captain would be of his crew, but agreed it would be an arrangement that would not compromise her position as one of the partners of the hotel.

So, Bob Hunt and his wife were a mystery to unravel.

In their own ways, the Hunts were still slight mysteries to each other. Marcia Hunt, née Lake, had been almost literally swept off her feet, having become Mrs Hunt faster than she might have said 'Jack Robinson'.

Bob Hunt had insisted her passport be changed to 'Occupation – housewife'. It had so much more dignity than the one she'd first travelled on to Paris with him, which said 'Occupation – dancer'.

Bob Hunt's first assessment of her had been correct. He had a similar way of judging race horses.

"Christ!" he exclaimed, as he saw her at a bus-stop at the end of Half Moon Lane in Herne Hill, London. "If they're not the legs of a dancer, I'll never place a bet on a horse again."

He touched the brakes instinctively on his Bentley as he homed in first on the high stiletto sandals, for which he'd always had a strong penchant, then upwards to the crossed legs, which seemed to go on forever. The pelmet skirt was short, very short, topped by a bomber jacket that encased an equally fine torso. She was blonde, her short hair bobbed in the style of Twiggy, the model of the day.

She's got to be a hooker, he thought, so his foot no longer quivered over the brake pedal. He'd never paid for sex, at least not directly. Then, on the ground at her side, he noticed a Louis Vuitton sports holder. *Hookers don't have sports bags,* he reasoned. His foot hovered again over the pedal, but he was now past the stop and looking back through his nearside wing mirror.

He was suddenly stunned by the sound of the horn from a large high vehicle. His looked in the rear view mirror, in which he got a full frontal view of a Hall and Co aggregate lorry. The driver's hands were flailing all over the place, which compelled Bob Hunt to accelerate out of the path of the oncoming vehicle. He indicated left and took the next immediate turn, which came upon him sooner than expected, allowing one irate lorry driver and one Bentley to avoid a collision.

In fact, Bob couldn't have cared less about the lorry. The young lady, however, he could not get out of his mind.

Back at the bus-stop, the girl was fully aware of the impact she'd had, especially from the fleeting glance she'd exchanged with the Bentley driver. She smiled. Gorgeous as she was, she didn't usually attract a Bentley driver. Such cars were normally driven by toffs who had their little woman alongside them anyway. More often she'd get a toot from a lorry driver, who would drive on and no doubt rekindle the vision when he climbed into bed with the missus that night.

When the bus arrived, she paid her fare to Piccadilly Circus and settled down on the upper deck to enjoy her familiar ride into town.

Bob, having three-point turned his car around in the side-road, sped back to the bus-stop. "Shit, she's gone!" he observed, looking at his Rolex. It was 3.08pm.

Now a girl like that looked organised. Whatever she did, whether the sports bag was for business or pleasure, she was likely to have some sort of pattern. She'd make a regular habit of getting to that bus-stop at 3pm each day. He'd bet on that. He'd look in his diary for tomorrow and try and come back.

Bob drove on to his appointment feeling freer than he had since his unpleasant divorce two years previously. She'd be wearing Chanel. Unlikely Estée Lauder, she'd have more style than that. Yes, her boyfriends would cover her in fragrance, and unfortunately probably their bodies too. Why not, she was a beautiful vision.

Bob Hunt had a habit of always getting what he wanted. Life had not come easily, but charm had, and, even at 58, he had the unique quality of being able to use that on male and female alike. As a much younger man, he'd habitually called anybody older than himself 'chief' or 'boss' when making a business arrangement. Bankers, he found, loved it, but usually told him there was no need to be so formal, and to use their Christian names. Start getting on Christian name terms with a banker and bring a bottle of bubbly into the equation and, he found, raising money was easy.

Females would be charmed by his manners in the first instance. He would always find something to individualise a lady on first meeting. He'd notice a stone in a ring, and say how attractive it was as an introductory comment, or a face on a watch, the colour of a nail polish, a perfume or the hang of a jacket. He would never fall for the cleavage trap. He would fix his eyes so as apparently not to focus below a pendant or above a smart Gucci belt, though 'to be sure' (one of his favourite expressions), he would have observed, and permanently noted, every single freckle, pore or brush of enhancing makeup in the breast area.

Bob's education had mainly been in the university of life. At 16, when war broke out, he had nowhere to go. Too young to enlist, he got a job in construction. When he was 18, he volunteered for the auxiliary fire service in the Stockwell to Central London zone. Whilst the prime objective was to put fires out and save the occasional life, he always felt sorry for families who had to watch their homes burn down, and then face the rude awakening that they had nowhere to live.

To say Bob Hunt ever did anything inadvertently was perhaps a mis-statement. However, when he used to call round to his uncle's estate agency in Kennington at the end of a shift and recount the extent of the damage he'd seen the night before, neither he nor his uncle had initially realised that, by suggesting to the displaced families that the uncle's business unit could probably re-house them, they were on the brink of commercial success.

Unbeknown to Bob, his uncle began to use his nephew's tales of the previous night's damage as a basis from which to approach the owners of houses in a road where a bomb had struck. He would offer to purchase their damaged property, and adjoining owners, fearing their homes might be affected by the next German attack, were often eager to sell too. Uncle bought cheap.

Bob soon got wise to how important his information was to his uncle, and sought a cut. The last two years of the war made the uncle an extremely rich man, and he placed Bob in charge of bringing in his own mates to rebuild, repair and generally smarten the properties up.

By 1947, Bob was beginning to be able to acquire whatever he set his eyes on in his own right. A wife was on his shopping list, and was duly acquired: a homely young woman with little aspirations other than to raise two children, which she did.

Bob extended his uncle's empire into new development situations and, lo and behold, money poured in. He bought a single leg of a racehorse, the front end of a greyhound and, with a developing knowledge of the turf, he set up a small chain of successful mares that carried his bets and increased his fortune.

Bob was a successful man, despite the inevitable divorce taking 33.33 per cent of all his recognisable assets. Well, he'd seen the breakup coming and had been more than careful in ensuring a number of nest eggs were tucked away for a rainy day, and for when he returned to bachelordom.

So, seeing and fantasising over a young lady standing at a bus-stop watching a day go by hurt no-one, apart from his lust buds.

He had made himself free for a 3pm visit to Half Moon Lane the next day. This time, however, he brought his binoculars so that he could track his filly from afar, as he did regularly with his trainer on Epsom Downs at the crack of dawn.

At two minutes to three, he realised he had not actually seen her move. Before, it was just a statue of a most beautifully carved body. Still and serene. If not modern, certainly contemporary, but not cheap. A beauty put together accidentally.

Now, as she strutted across the road, he followed her through the glasses. She arrived at the bus-stop, a quarter of a mile distant from him and completely unaware of his focus, and semi knelt to place her bag on the pavement, her knees together. Then, in slow motion, she raised herself to her 5' 9" height, plus heels.

Bob put the binoculars into the glove pocket, slipped the car into gear and set off.

She saw the dark blue of what she well knew to be a Bentley approaching. Her heart jumped a little. There was something about the vehicle that told her it was the one she had seen yesterday. She wondered if it would be the distinct looking, attractive middle-aged driver she had glimpsed the day before.

The car slowed. She could not do other than glance its way. The car stopped.

The nearside window lowered gracefully and the man leant across. "I'm not very good at this, but I'm sure I'm going in the same direction as yourself. It's a cold day, you're a beautiful young lady and if I promise I'm not proposing to molest you, would you accept a lift?"

Now, this was different. He had style, charm and charisma. He was very handsome and undoubtedly rich. What a nice touch, not "can I give you a lift?", the benefactorial approach, but "would you accept a lift?" What a lovely opening suggestion.

"It's kind of you," she said behind a smile. "But it's not cold, it's pleasantly fresh, and my mother always told me never to speak to men I haven't been introduced to, and certainly not to accept a lift in a Bentley… as beautiful as it is."

Bob was flabbergasted, and more so when the driver of the double-decker bus hooted up the back end of the car, remonstrating through the open window that it was his bus-stop and "not a parking zone for you and your great capitalist status symbol!"

Unfazed, Bob laughed. "Your mother was right. Here…" He groped in the glove pocket. "By way of introduction, this is my card. I'm Bob Hunt, by name, not by nature, and while I accept everything you say, I don't give up that easy. If I don't go now, I won't have a boot and your bus won't have a radiator!"

"You getting on, miss, or going in your grandfather's charabanc?" the conductor said.

She decided to take the bus option and climbed on board. Paid, but found the climb to the upper deck more difficult than usual in her flustered state. She fell clumsily into an empty seat, thinking that either she had gone bloody mad giving up on a lift like that, or it had gone really, really well. He was lovely. "OK, well, we'll see," she muttered as she delved into her purse for the fare.

Bob drove off. She reminded him of his most successful filly. Didn't appear to be a racer from the start, was slow to show appreciation of extremely special diet, digs and attention, but eventually was the best thing on four legs he'd had anything to do with.

That wasn't achieved without research which was, perhaps, one of Bob's best talents. Preparation was two-thirds of the required input to any competitive situation. Organisation was the remainder. So, prepared and organised he would be.

Marcia Lake knew men. Unfortunately a little too well, because since the age of 18 she had been gawped at by men of all shapes and sizes for a living. She always had clothes on, but in varying degrees of scantiness. Her mother was herself a frustrated dancer, actress and stage performer, and saw enormous talent in Marcia from a very young age.

She'd put Marcia through talent shows galore and had hoped she would develop on the classical side of dance. But she became too tall for ballet. Then her mother saw an advert in The Stage magazine for applications for the Bluebell Dance Troupe and borrowed sufficient money to get her to an audition in Paris just days after her 16th birthday.

The management team resolved she had the figure, poise, style and ability to get a touring place with the full troupe. The two years' experience was incredible but the strain of constant performance and travel took its toll and, after a particularly unfortunate performance in Milan, Marcia collapsed at the end of the show and was diagnosed with a slipped disc.

It was, in fact, irreparable wear to the vertebrae and the French team of doctors ruled that she'd have to quit full-time professional dancing with all its stress.

She'd had a limited academic education. Dancing was all she knew so, between her Bluebell retirement and her now 20th year, she had danced in night clubs for a living. It was all above board stuff, but rarely would a night go by without a punter sending anything from 20 quid to 100 to the dressing room to invite the blonde beauty to share a bottle of champagne after the performance.

That was never the ultimate idea. They always thought a body exposed in heels and sequins for their delight was flesh they could buy after hours. To an extent, at the levels of bonus offered, they were right, but Marcia did and always would keep her private life to herself. None of her colleagues knew whether she would 'do a turn with a punter' or not, and accepted it to be none of their business. What was apparent was that nobody ever came back for more of the same. Where her colleagues had regular revisits, Marcia never did.

So, having declined a ride in a Bentley, here she was top deck on a bus with the next pick-up line likely to be thrown at her by the ticket collector.

By God, she knew men. "Ticket dear, please." This wasn't the collector, but the higher-ranking inspector. "This will take you to the 'dilly dear, you know that?"

"Yes, I do," she said, holding her breath for his punch-line.

"Thank you for choosing London Transport, dear. Don't know why though, because the geezer you turned down was heading towards Monaco, we reckon. A car with a body like that and a young lady with a body like yours, well, you were perfectly matched."

"Thank you, and perhaps I might say that the trouble with you blokes is that you all seem to think that with a set of wheels and an essential engine, you can flaunt your wares in front of any young lady and get her into bed. So keep punching tickets and dream on, mate!"

"Oh clever lady, be like that!"

What she thought would happen was that tomorrow, Mr Bob Hunt, Chairman and Managing Director, Hunter Homes (as per his introductory card) would drive up to the bus-stop, drop his window, smile and tweak a finger to come hither, and damn it she would slide in beside him and no doubt have her butt charmed off. She suddenly realised tomorrow was Friday, the day she didn't work, apart from Sundays. Oh hell! Life was a gamble. If he didn't turn up, she'd still go into town, perhaps to the Academy Exhibition and then ring a girlfriend and have some supper out.

Next day, five to three. Out she strutted, across from one side of Half Moon Lane to the other. Sports bag downloaded onto the pavement. Not a hair out of place. She felt it was actually a little colder today. He'd probably have the air-con roaring.

So... 3.02pm, 3.03pm, 3.05pm – the bus was in sight. Where was the bastard?

"You getting on or not, lady?" the conductor said. Silently, disappointed, she got onto the bus. Why bother to go top deck? She scanned the lower deck, resolved the average age was 108 and so set off up to the upper deck as the bus pulled away. She had bought her ticket as she got on.

She settled down, planning her walk from Piccadilly Circus back up to the RA, which, had she thought it through, she might have tackled better in lower heels.

Feeling a tap on her shoulder, she held her ticket aloft for the inspector to scrutinise.

"Did your mother have a view on you being picked up on the top deck of a bus by somebody you're bound to have checked out by now?"

To her, it was like a Jussi Bjorling rendering of Nessun Dorma, Santa Lucia and Ave Maria, all merged into the most romantic rendition, to cover every conceivable pick-up imaginable. She'd keep cool though. Her next move could either place her into a controlling check-mate position, or a reverse judo submission. She needed pole grid position for the rest of her life, all in the one response.

Marcia half-turned towards him. She smiled into his face, whose charm increased with every sighting. With her left hand, she patted the empty seat alongside her and said, "Well, dear sir, you can join me as a reward for trying. My ticket says I get off at Monaco, though!"

"Bugger me!" he replied beneath a beaming smile. "So does mine, but it says I have to change at the next stop because the one behind goes via London airport. Why don't you join me? I can totally put your mother's mind at rest."

This time she couldn't decline.

He insisted on going down the bus stairs first. He said, "I'll lead. If the bus jolts, you'll fall on me." It also gave him a surreptitious opportunity to glance back at her legs. They truly did go on forever.

She felt safe. The chauffeur looked OK. Bob Hunt held open the rear passenger door of the car and allowed her to slide in first. He'd walked round to the offside by the time the chauffeur had switched the engine off and was standing in the road ready to attend to the door for his boss.

The door was closed behind Bob Hunt and the driver tactfully, and presumably on instructions, stayed outside the car.

Bob Hunt held out his hand and Marcia instinctively put hers into his.

"Hi, I'm Bob Hunt and I'll level with you. I really have no idea how to progress with this meeting."

They both laughed.

"Seriously, if you'd really like to join me in Monaco I'm sure I can get us on a flight, if not BEA privately. We could get there in time for dinner at 9.30pm, well, actually 10.30pm their time. You'll get your beauty sleep by midnight. We'll breakfast early and you can then decide the itinerary though to Sunday evening, when I'll get you back home."

"And if I said that's not quite how I'd planned it, what would Mr Robert Hunt, Captain of Industry, Chairman and MD of Hunters say?"

"He'd say he fully understood your point of view, but because you hadn't got this coming weekend fully planned, quite simply because you didn't know about it, we'd stick with my planning… but you could do next weekend's arrangements."

"And if I already have those made, which don't involve you?"

"Then I would ask you to consider changing them to include me. That is, unless there's a husband or boyfriend."

"And in that case…?"

"Then I'd say I don't want to be an interloper. Life's often about timing and if some lucky bugger is there before me… then… c'est la vie."

"You're certainly a persuasive charmer, Mr Hunt. Definitely you have an original style. But at which stage do you invite me into bed?"

"I don't."

In something of a state of shock she just had to reply, "Don't! Now listen, I've got two legs but neither have bells on. Please don't pull my leg."

"No! Seriously. Bed isn't the be all and end all of a relationship. It's a bit like a work of art that can hang to be enjoyed; the mere presence of such beauty is gratifying enough. You don't rip the frame and canvas off the wall and throw it under the sheets at the first opportunity. Art and beautiful things are to be cherished and not momentarily raped for self-satisfaction.

"If you invited me to your bed, I couldn't promise to be enough of a man to decline, but my three-day love affair thus far will be absolutely satisfied simply by being in your presence and breathing in your beauty.

"Oh, and by the way, I'm no crank or pervert, I have two children, probably older than you and I've slept with many ladies when invited. Do you know, I don't even know your name, and we're planning to go to Monaco."

"It's Marcia. Marcia Lake."

"Miss, Mrs or Ms?"

"Miss totally-unattached-and-swept-off-her-feet-Lake."

"So, what's the deal? My plan this weekend, yours next?"

"Yes, and I like the idea of being an artefact… and being cherished, and bed sort of only being on the back burner. And I like the idea that I'm in charge in that department."

"Marcia. Test me. You can. Bring your mother too."

"Mother's no longer with us. Her rules have been left behind. Do you know, Mr Bob Hunt, there's a side of me that's impetuous. Another one that tells me when not to trust someone. So the ground rules would be separate rooms and a lift home first to throw some things a girl needs for a trip like this into a bag. Pick up the passport, et cetera. One final question, though."

"Fire away."

"Mrs Hunt. What about her in the equation?"

"My wife's no longer with us. She didn't leave any rules behind."

It was like that until they got married three months later. Maria was right. Mr Hunt was an unusual one.

CHAPTER 10

Maria continued to review her alphabetical cards.

Monsieur et Madame Duval weren't going to be too interesting, nor difficult, it would seem.

Mr & Mrs French and family from Epsom in England had particularly wanted a guarantee that the pool would be fully operational, presumably to occupy their two young sons.

John Jones and his wife knew Mr & Mrs Bob Hunt. Maria hoped that wouldn't make the evenings too cliquey. Maria hadn't known what a turf accountant was and had looked the words up in one of the English dictionaries at the library. Gambling of any kind was off-limits for most Catholic Spaniards, so she was concerned what sort of person John Jones would be. They'd have to wait and see.

The Doctors Guibaud might come into their own should somebody have an accident or become ill. However, she and Marco had had the foresight to make arrangements with a doctor in Llanfranc, who had been appointed as the medical advisor to the hotel.

Maria glanced at her watch. Good God! Time was flying by. She had to finalise the arrangements for the grand opening by her very good friend, Carlos Sanchez, the mayor, who was sticking to his promise, for the following Tuesday week.

Carlos had also volunteered to 'leak' the mayoral special dignitary guest list to Maria so that at least all the important locals would have heard of the new hotel. If they turned up, that would be a bonus because they all networked and, presuming they liked what they saw, word would be up and down the Costa Brava in no time, especially with both a pool and tennis court, which the local social set were all agog about, keen as they were to see the area westernised to compete with the establishing resorts of France and Italy.

Maria thought it ironic that some of their early guests were, in fact, being drawn from France and Italy. She and Marco thought it was because their prices were very competitive, which she understood to be the case from her own research into others' tariffs.

They'd had 50 formal acceptances to the opening. José's RSVP had been one of the first: "Sñr José Romanez is pleased to accept the kind invitation from the Partners of the Hotel Playa to their opening on…"

It had raised goose pimples on Maria's skin when she opened the envelope. How could his response be so cold and unfeeling when they had shared so much together? How, on the other hand, could he risk Marco's questions had he responded as she would have liked: "Darling Maria, of course I'll be there to support your venture." So she understood.

She understood more when, at about 11 that morning, the local florist delivered a hydrangea plant in a container, with a note: "Best wishes for your success at Hotel Playa. If you show the enthusiasm I know you have for any venture into which you put your heart, yours will be the finest hotel in the land." It was signed "Yours" with a single "X". It didn't need signing.

On the night itself, even Maria's neat and tidy brain couldn't keep pace with the names attaching to the steady flow of guests who arrived, sometimes in droves of six or eight, as though individuals had been waiting under trees so as not to arrive alone.

José was the only one she remembered who announced himself formally as the Regional Director of Iberia Co-operative Insurance Company. As he shook her hand and bowed his head respectfully, he lifted his face with a quick wink and a beaming smile. Maria had turned to Marco and repeated the introduction, reminding him that Mr Romanez had provided them with their insurance. Marco thanked him for his company's support and in turn introduced him to Virginia, who had turned up trumps and made an appearance on the evening, despite having said it was not her scene.

Marco had responded, in the secrecy of their renewed relationship, that it was in Virginia's best interests to a) attend, and b) wear black underwear, in respect of which she'd get her reward later. She conformed.

"This gentleman," Marco explained to Pedro, who was the fourth member of the line-up, "controls our destiny. If you and I decide to burn the place down and run, then he will provide protection for these two ladies in our absence."

José thought the words were ill chosen because if it did now burn down, he would at least have to instigate an enquiry into this threatened arson. But on the other hand, Marco was right, it would be José's pleasure to provide all the protection Maria and her sister-in-law needed.

José had moved off to mingle but not before clasping Pedro's hand firmly and saying that he knew, from the information he had previously gleaned from Mrs Martinez, that Pedro had had major input into the design and conception of the project. If Pedro could spare a few moments during the evening, he would value a tour and an explanation as to how the resultant effects had been accomplished.

"The gated approach and the cobbles are so much more inviting than the concrete and tarmac I see so frequently through the length of the Costas," said José.

Pedro was flattered. "I look forward to showing you round."

The others had come for their introductions and passed on almost faceless and nameless, but Maria believed, as they headed off for a glass of sparkling wine, they'd be talking about the place behind their backs.

Jacques, the appointed head waiter, appeared by Maria's side. He whispered, "He's here. Sñr Mayor. He's walking across now."

Maria ran her hands through her hair, fluffing her sleek new style. She tugged a little at her blouse, exposing a respectable amount of Marilyn Monroe-influenced cleavage.

"Sñr Mayor," she said with a little curtsey. She then looked beyond Carlos, as though speaking to his non-existent companion. "So, you didn't teach me a lesson by inviting a formal companion to accompany you on this auspicious occasion!"

"Dearest Maria, there are no substitutes for gold and diamonds and the dearest of friends. No, of course I didn't."

Carlos knew Marco and Pedro and felt he knew Virginia too, but accepted the formal introduction in a dignified way.

Carlos's words were short, sincere and to the point. He wished the management and the hotel enormous success. He thanked the Martinez family for the financial investment they had re-injected into the area. He applauded that they had not just followed the competition in terms of matching amenities, but had had the foresight to introduce a modern sea water pool and all-weather tennis court for the enjoyment of their guests.

Marco excelled himself by keeping his response short and workmanlike. His sincerity was undoubted when he reached his conclusion "… and none of this would have been possible without the input of my business partner, Maria, whom you possibly all know… but if you don't, I recommend her to you… and also this very talented young entrepreneurial designer and business man Pedro, who happens also to be a chip off the Martinez family block… and to my wife, a big thank you." (Said with a distinct wink, which made her giggle.) "Please enjoy the rest of the evening and we'll welcome your comments and recommendations to bring tourism to Callella."

The applause was reminiscent of the new intake in the first year of a flamenco class, and then the wine flowed. Marco had to release extra stock to

Jacques, who reported there were 150 glasses in circulation. Marco looked at his watch and turned to Maria, who had been listening anxiously.

"I'd like to take the 151st glass for myself. It's a little before seven, I know, but I want to say cheers to you and Pedro."

Later, Maria was mingling and looking for José when there was a light touch on her left shoulder. "How did your son get on with the freebies?" a voice enquired.

She turned quickly. "Oh," she said, "it was embarrassing really. I gave them to him and he laughed and explained there was no need. If ever he needed any there was this very commercial pharmacist in Palafrugell who had the guys queuing up in the evenings for their supplies, and that he'd got plenty. How nice to see you. How come we invited you?"

"You'd be amazed. Ever since you came into the pharmacy in distress, I've been trying to find you."

"Come on, pull the other one. Firstly, I wasn't in distress and secondly, I don't believe you."

"Well, it's partially true. You're the sort of lady one doesn't forget in a hurry, but if you're Deputy Chairman of the Chamber of Commerce, as I am, there are a few perks, but this has been an especially memorable one."

Maria blushed slightly. Coming from such an attractive man, that was indeed flattering.

"I'm sorry," she said, "I don't know your name."

"Miguel. Miguel Mendes."

"Then, Miguel Mendes, we're delighted to have you with us, and if I may we'll tell all our guests about your late afternoon service."

They both laughed as though they were lifelong friends. "Better still, make sure your front desk carries a stock," he said. "It's sometimes a long time to wait from one night to the following late afternoon, if your clients were to become dependent on my service alone."

They laughed heartily again. Pedro joined them and met Miguel Mendes's eyes with some embarrassment.

"This is my son, Pedro."

"I'm pleased to meet you," Miguel replied calmly, but effectively and diplomatically.

José was suddenly standing alongside the trio.

"Hi José, have you been on the tour?" Maria asked, somewhat formally.

"Yes, and I'm thrilled to see everything you've achieved. My company's interests are in good hands here, as I've seen with this charming son of yours, Pedro."

"José, I'd like you to meet Miguel Mendes. He's Deputy Chairman of the

Chamber of Commerce."

"Have we met?" José replied.

"I don't recollect if we have."

"Are you local?"

"Yes, I'm a pharmacist in Palafrugell."

"Well, it's been a pleasure to meet you all. I ought to go and mingle with some of my Chamber colleagues." Miguel half-clicked his heels, bowed his head reverently and took his leave, but not before taking Maria's hand and thanking her for her hospitality.

José and Miguel: two staggeringly handsome men. Well, three, actually, including Pedro.

Most of the guests had left by 8pm. The comments had been most encouraging.

Marco took his leave, as did Virginia. "Exhausted!" he said to Maria. "Don't know where you get your energy from." Pedro was meeting his mates in town for a leaving celebration. Next stop for him was Madrid and his architectural degree, but not before he'd fulfilled his sports-directing, general factotum role for the hotel in its opening months.

José was also preparing to leave but Maria suggested they take an opened bottle of wine down to the poolside. Their first encounter together in such a public place had gone well, Maria was sure, that it showed that there was more to them than met the various sets of eyes focussed on them.

Miguel had been a disturbing influence to her. She'd felt it at their first meeting, but put that down to the circumstances of that encounter. *Oh,* she thought to herself, *I'm just being girlish. I've been working too hard.*

"So where's the changing room at the pool?" José enquired. "Pedro couldn't find the key."

"I see, I would have expected Pedro to have shown it to you. It was one of his ideas." She took the key from its resting place on the architrave above the door.

"If we're carrying your burglary policy, which we are, I'd not recommend that as a safe place to keep it."

"Sorry, darling fool, it's not normally. I put the key there earlier so that I could show you the place myself."

"So that's what fooled Pedro."

She opened the door. "I thought the lilo might save some bruising," she said as she threw both her arms around his neck. "How long has it been since we saw each other?"

"Four weeks."

"And I've yet to thank you for the anonymous hydrangea."

"Who sent you that then?" José said playfully.

"Well, I haven't found out yet but I'm going to give a huge gracias to the fellow when I do."

"OK, shit! I give in. It was me."

"Thank God for that…" she said with a giggle and a wiggle of her hips as she lowered her skirt, "…and watch your language, young man."

CHAPTER 11

Peter, or Pedro as his mother and uncle still called him, was becoming more used to his self-designed re-baptism. He was as comfortable driving his mother's Seat as Marco's Mercedes. The Merc was, of course, bigger and more powerful, and he drove it with a dignity the Seat didn't deserve. He'd passed his driving test first time, not to anyone's particular surprise. He had developed into one of those young men who, if they put their minds to it, could do most things. At 18, he was a sickeningly good tennis player. He swam well, but confessed to not really liking the water – because, his mother thought, of his childhood experiences concerning Paco.

He was an excellent footballer, both his team's main goal scorer and an accomplished defender. If there was a criticism, his sports master had said, it was that he worried a little too much about the adequacy of the half back line and was inclined to fall back a bit too far defensively, making his job of sprinting up front when the breaks came more difficult. So he was not an opportunist goal hanger, like some of the others. He ran the ball into the opposing goal mouth and quite often swathed through the others' defence to net a goal at the end of an exciting run.

His mother thought it was that excitement his band of female followers came to watch, although even she could see his shorts might have an attraction for a young girl too.

Academically, Pedro was brilliant. Maria felt proud that three days most weeks, Pedro would catch the school bus, alight at Palafrugell and meet her at the library. He would read selected books while he waited, which could sometimes be two or three hours. He'd then discuss what he'd read on the car journey home and continue to enlighten his uncle and aunt over supper on subjects about which they had no knowledge.

He had taken his university entrance exams early, and normally a place would be offered a year later. In his case, he had passed with flying colours, having submitted a thesis on 'The Environmental Needs of a Developing Industry – Tourism on the Bravas'.

The tutors at Madrid had apparently found it exhilarating and offered him an immediate scholarship. According to the headmaster at the school, they had done that to encourage Pedro to think about a four-year stint, which would include an MA from which they too might benefit.

The headmaster's preference was for him to stay on at school for another year. Maria proffered her view that moving onto a higher academic plane at this stage was surely the better route for someone she felt was destined for commerce rather than academia.

"But he'd also be head boy," the headmaster said, "and that would surely do his commercial career a bit of good too."

Maria thanked him but didn't fully agree.

"… and of course, we were expecting him to be captain of the football team."

Now that was a different matter. Not only would Pedro thrive on that, but it would bury the 'chiquito' bit for him well and truly. She might even condescend to bow to the 'Peter' preference too.

So, as Pedro drove into town for the farewell do for those who were not staying on, he focussed on the three months he would have left as a schoolboy up until Christmas. January would be a new beginning.

First, he had to get through his first spell of work as the hotel's Sports Director. That thought took him back just a couple of hours to his introduction to the chap who had put the hotel's insurance in place. André, was it? No, José. José Romanez. What a really nice bloke he was. He was interested in everything Pedro had shown him, and not just out of courtesy, it seemed.

Pedro had made José laugh with a tale of how he had talked Meribel, a girl from school he was going out with and who wanted to be a doctor, into doing a stint as a chambermaid/waitress. "Good God," she'd said, "I'm not going to go round and strip beds that are still warm from early morning copulations, or clean out the loos… and as for getting my bottom pinched by some Kraut while I serve his sausages… no, it's not my scene…"

"So, OK," Pedro had replied to Meribel, "you want to be a doctor who does the hospital rounds and says how unhygienic the toilets are without actually knowing how hard or easy it is to get them looking clean? Or whether a bed needs stripping when an incontinent patient has crapped in it? It's a golden opportunity to get your hands dirty and then, if you become a doctor, at least you'll know there's another way to life that you can understand."

"So, if I took the job, do I get to see more of the prissy Director of Sport?"
"Every day."
"Do I get to have a tennis lesson in my time off for free?"
"Yes, you do."
"Do I still get to give you a special time most nights?"
"Probably."

"Then I'll let you know tomorrow," Meribel had said, pulling Pedro into her welcoming arms in the back of Maria's Seat.

Pedro was still a bit bitter about Laura, and had not taken her news lightly. He was saddened that their relationship had not had the depth of a loving sexual encounter, which might have turned Laura heterosexual permanently.

Meribel didn't know the off-side rule, or the difference between a penalty and a free kick. But, at 17½, she knew what turned her on and had a body that looked to her in the mirror as good as any she had seen in the copies of Knave and Playboy and the like, which girls in her class had borrowed from their brothers. Her parents were devout Catholics. Her mother particularly had broached the subject of relationships with boys, just after her 17th birthday. "Look, Mother," Meribel had replied, "if I've decided I want to be a doctor, I'm sure I know by now that well, yes, boys will try to get you into bed and there are dangers of becoming pregnant. I also know, as does every other girl of my age, that if you break with your religious beliefs, you can make sex safer, but not foolproof. But what we girls have also worked out is that you can get a boy all the satisfaction he wants without going through the whole practical exercise." Her girlfriends were of similar minds, all bright, intelligent and healthy, with quite a sense of fun, certainly more versed in structuring relationships than any of their male counterparts, and more knowledgeable about how far they would go to keep the attentions of a lover.

Meribel had effectively propositioned Pedro, or Peter as she now happily called him. She'd made the first much-thought-through approach after following his movements to and from school on the bus.

She had worked out her timing so on this one late afternoon, Peter was already on the bus when she leapt aboard just as the pneumatic doors were closing, thus drawing attention to herself.

Peter looked up, as she had hoped, and focussed on that one blouse button that covered – yet also revealed – just enough of her charms.

"Wow, nearly missed it!" she said, pretending to be out of breath as she slid into the seat alongside him. Still breathing heavily, she gasped, "Oh, can I sit here?" and then leant slightly forward as though to regain her composure. "Oh gosh," she murmured as she hurriedly did up the attention-seeking button. "How embarrassing!"

She turned her face fully to his. The blush was not an act, it happened to be natural. The set-up had not been. Having composed herself she continued the conversation but she couldn't quite fathom if it was going right or the reverse.

"You're in the football team, aren't you?"

"While I'm fit, yes."

"I'm Meribel Gomez. But my friends call me Meri."

"Hi Meri, and don't worry about your blouse. It was lovely."

She could not do other than giggle.

"Could we see each other?" he said suddenly.

Then she leapt in with her killer blow. "You go out with Laura, don't you?"

"Well now," he said defensively, "no! I don't go out with her. Never did, actually, in the way girls mean by going out. We were just good friends growing up together. Why do you ask?"

"Well, all the girls think you do. But then we're a bit puzzled."

"Why are you puzzled?"

"Oh Peter, please don't push me, you've embarrassed me once today, that's enough."

"Come on, Meri, you started this conversation. What's the puzzlement?"

"They… and don't ask me who they are… but they say Laura is a lesbian and she must be using you as some sort of smokescreen to give her credibility."

"What?" He went quiet.

She left him in his thoughts for a full 30 seconds. She reached with her left hand to take his right one. She lifted the back of his right hand to her lips and gently brushed the hint of hair around his knuckles with a soft embrace.

"OK, so I'm probably the worst offender in thinking you're a hunk of a man. I've always said what's between a couple is up to them, but if you're saying you don't have any ties, and the offer's still on for us to see each other, the answer is, I'd love to. Hey!" she suddenly said in panic. "Here's my stop." She leapt up and hurried to the door.

"When?" he shouted down the length of the coach.

She climbed down the steps and ran along to where he was sitting. "Saturday."

"Where?"

"Write me a note. Give it to me secretly tomorrow."

There was the sound of the release of airbrakes. The bus moved off slowly. He turned to look out of the rear window. She waved. He sat back. *So it's because of Laura that they've all sort of given me a wide berth. I'll have some catching up to do.*

His secret note suggested they met at 7pm outside the bar in the town centre.

They met. Meri said she'd love a coffee in the bar. He had a beer. He suggested they walked. They ambled through the town. He hadn't known at what stage to take her arm, or hold her hand. Young men didn't get training in that. They found themselves outside the picture house. Would she like to see a film? "I'd love to," she said, even though she'd seen it with a girlfriend the previous weekend.

It was very dark inside the cinema and Peter found it much easier than he would have imagined feeling for her hand.

He rejected the seats indicated by the beam of the usherette's torch and continued walking to the very back.

"There," he said in a commanding way. *Wow,* she thought, *it's only the back row.* Well, that was fine, that's really what she wanted, because if any of the girls from school saw her there, it would increase her street cred enormously.

Thereafter, holding hands was the norm. They moved their joined hands often. On his knee, on her knee. *Hell, she has beautiful thighs,* he thought. *Wow, these are the muscles he scores his goals with,* she thought.

On one occasion he ventured to swap the hand he was holding hers with and put his arm across the back of her seat. She responded by leaning into his strong hold and her hair, which smelt of either lily of the valley or mimosa, he could never tell, was soft against his specially shaved cheek.

He was sorry when the film finished, as she appeared to be too. Outside they stood there, a little lost for a while in the suddenness of the brightness of the street lights. He was able to see her happy young face as she looked up at him.

"Where to now?" he said.

"Well, I've got these very strict and protective parents. I think it needs to be home. If you see me to the bus, that'll be fine."

"Bus, young lady? I've got a car near to the bar."

"A car?"

"Well, my mother's. I'm afraid it's a Seat."

"I'm sure she'll be beautiful."

"They both are."

"Both?"

"Yes, my mother and the car."

"Oh, I'm sorry. I know your mother's very beautiful. I've seen her at the football. I was only talking about the car. You seemed to be knocking the fact it's a Seat."

"Well! You see, I'm saving for a Ferrari."

They held hands and walked briskly to where the car was parked. She showed him the way home. "I'll ask you in next time," she said.

"So, I've passed the entrance exam. There'll be a next time?"

"There was no exam to take," she said, laughing. "Thank you for a joyous evening." She placed her left hand onto his strong, muscular thigh, leant across and kissed his cheek. "I'll glimpse you in the quad on Monday."

He was spellbound, as he had been when she'd left him stranded with his thoughts on the bus. As she climbed out of the car, he got out of the driving

161

side. There was a sudden chill between them as he walked round to her side of the car. "Don't touch," she said, "my mother will be looking out from behind the curtains. She'll already pounce on me and ask me if we screwed."

"How the hell can I not fall to my knees and ask can we, and when?"

"Well, dear Peter, we'll have to talk that one through but I agree we'll need enormous will not to." She let out an extremely cheeky giggle. "See you Monday. Thanks for a really delightful first date."

He watched her walk to her house. Her last riposte was still with him. *What the hell do girls mean?* he thought. *First they introduce the prospect of sex into the equation and then they play around with words like needing a lot of will power not to.* He had a last glimpse towards the house and received a little feminine wave. Back in the car, he pulled away slowly, then quickened at the end of the lane and drove down the B class road through to Callella.

"How was your evening?" Maria called out. She was reading in bed with a small side-light on.

"Oh, great. Went to the cinema."

Maria didn't need to ask what he'd seen because there was only one highly publicised film each fortnight.

"A crowd of you?"

"No, not a crowd," he called out as he headed to the bathroom. "Just the two."

"Oh," Maria replied with an element of surprise. "Tell me in the morning."

As he lay in bed, his hand falling naturally to his groin, he thought the evening through. She was fun. She was beautiful. Her body, he imagined, was great. She was soft, understanding, receptive and, finally, confusing.

If this was love, on balance, it was totally all right. The companionship of it all, her calling him Peter… it was all great. He'd had his moments of stimulation at the touch of her shoulder, the silhouette of her breasts against the half-light of the emergency exit sign in the cinema. He was satisfied, but had high hopes of more physical contact in the future. It looked as though it would be discussed on an agenda but he felt, for some inexplicable reason, in Meri's book it could wait. He'd expected a little more fervour perhaps. Maybe the evening was not sufficiently impromptu. But then, he reasoned, how could it be, meeting in public, walking the streets, holding hands in the cinema and being watched from behind the curtains.

He'd wait.

Four dates later Peter had stopped the car on the hill at the end of an uninhabited lane. The sun was going down and there was an early summer yellow-to-orange glow across the still sea. He was half-pondering the fact that

Meribel had put more into trying to beat him at tennis on the municipal court than usual.

As they looked at the view, he put his arm across the back of her seat. She moved across towards him, playfully put her hand on the gear change. "This is going to come between us if we're not careful."

Oh, good God! he thought. Meri was in one of her seriously playful moods.

"Would your mother mind if we went in the back?" she asked. Peter was nervy. "Well no, she's never said it's off limits anyway." Meri squeaked, "Goodie!" and in a flash she was sitting in the back of the car.

"Come on, chauffeur. Madame needs you."

Peter slid in beside her and it was then that they shared that first deep kiss, which in itself led to something of a post mortem, and his realisation that this was to be to his rainy day.

Meribel was still just wearing a tight-fitting tennis blouse and the tiniest of all tennis skirts. There was still enough evening light for him to see the slim legs that supported her 1.65m frame as she curled them up onto the rear bench seat. She took his one hand and put it behind her neck, with room for him to slip it into the back of the collar of the blouse, while she held his right hand onto her knee.

His defences were down. His tracksuit bottoms were hardly going to disguise his excitement.

"So," she said, with a little squirm, "that wasn't Latin enough for you," referring back to the kiss, and covered his mouth with hers. It all felt beautifully fresh to him, the nape of her neck, her smooth young thigh and now her wide mouth, her playful tongue. She'd read about the effect the modern French kiss would have on a man, and the article was right. "There, my darling Peter," she whispered. "We don't have to risk having babies, there's nothing for our mothers to know and we don't need the confessional." They kissed for as long as he could ever remember kissing.

CHAPTER 12

Maria and Sñr Martin had got on well right from the day the first guests arrived to fill at least some of the beds in the Playa. They had talked through routines, and despite the image he created – hefty in build, hair clean but a bit long, his breathing laboured on account of his asthma, tie always loosened and his top button undone, crumpled black trousers and shoes that looked as though they had marched through the desert with Rommel's battalions – he was a very organised man. Maria thought that was probably the school-teacher in him.

The plan was she would do the grand welcome and introduce the guests to Sñr Martin, who would get them to fill in the Spanish registration documents, take their passports and offer them a security box.

They had decided to accept Diners and American Express only. As they thought a number of guests would have cash and travellers cheques, they had built a small room behind reception which was more like the vault in a bank than a security box centre. "We'll charge for the rent on a box," Marco had ruled grumpily.

It was Maria and Peter's idea that they should give guests the comfort of knowing that prized possessions and cash were safe. José provided an underwritten policy, too, so they seemed well prepared for the expectations of the modern tourist.

Maria developed a '5pm daily meeting'. (She had read about the idea in an American management book they'd had delivered to the library.) She lined up Sñr Martin, the maitre d', housekeeper and Peter, when she could drag him off the tennis court.

She would go through all the arrivals and relevant information such as she had, and would outline the quirks and particular requirements of each. The staff were encouraged to remember the guests' names.

It was July 31st and in the next three days they would move from 36 per cent occupancy to 92 per cent. They forecast they would only have two rooms free. "That means," Maria said in her most reassuring, businesslike way, "we'll be welcoming 18 family units. I don't know much about the six Thomas Cook/Lunn Poly customers. They'll all be expecting an economic stay but remember, there's next year to consider, and our job's to impress them so much that when we drop the tour companies' principally loss-making tariff, they'll still come back, but under their own steam, with their wallets stuffed with cash."

She had made a point on all the booking confirmations of asking for approximate arrival times. It seemed all intended to arrive in the morning. There were early flights out of Heathrow and Blackbushe for the families on the travel agent lists. The French, Italians and Germans all appeared to be heading for one longish eight- to 12-hour drive to within four hours of the resort. They would make one stopover in perhaps the Narbonne/ Perpignan area and then have a leisurely drive into Palafrugell, ready to have lunch at the hotel the next day.

With this in mind, Maria issued instructions to Peter that she wanted him to hang around reception between 11am and 1pm so that he could have an early introduction to the guests likely to want tennis coaching or a game fixed up. She'd bought him a couple of Adidas outfits and had found a lightweight tracksuit top in pristine white with the words 'coach' in four-inch letters across the back.

He was almost better than the handsome doormen you saw in adverts for the Ritz in London. He cut a dashing figure and, if you could buy a smile like he had, most folk would be prepared to invest quite a sum.

Maria had bullied Marco, with more than a little help from Virginia, into decking the reception area out with mature tropical plants and cut flowers on the desk, from behind which she emerged to make her formal greetings.

The Cooks and the mother-in-law were the first to arrive on Saturday 31st. Maria was charm personified. "How was the journey... so lovely to meet you... I felt I already had from our phone calls and letters." She never missed out on including the total audience. "... And hello young ladies. Now I think you play tennis, don't you? Let me find my son Peter, he's the sports coach here."

Each time it was love at first sight with the teenage girls. A few of the mums, too, seemed suddenly interested in playing tennis again. Peter was a great hit.

Sñr Martin got on with the serious stuff of informing the Spanish Government who was here, and for how long.

The Browns were next to arrive with both daughter and son in tow. They too were as Maria had imagined. The younger generation flustered their way through being introduced to the coach, who was beginning to get used to the adulation. (It didn't cross his mind that the coaching life could ever be more rewarding than his intended architectural one.) So far though, all the arrivals had said they'd book up some time with him. Peter Brown was extra keen, as though he was looking for tough macho re-training.

The Sunday morning arrivals were the Admiral and family, comprising his wife, two sons and rather beautiful daughter. Maria put the children's ages at 21 studious years for Guy, the eldest; 19-plus years of over-indulged muscular activity for Philippe, not to mention his almost certain prowess for pulling the girls; and a delicious 18 for Michelle.

Michelle's competitive streak showed through immediately when she was introduced to Peter as 'the coach'. She held out a limp hand and simply dropped her eyelids with a certain bored come-hitherness, making it plain that if there was a spark of interest from Peter he'd have to make the running. Doubtless it would have been worth the pursuit.

Maria assessed Michelle as easy game, and that was through female eyes. Peter, Maria thought, had excelled in the little foray that had just been played out. He'd cut Michelle dead and turned to Philippe, enquiring if he played tennis. Philippe replied in the affirmative, but could not resist adding, "… and rugby, skiing, athletics, golf…" But then the old man ran sports shops, so every birthday, every Christmas, he'd do a little stock reduction, wrap it up and give his children the impression that he'd put a lot of thought and expense into the gift selection.

Yes, this family were sports and sex mad. Bedding girls, in Philippe's case, and young men in Michelle's, was just part of their curriculum vitae.

Mrs Carmel Parmentier seemed OK. Although it was not publicised, she had worked the till in the Admiral's first shop and was the frugal one in the family.

Maria found the Sylvano family from Italy a bit indulged. *Wait till Georgio sets his eyes on Michelle,* Maria thought.

Sñr Sylvano, whose first question was to ask if there had been any calls for him, was probably worried that the planned fulfilment of his family duties, with ten days spent with his wife for appearances' sake, would get in the way of the affair he was having with his latest plaything. He was clearly edgy but didn't seem the sort of man to have any qualms in the business area.

By late Sunday morning, the hotel was buzzing. The loungers were all being used around the pool. The folk who had been at the hotel for a week or so were assessing the new intake. They, in turn, were taking in all around them: the newly planted gardens, their fellow internees, the tanned bodies and those recently released from less sunny climes.

A few of the active types wandered over to the tennis court, which was set on a lower plateau from the gardens. Peter was busy already, coaching both the Cook girls.

The older generations were immersed in their pre-chosen holiday reading matter. There was the odd collapsed body slumbering on the chaises longues, recuperating from the journey, the clearing up of the office desk and the packing of freshly washed and pressed holiday gear. A few of the youngsters, at the age when they might have expected, or planned, to orchestrate a holiday romance, were contemplating appropriate mates. The discerning ones weren't bothering. They knew there would be a fuller selection of shapes and sizes at the local disco.

Occasionally, as if a starting gun had been fired, or a referee had blown a whistle, bodies would be heaved up from their relaxed poses and would be walked towards the pool's edge. The experienced would dive in from the pristine white stone pool copings; the less adventurous would descend into the refreshingly chilled water via the steps.

There were the odd pairs of conversationalists standing chatting in the shallow end. It was standard holiday chat, once the nationality had been worked out in a furtive study from the comfort of the pool surround: the language on the cover of reading material, whether the female members of the family shaved under their arms, the brand of cigarettes were all useful pointers.

Anyone from outside the UK spoke with whomever they happened to surface with or bump into as part of their exercise process. The Brits only spoke to those they had identified as being compatriots. "Where are you from?" "When did you arrive?" "Are you pleased with the hotel?" "Tell me, how are you coping with the food?" It was all scintillating holiday small talk. Observed from the terrace by Maria and Marco, however, it was just reward for all their hard work and planning.

"Marco, dear partner and brother-in-law, are you just a little proud now that you can see all this coming together?"

Marco thought for a few moments. "I'll take the credit for inheriting the Martinez estate and for doing the deal with the oil company. For the rest, I'll share the honours with you and Pedro and, more recently, Virginia, who's been trying so hard since you forced that holiday onto us.

"The balance, the pool, the court, the ambience, dear partner and sister-in-law, is down to you, for which I shall always be eternally grateful. That's providing we can make a profit and survive all the capital injections we've both made."

"Thanks, partner. That was very sweet," she said, and leant over to plant a soft kiss on his left cheek.

Their moment of intimacy was broken by Sñr Martin's shuffling steps coming through the sliding doors from reception out onto the terrace. They both turned at once.

Sñr Martin was normally a man in control, but now his demeanour was one of barely controlled panic, tinged with disappointed aggravation. Maria spoke first. "What's the problem, Sñr Martin?"

"Problem? Not *what's* the problem. *Who's* the problem."

"Who is the problem?"

"This nouveau riche type with the biggest Bentley I've ever seen, accompanied by one of the most beautiful ladies in the world who wants to know 'where the fuck is the doorman?' and, 'don't you have any bloody bellboys here?' and 'I want the key to my suite now, and I mean now, because this little lady needs a cold shower to cool her down so that we can start the day again. Right now I want some action. Call this a hotel, let alone credit it with any stars…' He was going what the English call berserk."

It was an outburst neither Maria nor Marco would have ever expected.

"Oh dear, Sñr Martin. Don't let that bother you. It must be Mr Hunt, but I have to say I thought he'd booked with his wife, not a girlfriend. Let me deal with this."

She beat her colleague back into reception, despite her high heels and tight black skirt. She sped across the marble reception floor, momentarily blaming Peter, in his Pedro days, for the design as her heels produced a sound of rapid staccato gunfire, which made Bob Hunt turn to defend himself against this unexpected attack.

Maria was in full beautiful flight, her hand already extended in greeting, as if to calm troubled waters between warring factions.

"Mr Hunt. It must be," she said, ensuring her body brushed his as she shook his hand. He was, broadly speaking, as she had imagined. "Now, it seems you've had a bit of a journey. Let me help you overcome that."

As she said that, a vision of statuesque beauty slinked through the open entrance doors. Maria couldn't help but stare, taking her in from toe to top: smart black sandals, slim, polished legs displayed by a short skirt, a virtually uncreased pink blouse hugging a perfectly formed torso, from which sprouted a youthful, equally uncreased neck topped by an astonishingly beautiful young face, framed by blonde groomed hair.

The beauty spoke and extended her hand before Maria had been able to completely take in the whole vision before her.

"I'm Marcia Hunt, and I do apologise for my husband's outburst. He's just not an easy traveller. Perhaps you could get him a cold beer? I can check us in, providing he apologises and actually decides to stay in this hotel. But as I said to him, it's a Sunday summer afternoon and at least we're here in one piece, which frankly comes as a surprise."

Maria laughed. "I'm Maria Martinez. Let me get that beer and I'll leave you to check in with Sñr Martin. Now, can I get you a drink too?"

"I'd love a Coke. But first, where can I have a pee before I ruin this beautiful marble floor?"

Maria was shocked by the sudden familiarity.

Peace and harmony were quickly restored. Bob Hunt loved the suite, thought the view was spectacular and greatly appreciated the fridge, inwardly hoping the break on this occasion would redress mistakes of the more recent past.

Bob's wooing of Marcia had been quite overwhelming to her as, to be fair, it would have been to most girls of her age without a career and pretty well no hope of amassing a fortune unless she was fortunate enough to marry one. Marcia's intent was not, however, purely monetary. She had actually been impressed by Bob's attentiveness and good looks from the beginning. Whether or not his pick-up approach would have been the same made through the wound-down window of a Ford Cortina she hadn't had to contemplate, because it wasn't.

Then, he was attractive and certainly didn't look the 40-odd years senior to her, which he was. As their initial meeting had been torrid, so the months following were too. Bob followed the Formula One race circuit and every other weekend took them around the adrenalin-fuelled tracks of Europe.

A weekend in Vegas away from fast cars was fun, and a private weekend on a friend's boat in Palma, Majorca, was destined to impress any girl. But Marcia was not just any girl.

Her upbringing in the Bluebell Troupe had given her the benefit of a chaperone. The management of the dance team was bright and modern, so the girls' protectors were not just there to turn away male suitors who fell in love with the dancers over a few glasses of champagne and then demanded to take them to their beds. They were conscious, too, of the dangers from within, so as soon as they saw two of the team walking along hand in hand, they were straight in to ensure a mass chorus line of lesbians did not out itself.

As a result, Marcia, despite all appearances, had hung on to her virginity. It was her saving for a rainy day. In Monaco, Majorca, Vegas, she had accepted the reasonableness of sharing Bob's bed and reacted generously to his requests for 'just a cuddle'. But when his male instincts got the better of him, even then she did not drop her barrier, simply responding with a kiss on the forehead, and a gently threatening, "Now come on, Bob, you promised…"

So, it was the prospect of having conjugal rights to her heavenly body that drove him into an early proposal, after just three months, which his family found outrageous.

Bob Hunt had made a living out of doing deals. He had a reputation for integrity but with this contract, which he intended to be for life, he had omitted to check that the terms and expectations formed in his own mind were agreeable to the other party.

They had a small wedding, largely because none of his blood relatives were prepared to attend. Both of his fledglings saw a huge chunk of their inheritances snapped away from them by a lovely pair of legs and a conniving brain telling their owner how best to use them. Little did they know that, indirectly, they were the catalyst for Bob's marriage proposal. On one of the occasions Marcia had been cut dead by Bob's daughter, she'd asked him why he thought that was. "Oh," he said, "it's probably natural really. They perceive me as an old man suddenly infatuated with a girl younger than his own daughter. They're bound to attempt to protect me from your wild ill-intentioned clutches."

"Do you think that?" Marcia enquired.

"No, of course not. I know I love you. There's a sincerity in you I feel I can rely on and a protectiveness in me that wants to keep you from harm."

"Would it help for me to tell your daughter how much I love you too and how, in turn, I'll protect you as the rest of your family don't seem to know how? I'm happy to sign a prenuptial agreement denouncing any entitlement to anything other than your love, affection and protection."

Now there's a fair deal. There couldn't be anything more kosher than that, he thought. "Marry me," he said instinctively.

"When?"

"On Friday."

"This week?"

"Yes."

"I don't have anything to wear."

"Then we'll get you a white Chanel suit."

"Wow, do I get to keep that?"

"Yes, for life."

"Then we'll marry, but I want you to understand it's not just for the dress."

They did it at Dulwich Register office, and celebrated afterwards at the Selsdon Park Hotel.

Her father couldn't make it at such short notice. Her sister and brother-in-law could, but they would have enjoyed the day far more if Marcia had tipped them off in advance as to her groom's age and wealthy status in life. "Neither are significant, if you love someone and want to care for them," Marcia told her sister Caroline, who was clearly taken aback when she first met Bob.

"Look, Ronald never stops pestering me for sex, which is really rather flattering, and I can pick and choose when I accept. Your 'young fella' might not be interested in a couple of years' time and you won't get to climax shopping in Harrods. I tell you, you should have thought this one through. There's a chance you'll finish up protecting the mattress in all the posh hotels you wheel him to, making sure he takes his pills and cutting up his lobster for him."

"You're a bitch of all bitches. This is my wedding day, Caroline. I'd like you to leave."

"Me too. Ronald, we're leaving."

"Oh, come on. I haven't had a drink like this in quite a while," her husband replied, clearly not ready to leave.

"I said we're leaving."

They did.

The other guests were mainly work colleagues. Marcia sat next to John Jones, who explained how he looked after Bob's 'fun' betting habits. He was a turf accountant, which Marcia asked him to explain. Generally she was quite bright and quick, but certain things had not reached her life and the circle she had been brought up in.

"Well, you know you see lorries going along the road with sort of large Swiss rolls on, which is rolled up grass cut from the field."

"Yes," she said.

"Well, I count those as they're put on the lorry and keep ledgers as to how many leave and how many get paid for."

"Really?" she said as Bob joined them. "I've just learnt my 'something' of every day, darling."

"What's today's knowledge?"

"I know what a turf accountant does."

"He's not a turf accountant, he's a basic conning bookmaker like all the rest of them. Thieving bastards. If it wasn't for him, I'd be a rich man."

"Maybe you're right," John Jones said with a smile, "but I'll lay odds you've got yourself a lovely bride here."

Bob explained later what a turf accountant really was. But not till after he had started the process of delivering his surprise, which all started to happen at 4.30pm. The Bentley arrived, driven by his chauffeur, André.

"It's time we left," Bob said.

"Oh, come on. Can't you get to bed just a bit later, just this one day of the year?" John Jones jibed.

Marcia looked at Bob. "So what do you say behind my back, dear husband?"

"Oh, you just have to not listen to most men, they're all the same. Besides, I'm hoping it'll be a special night for us tonight anyway."

Marcia's heart sank. She wasn't quite ready. Besides, it wasn't raining.

Their guests waved them off and they both looked back through the rear window as the heavy tyres rolled the quarry chip surfacing into the drive leading out of the hotel.

"Where are we going?" Marcia enquired.

"I'll tell you when we get there. You just be a good girl and wait and see."

His tone was quite patronising, certainly not one he'd used before. Could a ring and a few hours of security change a man that much? Surely not. They sat in silence, each contemplating the day. The car approached the bottom of Featherbed Lane, New Addington.

Bob glanced across at Marcia, who was sitting on the driver's side of the car. "See that, as far as you can see?"

"What, the fields?"

"Yes."

"Well, give me three years or so and there'll be up to 1000 houses there."

"What, yours?"

"Yup."

"Wow, how?"

Bob touched his nose with his forefinger. "Can't say. You'll see!"

He's making up secrets now, she thought, *as if he was my father.* "Bob, I really want to know where we're going."

"You're in a funny mood, Mrs Hunt, you've not always known where we're going."

"No, that's true, but we're now a declared item, we should share major decisions… we're heading off for a honeymoon. Supposing I don't like your idea this time?"

Bob didn't know quite how to respond. Particularly with the chauffeur's ears flapping in the front seat.

"André knows. You can tell Mrs Hunt… if you would."

"Biggin Hill, Ma'am," André responded, looking her full in the eyes in the rear view mirror, as chauffeurs have a habit of doing.

So, he was now playing avuncular games with her too. She calmed herself by humming a few bars of 'What a difference a day makes'.

"Well, all I can say, gentlemen, is I hope we're going to this new hotel on the Costa Brava Bob's turf accountant friend was telling me about. It sounds fabulous and a base for a really relaxed, informal holiday… and lots of activity too."

She turned and looked her husband full in the face. Bob Hunt had really been hoping Marcia would be turned on by the prospect of a private jet into Paris and then five nights surrounded by the luxury of the Ritz. She'd get lots of expensive salads in Paris and some retail therapy to match. Ordinarily, it was what she had loved in their short relationship. Now, all of a sudden she was into activity and sun and sea and relaxing and informality. *Women,* he thought, as they arrived at Biggin Hill. Well, she'd just have to make the most of it.

He'd also got tickets for the second night for the Lido, which he thought was a good idea because the Bluebell Girls were in the cabaret. He thought seeing them again after a long absence might make Marcia realise how much better off she was now.

As soon as they got on the plane, Bob went to the galley cupboard. "Glass of wine," he offered, "champagne, Perrier? What can I get you?"

Marcia thought he'd been drinking quite a lot at the wedding and would try and keep him off the booze if only on this, their wedding day.

"I'll share a Perrier with you, if that's what you're having," she suggested tactfully.

"I'll pour you some water. Mine's a whisky. My nerves need calming for tonight!" He patted her bottom playfully.

The flight went smoothly.

They had a car to the hotel, by which time it was coming up to 8.30pm Paris time. "Why don't you have a shower and slip into one of your Quants. We can go out to eat and I'll show you off to Paris?"

She'd already been shown off to Paris in her dancing days and by now she was tired. Her sister's comments were still playing on her mind, and she wished it was a case of slipping into a costume and having a leisurely swim to take the stress from the day. "I'm not really that hungry," she eventually replied, "I'd settle for some scrambled eggs and smoked salmon and perhaps a glass of Sauvignon. If I may. Room service."

Bob seemed pleased with that idea. Although he didn't intend to put sex out of his mind, he too was feeling a bit jaded. He'd get a bottle of Krug; Marcia rarely resisted bubbly. He'd have some oysters – well, they were meant to be an aphrodisiac, and he felt he needed all the help he could get if he was going to impress Marcia.

He rang room service and placed the order. They advised 45 minutes. "OK," he had said on the phone, "but I could go to the supermarket, buy the stuff, come back and have finished it in that time," he said edgily.

Marcia showed concern for this spate of impatience. She moved across to him as he replaced the receiver. "Here, baby," she said standing over him as he sat. She placed both arms around his neck and pulled his face into her cleavage. His breathing quickened at this sudden show of feeling, which also caused a twinge in his loins.

She released his head and slid down to a kneeling position between his thighs, which she had forced open. Raising herself slightly, she placed her left hand into the waist band of his Simpson Dak trousers, and found the toggle at the top of his fly zip with the thumb and forefinger of her gentle right hand.

She looked up into his face. "Now, if I'm going to get ravished after we've eaten, I'll need that Krug and I want to see that you've got the wherewithal to get rid of this virginity of mine I've been hanging onto for this very night."

Bob winced as she slipped her hand through the opened fly to his trousers. He clenched the muscles in his backside, took a deep breath and pulled his stomach muscles in.

"Hey," he said, pulling back slightly, "that's too nice. I need to save myself." She giggled, and took no notice. "Hey," he repeated and stood up, "a fellow can only take so much."

"Oh, go on," she said tantalisingly, "I'll go and get dressed for our in-house dinner, then we'll see."

She went to the wardrobe where the young maid had helped her to hang up her clothes amidst gasps of, "Magnifique, oh trés jolie, oh Madame, c'est vous exactement!" As they'd put her mainly black underclothes into the drawer, the maid was even more filled with adoration. "Oh Madame, c'est pour votre mari!"

"Oui, je pense," Marcia replied, remembering a little of her Bluebell French.

Now, without the encouragement and enthusiasm of the maid, it was up to her alone to select what was going to please Bob. She picked up a matching set she knew complimented her cleavage, with briefs that were more like the shortest of short shorts. She had a matching suspender belt and nearly black stockings. Her high black sandals with diamante clasp would enhance the outfit, which was to be hidden initially under a short black negligee.

Marcia changed in the opulent bathroom its cut-glass mirrors reflecting her gorgeous image back at her. As she stood in front of the full length one on the back of the door, she went into rehearsal mode. She hadn't really needed to remind herself of the routine. Without realising it, she had actually purchased the replica underclothes that were standard cabaret issue. Nobody in the troupe would have contemplated wearing that sort of gear out in the real world.

"How scary," she said to herself. This was no longer for the gratification of a large male audience, but her own one-man show. Her husband, no less.

She slowly slipped off the negligee and let it fall to the floor. She felt exposed. She put the right hand forefinger and the longer middle one into her mouth. Dropping her head slightly to let her hair fall forward she gasped seductively into the mirror. "If you haven't spent yourself by now, Bobby," she told the mirror, "I'd be surprised. I told you it isn't my rainy day yet." And she threw her head back in happy laughter. *My dancing days may be done,* she thought, *but I'll make an actress yet.*

They dined by candlelight, although Marcia had to persuade Bob to eat, as he said she had turned him on too much and his appetite wasn't for food now. He was drinking measures of whisky while she sipped a glass of Krug. He forced the oysters down, hoping each one would have its magic effect.

And so began the first act of the Hunt Mark II marriage.

Marcia went straight into her rehearsed performance. Bob was almost foaming at the mouth as she slipped out of her negligee and let it drop to the floor. The whisky was doing a lot of the talking for him. His eyelids were heavy and he kept licking his lips, dry from the effects of the alcohol, as he took in the scene she had set up from the other side of the room.

Marcia strode towards him, catwalk style, to where he was sitting on what appeared to be an antique sofa. She was playing out one of the Club routines from her last dancing job, which she had been forced into performing many times with a 'volunteer' from the audience. She'd hated that, but it was her role to wind up her stooge to a level of excitement that was contagious to the rest of the audience. But in this real life act, her aim was to raise Bob's excitement level to the point where he'd be able to complete the act.

Suddenly Marcia let out a scream. "Bob, you've been! How could you do that to me? It's such an important day in our lives. Can't you see that?" She shook (which even she thought was a convincing outburst) and then sobbed.

Bob tried to redeem the situation by laying Marcia back on the couch. He started to caress her body. She ripped his hand away, swung her legs to the ground and stood up.

Pointing a finger at him, she said, "Look, you had your chance to make me feel nice and you blew it. As you've always said, take chances when they come, they rarely get repeated, and you didn't take that one."

She caught a glimpse of herself in one of the saloon mirrors. "And look at me. It's the last time you see me putting on a show like this for you."

It was as if the stage directions had then indicated that:

Leading lady stamps her foot

Exits rear left into bathroom

Set pauses for three minutes

Spotlight from high centre to focus on leading man sorting himself out after mishap. He pours whisky

Leading lady re-enters, no make-up, drained of emotion, wearing white hotel robe

"I'm going to bed. That's a real nuptial experience."

Curtain

End Act I

In truth it was the prologue to Marcia's disappointing introduction to the Bob Hunt Marriage Mark II.

It was three days before they spoke again. The truth was, Marcia had spent her life nurturing her figure and she was scared of spoiling that by a pregnancy. She had therefore avoided intercourse, and wished to continue to avoid it. It had no place on her agenda, except that she had allowed herself to add a touch of reality in return for Bob sweeping her off her feet.

They were back at home and Bob had promised not to have a drink for 24 hours.

Marcia sat him down. "I'm concerned," she said, "you've changed personality. You get aggravated quickly. You're drinking too much. Your brain's not as sharp as when we met. But I'm really very fond of you, despite Paris. Would you do me a favour?"

"It depends."

"That's what I mean. Just a few months ago, I'd choose you a tie and you'd wear it and say that you could trust everything I did for you. Now, there's always an 'if' or a 'but' between us. And anyway, the favour's in your best interests."

"What's the favour?"

"I'd like you to see a doctor."

"But why?"

"I think you need to, just in case there's a physical reason for your mood swings."

"OK."

Two weeks later, Bob was diagnosed as 'advanced diabetic'. It was too far developed for tablets to help, so he was put on insulin injections, initially given by a district nurse but then by self-administration. He had only recently received the diagnosis when he made the booking with Maria.

In the hotel foyer, the cool beer seemed to have returned him to rationality. Marcia suggested a rest would do him good, so he and his wife adjourned for a siesta.

The Hunts elected to take the stairs to their room. Maria watched Marcia's body move, envying her sylph-like figure. Exercise was the answer, Maria resolved. She'd been a bit desk bound, and was having rushed meals fitted in between her obligation to the library and the hotel.

Marco and Virginia still tended to eat in their private quarters away from the hotel and it was almost now a family tradition that Maria and Peter, if he was free from his duties with Meri, would join them. They usually ate early so that Marco and Maria could mingle with their guests in the evening.

This first, really busy Sunday they had lots to talk about. How the checking-in had gone. What an asset Sñr Martin had been. How Peter's coaching was progressing, noticeably, as Maria pointed out, with a retinue of teenage girls.

"Are you sure they want to improve their tennis?" Maria had asked cheekily.

"Mother, please, leave me with my professional pride. Of course they do."

"I wouldn't be so sure. In the main, I think they all want to get closer to that body of yours."

"Well, tough luck to them. Nobody gets to that unless I want them to," he said with a smile.

"We'll see," Maria chirpily challenged. "Did you see the arrival of the Queen of Sheba this afternoon?"

"Mother, you talk in riddles these days. Who's the Queen of Sheba?"

"Marcia Hunt. Well, it's actually Mr and Mrs Hunt. They're English. He's, I'd guess, in his 60s and she's about 22. I could look at their passports to be sure. He's obviously loaded and let me tell you, so is she!"

Pedro started taking an interest, but tried not to show it. "What's loaded, for her? Do you mean she's got loads of money too?" he enquired.

"Well, probably not before Mr Hunt got hooked by her."

"Mother! You mustn't say things like that. No girl these days gets married just for money… she'd be landed with a marriage of convenience but a life of inconvenience. So, what do you mean she's loaded?"

"Well, wait and see. You might just not find her attractive, but let's see what happens if she tries to take tennis lessons from you, and whether she wants to improve her tennis or flaunt herself in front of you. Let's see how human you are then."

"Mother. Let me make it quite clear. She'll get tennis lessons, that's all. She can go and get herself into the Playboy calendar if she wants to show off her body."

"Well, Pedro, we'll see. Could you do me a favour while you're down from university? Could you spare me some tennis lessons? I'd like to get started."

She wasn't prepared yet to tell him she had already started at the municipal courts in Palafrugell when the library closed for siesta. According to the teacher, she was a natural. Maybe she had passed on the sports gene to Pedro. She doubted it was Paco; he was more of a marksman than a sportsman. Anyway, it's always nice for a mother to think she's responsible for her son's attributes. It's part of the natural bond, a bond that is tested when the son marries and the mother faces losing his affection to another woman.

To Maria's request for Pedro to help her new fitness regime, he answered, "Willingly mother. But I'll warn you now, I'll get you running around a bit. My coaching's not for the faint-hearted."

Their meal finished, Maria popped across to the hotel bar. Peter had a date with Meribel. Marco and Virginia decided to walk round the grounds to check what the next week's various programmes of gardening and maintenance should be.

In the bar, the Admiral was networking. He spoke several languages socially and was explaining that on the coming Friday he might organise some competitions. There would be three teams of eight, made up of all generations.

Two of the team would play singles and doubles tennis. The whole team would swim individually or in relays. And there would be a four-person boules team, pétanque, he also called it, explaining the game to his audience.

"Oh yes," the Cooks agreed excitedly. "We've played that in France. I think in England the nearest we have to it is bowls. Oh fine, yes, I'm on for that," Graham Cook volunteered.

It always takes one persistent organiser in a family hotel to get things going. He or she starts by being absolutely unpopular but once the five-a-side football or hockey has been won, or lost, their efforts tend to be more appreciated and sometimes there is even clamour for more.

At least, Maria thought, things were moving. There were casual chats on the terrace in groups of fours or sixes. People were mingling.

The youngsters were forming themselves into like-for-like groups across a noticeable age span of about three years' difference. The youngest, she noticed, tended to be female, probably because they were more mature for their age and could fit in with their 'seniors'.

The music they had chosen was pleasant, as if selected not to offend. James Last's 'Classics up to Date' appealed to everybody, by all accounts. The Carpenters, Perry Como, Neil Diamond, Percy Faith's orchestra… all got a casual foot tapping.

If no complaints signified silent approval, then the clientele enjoyed the food. Most guests hadn't gone to Spain for the food, but the combination of inclusive breakfast, table d'hôte and à la carte menus seemed to keep everyone happy.

Bob Hunt did like all the wrong foods for a man who should be watching his health. He and Marcia were exact opposites in the culinary stakes. He was a fried breakfast merchant with far too much coffee; she ate like a rabbit, mostly green salads, virtually no meat and sometimes a light fish. She drank water, and occasional white wine or champagne. He drank frequent whisky, red wine and brandy.

As Maria walked through reception, Bob Hunt appeared with Marcia on his arm. "I'm sorry about my behaviour earlier," he said.

"Oh, let's be honest," said Maria "Travelling *is* a pain."

Marcia piped in. "Well, actually, if my husband doesn't admit it, I will for him. Our problem is that he doesn't like driving on the right." She leant across and touched Maria's forearm, as girls do when they confide in each other. "Actually, he forgets and when we left the Palafrugell Road at the turn off to the hotel, we'd travelled about three quarters of a mile before he hit the brake, swore and accused me of not watching the road."

It was Bob's turn to confide. "To be honest, a holiday to me would be not having to drive. In the UK, I have a driver because when I drive myself, I look at all the pretty girls waiting at bus-stops." Marcia giggled for some reason not known to Maria. "Tell me," he continued, "do you have anyone who would drive us for a couple of afternoons? Ideally someone who speaks English, wouldn't be frightened of a Bentley, or my wife."

"That sounds like a job for my son Peter. Have you met him yet? He's the tennis coach."

Marcia became excited. "No, but the coaching was high on our agenda."

"*Our* agenda?" Bob interjected.

"Well, yes, *my* agenda. I used to play at school and I'd love to get it going again. Where can I see him?"

"He'll be around in the morning. If you don't find him, I'll get him to find you." Maria thought what fun this was. She wondered if she'd be proved right, and if Pedro would be smitten.

Bob Hunt said, "And we spoke on the phone about a boat trip…"

"That's right," Maria remembered, "I think it would have to be a weekend trip. Actually, I have a friend who doesn't normally do charters, but has said he would be pleased to. Just give me a suitable date and I'll see if I can fix it."

"Let's say Saturday week. That'll split our stay."

Maria said she'd try, which gave her an excuse to phone José. She hated just ringing and saying she wanted to hear his voice, which she did. So this would be a golden opportunity. She'd call on Monday, when he would be in Barcelona.

Señor Martin came on duty. "How's it going?" he enquired, ever the true professional.

"All the guests seemed to finish up in the right bedroom, and the youngsters appear to be planning their nightlife."

The Admiral's kids were ring leaders in that department. Guy, Philippe and Michelle had already sussed out the discotheque in Llanfranc, which was closed on Sundays, and were doing their best to get a crowd together for a visit. They were networking any of the youngsters from about 15 to early 20s.

Maria heard Guy explaining to the Cook kids, "They have this amazing dance orchestra there, it's all live, it's called the Costa Brava Orchestra. It's really a Spanish big band and the main drink, apart from beer or sangria, is a thing called cremate. It's a sort of liquor they set fire to and it burns with a blue flame.

We'll all go tomorrow. Anyone who needs their parents' permission, you can negotiate that during the day. Say we'll look after you. For those who can't get permission, we'll tell you how to get out without them knowing."

Maria thought: *dangerous, but fun if you were a teenager.* God, that didn't happen in her day!

Peter had realised that teaching tennis was not just a matter of standing in the middle of the court and making the pupil rush around. You had to plan your lesson and concentrate hard on helping the client improve.

He found he had to be very fit to cope with that, and it was sapping his energy – as were Meribel's attentions. Their relationship was growing stronger and it tended to fit into a pattern, with the pair of them usually finishing up in the back seat of the car. They knew each other's bodies well by now and had developed a range of risk-free lovemaking, which produced satisfying climaxes for both of them. Sometimes in turn, and occasionally simultaneously. As he tackled the uphill section of his morning run, he did think perhaps he and Meribel were taking a bit too much out of each other. His legs felt dog-tired after the previous night's antics. If he was going to stay fit for the busy six-week season, he'd surely have to feign a few headaches or upset stomachs.

His daily running circuit was about six kilometres. He ran the local footpaths and then some road and the final run into the hotel, which he liked to sprint. At 7.30am, nobody else was usually up. But on this fine morning, about halfway up the steady incline towards the hotel, he saw a figure striding up the hill. He'd now got a target to catch up with. Maybe it was one of the French chaps, Guy or Philippe.

Whoever it was, they were fit. He was making ground but doubted he'd overtake them before they reached the road. He tightened the muscles of his buttocks and picked up the pace.

Two hundred metres behind, he decided it could even be a female. Maybe the French sister. Now that was a prospect! She'd probably jump him into the woods by the roadside and screw his butt off. Whether he'd like it or not was another matter, but from Peter's experience he had Michelle on an 'easy' list, which some days might be welcome, but today not.

He closed to 125 metres, now perspiring strongly. Ahead of him was no diet-conscious jogger; this person was a serious runner. They'd reach the road perhaps a minute before him, time enough to go left or right and disappear from his sights. He might never know whom he was inadvertently pursuing.

He took a short cut across country, which he usually only reserved for when he was feeling particularly lazy, and burst through a gap in the hedge into the road and onto the track, which was higher by a metre than the ditch he would have to leap to get back onto for the last stage of his morning circuit.

Suddenly he was confronted by the most beautiful pair of legs he had ever seen. Oh, how female they were! Lightly bronzed, not over-developed, polished to a high shine. The thighs from the rear disappeared into nothing more than black elasticated hot-pants, stretched taut by the posture of the person who had been poured into them. He was now in no doubt. It was a hell of a female form he'd been chasing. *That's Michelle,* he thought again. The lady was bent into a standing jack-knife pose, her head tilted downwards and arms hanging limply towards the ground, seemingly recouping some much needed breath.

Peter stopped and walked slowly round the statue. He was none the wiser. A shock of stylishly cut blond hair hung forwards. He thought he'd better speak. Maybe she had overdone the hill. Certainly her curved back was heaving.

"Estás bien?" he said gently and quietly.

The bent body started to straighten with balletic grace. The lowered head rose, followed by firm athletic shoulders. The chest, as it was turned more fully to face him, was beautiful. Peter guessed it was braless, a speculation confirmed as the young lady stood upright, allowing a full view of her close-fitting, skimpy white T-shirt, with diamanté studs around the neat round neck, indicating Chanel was the designer.

She spoke. Just a simple word. "Pardon?"

"Are you English or French?" he asked.

"English."

"Are you OK?"

"Yes, of course I am. It's just that I'm lost. I thought I'd done a completely circular circuit and that I'd come back to the hotel."

Peter was on for a game. "Which hotel do you want?" he enquired.

"The new one. The Playa."

"It's the best part of a mile, I think in your language. I'm heading back there too, but I'm out for a run. I don't jog, so if it's alright with you, keep me in your sights until I turn left onto a cobbled road. If I've lost you by then, just jog on and you'll come to it. OK?"

Bloody cheek, she thought. At a personal best of four minutes 58 seconds, she'd expect to match any amateur. She'd run this young man's backside off.

"Oh, by the way, my name's Peter. I work at the hotel." He held out his hand in greeting.

"Marcia. Marcia Hunt. My husband and I arrived yesterday."

He needed to act this one out. He'd never heard of her, never been warned he might find her so attractive… this was his confrontation with the Queen of Sheba, trumpets blasting, et al.

"Oh, I must have missed you checking in."

He looked left up towards the hotel. "Is your husband up ahead of you?"

Marcia looked shocked, even a bit annoyed that word of her presence had not spread like wildfire ahead of her.

"Well, you could say that," she said.

"Oh well, I look forward to meeting him. It's a bit tough on you, leaving you behind in uncharted waters alone. I'll give you a clue. If you'd turned right, you'd have had to stop at the frontier in the Pyrenees, and if you haven't got your passport on you somewhere, you'd spend your holiday in jail. See you back there!" He turned and sped away.

This was a race. He knew it, so he accelerated at the imaginary starter's pistol to get a firm lead in the first 30 seconds. He'd rather taken her by surprise. Her rhythm was broken from the off. Peter pushed harder and harder, hugging the various kerb lines so well known to him from his morning canters. He always did run the last mile hard, but wasn't wrong in his reckoning that Mrs Marcia Hunt knew just how to use those legs to good effect.

Although he arrived back a full 200 metres ahead, she had gained an impetus of a fair few seconds out of determination and temper. Well, less temper, perhaps. Annoyance. Men looked at her. Always had. But not Peter. *Perhaps he's gay*, she thought, but then reasoned that he couldn't be. Then again, she conceded to herself, it wouldn't be the first time that somebody with such beauty and apparent masculinity had got their genes mixed up somewhere along their development. But not him. Somehow she didn't want him to be.

Peter burst through the reception doors almost straight into the arms of his mother.

"Morning darling…" she said, before being over-talked.

"Can't stop. On a mission," he panted, and thank God there was one, he thought. Michelle was booked in for her first lesson at 9am, but she was in the reception area already, pristine in short white skirt and Adidas top. Peter stopped in front of her, taking control of his heavy breathing.

"Are you ready already?" he said.

"No. I was about to get a light breakfast," Michelle replied as if she shouldn't really. As she said that, Marcia broke the invisible tape across the entrance doors and burst into the reception area.

"Morning, didn't realise you're a jogger," Maria said with some contentment, suspecting Marcia must have pinched Peter's bottom and sent him charging back to the hotel in shock.

"Running is part of my makeup," she said calmly. "If it hadn't been for that young man, I could have landed up in the Pyrenees."

"In the Pyrenees?"

"Yes, I could have made the wrong turn. It seems he might be your tennis coach, talking to the girl over there?"

"Oh him, yes, but only sometimes. I'll let you into a secret." Maria leant forward and touched Marcia's slightly sweaty left forearm. "He's my son when I approve of what he's doing, but when I don't, I disown him."

"And at the moment?"

"Yes, I disown him."

"Why's that?"

"Well, I think that young lady is trying to get him to be her holiday distraction."

"Will she succeed?"

"No, I wouldn't think so. He's got a lovely girlfriend of some permanence."

Marcia smiled, "I must shower. I'll speak to… what's your son's name?"

"It's Pedro, now known as Peter."

"Why's that?" Marcia asked.

"I think he wants to be anglicised. He finds Pedro a bit fisherman-like."

"He certainly speaks very good English. Is sport his life?"

"Goodness me, no. It's just a holiday fill-in. He's just starting an architectural degree at university."

"My husband would find Peter interesting."

"Why? Is he an architect?"

"Good God, no. He develops property, but he employs architects and says they're a useless bunch of gits."

"Gits… what are gits?"

"I guess they're architects. No, I'm pulling your leg. It's a slang name for somebody who's is a bit stupid, useless, does silly things."

"Well, I must tell Peter not to do any of those things. I don't want a git in the family."

The ladies chuckled together. Peter had extricated himself from his 'mission', which had had its uses. At least he'd got his breath and composure back.

He walked back through the reception and unleashed a broad smile at his mother and Mrs Hunt.

"You won," Marcia said by way of greeting.

"Won? Won what?" he replied in a soft tone.

"The race."

"There was no race."

"Don't you believe it. I'm a competitor. I was racing. I really hate losing. Losing anything."

"I was just exercising, as I thought I'd explained. I always have an agenda and I like to stick to it."

"How can I fit into your agenda for some coaching?"

"What do you need? Are you a complete beginner… intermediate… what?"

Marcia's parents had poured such money as they could into her education. Her father earned cash in his small building business and that largely went into educating their two girls. So Marcia was not just a pair of pretty legs. She'd excelled at sports at James Alleyn's in Dulwich, to where she'd won a scholarship. It was there that she played first team tennis at the ripe young age of 15. There, also, that she was told if she was going to play first team tennis, she'd need her grandmother to go shopping with her to buy some knickers that actually covered her genitalia. She was getting too much attention from the dads who supposedly came to watch their own daughters but enjoyed the subconscious display Marcia put on for them.

"Let's say intermediate, but wanting to do better."

"How's 12pm seem to you. Too hot?"

"As long as you buy me a shandy afterwards, it's fine."

So Peter wrote it down in his diary.

"Oh, by the way, do you have your own balls?" There was a pause. Peter wondered if she was being intentionally suggestive. On balance, yes, she probably was. It was building up to be her little game with him.

"Boxes of them," he replied nonchalantly.

Maria couldn't help getting involved. "That's supposing Michelle doesn't lose them all in the meantime," she interjected.

"I wouldn't be a very good coach if I allowed that to happen, would I?"

Marcia went into serious mode. "Peter, would you like to earn a few pesetas by driving my husband's car one afternoon and acting as our guide?"

"Sure! I don't teach on Wednesday. How would that be?"

"Magnifico!" Marcia broke into tourist Spanish. "I'll see you at just before 12pm."

"Yes, fine," Peter replied.

Not "Yes, I'll look forward to that," Marcia thought. It's as though this guy is missing out on me. If he was gay he'd be over attentive. What is it with him?

She turned and walked away. Peter's eyes followed her towards the stairs. "So, you agree. She's ravishing," Maria said with a grin.

"Listen, Mother, she's Mrs Prima Donna Hunt to me, whose lessons and chauffeuring are going to buy me a few pens and paints for uni. Now, if we're looking for playthings the hotel has attracted, consider Michelle, she's a real danger."

"OK then, but make the most of those beautiful green eyes, my son, before Meribel scratches them out," Maria said in a maternal way. Somehow she would have preferred Pedro having extra-curricular fun with Marcia than with Michelle.

Meribel was not enamoured with her temporary status in life. She'd largely taken on the work to please Peter and to get brownie points from Maria. True, the money would come in useful, if ever she didn't feel tired again.

Chambermaiding was exhausting. Maria insisted the mattresses be turned every week, which, single-handed, was a hard job. Rarely a day went by that Maria didn't inspect a couple of rooms at random. Meribel had no idea that toilet rolls should have their ends folded into arrow heads to signify the maid had bleached the toilet, cleaned the seat and left her stamp on the toilet roll. She objected to the fact that all the teenagers just appeared to get out of bed, dump their nightclothes together with the previous day's cast-offs and push off to enjoy themselves. They took up most work time and yet they'd be most unlikely to tip.

Meribel found she had to pick her time to do the Hunts' room. Up until 11am there was a 'no service required' sign out on the door handle. She had presumed at first that they stayed in bed bonking until then. But that never looked the case. Mrs Hunt's trainers and running gear were always a little warm when Meribel moved them around to tidy the suite. It seemed Mr Hunt read a lot of newspapers and magazines about horseracing because those were always left spread out on the floor.

She'd only seen Mrs Hunt a couple of times but, judging by the underwear hanging on a line in the bathroom, she was a very sexy dresser. Having seen a tennis racket in the room, Meribel was upset to think that at some time most days, Mrs Hunt would be getting Peter's undivided attention, which was more than Meribel got these days.

Both she and Peter were clapped out by the time they got together after she'd finished her evening stint of waitressing, and she longed for the season to come to an end so that they could all get back to normality.

Still, workwise, it was good experience.

At least Bob's evening drinking habit took the pressure away from Marcia, lessening his chances of taking her virginity from her. She had her sights set on a new rainy day, on which Peter would suddenly notice that she was the most beautiful female creature on the Costa Brava and demand to sleep with her. These were dreams she needed.

Bob Hunt didn't often go to the pool. While Marcia was out running, he studied the other form more readily available in the sport of kings. He'd telex his bookie mates with his instructions for the working day and then wander down to enjoy Marcia's workout with this young Peter chap who appeared to be doing so much for her tennis. It would then be time for a pre-lunch drink. Lunch, then a siesta under the shade of the trees, rarely joined by Marcia, who liked to top up her tan by the pool in the full glare of the sun. Most of the other male guests sat in various disguised poses of voyeurism. Bob usually made out he was asleep behind his heavily tinted sunshades, when in fact his eyes constantly scanned every pore of his wife's beautiful milky skin, every ripple of each taut muscle as she turned over to encourage the sun to tint every inch of her body.

Georgio Sylvano Snr was among Marcia's regular audience. He was brazen in his approach, as befitted his Italian blood. He would, in his mind, simply undo the clasp of her bra top, slide her pants down, service her and then sleep it off.

Philippe needed to control himself a little more. Doubtless he didn't know he did it, but he played with himself a bit, principally while watching Natasha, the Cooks' elder, convent-bred daughter. Occasionally his eyes and thoughts wandered to Marcia, but when his brain cleared from the sensation of the smoke the night before, his real eyes were for Tash, her one-piece costume and her young untouched body.

Maria glanced down at this now familiar scene. It was working. There was overall calm. Their guests were relaxed. The recipe she, Marco and Pedro had worked on seemed a success. She was looking forward to the break she'd get, albeit for only part of a day, when she and José took the Hunts out on the 'Maria de Rosas'. She hoped the queasiness she was feeling from all the strain would go by the weekend. She could never have contemplated that the non-stop thinking, planning and execution of their master plan would make her so irritable. She needed a few hours off.

Maria had thought too soon that everything was going smoothly.

Little did she know about a storm brewing up in Milan, Italy. Gina Oblobida, Georgio Snr's latest PA, whom he'd recently managed to entice into bed at his flat near to the works, where his wife accepted he sometimes had to stay over, was missing her boss and was restless.

Gina had been quite put out when Georgio announced he had no alternative but to placate his wife and take her on holiday with Georgio Jnr. She cried and accused him of not loving her but finally, against a promise that he would take her on his next business trip, she had accepted the situation.

At home, just outside Milan, she was now having second thoughts and had arranged to have a drink after work with Georgio's principal business partner, who had seen all this before, of course. Gina sobbed through a couple of Martinis with lemonade and begged Lorenzo Miedini to invent a business excuse to call Georgio Snr back.

"Look, that's OK for you, but you could get my friendship with Georgio into bad straits if I do that."

Gina was a dealer. "Do you want a really nice night yourself?"

"What, with you?"

"No, not with me. I'm for Georgio. No, I have a friend you'd like called Tina (who owed Gina a huge, really huge, favour) I'm sure she'd see you have a good time. You'd have to get Georgio back first, though."

Sñr Martin handed Maria a telex. "This looks bad news to me. We might lose the Sylvano family booking."

Maria read the telex. "Serious fabrication problem. Need your urgent input. Can you get back for three days of tests?"

It was signed by one Lorenzo Miedini. Maria had the telex sent to Georgio Sylvano at the pool. She watched him read it and then hand it to his wife, who went crazy. But within 30 minutes Sylvano was checking out alone, paying in advance for the rest of his wife and son's stay.

From then on, at two-hourly intervals, Mrs Sylvano appeared at reception asking if there were any telexes for her, or any calls she might have missed while out shopping. She was intent on hurting her husband in the wallet, the way she knew best, while she waited for him to make contact.

CHAPTER 13

Bob Hunt and Marcia, for different reasons, were looking forward to their drive 'out and about', as he had called it. Peter at the wheel would, they both thought, make it all the more enjoyable.

Marcia had said that Peter ought to go for a drive before the outing. Just to get used to the car. She said she wouldn't hear of Bob taking him. "Unless you're really drunk, you'd find showing somebody how to drive four million pesetas' worth of car just impossible. Do you remember the first time I drove it? We didn't speak for a week after. You remember you bought me my Rolex as a making-up present."

He agreed. So the introductory drive was to be that Tuesday evening before dinner.

Pedro thought it really unfair that Marcia would take such an opportunity to try to make herself (well, her body, in reality) a centre of focus. But his Catalan resolve ensured he would still not fall for the ploy. If ever he had been offered something on a plate, it was Marcia. But the more she tried, the more she made her interest in him known, the more he resisted.

Of course he found her beautiful. No hot-blooded man would not. He was just used to doing the running and making his own choices. Maybe it was the originator in him that made him want to shape and design his future rather than having it done for him.

Even to take Peter out on his Bentley familiarisation trip, she appeared in a white mini skirt that complimented her bronzed legs. Her black voile top was slightly off the shoulder, and he thought momentarily that really it should have been ripped down to her waist. He couldn't be sure, but he'd have said she was wearing a strapless bra. Through his learning curve with Meribel, he'd become quite well versed in women's underwear. Meribel seemed to collect magazines on the subject.

He had noticed how beautifully Marcia's upper half moved when she was playing tennis. She flowed. Never bobbed like Michelle or Meribel. He supposed those couple of years' experience, plus the most expensive underwear when she did wear it, made all the difference.

They walked to the car. He could hardly believe it. *What a car,* he thought, *with an outrageously beautiful driving instructor to go with it.*

"First, let me show you how to get in," Marcia said with a girlish giggle. "Watch this."

She was enjoying the role reversal of teacher/pupil. Peter was always forceful in his lessons.

"I'm sorry," he'd say, "nearly but not completely right. Here, try again, left foot comes across while weight is on the back foot. Throw the racket high and far over your right hip. Hand comes through. Weight goes onto left foot and as the racket head hits the ball… *rooolll* the right wrist over for top spin. Good. Excellent! You've got it!"

Now it was her turn.

"Hold the keys extended in the right hand. Perfect! Now point towards the rear-view mirror. OK, now push the pad slowly until you hear a click. The click means the door is open. Next, you open the passenger door. Good. Now, I'm going to put my bottom on the leather seat and in one sweep, swing my knees into the air. One tip for you during this exercise: don't try and look up my skirt. That's for tennis! Besides, it might be embarrassing." Peter by this time had freed the doors. "Good! Very good. You make a tennis player out of me and I'll make a driver out of you," she shrieked with laughter.

He smiled ruefully. "OK, how do you serve this thing?"

"Oh Peter! I never thought you'd ask."

"Mrs Hunt… please, let's be professional about this… I'm here to learn about the car. Please show me how to start it."

"Call me Marcia and I will."

"No. It's Mrs Hunt while I'm working for you and your husband."

"OK, Peter. You're too nice to argue with. It's just like any other car. Put in the key and turn it. The difference is you won't hear the engine. So you look at that dial there and if you see it's moved off zero, the engine's running."

He turned the key. His keen sense of hearing actually did pick up the engine running.

"It's automatic."

"I guessed it would be."

"Select the R, that one there." She leant forward, which made Peter tell himself that whether she was offering herself on that plate or not, he must be mad not to be accepting such overt advances.

She wasn't like this to Guy or Philippe, or anyone else in the hotel. Surely she'd get kicked out by Mr Hunt if she was like it all the time. *Maybe she sees me as a challenge,* Peter thought. Anyway, he had a job to do.

He found the Bentley big but quite beautiful.

Marcia showed every confidence in his ability. She leant across again and played with the dashboard. Soft music came from the speakers.

"What's this?" he asked.

"It's a selection of popular opera duets – La Bohème, Madame Butterfly, and a number of others."

"This one's beautiful."

"It's 'Your tiny hand is frozen'."

He listened for a minute or so. "It's unhappy."

"No, they're happy. You're a funny soft one, Peter. Would you say you're an artist?"

"A creator, yes. I've never had time to be an artist, as such."

"Perhaps you should try."

"It's about having time. Perhaps at university, I'll create something. When I'm not having the pleasure of teaching young ladies to improve their tennis."

"Do you think I'm improving?"

"Yes, of course."

"Why haven't you told me?"

"You know without me having to tell you."

"Peter, can I teach you one small lesson in life?"

"Mrs Hunt, nothing you teach me is likely to be small. I'd say whatever you say will have a lasting impact on me."

They both laughed at the prospect. "What's the lesson then?"

"However good or kind or gentle a lady is naturally, she still needs confirmation from time to time. I've never raised more than a 'Yes, it's coming' or a 'that's better', I've yet to get a grading from you."

Peter pulled into a lay-by. "Well, just so as you know, Mrs Hunt, in random order:

"Legs – excellent.

"Hips – brilliant.

"Waist – delightful.

"Chest – the best.

"Neck – lovely.

"Face – beautiful.

"Hair – perfect.

"Flirtatiousness – if there is such a word – outrageous."

"My, you have learnt a lesson for life," she said coyly.

She raised her left hand to her lips, kissed it and then placed it on his forehead. "… And I've learned you're a very serious young man who doesn't want a young married woman flirting with you. So I promise I won't. I value your friendship too much."

Peter really could not work this one out. He suddenly felt she was winning.

"So, diversions over," he said. "Let's get this show back on the road. You'll need to tell Mr Hunt if I get the job tomorrow or not."

"With those compliments you've given his wife, how could you fail? We'll leave at 2pm after a light lunch. My lesson's at 11am. We'll play a five-game limited set towards the end and I'll get you to deuce in three of the games. I might even take a game off you. Now I know you can take your eye off the ball to assess my body," she said, laughing. "I'll concentrate on the tennis and leave the flirting up to Michelle during her lesson between 10 and 11. Or even your girlfriend tonight. What's her name?"

"Meribel."

"Yes, I'll leave all that to her."

The next day she reached deuce in three of the games, but didn't take a game. She then appeared as a two-some in reception just before 2pm. Mr Hunt was wearing light grey, neatly creased trousers and a light yellow Lacoste polo shirt. Marcia had on a cool gingham A-line Mary Quant dress.

"So, you're the driver, Peter. Would you like me to sit up front and co-pilot with you, or would you prefer the more gentle Mrs Hunt, who definitely has the better knees, alongside you?"

"Without wishing to offend Mrs Hunt, I think I'd benefit from your experience up front."

"Suits me. Marcia, you're in the back. But listen to every word. No dropping off. We'll ask you questions later. So, where are you taking us, Peter?"

"Oh! I thought you'd have an itinerary."

"No, just show us some Spanish culture. That will do us."

"Then I think we'll start where the Romans started." Thank God for Marco and their buying trip to Ampurias.

They pulled away. Bob Hunt leant clumsily over the dashboard and turned on the cassette player. The Bohéme duet came on automatically. "We won't want this rubbish," Bob Hunt said, ejecting the tape and slamming in another. Herb Alpert boomed out. Peter looked in the rear-view mirror. Marcia raised both arms in total submission and smiled.

"You like this stuff?" Bob Hunt said to Peter, pointing at the tape deck.

"Fine! But we ought to have it low so that I can hear you, and vice versa."

"Or even off," came a voice from the rear.

"No taste," was the retort from the front passenger seat.

Peter took them the country route to Ampurius. They rounded one bend in a valley and suddenly all hell let loose from the back seat driver. "Stop! Peter! Stop!"

Peter hit the brakes in reaction to the apparent emergency.

"Just look at that! Isn't that amazing?"

There ahead of them were about ten acres leading up to the vines on the far hillside, absolutely covered with rows of sunflowers.

"That has to be one of the most wonderful sights I've ever seen," murmured Marcia. "They're statuesque. They look almost human standing with their head bowed to shade their eyes from the sun high in the azure blue sky."

"You're being a bit dramatic, darling."

"Let's go and talk to them." Marcia was out of the car like a flash. As she ran across in her red leather sandals, she paused and beckoned for Bob and Peter to join her.

"Bugger that," Bob said. "You go, Peter, she'll have you talking to the flowers, you watch. I'll just sit here and have a cigar. Correction, I'll just go and sit on that fence and have a cigar. 'We' are not allowed to smoke in the car any more. In fact, I'm bloody lucky to be allowed a smoke at all. Don't you know it's bad for you and besides, it makes the car stink – well, that's according to Madam."

Peter walked into the rows of large headed plants, which were equal to his own six-foot height. Marcia turned as she heard him approach.

"I knew you'd come at least." She looked younger, with a sort of gold glow that Peter thought was a reflection from the luminous petals surrounding the dark faces, which were being raided by working bees. She was clearly excited.

Peter stood next to her. "I've been talking to them, you know, just light chat," she said. "But they don't talk back."

"They're Spanish peasant plants. Did you speak Spanish to them?"

"Well, no, I thought they'd be prepared for tourism. Could you ask them in Spanish for me how they are."

"La Señora Hunt quiere saber ¿cómo estáis?" Peter clenched his teeth and, as if he were a ventriloquist on one of those European music hall shows, he squeezed out, "Estamos bien. Hace mucho calor y no hemos tenido una bebida verdadera por dos meses."

Marcia started hopping up and down. "Quick, quick! Peter, they spoke to me. What did they say?"

"They said, 'Why's the English lady so excited. Hasn't she had a conversation with a sunflower before?'"

"Peter Martinez! You're a bastard. They didn't say that at all. What did they say?"

"They said it was very hot and they hadn't had a real drink for a couple of months. The big fellow over there said that most of the tourists who drop by are old fuddy-duddy types on some sort of pensioners' day trip up from the Costa Brava, but they've never seen anything as beautiful as you."

"Did he really say that? Which one?"

"The big fellow there with a grin, and the erection." (*Christ, what on earth made him say that? Was she weaving some sort of spell over him? Please God, rub that out.* He hadn't felt himself blush for years, but it seemed Mrs Hunt had not heard. Maybe it was God's work to make her not hear.)

"Oh, did he!" Marcia walked across to where Peter had indicated the admiration had come. She took part of the upright stalk in her left hand and placed her right one slightly above the other as though holding a microphone. She went up onto her tip-toes, pouted her lips and kissed the richness at the centre of the sunflower's face. She turned back to Peter. "There," she said, "that's what he gets for being so kind."

He started to roar with laughter.

"So you think I'm stupid, just like Robert does?"

"No, Mrs Hunt. Not at all. Only that old codger just pollinated all over your face. Here," he said and, beckoning her over, he took out a crisp laundered handkerchief and wiped her face. There was a patch that was a little more stubborn. He dampened a corner of the cotton and rubbed the area gently, successfully cleaning it off.

"What do you call a sunflower in Spanish?" she asked.

"Girasol."

Marcia took his hand and, holding the back of it against her body, she brushed it first down her left breast and then down her right one. Peter could feel the firmness through her unseamed bra. "… And that, Mr Martinez, is what you get for being kind and gentle and entering my fantasy world, and the name of the upright gentleman who stimulated it is Mr Gira Sol, so don't forget him."

Peter's legs had weakened considerably and he wasn't quite sure whether he was finding it difficult to walk. It was either shock or temporary anaesthesia generated from Marcia's inner self. She was a temptress, perhaps even a witch. But his resolve not to be caught up in her beautiful web was becoming stronger.

They walked back to the car and found Bob still sitting on the fence looking in exactly the opposite direction. He turned as he heard Marcia's running footsteps across the light gravel. She ran to him and held her hand out for his.

"Darling, they talked to me."

"I didn't doubt they would."

"No, really, I know they did because I couldn't understand a word, so Peter translated for me. You see, they only speak Spanish."

"I'll have to buy you an English sunflower when we get home and then you'll be able to chat to your heart's delight. So," Bob added when Peter joined them, "you got to talk to the flowers after all."

"We did actually."

"Then come on, let's get moving otherwise all the other bastard ones will want to join in and we'll be here all day."

Peter opened both passenger doors. He watched Marcia slide in, then closed each in turn with a determined thud. As he climbed into the driving seat, Marcia put her forefinger to her mouth and said, "Shhhh… Peter, you woke that one up over there."

Peter glimpsed into the rear-view mirror and smiled back at her. The music started where it had left off when they stopped.

"Darling, just for five minutes could we have my opera?"

"You into opera, Peter?" Bob demanded, looking at Marcia in the rear-view mirror.

"Yes, I am actually. Duets particularly. What do you have?"

"These are duets, aren't they, Marcia?" Bob asked.

"Yes, you know they are."

"Then it will be duets for the duet who reckon they appreciate good stuff. Where's the sea from here?"

Peter drove off. "Bye-bye, my beautiful sunflowers," Marcia said, waving gently as they passed. She remained silent with her thoughts, wedged behind Bob's seat. Peter looked in the mirror again. Marcia was blotting a tear from her cheek.

The music playing was now 'Guantanamera'. Bob obviously didn't know his duets.

Bob Hunt turned the music down. "Marcia tells me you're not really a tennis coach or part-time chauffeur. She tells me you're going to be an architect. Is it too late for me to change your mind?"

"Change my mind? Why would you want to do that?"

"You seem a nice bright lad. Why waste your time?"

"Waste my time? It's what I love. I love to create."

"Balls!"

"Robert!"

"I do say balls. In the real world very few architects actually do create. If we left them to their own devices, they'd create havoc and we'd all go broke."

"Why do you say these things, Mr Hunt?"

"Well, I'm a developer. Don't know what you'd call it over here. So what I do is find a piece of land and decide it's got potential and then it's down to me to decide what we build on it to then sell."

"You, and your expensive colleagues, Don Christie, Geoff Hodgson and the others… You don't do it alone," Marcia interrupted.

"I bloody almost do." Bob Hunt was getting irritable. "Once I've come up with a concept, then of course the others have a role to play. But the point I'm making is that the architect bats about third or fourth in the team. Now, when I was your age… how old are you, Peter?"

"Nineteen," Peter said, possibly wanting to appear nearer to Marcia's age.

"Oh, I'd have thought you were in your early 20s. I'd watch it if I were you, you're not wearing too good. Anyway, when I was in my early 20s I wanted to be the team leader. So I bought a piece of land, told an architect what would sell on it and before it was built, I'd sold it. Then another piece of land. Twice the size. This time I had to bring in a financier, that's number two in the team, and then an architect. So, he went down to number three. Then I needed a builder with speed and technique. He took over as number three and the architect became number four. So it goes on."

"But in my case, I intend architecture to be my base. I'll have the concept and the architectural ability on the one hand. A sort of dual role number one spot. Then I'll bring in a development team in as number two in my team, then banker, engineer, marketing, sales, legals…"

"Christ, Marcia, wake up! This guy's got it all worked out. How well do you know this area, Peter?"

"I've known it since I was a kid."

"OK, let's play a game. Marcia can be the judge. In the boot there are some sketch pads. We get one each. You find us a piece of land and we'll have an hour each to design a land use. Marcia can get some extra tan time in. Did you bring a costume?"

"Yes, I did actually, just in case."

"Thought you would. OK, so we all get an hour of enjoyment." Peter drove to the coast where he knew there was a sprinkling of original farm cottages.

"Here's the spot," he said, "let's say 800 metres either side of where the car is now and 800 metres inland to the foot of the hills, because I'd guess the mayor would give planning for that. Not for a hotel complex, housing generally."

"It's a bit flat, isn't it? Couldn't we include a bit of that hill to give it some relief?" Bob asked.

"No, I reckon we have to work inside the million and a quarter square metres."

Peter had to convert that to the 1.15 million square yards or so that Bob would be used to.

"You go over that side. I'll go over here. I don't want you cribbing off me," Bob ruled.

Marcia chirped in, "… And my part in this male game of yours is to be just here, close to the car, so that I can hear the music. I might just be inspired to go topless, that is if Franco can't spy on me now from where he is. I'll do that just to put you off what you're doing to show who the real number one leader is in this team."

"Go on, love, do that. When we're working, we blokes don't let things like that distract us."

"No, I've noticed," she replied curtly.

The hour started. Bob Hunt from the off was sketching outlines on his pad and had pages of calculations. Peter did not touch the pen and paper for a full half hour. He moved around, whereas Bob was static. He walked back inland the 800 metres or so. It was horribly flat.

Bob reasoned there wasn't enough sea front and so influenced a development on a part village style with six storeys of flats at the back end of the frontage. He gave over a central area to a small play park.

Generally he saw family housing units for tourists to buy and let of about 1,200 sq ft – 120 sq metres – with private terraced garden areas of about the same size. So his unit floor plan was about 2,500 sq ft, say 230 sq metres. As roads, in his experience, would take up 15 per cent space, his final development solution produced some 300 houses built on roads that led down to the sea, and 50 odd flats in the high rise. Bob leant back, satisfied. He'd done all this before.

"Marcia, ask young Peter if he's ready. Oh! So you really did go topless. They look good. I hope you didn't put Peter off. I did see him pacing around."

Marcia called across to Peter. "Are you ready yet?"

"Well ready! But please, Mrs Hunt, I'd feel more at ease if you weren't topless if we're going to congregate over there."

"I understand," she said, sitting up slowly and taking her time as she dropped herself into the bikini top then straightened up as she fastened the clasp. "I'll judge your ideas over here please, gentlemen. Who has a coin?"

Mr Hunt only had notes, but Peter had a coin. They tossed for first presenter and Peter won the toss. "Does that mean I can ask you to present first?" he said, turning to Bob.

"No it bloody doesn't," he replied, turning to Marcia. "I'm not sure I want Peter to teach you tennis any more. He's too competitive."

"Your presentation may start now please, Mr Martinez," Marcia announced.

Peter had turned his sketch pad into a flip chart. He sat cross-legged in front of the Hunts. "I call the development 'Girasol'."

"What the fuck's that mean?" Bob Hunt challenged him.

Marcia's back prickled.

Peter, however, felt he was responding for himself and for Marcia. "It means to me a flower, a centre, a house, a number of houses that follow the sun, something portraying immense pride."

"Christ! I thought we were coming up with something for people to live in and for us to sell. OK, carry on. Mine doesn't have a name. I'll leave that to the marketing team."

"So," Peter carried on, "we have a lot of sea frontage, likely only to benefit 100 or so properties if built as a ribbon development. That would then leave the remainder of the development without a direct view of the sea, and therefore they could be anywhere. Not necessarily by the sea." He flipped his chart. "So, what we've done is to make the most out of the otherwise flat terrain and built canals in from the sea like this," he said, illustrating a sheet with just water.

"The area at the furthermost point inland is a marina lagoon, so access to the canals is from the rear, leaving the sea front absolutely free as an amenity area, undisturbed by cars or boats. The access roads to the properties need only be single carriageway stuff, to develop a more leisurely feel as everyone's driving slowly. Each house has its own berth and they all get the sun morning and late afternoon, front or back. There are no gardens so that anybody living or renting can maximise leisure time. The designs look like this…" He turned to another sheet.

They were Catalan-styled terraced houses. Painted shutters and pastel coloured, he explained. There was a huge amount of work to show for just an hour's input.

Bob Hunt sat transfixed. "What do you think, Marcia?"

"Well, there's nothing to compare it with at the moment. But it's young. It seems innovative to me. I can see if you're building a leisure/holiday complex, you don't want to give the husbands the headache of loads of gardening. Play on a boat maybe. That's leisure. Darling, let's see yours."

"Well, you've got to understand, I just set up the raw embryo. The guys in my team do a bit more visualising. I principally concentrate on numbers and economics and I'd want to quiz Peter on that aspect of his idea, because playing around with water is the death of many a developer. I've done mine on a single site plot by plot layout basis."

He opened his pad. "Here's the sea. I've got two sort of gateways to the overall development. That's these blocks of flats at each end. Punters love flats by the coast so there's little or no upkeep. I think it's worth developing the seafront itself. That's what people like and although Peter has a point about the back development, I've given them gardens, more for kids than gardeners.

Anyway, overall, I get 300 houses and 50 flats. The houses could look like Peter's if that's what the local knowledge would produce. What do you think?" He turned to Marcia.

"It's like the Bognor scheme you did, and Eastbourne, and didn't you do one in Bangor in Wales?"

"Well, it worked there, didn't it? Peter?" Bob canvassed the inexperienced opinion.

"Well, I obviously don't know Bognor or Eastbourne and as you've said, you know the game. Conceptually, I go with mine, but you're the businessman."

"Peter, how many units do you get?"

"Well, I've got a calculation sheet that produces 480 houses, plus private berths and a marina for 50 moorings and a local shopping area providing about 1,000 square metres of essential support retail."

"Do you?" Hunt stated pensively. "Look Marcia, what do you think? Why don't we call it a draw?"

"OK with me," Marcia said, "they're so different. How about you, Peter?"

"Fine with me, Mrs Hunt, it was fun."

Bob Hunt relaxed.

"Peter. I do say, I like the name of your development. Where's it from?"

"Oh! It just came into my head," he said with a broad smile.

"It's been a hectic afternoon," Bob Hunt pronounced. "Fun though. Tell you what, Peter, I'm really very, very impressed with your approach."

"Thank you, Mr Hunt."

Marcia smiled approvingly. "Turn your backs, chaps, I'm going to slip back into my dress."

"Thank God for that. Clearly you distracted poor young Peter. He was beside himself."

Peter was indeed beside himself – not due to the distraction of Mrs Hunt, but because he felt that his idea was far better than Bob Hunt's, whose scheme was such old hat. It took no account of the flat terrain and produced a smaller scheme.

But no matter. His job now was to drive them back to the hotel. The first part of the road back was virtually unmade, so he had to ensure he drove calmly and smoothly. Bob had fallen off to sleep by the time they hit the tarmac, his head slumped almost onto his chest. Marcia seemed to have her view still fixed through the rear quarterlight. Quite what she was studying so closely, Peter couldn't work out. The last mile or so of road was lined by a high hedgerow, so she must have been staring into space.

Peter recognised they were approaching the sunflower fields which would be on her side of the road on the way back. Just around another bend, he calculated, Marcia would suddenly come to.

He slowed the car. Suddenly the burst of gold and yellow hit her. The deep brown heads turned and looked up towards her. Marcia shot a glance through the mirror to him. Their eyes met.

"Gracias," she whispered and then leant forward. "I need to explain."

Peter shrugged his shoulders, lifting his hands from the wheel in a gesture of not understanding. She whispered again, "I'll explain," and put a finger to her mouth.

They arrived at the hotel at about 6pm. Bob Hunt thanked Peter profusely. "You're a bloody good driver for a young fellow," he said. "Perhaps I could borrow your sketches overnight. I'd like another look at them."

"I took them out of the pad. I've got them loose," Peter replied.

"That's fine. I'll look after them. I won't do them any harm."

"No, I'll hold on to them if you don't mind. I've got some thinking to do to crystallise my ideas."

"Well, son, do persevere. I really think you've got a natural talent there. I'll say it again, give up architecture now. You could make yourself a lot of money in the right development camp."

Marcia turned to her husband. "It's time for your medication. Why don't you go on up? If Peter gives me the keys, I'll park the car."

Peter was by now holding the door open for Bob Hunt and was out of the car.

"Good idea. I'll have a bath before dinner. I feel a stiff whisky coming on. Cheers, Peter. Thanks again for driving and the tour, not to mention our little competition." He walked into the hotel.

"Here, I'll park it. Hop in the front for a minute!" Marcia beckoned to Peter to get back into the car.

She backed the car away from the front entrance and swung the big beast into its usual parking slot. Disengaging the automatic, she placed it into park and applied the handbrake.

"Peter, your scheme was wonderful. It was exciting, young, vibrant and I can see it'll have a natural beauty about it. You designed your own personality into the project. The youth, vibrance and beauty are all you. Now Bob won't get you, or the scheme, out of his mind. I could tell he was shocked by your natural talent.

"But he needs the further discovery of what you can give and the exploitation of your talent to be his idea, not one stimulated by me. He's a stubborn man. If I really want him to do something, I feed the idea into him so that it comes out as his suggestion. Then it happens. One day I'll tell you about him. In the meantime, trust me. Do your degree. He's envious, he has no academic qualification and quashes anybody who has. None of his co-directors is qualified. With a formal training and your undoubted talent, I promise you, you'll make a fortune, but more than that, you'll create environmental legends wherever you practise your art."

"Mrs Hunt, one of the sunflowers said, 'Wow, that's a lady and a half'. He was wrong: you're twice the lady of any other, in both mind and body."

"Thank you, Peter. And forgive me for supporting my husband. It's my part of a deal."

"I'm on a day off tomorrow. Can you get by on the tennis court without me?"

"I need to learn to, in under a couple of weeks we'll be waving adiós."

Marcia felt a bit low as she walked back to the hotel. She'd followed her impetuous nose and been bowled over by Bob's early attentions. Now she knew the complexities of his personality. He was, deep down, a very kind man but when you're brought up as a street fighter, even as the body gives out you need to be told you either could still win or, in the megalomaniacal world he lived in, have actually won.

That was the supportive part of Marcia's role, a role in which, she understood, Bob's first wife had failed. The moment his adulation started to wane, she saw the reality of being told to pack her bags, as proved by the experience of Bob's first wife. After all, she was not satisfying him in bed, but at least in that department she was keeping his interest alive. There was a game on, he often told himself. His diabetes was helping him to bide his time. He got sufficient satisfaction from feasting his eyes on her body, and her occasional 'treats'.

Her stage experience had taught her how to be looked at. In her most recent club appearances, she had been topless and required to ooze genial eroticism for her anxious audience. So, what was new in a one-girl, one-man show? It certainly paid her well in terms of lifestyle and, in any event, she loved the kind side of her husband.

As Marcia crossed the reception area, Maria was adjusting a large vase of gladioli on the antique side table in front of the gilt mirror they'd shipped in from Madrid when she and Pedro went down for his final scholarship interview. They'd laughed at the fact that they had both looked at the old frame, touched the curves and scrolls and fallen in love with it but, amazingly, neither had seen their own image in the mirror itself.

"Well, that proves it's beautiful and not necessarily functional," Peter had pronounced.

"On the other hand, it might be saying to us that neither of us wants to see ourselves looking old," Maria had replied.

"Hola," she said, as she saw Marcia come through the doors. "That's a pretty outfit. How did it go? Is the car in one piece?"

"Thanks. It went really, really well and yes, of course, the car's in one piece. It had your genius son at the helm."

"Peter. My genius? Come on, he's bright, but not a genius. He can't play a violin, for a start."

"Seriously, Maria, he has such a talent."

"Really? Tell me what happened to bring you to that conclusion."

Marcia told Maria about the competition, and Bob and Peter's ideas. "Now Bob, remember, does that for a living. He's quick and extremely successful. But Peter, well, I think he must have that same initial ability to visualise a fourth dimension, the dimension beyond breadth, depth and width, the 'yet to become' factor. He came up with quite a scheme.

"Suggest to him that he shows you his sketches. They're lovely. The problem I have with Bob (but you haven't heard me say this) is that he's a realist and he knows very well that his ideas are flat and old. I'll have to let him spell it out in his own way. He'll sulk a while but, you watch, Peter to him will be like the prototype of a new car. Bob will want him for his talent, and my Bob, when he wants something, doesn't know how to let go."

"Well, it's exciting to hear that, but you'll find Peter's very determined too. His next three years are planned, he'll not change those."

"I can believe that but I'll make a forecast."

"What's that?" Maria said, almost protectively.

"Bob will book up to come here in the summer of each of those three years. He likes it here anyway, it's suiting him very well. He's relaxed. But he'll make out he's the one who's discovered Peter's talent and, a bit like sowing a sunflower seed, he'll want to see how it grows." And she told Maria about the field of sunflowers. "Maria, you have a lovely son. He's very dear to me already and I've only known him less than a week." She thought: *But then I'd only known Bob less than a week and we were on a crash course to marriage.* "Anyway, I must fly. Bob might have drowned in his bath. He drops off to sleep in it. Oh dear!"

Maria thought how happy Marcia was. Obviously she was proud to hear her singing Peter's praises so highly.

She'd best set the music up for the evening. Percy Faith – Summer Place, from about 7pm. Then James Last, Herb Alpert and finish the sequence with Neil Diamond. And the evening menus hadn't been set out yet.

Maria turned quickly to walk to the office and suddenly felt giddy. The dizziness soon passed. She looked into the mirror. *God, I look rough,* she thought. Maybe she'd been overdoing it. She'd see how it went but might pop along to the doctor's next week.

"Hi, mother," came Peter's voice from the staff door into the reception area. "How's things?"

"Fine," Maria responded. Well, what point was there in telling your son you've been working too hard and you need a break? "Fine," she repeated. "And how was the afternoon?"

"Interesting," he said, with a rueful smile.

"Oh! Interesting. What's that mean? You discovered I was right about Mrs Hunt being just about the most attractive young lady you'll ever get that near to."

"Come on, she's a client. A friendly client, I'd have to say, but if I want to gawp at sexy ladies I can always get you to buy me a Playboy. No. 'Interesting' with Mr Hunt, actually. He issued a bit of a challenge regarding the conception of a development idea up on the coast."

"How did that go?"

"Oh, it wasn't serious. It was hypothetical, but let's put it this way, I wasn't dissatisfied with the outcome."

"Did Mr Hunt have a go at the same idea?"

"Well yes, in principle."

"What was his like?"

"Well he thought it was fantastic, and I doubt anybody who works for him would ever criticise his ideas. I suppose if he makes money out of them, well and good. But I'm in danger of designing something that isn't in accord with the market. That's the problem if you're an innovator. I wonder how many engineers have argued with their bosses that a three-wheel car could have advantages over a four-wheel one, only to be told the market expects four wheel ones. Maybe Adam got his ears boxed for suggesting, when God made him a soulmate, that she should only have one breast."

"Pedro! Really! You'll get turned to stone one of these days."

"I just have this feeling in my bones that I'm not going to be your conventional architect. But I'm totally convinced what I suggested this afternoon would create a demand. We'll see. It was a fun exercise anyway."

"What did Mr Hunt actually say about it?"

"Well actually, I think he couldn't take it all in. We'll have another look at it together. I want to speak to Marco about it, too."

"Do you ever wonder what your father would think of it, or of you, dear?"

"Don't go soft on me, Mother. The answer is yes I do, of course, frequently."

"And the answer?"

"He says, 'Be yourself. Stay different if that comes naturally'. And, do you know, he's sometimes standing behind the goal. He acts as a target behind the net. He's guided me to loads of penalties. He's there when there's a mosquito or a moth fluttering around and he tells me it's OK to kill them."

"And do you?"

"No… no. I say to nature's little nuisances they've done nothing to hurt me. And it's just as well bigger things than me don't go round stamping and swatting me to death all day."

Maria put her arms around Peter's neck. "Stay lovely, Peter."

"With you around, I can't help it."

Upstairs, on the first floor, Marcia breezed into the suite. "Coo-ee!" she called out towards the bathroom. She knocked; she'd learnt to be prudent because at certain stages of Bob's ablutions, he was very sensitive.

"Hi," came the response, which meant the all-clear to come in.

She entered. Bob was lying full length in the bath, a towel rolled as a pillow behind his head.

"I hope you weren't dropping off," Marcia said in a matronly manner, as she sat down on the edge of the bath.

"I'm wide awake," he said, "my brain's racing like it hasn't raced this year, at least since the day you picked me up."

"Bloody cheek! *You* picked *me* up. Why's your brain racing?"

"It's young Peter's design."

"Well, as I said, it was OK."

"No! It's actually not just OK. It's brilliant."

"Why didn't you say so?"

"Well, he's a confident young man. I didn't want him to think it was too easy. It must have been a freak of a good idea. You see, if you pursue the idea of the holiday development, you know it's all calm and no rush, you do only need single width roads, and gardens would get in the way. That adds back about 50 per cent of the land use I'd set aside for those elements. Bringing the sea to everyone's back door means, as he explained, no-one needs the sea to look at from their front doors and windows… I could go on… and the small shopping centre, possibly a chandlery, a baker's and general store, a little sports shop. I think he and I could really make something great together. You know that site I'm looking at in New Addington? It'll be for young people so it needs young ideas. Innovation. Kids won't want homes like their parents, and I've built a lot of their parents' ones so I mustn't presume. You were wrong to say Bognor worked. Yes, it worked in a previous generation but not necessarily this next one."

Marcia was so pleased for Peter that Bob could appreciate his ideas. She stood up, peeled her dress over her head and slipped out of her bra and pants.

"Move over, genius. I don't know how you work all these things out. You're very clever to recognise talent. That's an art."

She slid into the bath alongside him.

"I was good at sorting out the talent below all the clothes you had on when I first saw you too."

"Oh, very."

"Come on then, let's see that real talent work," Bob suggested yet again.

"No, it's still not a rainy day. Not for me, but I'm happy it's going to be nice for you though."

Peter had showered off some of his thoughts about Marcia. He really found her hard to work out. One moment she was there for the taking, the next she was all her husband's property.

He put on some casual slacks and a shirt, not intending to go into the hotel that evening. He needed to speak to Marco.

He arrived at Marco's private terrace on the stroke of 7pm. "Just in time to join me," said Marco, who was sticking rigidly to his deal with Maria on the drinking front. "Beer?"

"Yes please."

"How d'you like owning a Bentley?"

"Great. They're a bit big for the lanes, though."

"Where did you get to?"

"That's what I wanted to talk to you about, actually."

"Why, did you get lost and you wanted me to come and pick you up?"

"Almost. You remember the road from Ampurias back to the sea? It terminates in an open bay with just a few little farm cottages, a reasonable beach, but it's very flat with rocks at one end."

"Yes, it's Banas."

"Did you say you had an old cousin who owned the farm?"

"Yes. Old José."

"We need to buy him out."

"What? Peter, we were stretched to build this hotel. I'm not sure we have the money for that."

"We can put a proposition to him."

"But there's no way he would move at his age."

"He doesn't need to. But he's probably finding it difficult to keep the land under control now. It can't make him any money."

"What sort of proposition, you dreadful conniving Martinez?"

"We went to the bay this afternoon, and out of a fun challenge from

Bob Hunt a huge opportunity arose to develop the area into a holiday home resort. Well, we'd need to get building permission and I reckoned if Mother spoke to Carlos, he might just know the mayor of that region, who might use his influence and consent to a really good scheme. Sort of award-winning stuff. So the proposition is that we offer to buy Old José's land, but conditional on getting consent to build."

"But how on earth would we do that?" Marco asked. "Carlos would need us to fix the price."

"OK, so there's no infrastructure. Electrics would be expensive, so would drainage. I think there would be water below the land that would need pumping. We offer him 15 per cent of a development partnership."

"But we'd still need to raise that 15 per cent to do the deal if we were lucky enough to get the permissions."

"No! Your cousin gets a promise of 15 per cent. If, when we have permission, we can't find the money or a partner with the money, he still has land with a valuable consent. If we don't get consent, he is as he is. A farmer with an increasing problem."

"Dear Peter. You're so like your equally dear mother and you're determined like your father. It's a crazy idea…"

"Let me stop you there. Here's the crazy idea this far." Peter produced the sketches and plans.

Marco was absolutely enthralled. "Why call it Girasol?"

"It means, as you know, follow the sun, and that's what the houses do. They're all sunflowers, only made out of blocks and tiles."

Marco was about to deliver his words of praise when Maria walked in. "Hello. You boys drinking already?"

Marco looked and realised he hadn't yet supped his drink. "We've been waiting for you. A sherry?"

"No thanks."

"A Martini, white wine?"

"No, water please. Just water." Marco put the glass of water in front of her.

"Pedro's been entertaining me with a scatterbrain idea."

"Oh yes. What's this one?"

"The Girasol development."

"The what? What follows the sun?"

"The housing scheme we're going to develop."

"Is this the scheme Marcia Hunt thinks is so brilliant?"

Peter was stunned. "She didn't seem so impressed."

"Oh, she was! The problem you have is that Mr Hunt thought it a stroke of instant genius, too. But he's a man who's jealous of guarding his reputation. You watch. Give him a day or two to get used to the fact that your ideas were better than his, and you'll hear all about it. It's the way he does things, apparently."

"You really do surprise me, Mother. But he's too late."

"Too late for what?"

"Uncle Marco and I have already established the principle of a partnership. Can you spare him some time off tomorrow? We need to go and set up the deal with our distant cousin. I'll explain your part in all this later."

"No! I don't want to wait. I might not like the part."

"OK. All you have to do is to put Carlos on your arm, go and see the local mayor and get the building consent. As easy as that," Peter assured her.

"Yes. My bones tell me. As easy as that," smiled Maria. "OK then, what's Mother's cut?"

"Cousin gets 15 per cent of development cost," said Peter. "You get ten per cent of profit. Marco and I get 30 per cent of profit each."

Marco chipped in, "That leaves 15 per cent not spoken for."

"That's for the greedy banker for putting up 85 per cent of the cost."

Marco chuckled. Maria said, "I hope you're not disappointed."

"If you don't follow your hunches, you'd never learn to walk in the first place," Peter responded.

Maria drew a deep breath. "Why didn't I join an ordinary family who just wanted to stand still?"

Peter looked at his watch. "Hell, it's 8.30!"

"Are you seeing Meribel? You could ask her to go with you tomorrow."

"No, she's got her father's birthday dinner. I'm slipping out with Guy and Philippe but I'll try and call her about tomorrow. It's her day off."

"And Michelle?" Maria asked.

"I don't really know, she may tag along with a few of the other younger guests. They fancy a disco."

"Watch Michelle, Peter."

"I have," he replied behind one of his broad smiles.

"She'll have you for breakfast, if you're not careful."

"Shall we leave about ten, Marco?"

"Sure, Pedro. Ten on the dot."

The youngsters had arranged to meet down by the tennis court and had gathered around the bench seats. Guy was there, and Philippe and Michelle. When Peter arrived, Michelle showed some excitement.

"I'd said you wouldn't come," she announced.

"Why did you think that?"

"I thought Mrs Hunt would have held you back in the back of the Bentley to do evil with you."

"Why do you say that, Michelle?"

"Because if I had access to one of those and had paid you for an afternoon's work, I'd have done that."

Peter laughed. "But then if you had an Austin Mini and asked me to drive you around, I'd have resisted and run a mile."

"Do you really mean that?" Michelle asked in a deflated way.

"I really do. But don't worry, I'll be brave enough to dance with you at the disco because I know we'll be walking home."

"So where's the action?" Guy asked.

"I'd guess Llanfranc. There's a disco called 'Stars'. It's out in the open and they have a 15-piece Costa Brava Orchestra who'll play local music in the early part. Then they throw in the disco."

"Sounds good."

"When's it open?" Philippe asked.

"About ten," Peter replied.

"So come on folks, let's go across to Llanfranc and buy a couple of drinks to get in the mood."

Peter found Michelle next to him. She whispered, "Make me a promise, coach."

"What's that?" he replied softly.

"Look after me, please. I don't want to get hurt."

He really didn't understand. It was like a plea from a young child, scared of some underlying threat.

"Behave and I will," Peter replied. He realised he was not really a part of this gang, whose members had joined up to make the most of their holiday. It was probably because he was working at the hotel and hadn't been out with them before. He seemed older in outlook, too. Even more mature than Guy. He was later to learn what convoluted rebellions the three Parmentier kids were waging against their domineering father.

When the children were very young, the Admiral had ruled that: "the eldest will be a successful businessman, the second son a supreme athlete and the daughter a star." Faced with such constant pressure, it was only a matter of time before they resisted.

A few jokes flew round, and over Peter's head, about the Cook parents' disapproval of their daughters going out at night. En famille, they took to their beds by about 9.30pm.

"Well darlings," the mother would say, "I don't know about you but the heat's taken it out of me today. Who's for bed and a bright, early start?" The grandmother always jumped at the suggestion, and it meant Mr Cook could get back to what he really loved to do most, read in bed.

Mrs Cook would be out like a light, face glowing from an overdose of sun. The daughters went to their rooms and would argue between themselves that Tasha really shouldn't sneak out after hours but, providing her younger sister could use her tennis racket the next day, she wouldn't split.

Tasha slipped into a really short mini-skirt her parents had no idea she owned, took off the bra she had worn to dinner, removed the band that had held her ponytail in place all day and, with a quick flip of a comb and a dab of lipstick and mascara, transformed herself into a very sexy teenager. She wondered if it would still be Philippe who provided the attention. It should be, because they had kissed the night before, which had given her great pleasure. Her natural instinct was to keep his hands under strict control. She had no experience in such matters but it seemed to her he was gentle, and the little twinges of excitement from the night before led her to believe that if he was allowed a free roam, that too would be pleasurable for her.

Her mother had always advised her not to get embroiled with young men until university. But her instinct was to find out more about what she could be missing out on in the next five years. "Hell," she had said to herself, "that's 30 per cent of my life gone, already passed by, if I take mother's advice. I'll try a little and then decide."

She skipped down the rear fire escape, across the lawn and headed down the path to where Philippe had said he'd wait, in the note he'd slipped to her earlier that day, while her parents were enjoying a siesta.

Thank God they slept deeply any time they closed their eyes. At least during their slumbers she got some free time.

"Hi, cherie!" came the heavy French accent from within the bushes.

"Où es-tu?" Tasha whispered. At least the intermixing was doing her French some good.

"Ici, à droit."

She walked into the total blackness from where the voice had come. Philippe's hand took hers. His eyes had become accustomed to the depth of darkness during his ten-minute wait. Quite naturally, she threw her left arm over his right shoulder. His own arms seemed to become octopus tentacles wound round her waist, grabbing her bottom, gripping her shoulder.

They kissed for two or three minutes, but it seemed like hours… Tasha felt slightly dizzy for lack of oxygen. She felt a hand on her right thigh, then she was being lifted off her feet and lain on the ground. The hand ran higher up her thigh and lay flat on her stomach. She pushed Philippe away.

"Mais, ma cherie. C'est extraordinaire, c'est nécessaire. Je t'aime." This was all flattering stuff but scary. She whispered, "Plus tard. Plus tard, peut-être."

"Oh! Always later is what you say," he said, with a tinge of frustration.

"Let's go find the others," he determined. "Here. One more kiss, please." There was less fervour about this kiss. He was calmer, she more in control of both her own feelings and the situation.

When she lay by the pool with her parents and loyal sister the next morning, Tasha questioned again why she had done what she then did. Coolly and calmly, her hand had strayed onto his right thigh as they knelt, holding each other close. His lips had pulled away slightly in surprise. As though magnetised, her hand moved to his fly zipper and stroked slowly upwards, feeling all the goodness straining against his tight-fitting jeans. He had winced as his tongue pushed between her lips.

With both hands flat against the points of each shoulder, she eased him away. "Comme tu as dit… let's go and find the others."

She was up on her feet, holding his hand and now guiding him out of the bushes. There was a light on the path… she stopped and brushed the back of her skirt down for fear she had picked up some strands of the dying summer grass. She turned her back to Philippe, lifted the front of her mini skirt and pulled down the dishevelled blouse, then smoothed out her skirt again.

Philippe moved closer behind her and pushed both his forearms between her arms and her rib-cage. She moved her hips forward and with one hard jerk, thumped him in his private parts with her firm, rounded teenage bottom.

She turned to face him in one continuing movement and wagged a finger in his face, although she was smiling broadly. "Singe," she scolded.

They joined the others in Toni's bar. Philippe bought Tasha a Coke and a beer for himself. The others were imbibing a mixture of drinks, the boys mainly on beer and the girls either white wine or Bacardi and Coke.

Michelle's eyes already looked glazed. Peter moved across to where she was sitting at the bar, and put an avuncular arm around her shoulder.

"Don't drink any more," he said.

"I have to," she replied, still staring ahead and sipping from the glass.

Peter sensed her body was shaking. Not overtly, but it was gently pulsating all over. He turned her to face him on her bar stool. "You OK?" he said, holding both her shoulders.

"It's… I don't know what you call it. I'm cold. Guy is being unkind to me."

"What's Guy got to do with it? He's over there talking to that Spanish fellow."

"He's more likely fixing a date with him," she said.

"With the boy?" Peter asked, surprised.

Michelle crooked her little finger into a bent shape, implying only one thing.

"Queer?" Peter asked.

"Of course. Did you not know?"

Peter thought deeply. Well, he supposed now that it was mentioned, Guy never seemed to talk to the girls. Peter had just presumed that, as all the girls seemed younger than Guy, there was nobody compatible.

But queer? He'd never worked that one out. Then again, he realised he had never knowingly met a queer man, or been in one's company before.

"Why's that make you say Guy is being unkind to you?"

Michelle looked Peter full in the face through her deep-set, glazed eyes. "He won't let me have a smoke."

"I'll get a packet of cigarettes for you."

Michelle started to laugh. She lifted both her hands and placed them on the sides of Peter's temples.

"Oh, dear sweet Peter. If cigarettes satisfied me, I'd be happy. I need pot."

Peter was flabbergasted. "Oh my God. You're too beautiful, too young for that."

"Screw me and that'll take my mind off it."

Something within Peter snapped. The truth was that Marcia's spell had far from worn off, and the brief glimpses of her body she'd allowed him had made him realise this was more meaningful, more mature, than one of his adolescent encounters, even those he had enjoyed with Laura and Meribel.

Michelle was beautiful, it was true. There was probably not a young man within five years either side of Peter's age who would not give their eye teeth to be in his position now. But...

"Screw you, be damned. You need help. Guy should be helping you. Philippe. Does Philippe smoke pot?"

"No, he's clean. He's the sportsman. Guy's the business scholar and he brought the pot habit back from university. I was introduced and it seemed to give him enjoyment to have somebody to share it with. Now I need it. But as I said, screwing would help."

"What did you mean earlier, that you don't want to get hurt?"

"Well, when I smoke, and I think it's the drink with it, I sometimes don't know what I'm doing. I either fall over, or get tangled up with some guy. When they realise you don't know what you're doing, they do strange things with you. If you don't submit, they hit you. Then they leave you in a heap to recover."

"What helps you recover?"

"Sleep. First the nightmares, then the dreams. Then nothing until the morning. Then your body aches and you feel sick and you vow never to smoke again. Then it's something about the loneliness of the evening into the night. You need to feel good again. It gives you confidence and you're on the roller coaster."

"Let's get some air," Peter suggested.

"Will you help me walk, coach?"

"Sure, put your hand round my waist."

"Are you going to screw me then, after all?"

"No! I'm going to comfort you and show you that you don't need pot, or screwing, or drink."

"OK, clever bastard. I've met types like you before. You get me through this night and then you walk out and leave me back where I was."

"That's possible. But I know a man. He can probably help. Leave it to me. I'll promise to get you more than 24 hours' respite. I know this beach just round the bay. We'll relax there."

Michelle giggled. "Oh goody. You're like the rest of them. So I do get screwed after all."

"Michelle. You do not get screwed. Hear me? You do not get screwed." He felt her shrug her shoulders.

They reached the bay. A sun lounger had been left out. He carried her across the beach and lay her on the taut canvas. He propped the back of the lounger up and lay down beside her.

"Now your job is to just cling on. The hunger will pass, the drink will be dissipated into your bloodstream, you'll dream. I'll be here when you need me."

She seemed calmer, the adrenaline was subsiding. Peter needed a master plan, though. He was committed to Marco in the morning.

His best friend in the world was certainly his mother. Could he trust her with this problem he'd walked into? He thought so. She had a rapport with the pharmacist Peter had met at the hotel's opening shindig. He had seemed a very professional chap and talked about his clinics and alternative therapies. He'd know where to get help and maybe, in the cool light of a couple of days, he could get Michelle to confide her problem to her parents. They'd surely help. Probably help Guy as well.

Michelle stirred. It was about 3am. She sat up, startled. "It's true then. We've been lying on this beach. I thought it was all a dream."

She seemed controlled and was no longer shaking. Peter realised this must be the 'cold turkey' he had heard about.

Michelle let out a sudden squeal. "Bastard!" she said, lunging her hand down between her legs. She looked him fully in the face, though now not through glazed eyes. "No, you're not. You're not, you're not a bastard. You haven't done it."

Peter laughed. "That's right. I haven't. How do you feel about walking?"

She stood up, started to unbutton her blouse and discarded it. She slipped her skirt and briefs down in one single movement. "If I'm going to learn to trust you, coach, you'll need to prove it. Here, we're swimming."

She undid Peter's shirt. Loosened his belt, unzipped his fly and slid his trousers and pants down as deftly as she'd undressed herself. She looked down. "Don't worry, it's because you like what you see. It'll go," she said confidently. "At least that shows you've got normal feelings."

They swam closely without touching. The moon sprayed a shaft of light across the calm sea. "What's that?" she said, pointing out to sea and treading water calmly.

"Oh, they're fishing boats. Out there with their masters, making a living."

"They look beautiful, silhouetted against the moon's rays."

"Michelle, they *are* beautiful. The fishermen are beautiful people too." Peter used his sweater to first dry Michelle off, then himself. There was no hint of any sexual expectation.

"How do you feel?" Peter asked.

"Good."

"In need of a smoke?"

"No, for the first time in ages I've gone through the barrier. A friend of mine I used to share pot with says she's cracked the habit. She said if you ration yourself to a smoke a day and you take it at roughly the same time, you get like an animal in a zoo and you expect feeding time. If you can break the routine, you can break the habit and the need."

"What happens tonight?"

"I don't know. Can you be with me?" she almost pleaded.

"Of course, but I'd like Meribel to be with us too."

"OK, three-in-a-bed stuff."

"No, two caring friends keeping control of an insatiable young lady who needs help. I'm going to take you back to the hotel."

"Is that where I get screwed, coach?"

Surely he must have shown her that was furthest from his mind. He'd passed his test of trust.

"Nope, it's where you get put into my bed to go to sleep, with my mother in the next room one side and me on the couch on the other. We'll get you through the night and then tomorrow take you along to this friend who may have an answer to get you through the barrier long-term."

"Peter, you're a lovely friend."

"That's as may be. If you see either of your brothers with a bloody nose and a sorry look on their face, that'll be because they've agreed to be your best friends too, but influenced by me…"

"Peter, you're still a lovely friend, even though you threaten to beat up my family."

"… And then I'll have a word with your mother and father and tell them to take more care of you…"

"Merde! Please don't!"

"We'll see."

CHAPTER 14

"Who the hell's in your bed then?" Maria said loudly, having poked the body on the couch and found it to be Peter.

"Michelle."

"Michelle! Good God! Meribel will crucify you. There are some lovely girls around who don't actually flaunt their bodies to the first Spanish tennis coach they think they've fallen in love with… girls with a bit of class. And here I am with this French tart in between the sheets I've washed and laundered for you. How can you hurt me this much?"

"Mother, let me tell you the whole story. I'm looking for your help."

Peter explained everything to Maria, who gradually settled into the conversation. She interjected just the once. "So, did you sleep with her?"

"No, Mother, and let me continue…" which he did, telling her the whole story. Could her pharmacist friend help? Peter reminded Maria that Miguel Mendes had talked of alternative therapies, and was very modern in his thinking.

"Let me make the position perfectly clear. I think Michelle is a young spoilt French tart… but because I love you, of course I'll help. But if I find in two or three months' time you've got her pregnant, then I'll be the first to chop your balls off."

"Mother! How can you think such things and what's more…"

He was interrupted from the now open doorway to his bedroom.

"… What's more, Mrs Martinez, you have a wonderful son. Yes, OK, I am a bit of a French tart, but Peter is soft and kind and didn't try to use me. He stopped me getting hurt and helped me over a number of barriers. You're a very lucky lady. He loves you. As for me… he's my tennis coach and a disciple sent by God to save me. I think he's on the way to doing that, so there's no need to chastise him."

Maria moved to the doorway, put her arms around Michelle and swathed her in one of her crisply laundered sheets.

"So…" Maria said. "How do we get you through the day? What about your parents? Will they help?"

"That's two big questions, Mrs Martinez. On the first one, I need to be kept busy, probably with people. Maybe at the pool. Hopefully Philippe will help. Secondly, will my parents help? They're lovely and in their way very loving. But there's only so much of their attention they can give me. So the answer is probably not. But if they knew Guy was queer and addicted, and I was close to being sick, I've no doubt they'd come to the rescue. They might just die of shame in the process. In the end, my father's a great team person. Teams are numbers to him and there's no such thing, in his book, as a team of one. So I doubt they can help."

"OK, then let's put you under the command of Philippe, and late this afternoon I'll take you to see Miguel Mendes. We'll see if he can help. In the meantime," Maria said, looking at Peter, "you have an appointment with Marco and his cousin. That's important. I'll take Michelle under my wing."

Peter crossed the room and placed his strong right arm around his mother's shoulder first, then his left around Michelle's. "So, listen girls, I'll need you two to square this mess with Meribel… otherwise she'll be the one to chop my balls off."

The three of them giggled. "What a night!!" he said.

When Maria had indicated she was not disposed to go and see the cousin, Peter had phoned and asked Meribel to go with him and Marco. He had arranged to pick her up at 10am. He'd asked her please could she wear a short skirt because he'd bet any older member of the Martinez family would be more malleable to a deal if he had an attractive young pair of female knees to ogle during the negotiations. They'd call back to pick up Marco on the way and they'd be at the beach farm by 11am.

Peter envisaged them wasting a lot of time while Marco and cousin José reminisced. They'd drink coffee and then, only if a deal was concluded, cousin José might break out a bottle or two of his best homemade wine.

Peter's perception was not far wrong and Meribel's skirt certainly worked. Cousin José nearly wet himself. He was waiting at the passenger side of the car where he had seen Marco sitting as they drove up the drive. Marco wound the window down and joked was he really José Martinez, his cousin from so many years, because he looked so young that Marco hardly recognised him.

Marco always had been the con-man in the family.

Meribel swung open the rear passenger door and lifted both knees and thighs high into the air to clear the step into the rear well of the car, all for the benefit of cousin José. And benefit he did indeed, showing his appreciation as he drew in his smoke-laden breath for long enough to enable Marco to have a peep at as well. Peter came round from the driving position and broke the silence of the older men's gawping.

"Good morning, sir," he said holding out a strong right to his distant relative. He'd got into the habit, a habit which in fact was to last him a lifetime, of calling an older man on first meeting 'sir'. Professional people, or those he thought might enhance his career, he was more emphatic about. Ladies were the same. 'Madame' slipped smoothly off his tongue, and he later found that, on better acquaintance, "Morning, young man," or, "Good afternoon, young lady," won him a special place in their rather gullible hearts.

"This is my good friend Meribel. Meribel – cousin José, cousin José – Meribel."

"Good morning, young lady." Cousin José clearly meant it. "It's good to have some young female blood on the farm. My Carla will watch your every move," he said, touching her cheek with his well-worn forefinger. "She's known all 52 years of our married life that her challenge would come from a young beautiful lady who would sweep me off my feet. I think any rivals who've come onto the scene have been poisoned and buried at sea, because as soon as they've appeared, she's made sure they've vanished."

Peter swallowed hard. He hadn't heard the expression being buried at sea for a few years. Visions of Paco rushed into his head. He never knew quite why, but often such visions conjured up a snapshot in his memory of them standing over a young boar, with Paco instructing Peter to kill it.

Dear father, he thought, *watch me deal with this old boar.*

Cousin José took Meribel's arm and said, "Let's take you inside and get you poisoned quickly. If Carla's any judge, she'll know it's you who's been sent to take me away from all this."

Peter's prediction as to how José would hold court for the first hour or so was spot on. First, the story of his father on the farm teaching him as a boy to harvest olive trees, then the tragedy of his father dying. "Yes, over there in that field you can see, he caught his arm in the harvester and bled to death. Shouldn't have been trying to free the blades anyway. Bled to death. Nobody knew till he didn't come in for breakfast at 9am, which had been a habit of a lifetime."

Next he recounted the circumstances of meeting Carla and yes, how she had been a perfect wife, save that she couldn't give him children (she'd never told him that it was he who was sterile. She'd had tests and was perfectly satisfied of her capabilities). Finally it was the Civil War and his leg. Marco had forecast that once that one was out of the way, he'd bring up the subject of the sale.

José was 32 and had been married for 12 years when the generals of the Spanish Army led their troops in revolt against the Republican government.

He'd been one of a number who thought God and history were on their side in their bid to overthrow the oppressive government. If he had been given ten pesetas each time he told the story of how he fought in the battle to seize power in Barcelona and lost, he would have been a very rich man.

His one visit to Majorca had been as part of a Republican expeditionary force of Catalan troops, which went there via Ibiza in 1936. He'd been part of the march on the Nationalist garrison when they had been attacked by Italian Nationalist support fighters and bombers. The result was that he'd left his leg in Majorca, which had always been his sickest joke, and had been returned home, and back to running the farm they were now discussing.

"So, enough of all that memorabilia. What's this land deal you want to try and do with me?"

Marco took the helm while Meribel shuffled on to her left buttock as she sat next to Peter on the sofa, slid her feet round on the solid hardwood flooring, and more directly under her knees, which had the effect of raising her pillar-box red mini skirt two to three inches higher up her tanned thighs. *There now, cousin,* she thought, *let's see if that gets you poisoned for looking, or me for making you.*

Marco painted a picture of Peter's background, his natural eye, and how he had seen cousin José's land and perceived it was not performing as economically as it might have been. It still produced good olives, but then so did millions of acres in the deep Spanish south, where they harvested commercially at great profit. Likewise, the vines... and so, while it would be an uphill climb with, in their view, a 50/50 chance of success, Peter was prepared to input his conceptual ability, which made Meribel giggle. It was not his conceptual ability she knew him for.

"So," Marco reasoned, "Peter would input all of that into his side of a deal. If it was successful, the land could either be sold or held and developed if the capital could be raised. Peter would put in his own expertise free and pay you 15 per cent of any land value to pass over the territorial interest into the deal."

"Fifteen per cent!" cousin José almost screamed. "Even I, a poor farmer, know the land is worth 25 per cent, if the cost of building a house is even as much as 50 per cent of the final value and allowing 25 per cent for profit and other costs."

"No! No!" Marco argued. "Here the building costs will be huge. There's no infrastructure, if we get permission we'll need roads, electricity, water, maybe gas, drains. All that will take the building costs up to 70 per cent, so if there's 30 per cent to split, Peter would have in mind 15 per cent each."

José scoffed. "It's 25 per cent."

"Look, this is family," said Peter "OK, I'm going to make a suggestion to remove any bartering that might only lead to ill feeling. Eighteen per cent. How do you feel about that?"

"How do I feel about that? Ill! That's how I feel about that," José scoffed again. "Look, I agree, it is family so I'll put an end to it. It's 20 per cent or nothing. No deal, no chance of development and Carla and I will be left in peace, as we are, and where we're quite contented. If there's a deal I suspect all that'll happen is that Carla and I just die rich. That is, unless this young beauty wants to run away with me in anticipation of me becoming very wealthy."

Peter had a lot of his mother in him. "Twenty per cent is tight. How would you feel, as a principle, to agreeing that if, and I do say if, we get consent, you include in that deal an option for first refusal on the farmhouse. That's only first refusal to match any open market price you get offered as and when you and Carla retire, or you or Carla just want to sell. How about that?"

José thought this time. For a poorly educated man, he thought well. "To you, with development, the farmhouse must be worth more. I'd agree 20 per cent and an option for first refusal at any offered open market price, plus five per cent. Meribel, my beauty. Tell your two accomplices that's final."

Meribel realised she now had a part to play again and turned to Marco and Peter. "I think this gentleman said that's final."

"If I accept, subject to the lawyers putting a contract in place after a family handshake," said Peter, "do we get to seal it with some of that wine I understand you've got hidden away?"

"Yes. But only up to two bottles."

"Three, if we need a third," Peter added tantalisingly.

"If you're like this, young man, with flesh and blood, what are you like with those outside the family?"

"I'd go for 100 per cent and all the wine stock," Peter laughed. "But I'd divide it amongst the relatives."

Cousin José stood up. "I'll seal that deal with a handshake from both of you, Marco and Peter, and a kiss on each cheek from Cleopatra."

"Done," said Peter, who stood up and shook José's hand. Marco followed suit. Meribel remained seated.

José said, "Come on, my dear, a kiss on each cheek."

Meribel looked up unmoved. "This lady didn't agree terms, she wasn't asked to agree terms and won't agree to those terms. It's a one per cent share for each kiss."

The three men looked amazed. José thought: *is she serious?*

Marco was thinking: *how can she be serious?*

Peter thought she might be half-serious.

The three looked on in silence. Meribel broke that silence.

"Look," she said, "the impression I have is that the Martinez family don't give their females enough say in family matters. You all presume women will agree with their menfolk. But we're in the mid-20th century. The world's gradually giving us more rights. Yet all it needed was for me to be asked for a kiss on each cheek and, providing I acquiesced, to be thanked for that, and for it to be accepted as the deal clincher."

José said, with some embarrassment, "You're right. My humble apologies. Would you seal the deal? But we can't afford two per cent." She stood up, leant forward and said, "By all means."

"What the hell are you up to, old man?" Carla walked in and screeched. "I came to see if you'd all like coffee and here I find my wayward husband embracing a child young enough to be his grand-daughter. Won't you ever stop looking for a replacement?"

Peter stepped forward. "Now listen, we're just celebrating a deal that will give you enough money in your retirement to surround yourself with young men. I was just coming to get you to beg a kiss on both cheeks from the remaining member of the family."

He leant forward and Carla wilted, raising each cheek in turn. He whispered, "… And I thought I'd try and book first place…"

She slapped his shoulder. "You're a cheeky one! You're a real Paco son!"

They drank the three bottles of wine as an aperitif and continued it over lunch, which Carla had prepared in advance of their visit. Salads, a good leg of beef, crème caramel and lots of coffee, with a few brandies for Marco and José. Peter was driving.

They left at three. Peter drove 300 metres through the fields of the farm parallel to the sea. He slowed and stopped. "All this," he said, turning to smile at Marco, "for 20 per cent."

Marco stretched his hand across. "My son, you did well."

Meribel interrupted from the back. "Did well? On the way here you'd decided to go up to 30 per cent, hadn't you?"

Peter turned towards the back seat. "Meribel, my sweet, your thighs got us ten per cent off and I'd cut you in on a deal if I didn't think you'd learnt the lesson of a lifetime for free."

"What lesson's that?" she asked.

"That with a body like that you could get yourself an empire. But if you decide to work for a living and do become a doctor, remember to be flexible. Things and moods change."

"True," she said, "you can't learn that from a book. You're right. Thank you. Oh, and about that empire. I'll get that whether I'm a doctor or not, with this body." And she wiggled like he really liked her to wiggle.

The three laughed and began the drive back. At about the halfway point, Meribel suddenly said, "About the odds of success – are they really 50/50?"

Peter addressed her question through the rear-view mirror. "Good God, no!"

"What, worse?"

"No, I'd rate the chances as 100 per cent in favour."

She was stunned. "A hundred per cent!"

"Yes, sure."

"Wow, how?"

"I'm good. Watch me do it."

They continued the journey in silence.

Peter dropped Marco off at the hotel before he and Meribel headed for the beach. There he explained about the previous night in fine detail. Meribel said she understood and believed every part of the story and agreed to play her part in helping Michelle. They stayed on the beach and watched the sun go down in silence. Peter seemed spent and elsewhere in his thoughts.

Meribel wondered whether to suggest going to a lane in his mother's car, but rejected the idea. She'd not seen him quite like this before. He was distant.

Peter got back at about 9.30pm and found Maria socialising with a few guests. He was keen to know how things had gone. In fact, Maria had got on fine with Michelle. After Peter had left, they'd sat down and had a coffee together.

Maria had taken the plunge. "When did you first take drugs?"

Michelle explained she'd been going through a lack of confidence phase. She had felt unwanted at 16. True, she was certainly wanted by all the guys she knew. They wanted to grope just about every part of her developing body, but as soon as they'd had their experience, it was back to football or rugby or cycling, whichever was their male pursuit. None ever said, "Thank you," or stayed around to see if she was alright. None just wanted to talk or hold hands.

Her parents, and especially her father, weren't interested in teams of one only, as she had already explained. They saw their children as a team of three. None were individuals. None had personal differences or problems. Hence Guy's nascent homosexuality and drug use went unnoticed. The Parmentiers saw Philippe as representative of how the team was performing and, because Michelle seemed popular and in demand, she was presumed to be alright and did not need attention.

She had trouble with her studies too. Despite not being naturally academic, she was expected to attain high results. So it was not, perhaps, surprising that she had turned to something else for comfort.

It was Guy who introduced her to drugs, in fact, by way of blackmail. Michelle had got home early from school one day when both her parents were out, and had slipped into the kitchen to get a glass of water.

Guy's jacket was on the back of a chair and there were two glasses on the kitchen table. *Good,* she thought, *Guy's home.* She hated an empty house. She wondered which of his friends he'd bought home with him. He'd be nice. All Guy's friends were. He'd be interesting, too. She might even be able to sponge a cigarette off him as a number of Guy's friends smoked.

Upstairs, seeing the door to Guy's room shut, she thought nothing of opening the door and walking in. It was that kind of family. She'd come across Philippe once before playing with himself, but found that quite natural. She'd just laughed and said if he wasn't careful he'd go blind.

This time, however, it was quite different. It was totally unnatural to find Guy and whoever it was, but very male in any case, curled up together on the bed, stark naked. Michelle was shocked in the first instance, and disgusted in the second. She just closed the door and left, but not before Guy had seen her.

Michelle had run to her room. Being the female sibling, she was allowed a lock on her door. She'd turned the key and thrown herself onto her bed in tears.

Minutes but not many minutes later, there was a knock on the door. She was too repulsed to even acknowledge it. Doubtless Guy would be full of his clever explanations. He'd always talked himself out of difficult situations and, it now seemed, into them as well.

Michelle was finding it hard to come to terms with the situation. She had arrived home in a low state anyway, and the scene in Guy's room was the final blow. She took a shower. To make matters worse, she had that tell-tale ache in the pit of her stomach. She'd be 'off games', as the girls at school called their cycles, by the morning.

She threw on a pair of tracksuit bottoms and a T-shirt, put her hair up in a bun and went downstairs. Her stomach turned with envy as she picked up the cigarette smoke in the air. There was a lightness in it, though, she had not known before.

Coffee, she thought as she went into the kitchen. The sight of Guy and his friend stopped her in her tracks, especially as at first glance this stranger to their home, this intruder in her life, their family's life, was, to say the least, majestically beautiful.

If it was a TV quiz game where she had to recognise and remember as many things as she could in a ten second glance, she would have done well.

She was meticulous in her appraisal. Partly from the hatred she felt, but also because of a powerful attraction. She told herself she must not be interested, this was an animal in her midst. She took in the jet-black shining hair, wavy from the right-hand parting; the curls at the nape of the neck. His forehead was smooth and tanned with shaped eyebrows most girls would have given their eye-teeth for. He had piercing blue-green eyes with bone china whites. His nose was sculptured, strong and full of purpose. The gleaming white teeth were framed by sensuous Mediterranean lips and the smile, which exuded power and friendship, created a dimple in his lightly bearded chin. His neck was strong and tapered into an open collared white shirt.

Michelle had always considered Guy attractive and as kids they had joked about both he and Philippe marrying beautiful princesses, who would introduce her to their crown prince brother for the 'happily ever after' bit. So there was no disappointment in the beauty that this incumbent brought with him. It was just a gender problem.

They both stood as she entered the room. Guy broke the silence. "This is my princess sister Michelle. Michelle, this is Michael, actually Mike."

Mike was a singularly appropriate name for such masculinity, she thought. He held out his hand, smooth and immaculately manicured. It was welcoming, strong and, so it seemed to her, supportive.

She hesitated and then put her right hand into his. "Well, Mike, I can't say I'm not a bit shocked. But maybe it was my fault. I invaded Guy's privacy. I suppose I ought to say something like, any friend of Guy's is a friend of mine, but I had no idea, well I suppose I've got to say it… I had no idea Guy was queer. I suppose you don't happen to have a cigarette, do you?"

Guy intervened as Mike withdrew his hand. He looked at Mike with a deep, quizzical stare. "Perhaps Michelle ought to have a treat."

"Treat?" said Michelle.

"Here, you'll learn to love us both too."

Guy passed her a roll up. Her first step on a dangerous road she now dearly wanted to get off.

Maria had been listening intently. "Wow, so that's how it started."

"Well, actually from then on it was blackmail really. Guy said my parents and Philippe, in particular, weren't ready to learn about his sexuality and that he preferred I kept their secret."

Michelle had said the family should know, whereupon Guy became bitter and said if they were to know that, then they should also know about her smoking pot. And so it began.

"We'll go and see Miguel Mendes this afternoon. You go to the pool. I'll be around. You'll be OK?"

"Yes, I know I'll be fine now."

She got up and walked round the table, leant forward and kissed Maria on the cheek. "Thank you, Mrs Martinez."

"It's Maria."

"Thank you, Maria."

CHAPTER 15

As Guy was coming out of his 'happy' state from the night before, Philippe was pretending not to recognise Tasha across the pool, even though they'd had their own natural happy hours the night into the morning before, unbeknown to her parents. When Michelle was on the way to see Miguel Mendes with Maria, the Admiral was organising the final touches of his great 'jeux sans frontières'. It was strange, really, that someone so hell-bent on team activities could not see the inside track on his own family *équipe*. Still, as he used to say, "It takes all types to make the world go round." He was certainly one of them, as were his offspring.

He'd picked three team captains. Philippe was his first choice, Georgio Jnr his second and Tony Fletcher, an English university student staying at the hotel, the third.

The intention was that the major focus would be around the pool. He had organised three lilo rafts which each of them would treat as a boat. They'd elect one team member under the age of ten to paddle two lengths, one between ten and 15, then 15 to 21 and the final two lengths out of eight would be paddled by a team member over 21. The Admiral had imported in his luggage floating lemons, which he'd throw into the pool like ducks at a fairground sideshow, not to be collected on a hook at the end of a bamboo pole, but by hand. Points out of 40 would be awarded for the number of lemons collected from the water in each age group within a timed minute.

A grand tennis tournament was organised for singles, doubles and mixed doubles and then the crowning glory was a select four-person older generation game of boules, which the Admiral fully expected the French to win.

"What a pain," Geoffrey Brown said to Sonya when they'd first heard the great event was to be held on their first Friday. But since he had been put in the same team as Marcia and, not surprisingly, in the over 21 group, he was becoming quite keen and competitive about the whole thing.

Bob Hunt had expressed the opinion that it was all an intrusion on their privacy and a typically childish French exercise to exploit their own competitive instincts and abilities. "Boules, fucking boules!" he cursed. "Who's going to play that stupid game other than the frogs themselves!"

Marcia didn't agree. She'd learn the game just for the fun of it.

"Then you'll dress the part," Bob ruled. "I don't want all those friggin' Frenchmen ogling down your blouse."

"Bob, don't be so narrow, they can ogle me at the pool all day long."

"I know, and they do. But I'm not having them make up their own party games and using your boobs to break the sheer boredom of chucking a few pounds of lead a couple of yards down a sand patch."

"What about the tennis?"

"What *about* the tennis?"

"Well, if what you say is right, then the ladies' doubles will have a huge audience."

"Are you playing in this berk's tennis extravaganza too?"

"Yup."

"I reckon you still have a hankering to show your body off to the world."

"Maybe I do. It seems it's not getting appreciated by this one-man audience."

"Now that's not fair. You know it bloody is."

"Then maybe it'll be appreciated all the more when you know all the frogs are after it."

"Well, we'll just have to see, won't we!"

Marcia put Bob's edginess down to his diabetes. He'd been seeing a new consultant in the UK who was trying to convince him to inject insulin and cut down on alcohol. Neither idea found favour with Bob. He was, and was always likely to be, his own master. Marcia had been told by his close friends that that was the downfall in his first marriage.

Marcia struggled with that too but had to come to terms with it. And if the loving side of their relationship had not outlived the infatuation, then at least the security she had gained outweighed the loss of the intrigue that had characterised their first three or four weeks together. After all, she had never had anything other than the shortest term relationships, it seemed, even with her parents. So, that element of life was hardly missed. She'd never ever had any financial security beyond the day after pay day, so to be able not to worry about spending money, whether at Marks and Spencer or Harrods, was a real luxury. The greater bonus was that she could change environments and climates without relying on her agent, or the demands of public acclaim for the Bluebell Troupe. Bob's mood swings were tolerable and his jealousy was something of a compliment.

Bob had started their relationship by being attentive and that aspect had stayed. So, on balance, she was pleased to be Mrs Hunt. But she would play boules and if her boobs did roll around a bit, that was a necessary part of the game. Likewise, she'd play tennis as a compliment to the time and effort Peter had invested in her. She'd been asked to pair with Michelle, so there was another challenge. They would certainly have the prime audience and she needed to believe it was Marcia Hunt, on stage, the crowds would be paying to see.

Despite being under the eagle eye of Maria, who was keeping her under surveillance as she had promised Peter, Michelle had warned her father, when she saw him fleetingly at the pool on the Thursday, "I might just not be up to the tennis, Papa."

He said, "Don't be a child! Of course you will be." That would have been that ordinarily, but on this occasion he added, "Why on earth's that?" Why should any of his kids not be willing or able to perform at peak in their respective sports, as he'd trained them?

He'd given up on Guy, but at least he was still an excellent skier and had yet to lose any amateur event.

Philippe, on the other hand, floated from sport to sport as his mood took him. He'd lost some of his athleticism since discovering girls. The Admiral had often thought that if there was a sex Olympics, Philippe would take a lot of beating. He and his wife often discussed Guy's lack of interest in girls, concluding that it must be because of his involvement in academia. If the kids had taken on their mother's genes, they might have turned out to be relatively unathletic, but dextrous in front of the keys of a till. Her main attraction for the Admiral had been her retail management ability. He would have stocked every brand of sports gear in their shop, had it been left to him, but his wife had suggested they offer sole dealerships with a handful of the major suppliers in exchange for better trading terms. Dunlop had been an obvious choice as, apart from tennis equipment, they did a strong line in golf gear. Their sports plimsolls were still the best and, of course, they had major advertising programmes centred around their motor sports activities.

Adidas were coming along and Fred Perry had already established their mark, but without Madame Parmentier, the Admiral would have been lost. Stock control before she came on the scene was a number of unopened boxes delivered and opened 'on demand'. She had advocated putting all the stock within the shop sales area, which meant a huge saving in time.

'Eiffel Sports', as they had rather unimaginatively called the shop, developed their brand and they opened four shops within the first four years of their marriage.

Carmel Parmentier had only taken four months off to care for each of their children as they came along. The kids had known au pairs better than their mother on all days except Sunday. That day, their father took over. Most Sabbaths were full-on training days as he developed each of their natural attributes.

The Admiral had not, however, left a slot in his agenda for helping Michelle through her current problem, or diverting Guy away from his path in life, which had caught Michelle up in his complex and dangerous web.

Maria picked Michelle up in the foyer at four, as planned, and drove her into Palafrugell. They chatted like sisters, or as natural mothers might chat with their daughters. Maria described Miguel as a 'lovely man', and told Michelle a little about his interest in both traditional and more alternative medical remedies.

Maria had no doubt that he would be able to help Michelle, who took to him instantly. Miguel's kind eyes shone above his crisp white tunic. His hands were soft yet strong to the touch, his voice was calming and his manner confident.

"So, let's see what we can do to help, Michelle," he said kindly. "Do you want to come off the weed?"

"Yes I do. It hurts me too much."

"Then if you want to be cured, and I want to help, and Maria encourages us to achieve what we set out to do, I've no doubt whatsoever that you're as good as cleared. But go backwards, cheat, and break my rules, then you're by yourself. OK with you?"

Michelle had no doubt. She smelt the scent of success already.

"Yes! Alright with me. I'd appreciate your help."

"Great, let's get on."

Miguel had told his assistant not to disturb him. She wouldn't. She'd broken that rule once and got such a dressing down that she would never do it again.

He first took Michelle's blood pressure. "How anxious do you feel?"

"Very."

"OK, so that accounts for the BP being up a bit. That'll go down."

He asked what dope she was taking and at what frequency. How she felt under the influence and as it wore off. Whether she smoked. If she had a regular boyfriend and, most particularly, who she turned to for support. She told him.

"Is Philippe a previous boyfriend then, or just an old friend?"

Michelle laughed. "No, he's the younger of my two brothers."

"Does he know about your habit?"

"Yes."

"Does he have a view on it?"

"Well, he's never said too much. He's got used to our elder brother. He's well hooked."

"How do you view him being 'well hooked'?"

"It's up to him."

"Do you think he'd like help?"

"I don't really know. He's got another problem. He's homosexual!"

"There's not much wrong with that. Does the tendency run through the family?"

Michelle's back went up. "No, it bloody doesn't!" she said with some feeling.

"Great," Miguel said with some relief. "We've been talking ten minutes and I don't think you realise the understanding we've developed. Let me show you." He reached for the blood pressure reading machine. He wrapped the inflating band round her beautiful upper arm. He leant forward and brushed a furrow on her brow with the back of his hand.

"Relax, Michelle."

The words were soft. She watched his friendly lips curve around the instructions. Maria watched too, in something of a trance. He was magnetic. Calm, in control. A friend prepared to help.

He pumped up the sleeve and placed his forefinger over the pulse on her wrist, firming the hold by pressure from his thumb placed under her frail left wrist.

"It's 130 over 75, with a pulse of 60. That's very healthy. Well done."

"Why do you say well done?" Michelle asked. "I haven't done anything."

"Yes you have. You got het up over some of my questions, even angry when I suggested homosexuality might run in your family."

"I wondered if you wanted me to be that way inclined. Do you mind if I ask you, are you gay?"

Maria's eyes shot across to Miguel's face. She'd never even contemplated that possibility. To her he was the epitome of masculinity in looks, stature and humour. She'd have hopped into bed with him without question, if not for José.

"That's a fair question. But no! Categorically, I love the female form too much. On the other hand, I don't condemn homosexuality. If it's good for them then there's no way I have a view on it. I tell you what too, they're good for business. They're into condoms and creams and a few other little pharmaceutical supplies, which is more than you can say for your devout courting or married Spanish couples.

"Anyway, enough of sex, we're here to sort out our other little problem.

You'll have to remember I'm not a doctor or a specialist in drug rehab, but I'd say you can save yourself, at the stage you're at."

What a kind way of putting it, Maria thought. He was not going to take any credit for the help he was proposing to give her.

He then gave a lecture on herbal replacement therapy, psychology, the more updated version of healthy bodies and healthy minds, comfortable sexual expression and finding a focus for the patient beyond herself, preferably somebody with more need than Michelle herself. Guy would be ideal subject matter, or children, a focus subject unable to care or cope for themselves. Miguel recommended cutting out smoking totally. Either hypnotherapy or acupuncture would be in the programme. Probably yoga.

Michelle wanted to get on with it straight away, but hesitated with an obvious question on her tongue. "You're a good salesman, Miguel, but how long would you need with me if you agreed to provide all, some, or most of that treatment?"

"Would I be able to trust your resolve, when you're out of the initial phase, to say no to any opportunity or impulse?"

"I hope so. I think so."

"Then let's say a month."

"I've only got just over two weeks left down here with my parents."

Miguel pondered the problem. "And what's waiting for you back in Paris?"

"Well I'm about five weeks away from university. I'm due to start a degree in sports education."

"That sounds like the healthy body and mind bit," Miguel said advisedly.

Maria had simply been witnessing this whole exchange between Michelle and Miguel, but now she spoke up. "Supposing I were to say I'd have a job for you for a couple of weeks to extend your holiday, and you could go back to Paris a fortnight or so after your parents?"

"Then without even knowing what the job was, I'd jump at it." Maria turned to Miguel. "So that's settled. Could you accomplish the end product in five weeks?"

"If the patient promises to be self-disciplined, no problem." Miguel turned to Maria. "There *is* a practical side to this, however. In an ideal situation I'd like to see Michelle daily for the first ten days, maybe two weeks. The other aspect is that, while I'm seeing you during the day, when the pharmacy's open, my time will be paid for by my friendship with Maria, but I'll need to charge for some of the herbal medicines and a couple of other treatments I'm not qualified to carry out. Do you have any way of paying for those?"

"I'll ask my father for some pocket money, I'll say it's for drugs!" They all laughed as the tension lifted more and more.

"So, Michelle. When do we start?"

"When's the earliest?"

"Can you get back here in about two hours? Just as I'm closing perhaps. I need to make up a couple of concoctions."

Maria smiled. "Isn't there a queue round about closing time nowadays, then?"

"Yes there is. But the boys all like being served by my young female assistant these days. They don't believe me when I say the products are ultra-sensitive, but if she tells them they somehow believe it's said from experience. So they're happy, she feels good and I'm happy too. But they come back for more, so obviously all parties are satisfied."

"So is the interview and interrogation all over?"

"I guess so, I've got a pharmacy to run."

"I can't begin to thank you enough," Michelle said, relief in her voice.

"Tell you what," Miguel said, as though he was about to promise a child a toy if they behaved well on a visit to an aunt nobody liked.

"What's that?"

"We'll have four to five memorable weeks with ups and downs. After that we'll stay in touch, but if ever I get to hear you've hit the drugs again, I'll move heaven and earth to come and find you, and when I do, I'll put you across my knee and spank you so hard you'll hardly ever be able to sit down again."

"Is that a promise?"

"Yes."

"OK, that sounds too nice to miss. I'll skip the drug bit, but I'll be in Le Meridien in Paris, say in eight weeks' time. We'll fix the exact date and time nearer to the day."

Michelle smiled an expansive smile and stood firm in front of Miguel's desk. She leant across, allowing him the pleasure of a breathtaking tour of her upper body, previously shielded by her loose fitting blouse. He was suddenly aware of her beautifully soft left cheek brushing his and then the warmth of her breath as she moved to press her right cheek against his.

She held his hand. "Thank you for saying you'll save me." Then she turned to Maria and took her hand too. "… and to you, beautiful mother to a wonderful young man, thank you too."

They held hands for seconds that none of them wanted to count. It was as if a bond had been formed between them.

Michelle broke the silence. "I'm so relieved, I need to have a pee."

Miguel said, "Do feel at home. It's back into the shop and across to the left."

Michelle left Maria and Miguel. They looked across the desk.

"Thank you so much. You dealt with that beautifully," smiled Maria. "I think she'll do it, don't you?"

"Yes, I'd say so. I'm not sure I could survive the Paris trip though… Listen, I need to be quick. It's about you."

"Me? Hey! We're here for Michelle."

"I hope you won't be very cross with me?"

"Try me. You're in my very good books at the moment. I doubt you can do or say anything wrong," she said encouragingly.

"OK. Here I go. I'll take the plunge. Do you think it's possible you could be pregnant?"

Maria positively blanched. "Miguel! That's outrageous! That's my privacy you're talking about." She leant her head forward and put one hand over her eyes to shield the tears she felt welling.

Miguel walked round to Maria's side of the desk and placed both his strong, kind hands on her shoulders, the thumbs inserting gentle pressure onto the base of her neck.

"Look. You're right. It's an intrusion on your privacy. Unfortunately, God gave me a few talents I'd rather not have. One of those makes me sense pregnancy even more keenly than a toad injected with urine from an expectant mother. So call me a toad but, if you were pregnant, and maybe didn't want to be, I'd say it's just a glint in your eye and at this stage, if you'd come to see me for advice, there's a couple of herbs that can put a woman back onto her cycle without her really knowing anything about it. Perhaps just a few hours' rest during an abnormally heavy period. But forget I intruded."

As he said that, Michelle came back into the room. "Come on, Maria. We've got a couple of hours to waste. I'll start by buying you a coffee. Where's that girls' shop you were telling me about? Let's get you that new costume to show off in front of the Hunt woman at Sunday's sea adventure."

Maria stood, hardly able to feel her legs. They'd turned to jelly. "Let's go," she said, hardly giving Miguel a glance as she turned towards the door.

"We'll see you just before six," Michelle said to Miguel lightly.

As they left, Michelle linked her arms through Maria's. "Maybe we'll have a glass of wine rather than a coffee."

"Good idea," Maria replied.

They sipped their white wine with little conversation.

"Shall we look for a costume for you?" Michelle asked.

"I'm not sure I'm in the mood."

"Oh, come on. You've got to look good alongside Marcia the Hunt. José'll want you to. Come on, let's be positive. At this time of the year they may have a sale on there, show me where the shop is. I need something cheerful to wear too."

Twenty minutes' drive away, they reached Mercedes's shop. The bell over the door clanged as Michelle charged in excitedly.

Mercedes appeared from the rear stock room. "Good afternoon, Madam," she responded to Michelle's grand entrance, and then: "Oh! Mrs Martinez. How have you been? How's that husband of yours, still liking the bikini? Is the hotel doing well? When…"

"Hold on, Mercedes. It's 'fine' to the first one. Very well thanks, he's fine. To the third," looking sheepishly at Michelle, "the hotel's doing very well. Michelle here is staying with us at the moment and is probably going to do a couple of weeks' student experience with us. Anyway, how are you?"

"I'm really well."

"Have you had a good season?"

"Yes. Very good thank you. Fashions have changed so much that everybody is having to buy new this season. Now," Mercedes continued, "are you looking for something special? Are you, hopefully, both looking?"

Maria was first to answer. "I've got a hankering for a black one-piece."

"Oh, Maria, don't go backwards. You look super in a bikini."

"I've put on a little weight… you know, eating irregularly and drinking a little more with the guests."

"OK, I think I've got just the thing. What about Michelle?"

"I'd like a cheerful, skimpy bikini that makes heads turn."

"We don't have anything like that. We've got lots of cheerful little bikinis but it's the body they dress that makes the heads turn. If I'm any judge, you've got one of those. So let's see how we get on. We'll use both the dressing rooms."

Black one piece in the left. Cheerful skimps on the right… and if you step out and the shop fills with young men, I'd prefer you pay quickly and do your head turning elsewhere. We don't want to get the wrong reputation," Mercedes said, laughing.

Maria went into the left hand cubicle. She slipped out of her dress and glimpsed herself in the mirror. Her breasts were fuller. Her normally flat stomach wasn't. It had a distinct bulge. She realised Miguel had been right. She'd had her suspicions but wasn't prepared to contemplate the truth. José would be furious. It wouldn't be fair to wreck his already damaged life. It was hard enough bringing up one growing lad alone, without forcing a step-mother and baby onto the scene.

Nor would it be fair on Pedro and Marco to turn their worlds into some great crèche, expecting the men and Virginia to take turns while Maria couldn't function in her managerial role. She hadn't been sure if, when she had been sick in the morning, it was the paella Virginia had heated up from the hotel kitchen the night before. Now she knew.

When had it happened? Maybe when she and José had made love on the lilo in the pool changing room on the hotel's 'open night'. After all, she wouldn't have expected José to turn up with a condom and a party pack to that. In fact she would have been disappointed if he did start carrying them 'just in case'. 'Just in case' might encourage him to look at all sorts of other girls. She wouldn't like that.

"How's it looking?" came Mercedes's voice from the other side of the louvered changing room door.

"Just slipping into it," came Maria's hurried reply, as she stepped out of her underclothes and her daydream. She'd go and see Miguel on Monday and get some herbal treatments. She was off on Tuesday, so it wouldn't be noticeable if she rested a lot.

The black one-piece looked good. She felt a bit dumpy, but slipped on her heels, which lifted everything by a couple of inches.

Mercedes exclaimed, "Great!" which was endorsed by a "Merveilleuse!" from Michelle, who followed Maria out of her right-hand changing room. Maria turned to look at her.

"Wow, that's fantastic!"

Michelle was wearing the skimpiest white bikini, just about covering the essential parts of her lightly tanned, exceedingly slim body. There was a hint of a pattern of sunflower petals, which at a distance could look like polka dots. At the top of the panties was a band of sunflower orange, which was picked up in the colour of the string thin straps.

"That won't turn heads," Mercedes said excitedly, "it'll outright break a few guys' necks when they do their double take!

"Michelle, I know Maria's already booked you for a couple of weeks of student work experience. But my assistant's away on holiday in a week's time. If you have any time spare, give me a shout, particularly in the late afternoons. We get a number of husbands come in here when they finish at the conference centre conventions held through the summer. They buy saucy undies for their wives, but we often think they're really for their secretaries or girlfriends, and I'm sure they'd love to see them modelled. I'd pay 1,000 pesetas an hour, plus ten per cent commission on any sales you make, which I'm sure will be plenty, with a figure like yours."

Maria said, "That sounds tempting, Michelle. Keep an open mind. We'll see how things can be arranged. Now I'm feeling a bit like the ugly sister!" Turning to Mercedes, she said, "I'll take this one. Is there a wrap to go with it? Michelle, you go and get some clothes on, I'm worried one of those wayward husbands might come in and buy you, and the bikini. It does look terrific." She looked at her watch. "God, we've got to get back to Miguel's."

Mercedes's ears visibly flapped. "Which Miguel? Not Miguel Mendes, by any chance?"

"Why do you ask that?" Maria asked.

"Oh, I tend to think there's only one Miguel and he's in Palafrugell. Well, he's really the only Miguel in the world, actually. He's a genius. He's kept my body and mind together for, oh well… more than a couple of years now. Since he opened up. There's nothing that man hasn't done successfully. Is it Miguel Mendes?"

"Actually, yes. I've been suffering from migraines and he's gradually putting it right. Michelle's just along for the ride. I said I was popping in here after and she, as you can see, was tempted to come along."

They left with their respective parcels. As they walked back towards the pharmacy, Michelle thanked Maria for not letting Mercedes know it was she who was being treated.

"Mercedes is a lovely person, but I wouldn't trust her imagination not to get the better of her. Miguel's very professional. You'd never even discover who his other clients are unless you happened to bump into them there. He even has gaps of a few minutes between any medical appointments, to save patients passing in the shop."

Michelle went in to see Miguel alone to pick up the various prescriptions. She had taken a first dose of some liquid in Miguel's presence, which she said tasted terrible. "He said tennis tomorrow would be good therapy for me and he's given me some vitamins. He says coming off the weed will take nutrients out of my body. I might even lose weight, which I really don't mind at this time of the year, especially if I'm out looking for a regular boyfriend with a steady supply of good sex, both of which he's prescribed."

They left the pharmacy together. Minutes down the road, Maria stopped. "I meant to give Miguel a message from Virginia. You stop here, I'll pop back. I'll only be a minute. Don't get picked up, though, before I'm back." Maria entered the shop. The assistant said hello and could she help. "I need a quick word with Mr Mendes please. I'll only keep him a minute."

The assistant knocked and went into the consulting room. She returned quickly. "OK, please go through."

Maria entered as Miguel got up from behind his desk.

"You're a toad," she said, "but a decent, honest toad. If I pop in on Monday can you sort me out your special herbal package?"

Miguel kept walking and stopped immediately in front of her. He looked deeply into Maria's eyes, put both his arms around her and held her too close for both their comfort. She felt herself tremble.

"Am I forgiven for intruding?"

"Of course, I'll never not forgive you, and before you ask, that's a promise."

"Then I'm OK. Look, I've already made this potion up, you're to take 100ml before you go to bed on Sunday. The same on Monday night and then 50ml on Tuesday morning and again at lunch-time. Don't worry, you'll just have a very heavy period for the first 12-15 hours. Rest through that and then just treat everything as normal. Would you phone me late on Tuesday afternoon? Just to tell me you're OK."

"How much is this?" she asked, now stepping out of his arms.

"Oh, it's a present. It's just natural herbs I collect from the fields or mountains. Oh! And it was my idea anyway. You must catch up with Michelle. Take care. Good luck. Speak to me Tuesday. I'll be thinking of you."

The two contented women headed back to base. Both with their respective secrets from the world.

CHAPTER 16

The Admiral was awake at 6am. It was just light. This was to be his working day, and how much pleasure he would give everybody was his great motivation.

He'd planned that the competition proper would start at 11am, but there was free practice between 10am and 11am. He 'required' the team captains for a briefing at 9.45am and had threatened Philippe with his life if he was late. In fact his wife knew better than to allow the Admiral's blood pressure to rise unnecessarily, so her plan was to wake Philippe at 8.45am and get some breakfast into him to help him surface.

The Admiral had seen Michelle the night before and she'd reported fit for the tennis. He had reflected that he wasn't sure about the combination of his lovely young daughter and the ogle-attracting star of the hotel, that 'English tramp Marcia', as he had named her. Philippe had said this was unfair. Marcia was a very beautiful young woman, far too good for the old man who had obviously wooed her with his money. But she was no tramp. If his father wanted to see one of those, he should drive round the streets of the Paris suburbs at night.

"At times, my son, you are outrageous. My opinion is that anyone who marries for money is of a very common status."

"Excluding my dear mother, I suppose."

That really made the Admiral snap.

"Your dear mother and I did not marry because I had money!"

"True," Philippe said, baiting his father, "she's so intelligent that she realised you didn't know whether you had any money or not, worked out you'd got more money than balls, probably proposed to you, and since has created your mini fortune."

"Outrageous!" the Admiral raged.

At that point Philippe's mother appeared. "Mother," Philippe postured, "we're having a family discussion as to whether you married father for his money or his balls."

"Philippe! You're dreadful, where do you get such conversation from?"

The Admiral, normally short on humour, felt vindicated and smiled victory over his middle son.

"Anyway," Carmel Parmentier continued, "the answer is both. It was his money first, then his balls... that's his Slazenger tennis ones, Dunlop 65s, squash ones, football and rugby, hockey, table-tennis... none of them were instant cash, but with the right stock control and encouragement I knew I could turn them into money... so to resolve this family discussion and to prove what a wicked mischievous son you are... we married for both money and balls, and with sufficient love to bring up two loving children, and a third who's really very, very outrageous but," kissing Philippe lightly on the forehead, "very beautiful and a dear to us in his own way."

Philippe and his mother both roared with laughter. The Admiral sat in stony silence, his feelings far too hurt to allow even a hint of a smile.

As the Admiral continued to stew, he thought through the agenda for the day again. He'd invested in a new pair of Fred Perry long tennis trousers, end of the range, and an Adidas top, which he had said he would have laundered after the event and put in the autumn sale. That way it would cost the shop nothing. The money he had saved overall on the use of stock from their shop, he had put towards lollies for all competing children under the age of ten. He'd bought various gifts from the shelves of the sports shop chain for the older kids, and some bottles of French plonk for the adults. (The Spanish equivalent would have been undrinkable, according to his expert French palate.)

"Merde!" he suddenly exploded, as he nicked his chin with his Gillette three-piece razor. He could never work out which was the better route to take when he had things on his mind: to use an older blade and not get a close shave, or a new one, and risk cutting himself. He'd chosen the latter option today and the blood trickling down his chin was the penalty.

He no longer had to stick a cigarette paper over such an open wound. He'd managed to get a styptic block from his barber which, in theory, he just had to apply to the cut, under pressure, and it would stop. Usually it did, but for half an hour or so there would be a white chalk patch around the offending sear. He'd need to remember to wipe it off with a damp cloth. He didn't want the risk of dropping blood onto his borrowed top. So he'd be careful not to open up the wound a second time.

He appeared back in the bedroom from the en suite bathroom, took his neatly pressed slacks out of the wardrobe, and put on his Adidas top and Dunlop plimsolls, which he had whitened with Blanco before leaving Paris.

"Where's the whistle?" he said, rummaging through one of his sports travel boxes.

"I've seen it somewhere," came the wifely reply. "I know you brought it with you, because I've seen it. Try the drawer in the unit."

"Great." The Admiral put the gleaming chrome whistle into his mouth, unable to resist blowing it gently.

Mrs 'Admiral' got out of bed. She was a couple of dress sizes up on when they had married. Three kids in five years is a lot for any body to take.

She, too, had set aside white gear to wear. She had 'borrowed' a below-the-knee skirt, a matching Adidas top, similar white blancoed plimsolls with green Dunlop all weather soles, but she'd need a hat, she thought, sitting in the sun keeping the scores up to date. Although she'd be under an umbrella she would need to go out into the sun to alter the blackboard, to keep everything up to date.

As she went into the bathroom the Admiral commanded, "Don't be too long, I want to make sure you understand the scoring. We must check that out before breakfast."

Quite why, she didn't understand. There were three teams. It was to be three points for the team winning an event, two for being second and a single point for third. In the unlikely event of a draw, teams first and second would get 2.5 points each, which again didn't need an Einstein to understand. As she showered, she smiled to herself. *It's his day. He so loves to organise,* she thought.

His hope, one day, was to assist the French teams in the Olympics. When Guy showed little interest in sport and Philippe had burnt himself out staying up late with girls, his focus had been on Michelle. She had the slim build and flowing hair that would suit a long-distance runner, but in club competitions she'd always been beaten by coloured girls from North Africa. Tennis they all knew she was good at, but not good enough to play beyond a reasonable club standard. Her best chance was always to play mixed doubles. That way the opposing team would be wrenched apart by, on the one hand, the opposing male not being able to take his eyes off her bouncing boobs, and on the other, the female partner trying to win back her male compatriot's attention to the game.

Overall, the early established training camps the Admiral had set up for the kids every Sunday had not produced the hoped-for results.

Carmel put on Ambre Solaire in the bathroom and appeared back in the bedroom, ready for the fray.

"Have you put on Ambre Solaire?" the Admiral asked. She thought he was being protective and caring, for a change.

"Yes, of course," she replied.

"Well that's bloody daft, isn't it. You know how it smells, and you can never wash that smell away. The chances are now that we won't be able to put the top in the sale."

"Look, I'll buy the top myself out of my inheritance." Both her parents had died in the previous three years leaving a part share in their modest estate between her and her brother. It wasn't a fortune, but it did give her some independence now and again. "But I'll want the full 30 per cent staff discount."

"We'll see how it washes when we get home."

Michelle and Philippe shared breakfast together in the garden. Maria had let Michelle have space, allowing her to sleep in her hotel room by herself. Miguel had said that the night medicine had a heavy herbal sedative in it and predicted that Michelle would have an undisturbed night with sweet dreams.

As she put her head on the pillow prior to going to sleep, she had thought back through the day. Her longlasting memory was the kindness in Miguel's face and the tenderness of his touch.

Her body informed her that it was ready for sleep. She turned onto her side, placing her right thumb into her mouth. She felt secure. She could sleep.

That's how she awoke the next morning. She was calm and rested. She'd been brought up being forced to pray by her parents. Today there was no pressure.

"Oh God, thank you, thank you for life. Thank you for Pedro, Maria, and my beautiful Miguel. Bless Mother and Father for their blindness and Guy particularly, please help him, and Philippe, and as for me, thank you for helping."

Marcia had her work cut out, because she was in the ladies' freestyle swimming in the morning, ladies' doubles tennis in the afternoon and, for some reason unbeknown to everybody, boules in the early evening.

Philippe had not been stupid in picking his team. At least he'd got the two most beautiful women in the hotel and he'd squeezed in Tasha, without her parents having a clue about their relationship.

Breakfast with team captain Philippe had been quiet to start with. He always took a bit of pulling around in the mornings. Over his scrambled eggs he suddenly questioned Michelle. "Where have you been for the last 24 hours? The last I saw of you was on the night we went to the disco. You vanished, but then Peter did as well, so we all imagined you went off by yourselves. It'd be one way of getting free tennis coaching. Bright thinking."

"We weren't 'off'. Peter took me under his wing. Saved me getting into the weed at the disco and finishing up with me being hurt by some over-sexed peddler. Then Maria Martinez came to the rescue and took me to this lovely doctor friend of hers, who's into rehab in a wonderful way. We saw him and now, believe it or not, I'm already under his magical spells and in his beautiful hands."

Philippe changed from being accusing to compassionate.

"Shit, Michelle, I'm so pleased for you. Will it work? What about Guy? Could he help him?"

"Maybe. But I'm not sure he's got the resolve. Perhaps we can have a word with him."

"Are you going to tell Mum and Dad?"

"God, no! That's the last thing I'd want them to know about. I'll stay on a couple of weeks extra. I've been offered two student work experience jobs… careful, here they are now."

"Morning, Captain," the Admiral addressed his son, then turned to Michelle. "Morning, beautiful *papillon*, are we all up for a good competition, guys? I hope you got some sleep last night, Philippe. You look bright-eyed, princess."

"Morning, kids," Mrs Admiral proffered, "are you having eggs, both of you? They're good for you. Try and get some banana too, there's potassium in that." So the ever-clucking mother carried on.

"Team talk at 9.45am, Philippe, then free practice."

As the Admiral continued, Natasha Cook's father appeared.

"Got some bad news, I'm afraid, my elder girl is going to have to scratch."

Philippe looked up. Scratch? She was OK when he slipped her over her balcony at 3am.

"That's sad," Philippe said, "I think she's in my team. She's something of a diver, I understand. Dare I ask what her problem is?"

"Don't know, old chap. Her sister came through this morning and said she just wasn't up to getting up and certainly not to compete in the Playa Olympics."

Philippe was concerned. He'd slip out to the lobby and phone Tasha in her room.

She answered the phone.

Philippe showed relief in his voice. "Hi! It's me."

"Hi, gorgeous!"

"What do you mean? How can you be so chirpy? You're meant to be ill. I was worried about you."

"… and so you should be."

"What's wrong?"

"Not too much."

"Oh come on, how much? I hear you can't compete today."

"That's right. It's because we competed last night!"

"Competed?"

"You'd think so if you could see my thighs."

"Thighs?"

"Too true."

"They're black and blue."

"Black and blue?"

"Yes, anyone would think you'd been making love to a trampoline."

"Oh my God!"

"Yes, where you got a bit physical virtually jumping up and down on me… and don't get me wrong, it was lovely… you bruised me from my knees virtually to my hips. So if I'd walked out onto the diving board, the whole hotel would have known what I'd been up to, especially my parents. They're with me all day. They haven't seen me fall over or anything, so the questions would be like the third degree. Give me a day or so in trousers and loads of Nivea and I'll be back to normal."

"Will you surface? Will I see you? I had thought at least if we were in the same team we could talk during the day. At least I've now spoken to your father."

"I'll recover quickly. Don't worry. But I just couldn't face walking the plank in front of all those inquisitive eyes. I'll see you by the pool and apologise for letting you down. Then we're talking in public."

Philippe returned to the breakfast table where Tasha's father was still talking to Michelle and his parents.

"I'm sorry to hear, sir, that your daughter's ill. I'll probably take the team out for a celebration this evening, I was going to ask you if she and her sister would like to come along."

"Oh! Thank you," Graham Cook replied, "they don't particularly like going out. They're here to get refreshed after their heavy studies, and prepared for next term."

"Would you mind if I ask them, sir? You never know, they might just be bursting to see a little early evening Spanish culture. I'd guarantee my sister and I would look after them."

"Ask by all means. Please don't take offence if they decline."

"OK," Philippe replied. "Now, how do we restructure? Michelle, can you still dive?"

"Well, I haven't for a while, but I can have a go." Peter appeared at the table. "Am I likely to disturb some heavy team talk? Good morning. Buenos dias, how is everybody?" he said, pointedly looking at Michelle.

Michelle just could not resist. She stood up and moved round the table.

"We're all brilliant," she said, "and you, coach?"

"Yes, I'm good, thank you."

The Admiral turned to Peter. "We've got a girls' double partnership fully coached by you. Hope you've got them to a winning standard."

"Who's that?" Pedro asked.

"Michelle and Marcia."

"What, playing together?"

"It seems so."

"Wow, we ought to be selling tickets to get in! Does my mother know about this? She's bound to phone the local press if she did. What a coup! I think I'll stick around to watch that game. Who do they play?"

The Admiral was in his element. "The teams all play each other. Just one set… it's all we've got time for. Another year, if this works, perhaps we'll run it into two days."

"Heaven forbid!" Michelle chirped in.

"Too bloody true, I had to sacrifice a night out last night to lead my team into the event," Philippe countered.

The Admiral, still very serious about the whole affair, and now with his gleaming whistle hanging on a chord around his neck, turned back to Peter. "How'd you feel about umpiring the ladies' events?"

"I'd lose my concentration, I think."

"Well it's that or the men's."

"I'll go with the ladies. Sure, yes, that's OK with me. Who do they play against, is it the French doctor's wife with the English girl?"

"It appears so," the Admiral replied. "You'll have to excuse me, I've got a Captain's briefing to sort out."

Maria arrived at the propitious moment. "Morning, Admiral. Everything going to plan?"

"Well, only just. You'll have to excuse me, Maria, I've got a captain's briefing to attend."

"Of course, Admiral. Can I just say we're delighted by the effort you've put into this event. I'm sure everyone in the hotel is most appreciative."

Marco appeared. "Bonjour, mon Admiral. Tout va bien?"

"Oui, mon patron. Mais je vais au conférence de chefs d'équipe."

Turning to Michelle and Philippe, Marco said, "That father of yours, he really ought to be organising the Olympics. He's wasting his talent here."

Philippe laughed. "If the Olympics are in Greece, then my sister and I would agree with you, and pay his fare!"

They all laughed.

The Admiral shot off, his wife in tow, with clipboards, pens and chalk in plentiful supply.

Gradually the competing guests appeared.

The practice session was chaos, the kids couldn't understand the lemon collecting heats; too many people, male and female, were wanting to practise their diving, while the sprint swimmers were splashing lengths up and down the pool. Some serious French guys were practising boules.

Marcia and Bob Hunt surfaced. They ordinarily had breakfast in their room. They spied their friends who had arrived overnight, the Joneses, across the breakfast area on the patio.

"Let's say hi," Bob suggested to Marcia. Marcia liked John Jones, so agreed readily.

Bob greeted his mate John. "So we've got yellow team, red one, some other bloody colour, maybe it's blue, are you going to open a book on this Admiral prat's fantasy world? Very good to see you. Good journey?"

"Great! Tiring but good to be here, and now we gather there's a mini-Olympics going on. Which team are you, Marcia?"

"I think it's yellow. I'll only know when we line up behind Philippe, he's our captain."

"Son of prat, you mean," Bob volunteered.

"Bob's in a bad mood, as you've probably gathered. He hasn't been invited into anyone's team. There's no heat for drinking and being bad-tempered, is there, darling?"

"Oh, come on, Bob. We're all behind Marcia and the yellows, if that's what she is. What events are you in, Marcia?"

"Ladies' freestyle, ladies' doubles at tennis and the boules."

"What," John said challengingly, "you're not likely to be freestyle, surely it's breast-stroke with you?"

John's wife screeched with laughter.

"Sandra, I don't find that funny!" Bob interjected, with a pretty serious tone to his voice. "I don't like jokes like that about my wife."

"Bob! Why so serious? A few years back you'd have been cracking the breast-stroke jokes yourself. Marcia's proud of every part of her body. She just loves blokes seeing her."

There was then an uncomfortable silence all round.

"She's professionally trained at showing off her body and, if I might add a serious note myself, it's certainly worth it! So... who do you play doubles with?" Sandra quickly changed the subject before Bob exploded again.

"Michelle, the Admiral's daughter. She's an absolute cracker."

"Christ, that should encourage a full house. I think I'd best watch that game," John Jones announced, arousing a glare from his wife.

Bob grunted, "So now I'm married to a spectacle."

"There's Peter and Michelle and the team captain. I'm going to have a word. See you later, cheers." Marcia extricated herself from the discussion.

"Hi, coach," Marcia greeted Peter. "Hi partner, hi, Captain, all set?"

Peter replied, "All set? What, as in tennis? Listen, you and Michelle are going to have to be on your best behaviour, I'm umpiring your game."

Quite what had got into Marcia even she couldn't recognise. She raised herself onto tip-toe, lightly touching his arm with her left breast as she reached to whisper into his right ear.

"Michelle and I are going to play bra-less so that you miss the line calls and help us to win." She ended with a giggle.

"Mrs Hunt, I have the power to send you both off and give the match to the other side if I rule that either of you are improperly cheating."

"Oh, go on, you misery. Would you find either Michelle or me improper without a bra?"

Peter felt an awakening in his loins. Yet he was just not prepared to accept his mother's prediction that he wouldn't be able to take his eyes off Bob Hunt's wild and beautiful young bride.

In fact, he felt uncomfortable as Maria approached. "Mother," he said, involving her in the conversation straight away, "can you get these two wild young ladies to behave. They're threatening to sabotage my umpiring this afternoon."

"How can they do that?"

"Mrs Hunt, you tell my mother."

"Oh, I can't do that, it's going to be a secret between just the three of us."

Poor Peter was thrown. This was a woman who always seemed to get the upper hand with him. She was smart, confident and fiendishly attractive. *Stick to your own plan,* he told himself, *she's the one talking about her body, you're not.* But he couldn't help thinking about it.

"Well, I'm sure Peter will be fair to all sides," Maria assured Marcia.

"I need some breakfast," Marcia decided.

She located her husband and they breakfasted in polite silence.

"Are you still going to play Olympics with the frogs?" Bob eventually asked, as Marcia finished her croissant and jam.

"Yes, Bob," she said in a quietly determined way, "that's what I'm going to do… and I'm sure I'll enjoy your day on the boat on Sunday just as much. We're on holiday and we need variety."

Bob thought for a few moments. "Well, as long as you don't overstretch yourself. You haven't been swimming much competitively and it's going to be hot for tennis. So take it steady."

"Are you going to watch?" Marcia asked.

"Of course I am. I'm as happy to see your pert little bum and other bits and pieces rushing around as the next guy – certainly as much as John Jones is, apparently!"

Marcia leant forward and kissed him on the forehead. "If we win, you can kiss my tits to reward me!" she giggled, with a suggestive wink. Bob spent all day secretly hoping she'd win. He believed she meant it.

The start of the competition was designed around the lowest age group, lemon-collecting and lilo-rowing. The disaster of the early rounds was a pebble-retrieving heat. There were intended to be three in each team and as there was no skill required, the youngest three team members were elected. The Admiral stood on the side of the pool in the deep end and lobbed 50 or so pebbles into the deep. On "trois", the first competitor would leap in, collect as many pebbles as they could hold, surface, touch the foot of the second relay member and the race would continue for one whole minute.

The only miscalculation was that none of the first three contenders could swim to the pool bottom. They each returned somewhat panic-stricken with a barren catch. True to the spirit, the second team members, being very slightly older, collected five pebbles between them. The third collected about a dozen. Yellow had the most and were declared winners. The Admiral's wife carefully scored the three points.

The Admiral stood on the edge of the pool, perplexed, as he saw the majority of the pebbles still in the bottom of the pool.

He announced an extra item for the three more senior members of each team as a second heat of the same event. Only the Admiral knew the intention was to clear the pool of pebbles. Red won that supplementary event and although the yellow and blue captains lodged an official protest, on the basis that their teams had not trained for the event, the Admiral continued to stand by the decision that the event was fair (inwardly knowing that if he didn't do something radical, the pebbles might clog the filtration system, bringing the resort to a standstill).

Pedro happened to be passing the pool at the end of the male relay swimming event. He still actually hated water and sensed that was unlikely to change.

"Maintenant," he heard the Admiral shout, "les jeunes dames freestyle!" He saw Michelle get up from her chair in the shade of the pine trees, where the boules competition was due to take place in the late afternoon.

Even with a thick towel wrapped around her body, she had an alluring presence. *Was it her height?* he wondered. *Or perhaps her slenderness.* She allowed herself to be announced as a member of the four-lady squad, swimming in the freestyle event.

Marcia, too, was in the race apparently, to the bewilderment of both Bob and John Jones; she was swimming the backstroke, proving JJ wrong in his breast-stroke forecast, but right to the extent that she'd be showing off her body to good effect.

Marcia stepped forward in a black Speedo one-piece instead of her usual bikini. It took a lot to wear one of those and still look sexy, so full marks to her for at least that achievement.

Peter was suddenly conscious of a profound silence settling over the pool. It seemed that the breeze, rather than blowing, was vacuuming in the air. Every male and every female, until then taking only a peripheral interest in 'Admiral's day', had suddenly come to life, all simultaneously as one.

The males were all agog, drawing in their breath. The females seemed to be lodging a collective complaint to some far-off referee about the unfairness of Michelle and Marcia's beauty. "That body and that bikini just should not be let out into the world," Mrs Brown was heard to announce to her gawping husband.

Christ, Peter thought, *there's no way now I'll cope with line calls!* He glanced at Marcia and Michelle: Marcia, with her Greco curves, streamlined, one-pieced, leaving little to anyone's imagination; Michelle, angular, tall and Roman, with those endless legs.

Meribel was cleaning the Hunts' room. She hadn't learnt to love her temporary job, but Peter had been right to an extent: changing the recently slept-in bed linen had taught her to distance herself from the more seedy facts. She was now able to strip a bed without really looking to see whether the sheets betrayed a nocturnal romp or a bed-wetting.

Marcia clearly slept on the right, and hardly moved through the night; the sheets on her side remained quite crisp and unruffled, with a hint of Chanel perfume. Meribel knew it was Chanel because Marcia Hunt's side of the vanity unit was stacked high with it. Perfume, eau de toilette, body lotion, even an oil for the bath and a separate one for the shower. Meribel resolved that that brand of perfume would be high on her 21st birthday present list.

Bob Hunt's side of the bed was exactly opposite. The pillow always reeked of cigar smoke and a particular smell she had worked out to be Brylcreem. It was always stained, where Meribel had worked out that Mr Hunt dribbled during the night, probably amidst heavy snoring.

There's no way they're compatible, Meribel thought. On the one side the Hunts depicted disturbance, and on the other serenity and sweet-smelling calm.

If the luxury of a bed ever did present itself to Peter and her, there would be a single indentation in the centre. They wouldn't have 'his' and 'her' sides. OK, maybe she would turn her back to him as they drifted into slumber, but he would stay close, his arm draped around her waist giving her the security to dream freely through the night.

The head housekeeper always instructed the maids to strip the bed and then air the duvet over the balcony for a few minutes. That had become Meribel's routine. This day she opened the French casement doors onto the balcony. She had forgotten it was the Olympics. There were more people round the pool than normal. Her telescopic eye took her to the far end of the pool, where there was a queue of three rows of four people in a line.

She suddenly felt lower class. Left out of the celebrations because of her temporary status.

Her stomach heaved. There was something a bit creepy about seeing Marcia at the front of the middle line. It was Marcia alright because Meribel had seen the black one-piece a couple of days before in one of the drawers in this very room. At the back of the line she could see Michelle, whom Peter had asked her to befriend. There, too, was Peter, hanging around the edge of the pool in his smart white trousers and white plimsolls and his dark blue Fred Perry top. He cut a dashing image, his jet black hair positively gleaming in the strong sunlight.

The bugger's ogling Marcia, she thought, *and Michelle. I'll have him for that.* And she knew what she meant because she'd neutered a rabbit at the end of her final biology exams at school.

The Admiral blew his whistle and the first of each team jumped into the water. What a fool the Admiral was for putting the guests to all this trouble and drama. What idiots they all were for taking part. What the hell did Marcia want to do this for? She got enough adulation just by doing a circuit of the pool.

Marcia held on to the rail below the coping line. Meribel could see she bent her knees up into her chest.

"Prêt!" the Admiral shouted, and then with one blast on his whistle the three contenders threw themselves backwards into the air with arched backs and windmill arms flailing. The first length was neck and neck, but after the turn the shorter German girl in lane one took a lead and handed over to the red number two about a metre ahead of the field.

Amidst lots of splashing, and shrieking from the now involved crowd, the breast-stroke leg finished up with red and yellow about equal and blue out of contention.

There didn't appear to be a butterfly expert amongst them, making the fifth and sixth lengths a slightly uncoordinated affair, with the Admiral pacing the edge of the pool in line with the now almost equal contenders, panting and shouting that each was flagrantly breaking the rules.

Red handed over first then, surprisingly, blue. In slow motion, picked up by Meribel from afar and most men and their overseeing wives from the closer proximity of the poolside, Michelle became the focus. You had to hand it to the Admiral, at least he'd provided an unexpected spectacle to break the monotony of a two- or three-week break.

Meribel caught sight of Bob Hunt and John Jones about mid-way down the length of the pool, staring towards what she now saw was a polka dot bikini barely adhering to a sylph-like body. *Michelle.*

"Shit," she observed, "and look at Peter. He's positively beside himself! Fancy making himself look such a fool." Yet nobody had a spare glance for him. Male and female eyes alike were glued on Michelle.

Bob Hunt was taking odds on Michelle's top half not standing up to the 'G' force of the entry dive, while most of the women were inwardly willing the bottom half to give in to the drag so that Michelle would be thrown a towel to cover her humiliation.

At entry, in the event, Michelle's dive was well behind her two opponents'. But her stroke was dynamic, totally coordinated after years of Sunday morning training under the eye of her father, and the challenge of keeping pace with Philippe. Meribel could now see Philippe, who himself cut a dashing figure in his tiny little Adidas trunks. She could see that as team captain, he too was taking the games very seriously. He had his hands cupped over his mouth shouting encouragement to his sister.

"Gosh, he's well endowed!" Meribel breathed to herself. "I wonder why he doesn't seem to have a girlfriend out here. Maybe she could get a night off from Peter, she was owed one, after all, on account of his night out saving this very water baby's life – apparently. Or was that all a ruse?" She doubted it. She did trust Peter's integrity and loyalty.

There were now only centimetres between Michelle and the leader in the blue team at the turn and there was no hint of Michelle flagging. In fact, she seemed to be getting faster.

By the time she was within touching distance of the finishing line, she was a clear, beautifully-carved body length ahead of her two opponents. With one graceful push, she heaved herself out of the water, before the other two crawled into the shadow of her limelight.

Michelle was the heroine of the moment. Marcia engulfed her in a hug, then they were joined by the team's breast-strokers and butterfly representatives. The triumphant quartet would have done justice to any Pathé Newsreel at the real Olympics. Philippe rushed across and, enveloping the four in his powerful arms, they circled round and round, jumping up and down at the end of the pool.

The Admiral made copious notes in a little notebook, and then confirmed to Carmel. "Trois points les jaunes, deux les rouges, et un point le bleu."

Meribel stared into the back of Peter's neck. As if sensing her gaze, he looked back towards the hotel at that precise moment.

She gave a little wave. Peter held his hand quite close to his chest and waved back. Meribel held up a forefinger, indicating, "Don't go away, stay there," and disappeared back into the room. She'd looked into Marcia's drawers before and had a particular longing for her designer knickers. You couldn't buy such finery in Spain. It was still too much of a Catholic country; the emphasis was more on cotton for hygiene than silk and sex.

When she returned to the doorway, she stood in the half shade, holding a pair of Marcia's French knickers up to her hips. The black lace stood out against her pink uniform. Peter was panic-stricken. He shot glances to his left, where everybody was still watching the circling quartet in the arms of Philippe. *Thank God for that,* he thought; Marcia was far too involved to notice.

Where was Bob Hunt? Peter wondered. Over there with John Jones gawping at Michelle, no doubt. Certainly Bob wouldn't budge while there was the prospect of Michelle wandering about in her drying bikini. What the hell was Meribel playing at?

He turned back to remonstrate at a distance, half-angry, half-horny, but Meribel had gone. Not further, however, than behind the second bedroom window, which was still shuttered. "That's got the bugger's taste buds going!" she giggled to herself as she moved into the bathroom to finish cleaning.

She'd left the door to the suite open with a sign outside: 'Limpiar en el progreso'. She was leaning into the bath, cleaning the porcelain sides, when a sudden stinging pain on her backside made her kneel up in shock. Peter's tall physique was looming above her.

"What was all that about?" he demanded.

"You were looking forlorn and I thought you needed a bit of action."

"Action? What, fooling with the guests' underwear?"

"No! Oh, come on, Peter. Real action." She put her hand on the mound in his trousers that had noticeably developed.

She held out her other hand, inviting him to pull her up. In one deft movement her right arm went around his neck and she slipped his right hand inside her housecoat, which she'd slightly unbuttoned.

"I miss seeing you during the day," she said, pulling his hand upwards and onto her soft flat tummy.

"Not here, Meri," he said, somewhat unconvincingly.

"Where then?"

"In the laundry room."

"I'll see you in there."

"You go first."

He turned obediently, recognising he was acting like a well-behaved yet very aroused schoolboy. Yet this was adolescent desire that might lead to something physical.

Meribel closed the bedroom door, taking the cleaning utensils with her. She suddenly remembered the sign and went back to remove it from the door.

"Oh, I was hoping to find you on this floor." It was Marcia's voice. "I haven't got a key and I just have to get out of this very uncomfortable swimsuit."

Meribel inwardly jumped. Just a minute before and Marcia would have caught them in her bathroom.

Meribel opened the door. "I've just finished, actually."

"Thanks, darling. You do the rooms so nicely. Hey, I know this is only a fill-in job, and it's not what you're used to, and you must get fed up with bleach and lack of femininity all day. If ever you feel like splashing on some of my perfume, then do."

"I couldn't do that," Meribel said, surprised.

"Here, come with me." Marcia beckoned her towards the dressing unit. She picked up her cut-glass spray bottle with the bulbous perfume pump, took Meribel's left hand, turned her wrist over and sprayed it lightly. She repeated the process with the right one and then lightly touched the base of Meribel's neck both sides with a slight smattering of Chanel on her right forefinger.

"There. That'll make you feel very girlie."

"Thank you, Mrs Hunt."

"Marcia."

"No, I'm sorry. It has to be Mrs Hunt while I'm working. But thank you, anyway."

Meribel slipped into the laundry.

"Where the hell have you been?" Peter semi-exploded. "Don't tell me you've been using Marcia Hunt's perfume too! If you were a normal employee, you'd be fired."

"Listen, if you were a normal boss's son you wouldn't go round slapping chambermaids' butts and inviting them to deal with your pleasures in the laundry room, and jumping to wrong conclusions. Why I've been a hell of a long time is that Marcia Hunt came back just after you'd left."

"Shit!"

"Oh, so that's different, isn't it?"

"Well, she could have caught us."

"So what. She'd only have been envious, me getting attention when she doesn't."

"Meribel, what on earth has got into you? You can't go round saying that sort of thing."

"Peter, it's true."

"How would you know?"

"Look, I'm a cleaner, I do their room, right. I see their bed. There's no signs like in the other beds shared by married couples. I'm getting to be an expert, like you said would be good for me. There are signs when couples have been 'fornicating', if you want it put respectably."

"Signs? How come you're suddenly the expert?"

"Come on, Peter. When you have the luxury of a bed, which we never have, the tissues get used up, the sheets get soiled and crumpled, sometimes the pillows. Mr Hunt leaves his toilet bag open. His stock of condoms is intact. Their night clothes are as crisp as when they were packed. I tell you, it doesn't take a Master's degree to know that the Hunts don't do it. And let's get the stealing of perfume out of the way. Marcia Hunt put it on me."

"Why would she do that?"

"Peter," she said, disappointed, "you really don't believe me, do you?"

"Why would a lady like Marcia Hunt put her ritzy perfume on you?"

"Oh! Right! Well, when a girl tells another girl she's off to sow oats with the boss's son in the laundry room and she's conscious she stinks of bleach, then there's a certain *esprit de corps* which says you lend each other your perfume."

"Meribel, what on earth has got into you today?"

"Peter, I'm busy. Leave a note at housekeeping if our date's still on for tonight."

"Of course it is. But I want you smelling of yourself. Not like some Parisienne."

"OK, I'll splash myself with bleach. But I'll wear the knickers, at least you'll know what's packaged inside those."

"Do you mean you've still got them?"

"You'll have to wait and see, my sweet. You might, of course, never get to know."

"Look. If you've got them, for Christ's sake, put them back before you leave. It's stealing."

"So's giving Michelle and Marcia the sort of attention they're getting from you while I'm here learning the seedy side of life."

Meribel picked up a couple of clean white towels and, as she opened the door to leave, said, "Sorry, sir, I'm busy. I must get on."

As she walked out, she nearly fell over Marcia Hunt.

"Sorry," Marcia said, "what did you say?"

"Say?" Meribel replied. "I didn't say anything."

"Oh! I heard your voice and I thought you must be talking to me. I couldn't see who it was."

"Oh that. I stubbed my toe and I was telling myself not to be so clumsy."

"Fine. Mind how you go," Marcia said, continuing towards the stairs leading to reception.

Peter was disturbed by the series of events. He thought it was because the whole scenario hinged around Marcia. It somehow made it worse to think that Marcia and her husband were very probably abstemious. He didn't think Meribel would have got that wrong. She was a very intelligent, perceptive young lady. He supposed that with such an age difference, it was possible. Who'd know? But if Bob Hunt was abstemious out of choice, he'd have to be mad.

The perfume smelt wonderful on Meribel, but he also knew it smelt terrific on Marcia. He'd first noticed it the day he had driven her and Bob Hunt. It had seemed like a lucky potion, helping his romance with architecture through its innovation stage. Bob Hunt was certainly a lucky bloke.

The games broke for lunch from one till three. At 3pm it was to be the first of the three ladies' doubles play-offs. Red playing blue. Blue playing yellow. Yellow playing red. During the break for lunch the Admiral took Michelle to one side. "Well done, dear," he said, but she knew that tone, it was usually followed by "… but… if you…" Always words that demanded a better performance, rather than accepting it was the best she or her brothers could achieve on the day.

The tennis court, although set at a lower level, was only slightly shielded by pine trees. By three there would still be plenty of sun. Her father said she should wear a cap. She settled for an eye shield and Ray-Bans.

Peter grabbed one of Maria's old straw hats and fixed up an umbrella over the formal umpire's chair which he had suggested, would give the court that air of difference between a play area and a zone for serious sport. It certainly had that effect.

There was a casual number of onlookers for the basic red versus blue game. It was all a bit typical of ladies' doubles. Base line stuff with more yelps and squeals when the ball went out, and few volleys and smashes.

Blues won and were given a 20-minute break before playing the single set competition against the formidable duo of Marcia and Michelle. The yellow duo were true to what Marcia had threatened, even before a single ball had been served. Both wore very tight shorts. Both their T-shirts were armless and hugged firmly in all the right places.

Marcia won the toss and said they would serve; she would start. They had agreed that Michelle, who was undoubtedly the better player, would play at the net.

"Yellow to serve," Peter announced. "Service – Marcia Hunt."

There was loud clapping from the shadow of the pines. Both Marcia and Michelle looked across to where the sound was coming from. It appeared to be coming from Bob and John Jones, much the worse for a few lunch-time beers and a bottle of Rioja.

Michelle was not so sure. From beneath her sun visor she could make out the outline of a tallish man merging into the pines. She was overcome by an uncanny sensation, almost spiritual. She could make out canvas trousers and either a black or dark brown shirt, but the face was totally lost in the shadows. Then the vision in the trees lifted a strong arm and saluted.

"Service," Peter called, almost as if to say, "Come on now, team, I've coached you both into this."

Michelle put the figure in the trees out of her mind as she felt the air part to allow Marcia's really rather good first serve to whizz past her. French blue returned the serve quite gently back to Marcia, who played a massive forehand to her opponent's feet, which produced a yelp. French blue got a racket to it and played a short lob intended to go over Michelle's head. Michelle anticipated that play and was running back towards the baseline as the ball was high against the backcloth of the clear blue Mediterranean sky.

Michelle leapt and swung her racket hard towards the oncoming ball. The return split the blue partnership apart and the ball skidded low on the loose clay surface. There was a loud thunderous clap from beneath the trees.

"Fifteen love," the umpire called.

The set swung predictably to the yellow duo. Peter was pleased, although keen not to be seen as biased. His coaching showed, not so much in terms of technique, but in the power each of his pupils generated. He'd shown them how to hit firm and strong.

As the set ended, Michelle looked back into the trees to locate her fan.

Maria appeared, on a rare break from the bureaucracy of running a hotel at the height of the season. Señr Martin tended to come on duty about four, or a little earlier, which gave Maria a bit of free time, after which she would reappear more socially in the evening.

She strode towards the trees and Michelle's heart sank as she watched her greet the tall shadow with a tip-toe kiss on the cheek. She pointed towards Michelle and Marcia and the shadow moved forward. Michelle whispered, "Merde!" It was the beautiful Miguel Mendes! Here!

He and Maria approached Michelle. "Hi," Michelle greeted him, wishing for a moment that she was dressed more demurely for this refined older man. About mid-30s, she had worked out when she'd thought about him the night before.

"Well played. I was pleased to see you de-stressed. You're a good little tennis player. Well, not so little."

"I saw this figure in the trees. I had no idea who it was. I apologise if I didn't wave back. I just didn't know it was you. It's a bit unfair of you not to wear a white tunic, then I'd have known. Have you come to see Maria?" she asked.

"No, actually you."

"Me?"

"Well, yes, but it's a bit unfair. Mercedes, from the boutique, has put an advert on the side of a van that has been touring Palafrugell all day saying there's this goddess who'll be modelling her latest and greatest bikini here this afternoon. I can't resist either a goddess or a well-dressed bikini, so I came to have a peep. Now where's this bikini?"

"Bikinis are made for swimming. Come and swim with me in the sea, I'm sure Maria can lend you a pair of trunks. Then I'll buy you an ice-cream on the terrace. You've got 30 minutes. We've just got to beat the red team and then my competing day's over."

"Do you have a pair of trunks?" Maria asked.

"No, tennis was going to be my sport for the day."

"I'll find you a pair of Peter's," she volunteered.

"Am I Peter's size?" Miguel enquired.

Maria smiled. "I think you'll get in with a squeeze. Come up to the house and I'll chuck a pair out to you."

Miguel waved nonchalantly at Michelle. "Be sure to win."

"We will."

Michelle trotted back to link with Marcia. Their 20-minute refresher was over.

"Same strategy," Marcia said.

"Yup. Remember blue already beat red so we should be favourite. Can we try to make it quick? I've got a surprise date."

"Fine with me. I'm in the boules thing then, to be perfectly honest, I think I'll be done in."

"Wow, you're lucky, I wish that was going to happen to me!" Michelle replied mischievously.

Marcia patted Michelle on the bottom with her racket. "Come on, let's go and win, you cheeky young lady!"

Maria walked back with Miguel. "Hey! I think you've got yourself an adoring fan there," she said.

"Oh, go on! Really why I'm here is I've been worried about you both since yesterday. Are you alright?"

"Yes, sure. Apart from being sick this morning."

"Does José know? I presume it is José who ought to know…"

"No, and he must never know either."

"Shouldn't he have a say?"

"No."

"Well he should share the emotion in some way."

"No, he can be spared it. He's an honest man, he'd insist I have the baby, which would force him into marriage, which he's not ready for yet. So what he doesn't know about, he doesn't need to know about."

"OK, I won't interfere. We'll start you on Sunday evening, Monday or Tuesday will see you alright. Now let's see what sort of macho pants Peter's got to help me impress the young lady."

Yellows whipped reds, only Marcia conceding one service game. The Admiral was still to be seen making copious notes, no doubt for a post-mortem after the match.

Michelle played aggressively just to get the set over. Yellow won.

Michelle was quietly animated when Miguel appeared from the pool changing room. Being able to walk down the steps carved into the rocks had proved as popular as Peter had hoped it would be.

As they walked into the surf, Michelle stood with her full weight on a sharp pebble Miguel was near enough to catch her elbow and break her fall.

Already there was a bond between them. Miguel was thinking how crazy it was, not being able to get her out of his mind, and, unbeknown to him, she was of a like mind, telling herself she was hooked on the security he was promising to introduce into her life. But she'd play it cool. Withhold her emotions, give it time. Anything more might interfere with her treatment. God! His code of professional ethics might ban him treating her if he so much as held her hand. That happened to doctors, so why not… what was he… he owned a pharmacy, so presumably he was a pharmacist… but beyond that he had these extra powers with herbs and the like…

"Miguel, I've been thinking. You'll be treating me, but I don't know how to describe you professionally, in case I need to explain to Guy, for example."

"Let's swim and I'll think up something convincing," he said.

She became like a dolphin in the water beside him. Diving with an arched back, over and then under the gentle late afternoon waves. He followed her example, showing off his very flexible body. He was obviously fit, as she was, but he wasn't muscular. His moves were graceful for a man.

They were not out of their depth, they could both stand on the seabed. The salt water had obviously helped her foot. Any pain had receded.

"You're fit," she said.

"I work at it," he replied.

"What do you do, jog, weights, or do you have some magic potion in a bottle you pour over yourself, or a couple of Geisha girls walking all over you in your time off?"

"I wish!" he said. "Mainly yoga and a controlled diet."

"What! You can get like that sitting on your bum with your legs crossed?"

"Basically, yes, it's what you put into your mind."

"So what's in your mind about what I should call you, profession-wise."

They talked, and Miguel told her his views on alternative medicines and therapies, how he'd studied them, and their advantages, as he saw it, over chemical-based cures.

"I got motivated through my sister, who had a thalidomide baby. She suffered morning sickness and, rather than put up with it, like our mother had, and mothers before her, she went to the doctor, who prescribed this new and, who knows, insufficiently tested drug. The results, as I'm sure you've seen, were horrendous.

"She's got a lovely daughter with a golden mind, but a badly malformed body. I'd like to be able to help out in such situations. I teach... well you don't actually teach yoga, you explain it. So I explain yoga now as one discipline. I went to China and did two years of acupuncture, of the traditional kind, and I fool around with herbs. So, you tell me. What's all that make me?"

"Unique, I'd say."

They swam off over and under the waves again. Michelle pointed to a starfish just above the seabed. It was as if they could snorkel without the essential equipment. It was peaceful and gentle fun. They both surfaced at the same moment, she exhaling in laughter.

"So you're not medically qualified?"

"That's right."

"So are you allowed to sleep with patients?"

Miguel was completely thrown. She was a beauty, yet there was a side to her that was wild and obviously uncontrolled. He studied the salt water draining from her lovely skin. Her shaped eyebrows were glistening from the dampness, and her cheeks were fresh and lightly tanned and she pushed her hair back. She gave the impression of a Spanish doll in all its gypsy finery.

"Well!" she said. "That obviously needs a very considered answer too!"

"I can't answer that when I'm in Peter's swimming trunks. Besides, I'll need to keep some professional secrets from you. But by all means, keep asking the questions." And he lightly pinched her cheek.

"You're a bastard. You're a professional bastard who dabbles in black magic. That's what you are."

"Totally right, but one who agrees with Mercedes: there was a sight to see at the Playa which even a witchdoctor would find hard to resist."

"Do you know, I'd quite forgotten I'd got my beautiful bikini on. It feels as though it was made for me."

"My dear Michelle, I think perhaps it was. Now let's get back. If I don't get Peter's trunks back by six, I think a part of my body may become detached."

"Ouch!"

"Oh well, perhaps I can get another pair."

"What, trunks?"

"No! Balls."

She screeched with laughter. "Oh, my poor Cinderella!"

Maria was on the terrace in deep conference with Marco. He had initially been against giving the Admiral, or anyone come to that, the run of the hotel for such an organised event. He said it was a place to relax and thought it might just have introduced tension into the otherwise informal arrangements. Maria, on the other hand, said she thought they needed something to create a bit of fun and advocated that they ought to try it. So the partnership agreed, without a vote, to give it a try. If it failed they could set up a guillotine the following morning and behead the Admiral, which might prove a more popular event.

From the terrace, they could pick up the atmosphere generated by the boules tournament, which was ending, it seemed, in a very exciting climax. Marco was agreeing with Maria that the 'Olympics' event had been an absolute highlight since the opening ceremony. It also took pressure off the formal waiting staff, because the guests took their lunch from the buffet the hotel had laid on.

Marco had had no formal training as a hotelier, but seemed to have the attributes of a welcoming innkeeper in his blood. Maria would always be the organisational one, but she too was learning that to reinvest was the nature of the business. They were both agreed that they would entertain the Admiral and his wife to dinner with them in the à la carte restaurant, providing Carmel could get the chalk off her hands.

Peter appeared, still looking the part as tennis umpire, having handed the refereeing of the boules over to the Admiral.

Maria greeted him with a chirpy, "Hello darling. We've just been talking about inviting the Admiral and his wife to have dinner with us as a thank you for all the work he's done, admittedly a lot for his self-gratification, but it's been very successful."

"Yes, it surely has. It's been a busy day, but I agree. If he comes back next year I wouldn't have a problem supporting him. It's still going on, you know. Bob Hunt and John Jones have got a book going on the boules. Have you seen Marcia?"

"No," Maria said, craning her neck to look over the parapet towards the cool evening area beneath the pines. "Let's go and take a look. There are more men down there interested in this French sport than there are trees in the forest."

"This sounds like something we should see," Marco said, taking Maria's arm. They really had matured into being very good friends. In their partnership there had never been a cross word and, in his preoccupation with the busy hotel, his constant desire for Maria's body had receded. Maybe it was that Virginia was now preoccupying him in the bedroom arena.

As they walked down the path from the terrace they stopped by the old millstone Peter had brought back from the cousin's farm. It had just been lying around and Peter asked if they could 'borrow' it.

"You've got to hand it to Pedro," Marco said, "he's really got a great eye for design – and the girls, I might add. I saw young Meribel in her pink housekeeping gear the other day. I tell you, if ever I'm in hospital and she approaches my bed in a white overall and a stethoscope, I'll drag her into bed with me, providing Virginia's not visiting at the time. It would be a wonderful way to go."

"Listen, who knows, she might have married Pedro by then, that would make her your niece and I'm sure that would count as incest."

The rest of the stroll was punctuated with the odd, "Hasn't Manuel Carlos done well with that planted area? It looks so mature already," from Maria, and, from Marco, "Look back at the hotel from here, Maria, see how the sun's making the pink painted render look a strange hue of deep orange. Don't the pines reflected in the pool look lovely?" For a man with such little breeding, he had a certain natural appreciation for beauty.

"You're proud, aren't you, Marco?"

"Not as proud as Paco would have been, having got your investment to provide all this."

"Poor Paco!" Maria said. Her stomach heaved, she inwardly asked: *Forgive me, Paco, don't think of me as being disloyal, selfish. You were my first love and nothing can change that. Besides, I bet you've got the odd angel or two washing your clothes and cooking your meals by now. And I'd bet they haven't been able to resist going to bed with you either.*

The pines area was thronging more like a marketplace. Cheers and shouts of encouragement echoed out in French, German, Italian and English, and who could decipher the others in the midst of the excitement that had built up.

At the beginning of the boules leg of the Olympics, the Admiral let Marcia know that he was not amused by her attire. To spite Bob, and unbeknown to him, she had put together an outrageous outfit comprising a black off-the-shoulder blouse, tucked crisply into a bold red skirt, fishnet stockings and totally impractical black patent stilettos. To top it all, she'd acquired a little red beret and thrown a string of French onions into the equation.

"Mon Dieu! Mon Dieu. Qu'est ce que nous avons ici?"

Marcia spoke quite good French, in fact, practised when she was in the Bluebell Troupe in France. "Je suis ici à jouer aux boules."

"Quoi! Dressed like that. That's the attire of a tart in a fish market in Marseilles. Go and get something more appropriate on," the Admiral directed.

Marcia had said she had nothing more appropriate and that he should ask the team captains if they objected to her dress.

Philippe risked being written out of the family will. "Dad, she's great, it'll add a little fun into the end of a pretty serious day."

The other two captains agreed.

"Well, I don't want her like that at the presentations or in the photographs."

As it happened, Bob was suddenly very supportive of his wife's activities. He thought the Admiral was an old fart anyway and her attire would really get the betting going, as the punters were bound to expect she wouldn't even be capable of picking up a boule. So on this one occasion he would forgive her for her extrovert ways, especially given the compliments he was getting from the other men. "Tell you what, old boy, you might not live to a great age, but by God I'd bet you have a smile on your face before you go. Now my other half…"

The betting on reds, because they were a mainly French team, was 'evens', blues 2/1 and yellows were rank outsiders at 5/1. John Jones had to adjust the odds when he realised that the punters were placing bets, not on the basis of who, according to form, should win, but who they would like to win.

Marcia was in fact very, very good at the game. She was deadly accurate with her throws and, when it came to a heavy cannon to remove an opposing boule from its close proximity to the jack, she was devastating.

Marcia had her two final boules to place. The crowd fell into silence. Bob's wine- and whisky-laden voice broke that silence. "Allez les Anglais, allez!" came the chant.

The Admiral turned about, as though he had just got word on the bridge that they were being pursued by a lethal torpedo. "Monsieur, c'est trés serieux. Silence!"

"Silence, my arse!" Bob shouted back. "Allez les Anglais, allez les jaunes."

Marcia seemed unfazed by it all. By now she had shed her stilettos and was gradually wearing out the soles of her stockings on the dry sandy clay beneath the trees. Her first boule bombed her opponent's one from on high. She'd seen the French do that in practice, rolling the hand upwards in a sort of virtual au revoir. There was that now familiar heavy metallic thud as the two surfaces came together and then the satisfying sound of one heavy boule making its way off to land far away from its home jack.

It was red's ball doing the scurrying. Marcia's ball fell just the other side of the jack, where red's had been positioned to guard all the options. The drop, in those circumstances, was the only shot to play and even the Admiral conceded a clap as others around him whooped and cheered.

If she flighted her last boule there was a risk she might dislodge the one standing guard behind the jack. Philippe whispered, "That gives us the draw. What's your plan?"

"I'll roll this one round the outside with a bit of spin and bring it in close to the jack."

"Can I say?" Philippe said enquiringly.

"Well, yes, of course, captain."

"Here, come with me, we'll walk the course. You can do that. I'll show you the problems."

Philippe pointed out the area of small stones that had been thrown up by the constant rolling of boules through the early evening, just along the path that Marcia had marked out in her mind.

"Try that. You might be lucky. If you hit the stones at the wrong speed the boule will shoot left. So, OK, we get the draw, and share the points, which means we'd win the day's competition."

"So we win the day's competition anyway?"

"Yes, that's right."

"OK, so this is about winning this element of the competition and satisfying the bookmakers?"

"Well! Yes, I think that's right."

"So I'll give you plan two."

"What's that?" Philippe enquired.

"I'll plant one on to this boule," she said, indicating the originally short ball laid as a barrier by one of her team mates. "If I hit it just there," indicating a point the size of a franc piece, "I think it'll roll forward the metre, and finish close to the jack. Trois points."

"Marcia, you do that and you're a genius!"

As he said that Marcia looked up and saw Peter taking serious interest in the play. She caught his eye. Took the last remaining boule into her left hand, held it to her lips and kissed it firmly.

Peter was angry with himself yet again for allowing a twinge to shoot into his groin. It was not, of course, the fact that she was kissing an inanimate object in a meaningless way; it was that again he knew she was playing with his emotions. "Let's do it," Marcia announced.

She walked back to the mark from which she had to throw. She focussed firmly on the French franc she'd drawn in her imagination. Transferred the boule from left to right hand. A practice swing to get the weight right and then she burnt a hypothetical line in the worn surface along which her boule would travel, if she insisted firmly enough.

A final back swing, a fixed eye along the practised route. "Now!" she exclaimed as she let the boule fly under control. "Go! Go!" she screeched. It did. Her heart leapt. It hit a stone, but its course did not waver. The gap was closing. In mini seconds there was the dull metallic thud, which at least said she'd hit the target. Whether on the sweet spot or not would soon unfold. The target boule involuntarily set out on its path. There was no initial acceleration. It didn't need that. It just needed to hold its breath and close its eyes. She thought it had to travel three feet to be successful. Six inches and it would not have done its job. Four and she'd be a heroine.

Ten, nine, it looked as though it was running out of steam. It hit a slight downhill stretch not perceptible to the human eye. Eight became seven and six quite quickly. Its roll was beginning to die, though. It made five and then virtually stopped. She let out a silent gasp of breath and whispered, *go on you little bugger.* The boule rolled on what was for the English contingent 2 inches, and for others a devastating match-losing 5 centimetres. There it died in a heap of beautifully moulded steel.

The partisans leapt, Philippe threw his arms around her. He lifted her high as though to do a spin in an ice skating pirouette. There was leaping about all around, hugging and kissing, and this was a friendly fun Olympics. What would the real thing have been like? Bob parted the throng to get to this wife. He eventually managed it. They held each other, but it was not with the same camaraderie as intra-team. Philippe broke them up.

"Come on, team. I'll buy you all a drink. We are the champions!" They rushed as an untidy mob towards the terrace. Bob found himself watching as they all bounced towards the bar.

John Jones noticed the sadness in his eyes. "You OK, mate?" he said.

"Yeah, sure. They're all taking it so bloody seriously. I can't quite understand it."

"Oh, come on, mate," he responded with unusual affection, man to man.

"Think what you're like when you clinch a deal. You might not jump and dance around like a load of prats, but you do it your way. You'll pile champagne glasses high, and then get pissed."

Bob didn't accept the analogy, "Listen, it's one thing celebrating like that among your peers, even with the odd young bloke. But the young blokes follow their. The way Marcia's acting these days is the reverse. She's attention-seeking and leading rather than being led. She wasn't like that when we first met."

"Maybe she *needs* attention. Is everything alright with you in bed? Are you leading, or letting her choose the moment, the mood?"

"Don't be bloody daft," Bob retorted aggressively.

"Then you're OK. If you've got a young filly then you know as well as I do you show her who's boss and then let her go into the fields and kick around. If you don't get her under control, she'll be kicking all the time."

"Soppy bugger," Bob proffered.

"Come on, I'll buy you a drink."

At the bar there were five distinct camps. The French frog and his entourage, strutting like peacocks at the end of a successful day. The victors, slapping glasses together and basking in their glory. The two losing teams, trying to lift their spirits. Then Bob, and others, mere spectators, waiting for their moment of inclusion.

Recognising their similar plight, Sylvano's wife, who was also temporarily without her other half, saw Bob as the antelope who had not kept up with the rest of the pack, and was therefore easy prey for a hungry tigress. With her full bust a bit too exposed, she pushed across to him, threw her strong Roman arms round his neck and suggested they go to the pool to celebrate his wife's win.

"She is busy," she said. "My man busy too."

Bob had had a lot to drink. "Piss off. I'm watching my busy wife. Bloody behave." And he pushed her away.

It was now time to break up the party. The Admiral banged on the glass bar top with a spoon he'd lifted from an adjoining table laid for dinner.

"Mesdames et messieurs," he commanded. "J'ai le plaisir…" Bob thought, *Yes I bet you bloody do give yourself pleasure, you tosser.* "I have pleasure," he continued, "to congratulate all those who have today entered into the Playa Hotel Premier Olympics. It gives me special pleasure to ask Maria Martinez to present the cup to the yellow team, captained by my son and including my daughter." Where was Michelle? he wondered.

Maria presented an especially bright and shiny, exceedingly cheap trophy, which had been provided 'generously' by the Admiral and his wife. She thanked the Admiral for all the time and effort he had invested into the event and then announced, "My partner Marco and I invite the Admiral to make this an annual event."

There were whoops and much clapping. It seemed her sentiments had hit the sweet spot.

Maria and the head chef had laid on a buffet on the upper terrace. Marcia continued in her role as 'French tart', much to the annoyance of Bob, but at least within his sights.

"Go and change into something ordinary," he had suggested at one stage. The light sparkling wine had got the better of her, as she admitted the next day. She didn't remember, but well believed it was probably true that she had countered by saying, "Something ordinary. What, like the original Mrs Hunt?" This had put Bob into a horrendous temper, and he retired to their suite with a bottle of whisky and a bowl of ice, announcing that when she was done with her schoolgirl antics he'd see her in the dormitory. He then looked around for the Italian Job, as he thought of Señora Sylvano. She'd vanished, and in fact was having a bit more success with one of the loud German male guests on the beach.

"Shouldn't you be celebrating with your brother and the rest of the team?" Miguel asked Michelle as they sat in the swing hammock by the pool, from where they could see and hear the celebrations, and likewise the two shadowy figures now apparently humping in the sand like water buffaloes.

"Oh no, I won't be missed. I never am," she said.

"Why do you say that? You're in a family unit, you must be missed."

"OK, then, what about you? Are you 'missed'? Are you in a family unit?"

Miguel laughed, "No! and No! is the answer."

Michelle was half-satisfied by the response.

"So you're not missed by anyone? Is that what you're saying?"

"Yes, I actually think that's right, because I'm always there, available, transparent... so I can't be missed, and if you're asking in a very unsubtle way, am I part of a family unit... do I have a wife or a partner or a hundred dependent kids... no, I don't."

"So are you lonely?"

"Good God, no. I don't have time to be lonely. I treat all my patients as friends. I'm available from seven in the morning, to those who work early, until nine or ten at night. So when can I be lonely?"

"You looked lonely in the trees this afternoon. I didn't know who you were. But you looked lonely."

"Lonely, because I was watching you and I want to provide you with a friendship, of the most professional nature, security and a cure. So, yes, at a distance, of course I was lonely."

"… And now?"

"No, I'm not lonely. I can leave here knowing that we've bonded. That you're interested in being cured and I have a desire to cure you. Life's not about three dimensions. That is, it's not only for me to see the length and breadth and width of your face, or your body. My world's four-dimensional. The fourth dimension is measurable too, except you can't see it."

"Miguel, you talk in riddles, excuses for what ordinary people accept as non-existent."

"OK, I hear what you say. Have you got a cigarette?"

"Oh, clever. So it now comes round to you weaning me off the cigarettes, simulating coming off the weed. You're into trickery."

He took her purse. "I'm sorry, I know a lady hates a fellow to look in her purse. There's things like an emergency Tampax or a condom, a photo of somebody real in her life, or an overnight pair of fresh knickers, but it's a cigarette and a lighter or a match that I need," he said as he did indeed take out both a packet of Benson and Hedges and a lighter. He was not disinterested in the low quality condom he noticed and pushed to one side.

"Right," Miguel said, "how high is it to the top of my head, from my chin to here?" he indicated, touching the top of his neatly groomed black hair.

"Let's say 24 centimetres."

"OK. And the width between my ears?"

"Say 18 centimetres."

"And from my nose to here," indicating the back of his head.

"I'm guessing, 18 centimetres again."

"OK, very good, and how far are our faces apart?"

Michelle hesitated. "I'd be guessing."

"Don't guess. Establish the fourth dimension."

"Sorry, I thought that was the question. What's the distance of the fourth dimension?"

"Right. But what you need to do is to see the fourth medium. Here, would you light my cigarette, and remember, I don't smoke, so I might choke to death."

"Miguel, please don't do that."

"OK, so I'm a cheat. I've established in your mind that smoking can be dangerous. But we'll take that chance. Would you light my cigarette please?"

She leant forward and did what he asked. He drew in smoke and exhaled a few amateur breaths. The space between them filled with smoke.

"Touch the gap between us," he instructed. Michelle obeyed. "Now you can see the fourth dimension. No width, depth or height. Just a presence. How far would you say we are apart now?" Miguel asked.

"I'd say we're getting closer."

"No, dimensionally, how far are we apart?"

"Sixty centimetres, and closing," she said. "So if there's a fourth dimension, then there could be any number of emotions beyond the two extremes of love and hate, loneliness and companionship, and all those areas and volumes we've yet to identify."

"So in the gap between the shadow I was in the trees, and you were in the shafts of light on the court, there's space we might build in. That, simply stated, young lady, is where I hoped we'd be."

"Miguel, you're fun."

"Michelle, you're salvageable." He leant forward and kissed her forehead. "Now, how far apart was that?"

"Very close," she smiled. "Miguel, why aren't you in a family unit?"

"Questions, questions, questions," he said, touching the end of her nose with his forefinger. "First, am I allowed to screw patients, then am I lonely, and am I in a family unit? If you stick to the treatment and see it through, then I'll see about some answers."

"Oh, goody," Michelle giggled. "I'll settle for the one about sleeping with your patients first." She threw back her head with a burst of laughter.

CHAPTER 17

Peter glanced at his watch; it was 7.40pm. *Hell,* he thought, he was due to pick Meribel up at 8.30pm and he needed to shower and change.

He hadn't seen Michelle since the tennis and hoped Guy and pals hadn't caught up with her and diverted her back to the pot. Superficially, she'd been doing very well. She didn't appear to be suffering too much withdrawal. His mother had said they'd had a meaningful session with Miguel Mendes and that he hoped he could get Michelle through this chapter of drama in her life. She'd also explained about offering Michelle a job at the end of her official holiday.

"How about chambermaiding? I think Meribel's just about had enough."

"No, I hadn't got that in mind, Michelle's a brilliant sportsperson and I was wondering about her taking over the coaching."

"What! That's my bloody job!"

"Peter, please, language!"

"Well it is! What are you doing, firing me?"

"No, no, no. Listen, I've got this idea."

All the times in his life that he'd heard those words uttered by his mother, he had yet to hear one of her ideas that was not an exceptionally good one.

"Go on, Mother, what is it this time? We'll do donkey rides on the beach and you want me to take that over and sweep up the shit and spread it round the gardens?"

"Now I hadn't thought about that, it's a good idea. No, actually I had in mind getting you to do something you're good at."

"So I'm not a good coach now!"

"Pedro, come on, hear me out. Of course you're a good coach. What I had in mind is getting you up to cousin José's land. You talked about needing a land survey. If you had the survey you could start developing your ideas on site development layouts before you get to university in late September. Then when you get there, you'll probably have time and certainly have the facilities to progress with the design. You could have an application before the parochial council, perhaps by the spring, and that's important."

"Mother, that's a brilliant idea and I'd love that far more than telling lots of young ladies who want to improve their tennis that they probably shouldn't have taken it up in the first place.

"But as for the timing, I don't want to be pushed. I've got three years to plan the development, and besides, I've got a lot to learn. I've yet to satisfactorily design one house, let alone a few hundred and a hotel and maybe a local shopping centre."

"I understand that, but doesn't the planning application rely on an outline, a schematic presentation of the intentions, with a hint as to the character of the whole?"

"Well… yes."

"Right, so that could be fairly quick, say by the spring?"

"Yes."

"So listen… Oh, I nearly said 'chiquito', because when you miss a point I see the little boy who didn't believe a day in Rosas was happening and ran away so he wouldn't have to come to terms with it. It was then that you were my most 'chiquito'. Not when I was breastfeeding you and changing a nappy… Listen, darling, Carlos Sanchez is still in his second year of office as mayor. I think that runs out in September next year. As mayor, he chairs the parochial council and, to be quite frank, if I speak to him after he's watched my lunch-time tennis he'll do anything to help my life. For that, read 'our life'. So I think speed might be advantageous."

"Mother! Are you saying he's attracted to you?" Maria remained non-committal. "I see what you mean. OK, I'd really love to get my teeth stuck into it anyway. Do you think Michelle *would* do some coaching?"

"I'm sure she would and, if you want to know a secret, she's been asked to model some swimwear in the afternoons in a shop she knows in Figueras."

"What! Well I suppose they won't find a better figure and a greater extrovert. She'd be ideal for that job. OK, I give in, I'm fired."

So he'd be able to tell Meribel about all those plans, but first he needed to satisfy himself that his overseeing role was being effective.

At that very moment he heard Michelle's laughter during a lull in the general merriment around the bar. It came from the pool. He'd be so cross if she was bingeing again. He strode across to the pool area, where he picked out the silhouettes of two figures. One was unmistakably Michelle. She was standing in front of a low-level patio light.

Peter did not recognise the man beside her. "There you are, Michelle. I thought you'd be with the winning team celebrating."

"I am," she said with a giggle.

Peter was now close enough to recognise Miguel. "Oh Hi! It's Miguel Mendes, isn't it?"

267

"Yes, Peter. Pleased to see you again, and in fact a little embarrassed."

"Embarrassed! Why?"

"Well, I came across to watch the innocent games of tennis you put on this afternoon. I expect your mother's told you I'm going to be working with Michelle on her, well, let's say problem."

"Yes, yes, I know all about that. I'm sure we all thank you."

"Anyway, the patient demanded that her early therapy would be to teach me how to become a dolphin and, well, to cut a long story short, the options were either to join her nude and defenceless or take up your mother's offer to borrow a pair of your trunks." He pointed to the pair which Maria knew to be out of fashion with Peter, who was now wearing the more fashionable boxer style.

"You're very welcome. But I'd still like them back, and when I say that I mean right now. Immediately."

Miguel looked down. "Now? Immediately? Please become my best friend. Could I rent them for just another few minutes please, I'd hate to catch cold!"

The three of them laughed.

"Hang on to them for as long as you like," Peter offered. "They're obviously doing you some good, I've noticed Michelle can't take her eyes off you. Anyway, listen, I've got a hot date, I'm going to be late if I'm not careful."

Peter left with a wave. "Keep all this treatment up, guys."

Back in the garden accommodation Peter and Maria still shared, his mother was on the phone. She looked surprised to see him. "No," she said, "that's all fine. Are you there in 30 minutes or so? OK, I'll call you back then… Yes… definitely."

"Hello, dear," she addressed Peter, "I thought you must have gone straight out. Aren't you late?"

"Yes, but I came across Michelle with Miguel Mendes down by the pool making eyes at each other. I stopped to see if Michelle was OK and to reclaim my trunks, which I gather you loaned to Miguel."

"Oh, I didn't think you'd mind," Maria said.

"Of course I don't, but when they come back perhaps you'd incinerate them."

"Why?"

"Well, I don't want to catch anything."

"Pedro, that's terrible! As if somebody as clinical as Miguel would have anything to pass on."

"Mother, I meant more in the sense of catching Michelle's eye… the way she looks at him in those trunks!"

"Pedro, you're incorrigible! Go and shower, you smell. Meribel won't like that. Lavate bien." She crossed to where Pedro was standing, lifted herself onto her toes and kissed his cheek.

"Are you OK, Mother?"

"Yes, of course."

"You look tired."

"Darling, I *am* tired. We've been working very hard. We're fully booked and there are some real nightmares behind the scenes."

"Can you get a weekend off soon?"

"I'm going out with the Hunts on Sunday on a sea trip. That'll be nice. I've got Tuesday off next week and I'd like you out of the way. I intend to sleep all day. So I don't expect you coming back and playing your music."

"Yes, Ma'am," he said, saluting as he about turned towards the shower. "Who have you got to phone back?" he shouted as he stripped off.

"Oh, a chap about a boat."

"Then don't forget to call him."

Peter enjoyed first the hot water of the shower and then, as the immersion supply ran out, the crisp cold soft water from the spring. All the guests were complimentary about the softness of the water. Michelle had said it was better than any body lotion she had tried.

He hoped Meribel might be in a calmer mood. A little relaxing time with her would do him good, but not if she was as forceful as she had been earlier in the day. Away from the hotel and Marcia Hunt, it might be as it normally was between them. That morning she'd seemed to want to make some sort of point Peter didn't really understand.

Showered, dried, electric shaved and having kissed his mother adiós, he went off to find out how the land lay. As he drove away in his mother's Seat, he thought he'd have to have a word with Marco about how hard she was working. She certainly didn't look herself. She needed a break, maybe even a course of vitamins. Miguel Mendes might be able to recommend some.

"Sorry about that, darling," Maria began as she phoned José back. "Pedro came in a bit unexpectedly and I knew I wouldn't really be able to speak. So you were saying, you're having to stay over in Barcelona. What time will you leave in the morning?"

"Crack of dawn. I've probably got a full day getting the boat ready for the Playa cruise. Don't want to let you down with those rich guests of yours for Sunday. Do you think we'll get some time together alone? It's been six weeks and a chap starts to pine for his girlfriend after that sort of period of time."

Maria's stomach positively heaved. *Christ, of course he'll want to make love,* she thought. She just couldn't, physically and emotionally, she just couldn't.

She'd wait till Sunday and say she'd suddenly gone 'off games', possibly due to the excitement of seeing him again. She could still satisfy him alone, he'd be happy.

"Are you there?" came José's voice.

"Oh! Yes, sorry. I was just getting a bit sweaty thinking of being together again. I expect Bob Hunt and Marcia will want some time alone anyway. It wouldn't surprise me if we got to re-christen the cabin," she giggled.

José suddenly felt how much he wanted to see Maria again. She'd been a breath of life into what had become a melancholy world.

"I tell you what," Maria said, "I'll bring you a flask of coffee and a couple of sandwiches round about tea-time on Saturday, but no hokey pokey definitely, because I'll be on my way back to the hotel to cover the evening shift. Sñr Martin's off."

The real teenagers who should have been laughing were having a slightly tense time. Their pattern of life together was a bit stuck, like a 78 rpm record with an old needle. Peter reasoned it was because they were both working and had to grab time at the end of the day, when both were tired and neither was at their best.

Typically, through their early experimentation, they'd learnt to give each other satisfaction without putting Meribel at risk. That was the best of all worlds for Meribel, who would not have wanted to indulge if there was the slightest risk of becoming pregnant, however good the experience might have been. She dreaded having to confess to a priest.

Peter accepted the situation, but at times the male in him couldn't help thinking about Marcia and Michelle, and what it would be like to have sex with them. They'd naturally acknowledge how wonderful he was and beg to submit to him again and again. But these were mere adolescent dreams any young man would have conjured up.

So for Peter and Meribel, physical pleasure their agreed way was OK, but from time to time it needed spicing up. That, Peter thought, was why they niggled each other. They kissed and touched, then went their separate ways to their own beds. A night in a bed together would, Peter thought, do them both good, but that was not on their immediate horizon.

That evening they'd met as planned and touched lips in no more than a cursory way. Meribel went straight for it, unleashing what she had bottled up all day. "Are you less grumpy now that you've got through your performance before your entourage of adoring women?"

"Oh, come on, Meri! I've been stuck in the heat in an umpire's chair all afternoon, and it wasn't with adoring women, more aggressive German and

French men, arguing the toss over my line calling. I've had to watch a load of kids collecting plastic lemons and keep a megalomaniac French Admiral in his place, or else he would have had press conferences, dope tests and physicals. So come on, let's just have a little quality time. We're both tired. You've been stripping beds and nicking perfume most of the day. Let's relax."

"Nicking perfume!" she screamed.

"Meri, I'm pulling your leg, but if I might say now, it's lovely, it suits your personality. It's rich and it's spicy, and I had no idea Marcia Hunt had said to borrow it whenever you wanted to, to cheer up the grime and shit you have to work with... well, not have to work with... by working with us, helping us out. You still smell lovely."

"You're bloody pulling my leg. I've showered and scrubbed the stuff off. I didn't want a scene or to disappoint you. I can't see how you can still smell it."

"I've noticed with good perfume it gets into the pores and lasts for ages. It's Chanel all the way from here on."

Meribel moved across the front seat of the car and put her arm around Peter's neck. "Shall I level with you?"

"Yes, always."

"I'm jealous. You're out there all day in your smart coaching gear. You have girls falling at your feet, and to an extent you encourage them..."

"Meribel, I don't."

"... And there I am in shit, being treated like shit. The Bob Hunts of this world aren't falling at my feet, or the Philippes, they're more concerned with demanding a clean towel. I even have to clear the odd condom up from those guests who don't remember the night before."

"What! Do you? What do you do, throw them away?"

"No way."

"What then?"

"I pick them up in my rubber gloves and lay them on a tissue on the dressing unit. They can decide to throw them away if they want to.

"Anyway, enough said. I'm jealous. But now I've got you to myself, on this balmy hot night, I want to be taken into our field and for you to make me feel good, and let me do the same for you. I've got a bottle of Mateus to help us along the way."

Peter sank a little. They were in a rut. If it was cool or raining they'd be in the back of the car. On nights like this they had a couple of favourite out-of-the-way fields.

Peter plucked up courage. He felt he could see exactly where she was coming from. She needed attention. She needed cleanliness.

"Can we find a hotel?"

"Tonight?" She seemed shocked.

"Well… yes. It might make you feel, well, treated. A bit less sordid."

"Oh, come on. I can't wait for all that palaver of booking in you have to do, agreeing a name and then knowing you're just there for the convenience of a few hours. Let's just go to the field where we can see and hear the sea. It's not far. You'll have to wait, but I've got something special for you."

It was no more than ten minutes' drive. Peter pulled up by the gate as he usually did. Meribel leant into the back of Maria's car, grabbed the car rug and small hamper she had put together to go with the wine, and hurried to get out. She looked back through the open window.

"Hurry up. I'll be waiting for you."

As Peter locked the car up he reflected that if they did get to a hotel, he would suggest they went the whole way. "Everybody is nowadays," he had once put it to Meribel. When he thought about their indulgences, he was always left feeling he'd given in to Meribel's all-controlling influence on each occasion. The way she moved his hand from areas she decided she wanted to be off-limits, yet she could do what she liked, it seemed.

On this occasion, Peter had only got a couple of steps away from the car when he remembered Meribel had said she'd brought a bottle of Mateus for them. He hadn't seen her carry it into the field with her, so he returned to the boot. Sure enough, she hadn't taken it. He decided to open the bottle there, rather than have the fiasco of opening it down in the field. It had suddenly got dark and there was not much moon, so feeling his way in the field with a bottle opener would not be easy.

"So, honey, you bring your lady spirits, with which to lift her," Meribel quipped, trying to replicate the pose of Elizabeth Taylor lying on her cushion in Cleopatra.

Peter responded by pouring the wine into a plastic glass and handing it down to her. He did one for himself and slid down next to her on the rug.

"Santé," he said.

"Santé."

"Sorry about this morning."

She found a piece of firm ground beside her and placed her glass on it. "Here," she said, "let's make up." She took the glass from his hand.

"Could I have another slurp?" he said. "I don't know what you've got in store for me!"

"I can see what you've got in store for me, you devil," she said, rolling over slightly and placing a hand over the bulge in his buttoned fly jeans. "Wow, do all umpires have such big problems to cope with?"

"Only in mixed singles," he said, through a laugh.

272

"Mixed singles, surely you mean mixed doubles?"

"No, singles. You and me. Now. We're singles and we're mixed."

"Oh, too true. Thank God we are." Her spare hand went to the waist of his jeans. She was now deft at undoing his belt and then, button by button, his fly.

That was normally the point when his hand would make its purposeful journey over her knee and upwards along her thigh. Tonight there was an excitement about her. She was playful. She took his hand. "Come on, coach. This'll please you," she said as she guided his feel for herself. He was wrong about the surprise treat being that she was not wearing underclothes. His hand rested on what he sensed to be lace. She slid his hand onto her right hip. The lace turned to a more slippery fabric; *silk,* he thought.

"Hey, have you been out shopping?" She didn't answer, but continued to guide him, now downwards, back towards her thigh, which too was the consistency of what he took to be as silk, save that it was warmer and very slightly textured.

"Hey! What's all this about?" he said, looking at her now that their lips had found each other's and they were lying close and facing one another.

"They're for you. Do they feel nice? Aren't they clever," she said, pulling her skirt right up above her thighs and encouraging him to touch over and under the silk and lace still covering her tummy and bottom, yet allowing his hand relatively free movement to caress her.

"Where did you get these?" he enquired playfully.

"I thought you'd like them."

"I do, I really do."

"Tell me it's inside the wrapping that you really like. Tell me it's me that you want."

"Of course it is, of course I do," he said, kissing her firmly and passionately.

Her hand went inside his underpants as she pushed them firmly down. She was now really arousing him.

He caressed her private parts. They'd practised many a time but this was different. He found it very sexy and stimulating and they took each other to an exquisitely timed moment of satisfaction, with more fervour than normal.

They relaxed in each other's arms while they got their breath back.

"That was lovely," Peter said, breaking into the coolness after the heat of those moments.

"There, I said I had something you'd like."

"Whoever invented those knew what they were doing. Where did you see them?"

"Promise you won't be cross."

"If you're saying they were very expensive… How could I be?"

"I borrowed them."

"Borrowed them?" he replied, pulling away slightly. "Borrowed? Who from?"

"Marcia Hunt."

Peter pulled right back.

"Marcia Hunt!"

"Well, she's got loads of them. Mr Hunt won't be missing them. Just for one night. They'll go back tomorrow."

"Meribel! Are you seriously saying you've 'borrowed' Marcia Hunt's underclothes?"

"Only for you. I don't get to go to Paris to see these new things. You're right, they're bound to be expensive. I thought you'd get a kick out of me in Marcia Hunt's undies."

"Kick! For Christ's sake, how on earth can you do this! You've stolen her knickers!"

"Not stolen, silly, borrowed. What I do tomorrow is leave a note saying they got scooped up with the laundry from the room. With the bed linen and towels. She'll never know differently."

"Meribel. I can't believe I'm hearing this. You've defiled her."

"Silly, she's got nothing to do with it. I did it for you… to give you pleasure… just like if you'd turned up with something of your mother's and asked me to wear it… I would have done… if I knew it would give you pleasure, or security or something…"

"Meribel… I think the bleach must be getting to you. I'd never ask you to wear something of my mother's. What's going on in that normally clear-thinking brain of yours?"

"What's going on is that you're cooling! How do I believe that in a whole night and early morning out, apparently consoling and weaning Michelle off her weed, you didn't slip your hand into her panties. Even if you didn't… you're close to wanting to… or how do I know that when you went out driving Bob and Marcia Hunt, the old man, who we know does nothing for his young wife, didn't drop off to sleep after his lunch-time drink and she screwed you… you look at her all the time… I'm sure you fancy her… all the men seem to…

"So I just thought it might turn you on a bit more if you knew we were doing our thing. I felt the risks were fun… and I was right… you liked the effect. Maybe I should have just lied and said I'd seen them in a boutique and bought them, to give you pleasure… without bitch Marcia Hunt coming into it."

"Let's collect this stuff up. I'll get you home," Peter said sternly.

"What, just leaving it like this? You're upset because I borrowed someone else's knickers? Peter, that's pathetic."

"Look! Let's call this bad day a bad day, and get cleaned up. We'll need to talk through how you get the pants back into Marcia's drawer without her missing them; I don't think you can use the laundry excuse."

"Missing them! How can she miss them, she scatters them round the suite like confetti. I think she does it to arouse Bob, or to annoy him… maybe to get to me, to make me jealous, in my mundane pants which clearly aren't as arousing as hers, and she knows it."

"Meri, how on earth can you say such things?"

"Because a few days ago… there was no 'do not disturb sign' and I went into their room earlier than usual, room 28 were checking out and needed to be done later. I went in and found Bob Hunt sitting on the bed holding a couple of pairs of Marcia's pants. He looked embarrassed, and said to me, 'Do all girls chuck their knickers around for their husbands to tidy up?'"

"What did you say?" Peter asked with a degree of shock.

"I said, 'no, I don't think so, usually my mother comes to the rescue', and we both laughed."

"Meri, I don't think you ought to have conversations like that with paying guests."

"Oh, that's great, I'm expected to take on the personality of a chambermaid with no brains, am I?"

"Not with no brains, no. But a chambermaid role where you know your place."

"Peter, you're so naïve. If I was your average chambermaid, like that Tania Henriques, the gypsy girl who's just started, if I'd found a male guest sitting on a bed, playing or even not playing with his wife's panties, then what I would have done is get close to him and ask him if everything was alright, or could I help him in any way. I'd wait and there'd be a more than 50 per cent chance that he'd say, 'What more can you do for me?', and I'd giggle and say 'Oh Mr Hunt', and move closer. Apparently I'd rarely let him screw me, unless he waved a big wad of pesetas at me. But I'd let him fondle me for about 10,000 pesetas."

"Are you telling me that's what Tania Henriques actually does, or is that some fantasy tale?"

Meribel was like a scared animal trying to save its skin. It got worse. "Well, according to her, that's the sort of money she regularly takes when your Uncle Marco does room checks instead of your mother."

"Meribel, you really are going too far…"

"Be fair, Peter, you suggested I should be acting like a typical chambermaid. Yet you accuse me of outrageous behaviour just because I wanted to please you, give you a break, liven up our relationship..."

"What do you want then, 10,000 pesetas?"

"Would you get me home now please?"

He wished he hadn't said that, but he couldn't curb it. She'd tantalised him – at the expense of Marcia, he felt – and then breached a confidence, smearing the already tarnished reputation of his uncle. This would sour their whole relationship.

They walked solemnly to the car. "If I said I agreed I'd been outrageous, would you tell me you still loved me?" Meribel asked coolly.

"At the moment I'm confused. I've enjoyed our relationship, but I just don't understand why you thought something... something as personal as Marcia's possessions would give us spark and enjoyment. Yes, OK, any bloke would be turned on by silk and lace. But they should have been yours, ours even, not some identifiable other person's, who I have no need to consider in sexual terms."

"Oh, Peter, for Christ's sake, I've done it now, you've made the point, but you were quite happy to capitalise on the mood of the moment. What the hell's the difference between borrowing Marcia's knickers and borrowing your mother's car? We can grope in your mother's car without recrimination or defiling her, but put your hand inside Marcia's panties, with me in them, and some sort of self-righteousness comes over you. Maybe, after all's said and done, you feel some sort of guilt that you've had your pleasure with her, rather than me.

"But I tell you one thing... no... a number of things... if it had been her, then I doubt you'd have been the first. If it had been her it would have been to satisfy *her* shortages and demands... kid yourself not, it wouldn't have been to give you what *I* was wanting to give to you. And what's more, you'd have had to wait your turn for a return favour with her... but with me, whether in a cheap laundry room or your mother's defiled car, I'm always there for a return visit, I thought, in fact, for all time. That, my dearest Peter, I now doubt to be the case. Get me home please, I feel sick."

They took their respective seats in silence. Peter had put the rug in the boot and was feeling distinctly uncomfortable, unsure whether he had reacted adversely in haste, or whether his emotions were justified. He started the engine, slipped into first gear, second, then third as the pre-set radio took its charge from the battery and emitted the sixth or seventh bar of 'La Mer'.

Shit, he thought, it was their special song. The song that had been playing after their first sexual encounter in this very car.

"... and you can turn the bloody radio off too, please," Meribel pronounced.

They drove in morbid silence. There was a lay-by not far from Meribel's parents' house, where they usually stopped for a tender goodnight kiss.

Meribel broke the silence. "Could you stop in the lay-by please."

He did as commanded. She'd make the move, he was sure. She did. She slid her skirt up towards her waist, exposing her long legs, those beautiful silk thighs he knew so well. Hooking a thumb from each hand into the elastic woven into the panties, she slid them down, lifting her bottom off the leather seats of Maria's car. *Maria's car of all cars,* she thought, as her bare buttocks hit the coolness of the leather. She lifted first her left knee. He wondered why she always did that, but she did. With one final tug she slipped them over both her feet, which were bare, freed from her strappy sandals.

"I'll walk from here," she said. "Here, you give these back to Marcia, or even Bob Hunt. Say they may be expensive but they're a cheap pretence, just wrapping paper. Maybe they should pay more attention to the treasure inside."

She opened the passenger door and left, not looking back towards the car's searching headlights. Peter watched her turn the corner and waited for her to reappear. She did not.

What a mess. He'd gained a pair of Marcia's panties, but lost Meribel, he was sure.

He drove on. As for Tania Henriques... she wasn't what the Playa needed, whatever little extras she was giving Uncle Marco.

Peter normally felt a frisson of satisfaction whenever he turned into the hotel drive. The entrance, depicting so much history, always made his heart jump a beat or two. The crunchiness of the shingle and cobble drive always used to slow him down to a more regal pace and by the time he swung into a parking bay, he almost expected to hear the golden horns of Roman centurions blasting their welcome home to their Emperor.

He felt for the light switch below the dash of Maria's car and turned it off. His eyes acclimatised to the level of light, which became stronger as the shafts from the hotel reception drifted up to relieve the otherwise total blackness around him.

By God, he felt tired. Perhaps less tired than drained.

"Come and find me," came a voice from deep within the pampas bushes. He stopped in his tracks. It was a female voice, which he thought he recognised. His first thought was Michelle. He waited in case his senses were playing tricks with him.

"Come and find me!" the croaky, slightly slurring voice repeated.

"Where are you?" he called out, somewhat sternly.

"Coash," came the reply, "coash, is that really you?"

"Where the hell are you, invisible woman?" he called back. "For Christ's sake, don't wake up all the guests! Where are you?"

A giggle came from the pampas, muffled by the thickness of the gently moving foliage in the light night breeze.

"Coash, can you help me? Please coash."

He moved into the pampas.

"Peter. Coash, is it you? It is you!"

He came upon a form lying in the bush. "Christ! Marcia Hunt."

"Why are you always so bloody formal?" the slurred voice asked. Peter knelt down, both hands outstretched. Marcia had the benefit that Peter was backlit by the hotel lights.

"Peter, darling, I'm pissed."

"I think I can tell that," he replied.

"Don't be cross, coash. We've been celebrating the win and I had too much."

"Where's your husband?"

"Now you're talking like the young stud I'm sure you are. He's all tucked up in bed, probably asleep, so you and I can frolic."

Peter pulled at both her hands, which were now gripping his firmly. He levered her up until she was upright in front of him. She put one arm round his neck.

"He's asleep. Come on, coash. Let's have some fun."

"Marcia. You're pretty drunk. That's down to team captain Philippe, I'd guess. You're not in control of your senses. Let's get you to your room."

"You're a young fart, dear Peter. I'm married to an old one. Why am I surrounded by farts?" As she said that she burped. "… And burps." She giggled as she repeated "… Farts and burps… burps and farts."

Peter converted the hold of her arm around his neck into a stabilising limb upon which to lift her off her feet and carry her like a small dependent child towards the reception lights.

"You're so strong, coash," she said. "Are you taking me to your bed?"

"No, Marcia. To Bob's bed."

"Ooh. Spoilsport Peter."

As they hit the full lights of the reception area she screeched, "Ouch!" and closed her eyes.

Peter looked down at her in his arms. Her face was childlike. Not a single wrinkle. Her head went heavy. She had passed into either sleep or a drink-induced coma. Either way, she would need some reminding of events in the morning.

He pressed the lift call button with his left elbow. Within seconds the reliable

278

Kone lift appeared. The doors parted and he stepped in. He hit '01' with his same elbow. The doors closed and after an initial jerk, they glided upwards.

Peter looked down and kissed her forehead. There was not a flicker of a nerve twitch. She was out for the count.

He turned into the corridor towards the Hunts' suite. At the door he was able to free up a forefinger with which he rapped three solid knocks.

There was silence within. He repeated the knocking with a degree more force, now feeling Marcia's nine stone plus dead weight.

"So you want to come in. Eh! Marcia. Huh! So you left your young team-mates behind. Huh? So you know where home is after all. Eh! Well you should bloody well stay out there all night."

"Mr Hunt," Peter said in slightly more than a confidential whisper. "It's Peter Martinez. I found your wife in the garden. She's out for the count."

The door opened. Bob Hunt was framed by the corridor emergency lighting. It made his face seem grey and pallid.

"Peter, what the fuck are you up to then?"

"It's a short story really. I came home, parked the car and heard your wife's voice in the bushes. She's a bit the worse for wear."

"She was an hour or so ago when she refused to come up with me in favour of making herself look a fool with the son of that French frog. What's his name?"

"Possibly Philippe."

"Yes, that's the bastard. Cocky bloke. Doesn't do for a prat like that to win something and have such good looks as well. He had this little English filly falling all over him. Here, bring her in. Dump her on the bed. I'll do the rest. Thanks, old pal. I'm glad *you* found her. All the other buggers would have raped her by now. You're a good bloke. I'll thank you properly in the morning and make bloody sure she does too. Doesn't she just look a tart in that red skirt and bloody ragged fishnets? Have you got her other shoe?"

"Christ no!" Peter exclaimed. "But I'll show you in the morning where she might well have spent the night if I hadn't come along. It'll be there somewhere."

Bob Hunt took Peter's hand. "Thanks, pal. You're a good mate. Get to bed."

Peter's last thought as his head touched the pillow was: *What a bloody awful day.*

CHAPTER 18

True to her ever-supportive role, Maria had called out to Peter as he headed for bed, "Alright, Pedro?"

"Yes fine, Mother. You sleep well."

"You too, Pedro."

"Aren't you going to advise me to 'lavate bien'?"

"Oh, Peter. Skip it. It must be late," she said in a worryingly tired voice, he thought. That wasn't like her. He'd insist she had a check-up in the morning.

Maria was up early on the Saturday morning, and at her office desk by 7.30am. She was covering for Sñr Martin, who was having the morning off 'for family reasons'. She'd left Peter sound asleep.

She jotted down a few essential things on her day planner: fix dinner menu for Admiral and wife… arrange picnic for Hunts on Sunday… check flowers in restaurant… check arrivals/departures…

The phone rang. It was Meribel.

"Oh! Good morning, Maria. I thought it would be Sñr Martin answering this early."

"No, he's off. How are you, darling? What can I do for you?" She looked at her watch, realising Meribel should be on her way to work.

"That's it really. I'm afraid I'm not so well. I won't be able to get in."

Maria thought, *what a pain.* It was Saturday, they had a couple of turn-arounds – guests checking in to a room soon after the previous occupants' departure.

"Can I ask what the problem is?"

"Woman's stuff. I'm feeling very sick and my legs won't carry me."

"OK. Well, hope you feel better. Shall I let Peter know, or will you phone him?"

Meribel hesitated. "Well, I think that's another reason for me feeling so bad. I think I've blown our relationship."

"Oh Meri, I'm sorry about that. Do you need a peacemaker of a potential mother-in-law?"

"Thanks, Maria, you're a friend. No, it's just something I'd like to turn the clock back on. We'll see. But I'm a realist. We're going to get separated in a few weeks anyway and I'm sure Peter'll be needing space at university. Me too, I suppose. I want to just get my head down and get my medical qualifications… Peter might just be too much of a distraction anyway."

"I'll let Peter know. You never know, he might phone you."

Maria put the phone down. *Bugger it.* One key member of staff short on a busy day. She rang housekeeping and spoke to Tania Henriques, who was already in. She started at 7am.

Tania had been one of Marco's 'finds' resulting from a recommendation from a friend of a friend. In fact, in terms of putting the personnel in place for the hotel, which ordinarily would have been Virginia's contribution, finding Maria a potential chambermaid was his only contribution to the staffing arrangements.

At first, Maria was loath to consider any female introduced by Marco. He had always been prone to make his weekly visits into Palafrugell. Ostensibly, it was to do the banking but he'd then go to a café/bar where the local traders tended to gather to put the world to rights and lower the proprietor's stock of barrelled wine and brandy. He had been caught out by Virginia a couple of times after having climbed the stairs to the rooms above, either with the previous barmaid of the day or one of the girls who had been passing through.

In the case of Tania, allegedly she had run away from her Romany roots, where she had been ill-treated, and happened to find herself in Palafrugell.

Maria was sceptical about any suggestion of her being offered a job until she had met and interviewed her. She had had a pleasant surprise. Tania was clean, respectful and, judging by her hands, she had worked more with those than with her body, or so it seemed. Maria offered her a three-month trial, and to date, she had not disappointed. Importantly, Marco had not been caught leaving one of the empty rooms in which she had been making the final preparations for the imminent intake of paying guests. Hopefully, Maria had found a good match.

"Meribel's sick. Is there any chance of you doing some overtime to cover her shift?"

Tania thought for a moment. "It's Saturday, my sister's at home doing nothing. What do you say about her coming in and helping?"

It was Maria's turn to hesitate. The one thing Marco and she had insisted on was that all staff with access to the guests' rooms should be security screened.

"It's an idea," Maria said, "but she hasn't been security screened."

"Oh Mrs Martinez, come on, she's my sister. I think Mr Marco knows her, she did some waitressing here before the hotel was built. Ask him about my family's integrity. He'll vouch for us, I'm sure."

And if he bloody doesn't he'll not get to touch even my knee again, let alone the rest, Tania thought.

Maria thought for a minute. "OK, but she'll have to have a routine check before she leaves the hotel."

That was something they had introduced on an ad hoc basis. Guests would leave half-used bottles of suntan lotion, or an inch or two of gin or vodka and tell the chambermaids to take it home with them. The rule then was that the staff had to hand such leftovers in to the office and ask if they might take them home. That way they could check and control petty pilfering. The staff accepted the criteria and none objected to a body and bag search as long as it was by a member of their own sex. Tania had once asked Marco if he wanted to check her out at the end of the day. "It would be fun for everybody to see you playing with my body in public," she teased. Marco had resisted.

So it was agreed, and Tania's sister would be there by 9am. Panic was over. Surely it wasn't going to be one of those days.

Maria rang Peter on the intercom they'd had fitted.

"Hi! Were you awake?"

"Dozing."

"Meribel's been on, she's reported sick."

"Oh! Shit."

"Well, she says she's sick but went on to say you'd had a bit of a tiff. That's probably the real reason for her not coming in."

"Oh, hell!" Peter said. "OK, Mother, thanks for letting me know, I've got a couple of things that need sorting anyway. I'll be up and about. I'll give her a call and see what we can sort out. We're coming up to an enforced separation anyway, with university and all that. Don't worry about it. Sorry you've been inconvenienced on the housekeeping front."

"Oh, I've sorted that, Tania's sister Beth is coming in."

"Good," Peter said, suddenly feeling a rush of blood on hearing Tania's name after what Meri had told him the night before.

He made an early morning cup of coffee, grabbed a croissant and took them out onto the little terrace they had built in the garden area. He sat down at the wrought iron table they had found in a local farmyard sale, sipped at his coffee and contemplated the hot hazy morning, and life in general.

As much as Peter had resisted his mother's words about Marcia being a head-turner, particularly his, he really did have a thing about her. The Meribel episode the night before, and Marcia's drunken antics, had confirmed that for him. But it was not for her to know.

With that in mind, had he been hard, too hard on Meri? He'd best phone her. But then he'd get her mother first and he'd have to go through all the usual pleasantries. He didn't fancy that. Yet he'd best strike while the iron was hot.

Sod it! he suddenly thought. The iron being hot was the memory jerker. He'd got Marcia's panties. How was he to get them back to her?

He'd go to Tania's locker and plant them in her bag. Then alert the back door security to search her and her sister as they were leaving. They'd find them. Maria would fire Tania and Marco would be shot of his unsavoury little bit on the side, who he seemed to have got too deeply involved with.

No! None of that would be fair. Peter had no right to get someone wrongly accused, or even to ruin Marco's extramarital romps.

Back in his room, he picked up the jeans he'd been wearing the night before. Then panicked as he felt inside the left pocket for Marcia's pants. They'd gone! Hell, where on earth could he have lost those?

"Oh God!" he moaned. "Shit, in Mother's bloody car!"

He left the cottage and made it to the car faster than he had ever done before. But then he felt in the right hand pocket and unexpectedly felt the cool of the silk and the crispness of the lace. *Thank Christ for that,* he thought. He took the troublesome panties out and shook them, gave them a thorough inspection with a degree of embarrassment. He'd best rinse them out, but then how would he get them dried and back into Marcia's room?

His mother's hair drier came to mind. Back in the cottage he went into the bathroom, ran some lukewarm water and swished the knickers around. He sensed his pulse racing and was ashamed by the fact that he actually found it stimulating. He felt perverted. This was why Bob Hunt apparently played with Marcia's underwear. But then she was his wife and that seemed to make a difference.

He squeezed the tiny garment as dry as he could and shook off the surplus water. He knew where his mother kept her hair dryer. He wished, as he turned it on, that it could have been silent. Suppose his mother returned. What would he say?

"I'm just drying Marcia's knickers for her!" No. He'd just have hold the drier up to his hair and say he was in a hurry.

None of that forward planning was necessary. The expensive fabric dried quickly. He folded the borrowed goods into a handkerchief sized square and put them on the dresser in his own room. They were in the sun there. He stripped, went into the bathroom and cold showered. He put on his tennis gear and his tracksuit, he was sure he had some coaching, but he would need to look in his diary in the office.

Putting Marcia's belongings in his tracksuit pocket, he cursed Meribel. He looked at his watch and figured out the Hunts would probably be at breakfast. He'd check, and if they were, he'd take the office key and go into their room, plant the garment back where it belonged.

He closed the cottage door behind him. As he walked across the path, thinking of how the hell he'd got into this mess, he was reminded of Meribel the night before. Shit, he hadn't rung her. In fact, in all the washing and drying drama, he realised he hadn't given her a thought.

He'd best ring. He fumbled for his key, which he realised was now tangled in Marcia's undies. This couldn't get much worse. There was morning pollen around. He'd have to consciously remember that if he sneezed, he mustn't take the apparent handkerchief out to wipe his nose. That would be dreadful.

Back in the cottage he dialled Meribel's number. He really didn't feel like speaking to her mother.

"How are you, Peter?" she'd be bound to say.

"Oh! I'm fine. But I'll be better when I've given Marcia her knickers back."

The phone seemed to ring for an age. They couldn't all be out. Meribel was meant to be sick.

"Hello." Meribel's quiet and weaker than usual voice answered.

"Hi, it's me."

"Yes," she said.

"My mother says you're not well."

"If that's what she says, then that's what you must believe."

"Meribel. I'm ringing to see how you are. You're being a bit curt."

"Curt. Don't you mean 'hurt'?"

"Oh dear! Have I picked the wrong moment."

"Not particularly. Anyway, what do you want?"

Peter was staggered. This was a side to Meribel he hadn't seen before.

"Listen," he said, "I'd heard you were unwell. I'm ringing to see how you are."

"I'm fine. Actually I'm just very disappointed, I'm feeling shunned. My best intentions in the world have been thrown back in my face. That's it really. So now you know how I am you can go about your busy day. I'll nurse my hurt while you play around with your entourage."

Peter remained silent. He felt that whatever he said would be wrong.

"I see," Meribel said in a strange tone, "you're going to remain strong and silent. No apology. No remorse for having made me feel inept. OK, Peter. Have it your way… we're washed up."

"I'm ringing to see how you are… with the intention of saying we both made mistakes last night and that together we might patch that up."

"Patch it up!" she yelled. "A patch, dearest Peter, is a temporary repair, it can stem the flow of blood or a punctured tyre, even a rip in a parachute. It's not permanent. So you're looking for a temporary arrangement, no doubt with the treats that I give to you... or, more correctly, *used* to give to you. Cheers, friend... let's go our temporary ways."

There was a metallic thud. She had slammed the phone down.

He looked at the handset as though expecting to see a face in the mouthpiece. *"Go our temporary ways..."* Quite what that really meant he didn't know. Was she saying they'd separate but not 'divorce'? *I don't know,* he thought. *Girls... women... they're all so complicated.* They never seemed to accept finality.

Peter knew that while his own mother in some ways faced the blunt truth that Paco had died, she still expected, from time to time, that he'd walk in through the door as though nothing had happened. Yet he could understand his mother being in love with a ghost, as he himself still loved his father's image.

But Meribel's decision did seem final. They had reached their sell-by date. The next chapter would be new, with no reference to the past.

Peter had presumed the Hunts would be in for breakfast, but, suddenly remembering the events of the night before, he thought it more likely she'd be nursing a hangover or getting a lecture from Bob about her behaviour. So he'd bide his time.

But as he walked across towards the terrace, where breakfast was taken by those guests who preferred the elements to the air conditioning inside the restaurant, he recognised the back view of Bob and then Marcia behind her Ray-Bans. The Admiral and his wife were there too, together with the Cook family and a few Lunn-Polys and Thomas Cooks.

As Peter approached, Marcia went into deep concentration over the remnants of a croissant on her plate.

"Buenos dias, como estas?" Peter said in his strongest voice.

"Well, we could be better," Bob replied.

Marcia lifted her head and looked up at Peter. Although he couldn't discern what her eyes were saying, she looked a little like a forlorn cocker spaniel.

"Buenos dias, coach," she said.

Peter laughed. Bob beckoned for him to pull up a chair and sit down, anticipating that any further conversation should be between the three of them and not for general entertainment over breakfast.

Peter sat down and laughed again. "At least you can say 'coach' this morning."

"What?" Marcia enquired.

"Last night I was 'coash'. Coash this, coash that..."

"Peter, I'm sorry. I don't remember too much. We'd had some sparkling wine and then we went on to that dreadful poison, sangria, which you serve to kill people in Spain. I realised I'd had enough and decided to go up to join Bob, who'd made it perfectly plain he was in no mood to celebrate. I got to the foot of the stairs and felt the cool air coming in through the reception door and I think I must have changed course and walked back out into the front gardens for some air. All I can then remember is seeing the headlights of a car coming racing towards me. I think I must have stepped back out of the way to save being run over... and the rest isn't clear, but I know you were involved."

"Well, yes. That's right, I did run you over. I broke both your legs and one arm but, because I've got these wonderful powers of healing, which come from my mother having weaned me on sangria instead of milk, I was able to mend the damage and deliver you virtually in one piece to your husband."

"You're a rotten leg-puller. What did happen?"

"You recognised me and then passed out and I nearly broke my back getting you back to your room."

If they hadn't been hidden by her opaque shades, her eyes would have shown a sudden recollection. She could vaguely remember being in Peter's strong arms... and enjoying it. The power and comfort had led them into a fairytale embrace, she felt sure, which had lulled her into an undisturbed night's sleep. When Bob wasn't around, she'd ask Peter if there really had been any passion between them.

Peter noticed she was working something through in her mind. He wondered if he might suddenly plunge his hand into his trouser pocket, fish out the pants and say, "Oh, by the way. You'd best have these back." He still felt uncomfortable at his own arousal.

Bob broke the ice. "So there you are, Marcia, if it hadn't been for Peter you might have stayed out there all night and been eaten by the mosquitoes and all those bloody little lizards lying around the place. So you'd best thank him."

Peter saw that some inner thought had stimulated her as she stood up and came round the table to him. She leant down and kissed him firmly on the forehead. As she pulled back, leaving Peter bathed in the aroma of her Chanel, she just whispered, "Thanks, coash."

How this lady was always able to come out on top, Peter just did not know.

"Now I'm going to have a quiet day by the pool. Tell the guests to let their husbands ogle but I don't want to be bothered by them. Had we got a tennis lesson today, Peter?"

"No."

"So I won't need to cancel that. I've got to recover my sea legs to do justice to our trip with your mother tomorrow." She leant forward again and touched her cheek to his, placing her left hand on his thigh for support. "Seriously, Peter. Thank you for saving me from all those creepy crawlies."

Her hand was so near the knickers in his pocket, and she'd stroked his thigh almost playfully. This lady really was practised in making impressions.

Peter stood up. "I've got loads to do, I'm afraid. I'm not on holiday." Then, as if to leave a lasting mark on both the Hunts, he turned to Bob and said, "By the way, you remember the stretch of coast we looked at and where we played the 'how would we develop this' game?"

Bob thought for a moment. "On the drive. With the sunflowers. Yes."

"Well, I've bought it." He felt he could now say that because the options had been signed.

Bob looked flabbergasted. "Go on! You're pulling my leg."

"No. True. I have. I'll tell you about it when we've got more time... I must go."

Bob seemed stunned. Marcia too.

In a final gesture, Peter squeezed Marcia's left cheek playfully. "Thanks for last night," he smiled and walked away.

"You bloody sure you can't remember last night?" Bob said in a staccato tone.

"Of course I can't," Marcia said, offended.

"What's he bloody mean then?"

"Oh, Bob. He's a boy having his game."

"Boys don't go buying big chunks of good land, darling. That's men's work. And boys don't go carrying young senseless women around without at least a little fumble, either."

"Bob! Peter's not like that. Please don't say things like that."

"Well, I wish you hadn't got pissed."

"Look, darling, let's forget it. Come up and watch me get into my costume. I'll make you feel better. You're all strung up."

Peter saw them going upstairs as he was touching base again with his mother.

"So Tania's sister's covering, OK then. Who'll be doing the Hunts' room?"

"Tania."

"Well, tell her to leave it an hour or so. They said they've got some sorting out to do... I think for your trip tomorrow... and you know them, they never put the 'No perturbe' sign out. Tell Tania I'll let her know when to do it."

"Taking over housekeeping now, are we?"

"No. Don't be silly. Just trying to be helpful. It's Meribel's and my own fault for causing you this extra stress."

"Did you talk to her?"

"Yup!"

"And?"

"Mother. Forget it. I think we're washed up."

Maria came from around her desk and put maternal arms around Pedro's neck. "You don't have much luck with your girls, do you?"

"I bloody do. I escape their clutches, that's luck by any standards. I'm not looking for any permanency."

"Oh, Pedro! Don't leave it too long, I've always wanted to be a young grandmother."

"Well, I'm blowed if I want to be a penniless young student with a wife and family to keep. You'll have to wait, I'm afraid."

"I understand. But at least I now know you've got it in mind." She slapped him across the bottom. "We've both got to get on."

Peter went out into reception. He'd get his first hour of coaching out of the way and then... well, he smiled to himself, he supposed he'd be on laundry duty...

Maria told chef she wanted pâté and avocado and prawns or gazpacho as starter choices for their celebration dinner that evening with the Admiral and his wife, Marco and Virginia, Peter and herself. Lobster, John Dory or lamb chops for main course, and a crema Catalana, ice cream or cheese for dessert. She could confidently leave the wines to Antonio, the maître d'hotel.

What a bore, she thought to herself. But it was a small price to pay. She'd seen last night's bar takings when she cashed up that morning, and they'd served the most dinners ever.

She'd then got the Hunts' 'mini cruise', as they kept calling it, and then the dread of taking Miguel's potion. She suddenly felt a little flat.

Peter was half-hearted about improving the young Brown family's tennis game. He was distracted, kept looking up to the balcony of the Hunts' room to see if there was any movement.

Marcia suddenly appeared, like some statuesque Roman empress welcoming her returning triumphant armies gathered below her balcony. She was wearing a white one-piece, indicating she was bound for the pool.

All the guests tended to choose the same loungers every day. The Hunts' preferred spot had one lounger in the sun, another in the shade of the pines, and an extra upright wrought iron chair.

The Hunts' arrangement of chairs was still unoccupied. Without Marcia adorning the area, it looked dead and uninviting. But it would be occupied and alive soon, which would allow Peter to get his morning task over and done with.

Peter passed Maria in the reception. "Have the Hunts come down?" he asked.

"I think so," his mother replied.

"I'll go and check and tell Tania if she can do the suite."

"Thanks, darling."

Peter sprinted upstairs, two marbled steps at a time. He was never really a lift person. He found them claustrophobic. He swung into the Hunts' corridor. The room key from reception had got tangled up but he unravelled it. It turned smoothly in the lock and he entered through the outer lobby, closing the door behind him. He hesitated, wondering whether to put the safety chain on but decided against it.

He went through the sleeping area and stood behind the curtain to the open balcony door. He could see Marcia and Bob Hunt now firmly in their appointed positions. Thank God for that. They'd never get back before he'd returned Marcia's underclothes.

Peter moved to the dressing table. In the top left drawer there were handkerchiefs and scarves. Chanel wafted into his face as he closed that one and tried the next one down.

He felt the tinge of excitement a burglar must feel when finding where the valuables are stored. Success... there in all their laundered, folded glory were the sister panties to the ones he was now holding in his hand. White, pink and black items of underwear, resting from their exalted task of wrapping the most intimate part of Marcia's body; waiting their turn to be the next chosen one.

Peter refolded those he now had in his hand and slipped them between the top and second black layer. It was a bit like having chosen a card, then returning it to the pack for a magician to find in some secret way.

Job done, Peter thought with a sigh of relief.

"Your uncle loves black."

Peter shot round. "Tania!"

"Yes, Mr Pedro."

"What the hell are you doing here?"

"Mrs Maria said she thought the room was ready to be done."

"Well listen, young lady, you should always knock," he said crossly.

Not liking his tone, Tania said, "I'm sorry, Mr Pedro. I didn't think you'd be in here playing with Madame's underwear."

"Playing... what...?"

Tania was quick in her appraisal of the situation and saw it as a moment on which to capitalise.

"I don't mind, sir. I can keep a secret. But if ever you'd like to feel those things with the real thing inside, then all you've got to do is say... after all, you're young and I'm young... I'd like you to do that."

"For Christ's sake, Tania! You keep yourself to yourself. The truth is Mrs Hunt got very drunk last night and told Meribel she'd mislaid her underwear and didn't want Mr Hunt to know. We found it in the garden and Meribel was due to replace it, but she's ill and I'm having to do it for her."

"Yes sir, I see. So it's not how it looks."

"That's right," Peter replied, hoping he did not appear too flustered.

"So, I'm not to let anybody know about this, sir," she said softly. She stepped tantalisingly forward, as if she was Carmen offering herself to the village men. She smiled broadly. "But I'm still serious about you feeling me if you'd like to, Mr Pedro."

"One word from me to Mr Marco about you being too generous with your offers, Tania, and I think he'd probably fire you."

"Oh! I see, Mr Pedro. You want it to be like that then. OK, it's alright with me. But I tell you what, it would be more alright with me if my sister could have a permanent holiday job here…"

"I'll arrange that," Peter said.

"… and even if you don't want to put your hand in my underwear, I'd welcome an extra few hundred pesetas anyway. I'd love to be able to buy something like you've got there. Here," she added, "let me fold them properly and put them back into Madame's drawer for you. You won't know where they belong… there!" she said. "Now if you were your wicked old uncle I'd be made to slip them on. That's a duty with him but I'd see it as a pleasure for a young master like you."

"Tania, you're overstepping your mark, I don't ask for such favours, nor do I need to. Keep your little extra-curricular requirements where they belong and I tell you what I'll do for you!"

"Yes, Mr Pedro. What's that?"

"I'll do a trade with you. This little scene which you've misinterpreted didn't happen, OK? And I'll tell you what else didn't happen, which might otherwise cost you your job: you haven't breached the confidences of your employer, my uncle, by alluding to the pleasures you provide for him."

"Mr Pedro. You're very clever with words. I also think you're a very nice man and any girl who's allowed into your world of pleasures is a very lucky girl. My offer stands. There'll be a time you might want some fun with no strings attached. Maybe you'll throw in a few extra pesetas if you're happy, and for that you do buy guaranteed silence. You're right, I let it slip about your uncle, so we've got a deal."

She held out a latex-gloved hand, then removed the glove to expose soft white skin, long fingers with brightly painted red nails. He'd seen that colour before. Where? When? Then it dawned on him. The day before. The colour matched Marcia's French tart skirt.

"Tania. Did you get that nail polish where I think you got it from? From Sñra Hunt's collection?"

"You're good Mr Pedro, yes."

"That's theft, Tania."

"Do you think my nails look as good as hers?"

Peter thought hard. Where the hell was this going? This little vixen knew where she was coming from, but Peter was not sure he could read the situation.

"It's not a question of whether they look as good as Mrs Hunt's or not, it's theft."

"No. I've only borrowed it. Just like you were only borrowing her undies. You've put yours back. I can't. So, again, we're quits. We're two of a kind. Lost. Needing to borrow other people's beautiful things. So there's another deal, I think. We both keep quiet."

She was right.

Tania rested her hands on his strong forearms. "Now, the question is, again: do they look as good as hers?"

Peter finally gave in to the gypsy enchantment behind her constant challenge. "Equally, Tania."

"Thank you, Mr Pedro. And don't forget my promise. I look equally good with or without undies on too. The difference is, I'm on offer. I doubt she is, and even then, so they say, she's only playful. She's got a problem with doing what I do, and what I actually enjoy to do if it gives pleasure."

"Tania. One further thing. It's Mr Peter, that's the name I prefer."

Peter was being made to feel a bit too masculine for his own comfort. She'd kill his uncle if she went on like this with him. She'd get his blood pressure up into the record books. Peter would stop it here. Their deals were done. He'd been trapped into an arrangement of mutual silence.

Tania seemed thrown by his suggestion. She didn't know quite how to react. She wasn't sure whether he was encouraging her to be more familiar.

"Tell me, Tania. Is Mr Hunt on your favoured guest list?"

She came out of her contemplation and giggled like a girl who's just found out her boyfriend's weak spot. She placed her long right forefinger on Peter's nose and tapped it hard.

"Now, if Mr Hunt asked me if you'd been playing around in Mrs Hunt's underclothes, I wouldn't know," she smiled. "What's good for the goose is good for the gander and whether he's been in my undies is not for discussion and, sir, I'd like to say, not for common speculation either. We girls like our privacy, you know."

Peter went back into managerial stern mode. "We've both got jobs to do. Let's get on."

"Yes, Sir, Mr Peter," she saluted playfully, plunging her still bare hand inside her blouse to pull her bra strap back into place. He noticed she was wearing a short gold chain with a crucifix, which seemed to point to the promise of a deep, plunging cleavage.

Tania knew very well the effect she was having on him. She blew air into both latex gloves and, having puffed them up like cow's udders, started pulling them over her hands like a surgeon preparing to operate.

"You're right. Let's get back to work. Thank you, sir, for understanding. I enjoyed the interlude. You can leave me here, I'll not borrow any more, I know you've rumbled me," she said, with a broad smile.

Peter went to the window. The Hunts appeared to have died in their respective chairs. Marcia, no doubt, had sunk into the oblivion of her hangover and Bob into the boredom of yet another holiday book, his uncharged brain dulled by the absence of deals to clinch, and ducking and diving.

Peter exhaled a long breath of relief. Job done. He'd been propositioned loud and clear, but overall he could relax.

Tania was dusting and polishing as Peter passed her on his way out. "Now you make sure you give that an extra polish today," he said. "Yes sir, and it'll be just for you!"

Shit! What a 24 hours this had been!

Peter suddenly had his great awakening. He wanted to get rid of his virginity. Hanging on to it was getting in the way of his life, interfering with his rational side.

He jumped a mile when he heard his mother's voice.

"Everything alright, darling?" Maria said cheerily.

"Yup, under control," he tried to say convincingly.

"Oh, I sent Tania up. Was that alright?"

"Yes, as far as I'm aware," he said nonchalantly. He stopped in his tracks. "Mother, I can't see Meribel coming back, you know."

"Oh dear, we've got full bookings right through to school holidays. We'll need her."

"Did you say something about Tania's sister?"

"Well yes, for today. It's a weekend."

"Isn't she still at school? If she is she'd be available through the school holidays. Couldn't she do the job?"

"Peter, you're a genius! What a good idea. I expect Tania's still doing the suite. I'll ask her."

At four o'clock, Maria was at José's boat. As she approached, an imaginary veil indicating her widowhood lifted. She felt she was leading some kind of double Geminian life. At the hotel she was the organised, somewhat distant proprietress, efficient but nevertheless welcoming. With José she'd been able to expose her twin. Soft. Loving. Wild in thought and very welcoming too.

José, by design rather than accident, she thought, was working down on the aft deck, from where he would have seen her approaching. He waved her a boyish wave. Maria really hoped he was not expecting some quick sexual activity. True, they'd been apart for some while, and the last time they'd made love was in the changing room, which had had such traumatic consequences. She hoped he wasn't getting attention from elsewhere, so it would be natural for him to be expecting a bit of pleasure.

She'd vomited again that morning and she felt bloated. Was constantly having to pop to the loo. She didn't remember spending such a number of pennies in the early days of carrying Peter. She was tired, too.

She waved back to José, and blew him a kiss. José made out he was having trouble catching it, and when he did put both his hands around the invisible sentiment, he touched his lips with it. He swung over the side rails onto the jetty, avoiding the more formal plank entry.

He hurried to meet Maria, clearly pleased to see her. He bent and took the weight of the picnic basket from her, then kissed her cheek and took her now spare hand.

"Gosh, it's good to see you! I was beginning to forget what you looked like."

"Hi, darling. I was hoping you wouldn't stand back and say, 'Are you sure this is the Maria Martinez I know so well', because I'm feeling tired and haggard, worn out."

"Come on now… don't try and get compliments out of me that way… you look as beautiful as ever." He stood back, looking her fully in the face. "Haggard? Yes, I see what you mean!"

"You're a tease, José Romanez," she laughed.

José always had the power to make her laugh. They always had happy laughing times, even when just on the phone.

"Now listen," she said, "you've got me all day tomorrow. But I've only managed to squeeze an hour away from the hotel today, because of Sñr Martin's break. So let's get you something to eat…"

"Tell you what… I'll be happy to skip the food. I'll trade that for an hour in our cabin. That would do us far more good."

"Get on with you! I'm here for tea and to catch up on all your news, not for a romp… much as I'd like that too." Her stomach heaved as she said that.

It was far from the truth and she didn't like to lie to José. She had an almost constant headache, and had had for a couple of days. Her legs felt weak, her thighs ached. She had a feeling of sickness in the pit of her stomach, and the band on her knickers was uncomfortable.

"OK then," José said, with a tinge of disappointment. "So this is growing old together, tea and cakes on the aft-deck."

"José, please don't." She walked across and gave him a light kiss on the lips. "Give me a big hug, please." He did.

She spread a crisp white linen cloth over the table in the saloon and set out some picnic plates.

"I've just got two more screws to fix," said José, "and then I'll show you how we can meet Bob Hunt's fishing requirements."

The water in the kettle had boiled slowly on the Calor gas stove in the galley, and they sat down for tea. José was like a small boy with his new invention. He'd had the blacksmith in Palufrugell make him two tubes with flanges welded onto the back, which then clipped over the handrails at the back two corners of the aft-deck. Maria looked mesmerised. She'd been asked if she could work out what they were for. She wanted to shine intelligently, and knew that Pedro would have known instantly what they were for.

"Well!" she said. "I could guess and I could guess wrong. But what I'd say is they're very clever boys' inventions and Bob will know immediately. I doubt girls would ever guess, though."

José fixed his screws to the rail and went rushing off into the cabin his son used. He came out with a three-metre fishing rod.

"Look," he said to Maria, "what Bob does when he wants to pick up his gin and tonic is he stands the rod in the tube, and it supports itself. You turn this threaded spindle and it tightens up and even the highest jumping marlin shouldn't be able to yank it out."

To make up for her lack of imagination, Maria said, "Wonderful, José, you're so clever. Come here now and have the reward of a cup of tea and a piece of chef's fruit cake."

They sat and chatted. They both had a lot of news. José was under threat of being sent to London for a month's exchange at head office. Maria told him all about the 'Olympics', and that she thought Pedro had split with Meribel, and that the contracts had been exchanged with cousin José.

José had been bursting to tell Maria that his son had won the regional under-15 golf tournament and would automatically get to play in the next year's national schoolboys' event. Also, how he was doing well at school and growing up fast.

They chatted through their tea. Time flew. Maria suddenly caught a glimpse of her watch. "Good God! It's 5.20, I really ought to be gone."

"Don't rush. You're working too hard, you're looking pale. Phone through and get somebody to cover for you."

"The only person to do that is Sñr Martin…"

"Oh, sorry, yes I'd forgotten. OK then, it seems I'll have to share you again with the hotel."

"But tomorrow," Maria said, getting up and moving across to stand behind him, putting both arms round him and pulling his broad back into her chest, "we'll have all day. You said a 9am start. Is that still on?"

"Yes…" José replied. "… And I tell you what, crush up some Senokots and put them in Marcia and Bob Hunt's dinner tonight. Then they'll cancel and we can have some quality time together."

"You, my young José, are wicked. How can you think up such things?" Maria cleared the plates and put them dirty into the picnic basket. "Should I leave the rest of the cake?" she asked.

"Please."

"Then don't leave it lying around, or any crumbs, we don't want a crowd of rats coming fishing with us."

José took both her hands. "Love you," he said.

"Love you, too," Maria replied as they fell towards each other in a full embrace. She felt comforted. Then: "Let me go, let me go, you wild sailor! A girl's got to get back to work otherwise she'll lose her job."

"So if I don't let you back you'll lose your job, eh! That would mean you could come to Barcelona with me… oh, and to England."

"Get along with you! I'll see you in the morning. How's the weather look?"

"Great."

She scurried down the gangplank, turned and waved as she headed back to her car. She crashed out when she climbed in behind the steering wheel, but took a couple of deep breaths, started the car and drove back to the hotel.

Her veil fell back into place.

Dinner with the Admiral was predictable – at least at first. The chef excelled himself and Peter ate as though he hadn't eaten for a month. The Admiral held court and announced his plans for the following year. There'd be another Olympics, but with a few embellishments to keep the thing moving. Perhaps they'd cut out the diving, because it took so much time and was a bit slow.

How did Marco and Maria feel about a staff versus guest football match? He said he knew that Peter would be all for it. Peter remained silent, not wishing to show too much enthusiasm for anything the Admiral suggested.

Then, the Admiral surprised the four members of the Martinez clan. He pronounced that there should be some sort of end of sports day ball. Maybe even fancy dress. Peter placed a bet with himself that the Admiral either had a full Admiral's get-up, with his wife as a deck hand, or a Napoleon outfit, with his wife as a slightly ageing Josephine.

"What? Next year?" Maria asked.

"No. This year. Soon. It'll be good for your business."

They might have mocked the Admiral, but Marco, Maria and Peter all realised the benefits of building some individuality into the hotel. After all, they had set out to achieve a family resort, and what better way than to have some fun games.

The evening was a pleasant one, with Virginia particularly enjoying the food and the fact that Marco was sticking to his limited alcohol intake. He'd lost weight and now cut quite a dashing middle-aged figure. He generally wore crisply laundered white shirts and, as Maria had advised, dark trousers with the occasional matching jacket, which flattered his shape.

Maria had a difficult time when the Admiral began to wax lyrical about the various attributes of his three children.

"… and Michelle…" Maria interjected. "Where do you see her future?"

"Oh, she'll do a B.Ed in sports sciences, but during the course she'll probably run away with some exceedingly rich French prince and have children forever after," the Admiral forecast with some confidence.

Maria wanted to say, "… Or if that fails, she could turn to drugs, and a life of vice in order to pay for them."

"Has Michelle mentioned she's planning to stay over when you and the boys leave?" she asked instead. "Peter's got a project to concentrate on and Michelle's going to do a bit of coaching for us."

"Not a word. Secretive little lady," said the Admiral. "You sure you haven't lined up a Spanish prince for her to fool around with?"

"She's got such a stunning figure, there's a lady who runs a boutique in Figueras who's recognised her talents and has offered to, well, let her show herself off a little. Perhaps, though, I'm talking out of turn. I expect she's about to tell you both."

"Possibly," the Admiral offered. "You see, I don't think anyone's realised just how busy my wife and I have been with your big sports day. I expect she's been busting a gut to get to us to tell us. I'll ask her in the morning what her plans are."

Peter was not a major contributor to the evening. For a start, there was a generation gap with the other five diners, and then he'd got Meribel, Marcia and now Tania on his mind. He was not, he realised, too gutted by the Meribel situation. It wasn't going anywhere. The Marcia one he just really didn't understand. She was somehow totally out of reach, but at the same time completely available. At least that's what he thought. Then there was Tania, wicked little vixen and very available, he sensed, in a paid-for way. Surely he would never pay for a woman's attentions? On the other hand, if you could slip a girl a few hundred pesetas, get your satisfaction and not have all the emotional complications, it might be the better the option.

As the Admiral's voice droned on and Virginia squeaked her polite agreement with any topic of conversation, Marco watched the backside of the dessert waitress. The Admiral's wife lost herself in the Rioja white wine and Maria did her high-profile social bit, so Peter dreamt on.

Finally, Maria broke up the party. "Got a busy day tomorrow," she said. "We've got a fishing trip for a couple of the guests. Tell you what, Admiral, if ever you feel like getting salt splashed on your face, give me a shout. I have a friend who charters a boat."

Peter couldn't work out the depth of Maria's 'friendship' with José. They only seemed to see each other every couple of months or so. *So what*, he thought. *Good for her.* She was still young and needed affection.

As Maria stripped off for her nightly wash, she studied her body. Well, she'd take Miguel's potion the next night, and hopefully all would be restored to normality. She washed thoroughly, and dried herself vigorously.

She went cold as she noticed a smear of blood on the white Irish cotton towel she'd had imported for the hotel bathrooms. She remembered the same experience before she actually knew she was pregnant with Pedro.

In any case, Miguel's tonic was due to do its work, so why be concerned? She needed sleep. That was her main motivation as she climbed into bed and set her alarm for 7am. Early for a Sunday, but essential for a planned departure time from the jetty at nine. It felt good to put her feet up and rest her aching body.

CHAPTER 19

Maria woke before seven. She still felt tired, but a nice shower would sort her out. She had prepared what she was going to wear the afternoon before.

Looking out of the window, she saw it was going to be a typical Costa Brava August day.

Her legs still ached but the shower made her feel fresh and better. She wore wedge canvas sandals, which she knew José was OK with on the boat. She giggled as she imagined him having to tell Marcia that her stilettos would damage the deck. Marcia wouldn't like to be shoeless, her stilettos were almost a part of her.

Maria put on a crisp white sleeveless blouse with a halter neck. She tied a cravat in a single knot at one side and took her blue linen jacket from the wardrobe, which she would slip around her shoulders. She reflected on the vision in the mirror. With her favourite white trousers, she felt she looked OK.

She'd packed her little overnight bag, which included her new one-piece and a couple of girls' just-in-case bits and pieces. She put four hotel beach towels in another carrier bag. By 8.15am she was ready and set to leave via the hotel kitchen, where she knew the chef would have put together her picnic order.

The Hunts were having breakfast on their balcony, so Maria had fixed some light tapas for about eleven o'clock, then salads, cold meats and chilled salmon for lunch, with some suitably selected wines and fresh wild strawberries and cream, cheese, or cheesecake. Coffee could be brewed in the galley.

She packed the car and was away by 8.30am. She'd be a bit early but that would give her time to set things up and store the food away. José was sleeping on the boat overnight so he'd be there anyway. Spick and span, without a doubt.

He was. He cut a dashing image in his dark blue short-sleeved shirt, white shorts and white rope and canvas shoes. As Maria approached, he slipped on his white and gold captain's headgear, which she had bought him. The sunglasses and his angular chin and cheek bones added to the effect: he was the epitome of calm control and good looks. Her heart skipped a couple of beats. *I'm lucky to have this man's attention,* she thought.

298

"Morning, Señora," he announced, saluting.

"Buenos dias, mi capitan, everything under control?"

"Aye aye, Ma'am."

She'd climbed the plank to the deck. "If you'd get your silly sailor's hand out of the way I could kiss you, Captain," she announced.

"Now you're talking." He placed an arm around her shoulder. "My, you look good, and incidentally smell good. I've got an idea. Why don't I raise the anchor and we do a runner, then I won't have to share you with anyone else?"

"Because, my dear cheating José, we have a commission which should pay your berthing fees for the rest of the year, and besides, the Hunts are really looking forward to their trip, especially Bob. He felt a bit left out of things at the Olympics, which he was. So he's looking for a bit of equality, I think. All he needs to do is to catch a hefty great white shark, which he might even be related to, and he'll be away."

José had prepared the rods, hoping he too would get time to fish a little. Maria could navigate for a while.

The boat looked spotless, as always. There were a couple of lilos set up for the girls on the bow deck, and a good stock of booze supplemented by the hotel's special wines. So they were set for a good day.

Bob and Marcia had arranged for a taxi to pick them up at 8.45am. Bob so hated driving "the big wagon over all these cobble tracks" that he drove as little as he could. They drew up right at the quayside and when Maria spotted them, José beckoned them to come on up. Bob looked the part in pale blue slacks and white rubber-soled shoes, which José knew would leave rubber marks all over the decks, but felt he should not say anything, because at least they would do no damage to the sensitive timber decking.

Now how am I going to break the news to Marcia? he thought, seeing her stilettos. This should have been a job for Maria, but she was pottering in the galley.

Bob gave her a hand at the top of the ramp and José was about to issue the captain's instructions to take her shoes off when she put her full weight onto Bob's left arm and, in one deft sweep, whipped first her left then her right sandal off. She rummaged in her D&G bag and came out with the highest heeled rope wedges José had ever seen. They were white to match her tailored slacks. She had a large-collared, open-necked formal shirt neatly tucked into the waistband of the trousers, which were ostensibly being kept up by a Gucci fabric gold belt. The rather severe cut of her shirt was given a hint of informality by Marcia having left one of the buttons undone, thereby exposing sufficient cleavage to make any captain's day.

Maria arrived just as Marcia was bending to slip on her shoes, exposing more than the intended cleavage to Maria, who felt a twinge of jealousy. That would be a feast for José's eyes all day.

"Welcome aboard," Maria nevertheless announced. "Morning Bob. Feeling lucky, are you? Well, don't worry, I've had a word and they're arranging to send a whole shoal of fish straight onto your rod to wear you out before lunch. Then you'll get a siesta."

"Good on you," Bob replied.

They were all relaxed. José did some final stowing away and showed Bob and Marcia into his son's cabin and said to use that as much as they liked. As he passed Maria in the galley, he slapped the cheek of her left buttock, quite hard but playfully. It made her wince with pain, and she stood still for a minute. José had continued walking but, realising his slap had not been met in the usual way, he went back to where Maria remained.

"You alright?" he said.

She laughed. "Yes, fine. That slap seemed a little more stimulated than usual, I suppose you're excited by Marcia dangling her body in your face."

He sensed Maria had said that in fun, but with a heavy tinge of seriousness.

"Hey, don't put that one on me. The cleavage is for Bob and the fish. Anyway, you outdo her any time… is your bottom okay?"

"Yes, I'm just tender at the moment."

He sensed she was a bit sensitive, so he'd remember to adjust his reactions accordingly.

"If you've recovered enough, and I'm sorry if it hurt, can you pop up and get us untied. I'd rather not get Bob involved in the domestics. He might pull a muscle or fall in or something."

"Aye aye, Captain," Maria said, saluting as she turned and headed for the aft deck and their link with the jetty capstan.

The process of setting sail allowed Bob and Marcia to familiarise themselves with their temporary quarters. They had a quick recce, opening doors and announcing what they saw to each other. "Oh! A shower." Oh! That's a nice bedroom." "It's a perfectly adequate galley." "At least there's a loo!" Clearly they were buzzing with the excitement of the new environment. Bob, after periods of rest, always thrived on change and the challenge of new situations. He was not one to stand still.

"Come on, guys," José called from the bridge.

The Hunts dutifully obeyed orders and climbed to the wheelhouse. Maria had prepared four coffees, served with some shortbread biscuits.

"Right," José instructed, "when we get to the sea wall we need to either turn left or right." Maria blanched at hearing this instruction again. It took her back to her first voyage and the vision she'd had. She strained her memory. Was it right or left she'd instructed? So what. It wouldn't happen again. Anyway, they were being paid to do what their client requested them to do.

Marcia felt her wedding ring. It seemed the main purpose of the trappings of her marriage now was to enable her to remember which was left and right. It was invaluable in the car, because she suffered from a mild form of directional dyslexia. She'd never had it investigated but she knew it was a weakness. In her dancing days she always wore a bracelet on her left wrist. That was fine until one day she was told by the choreographer that she wasn't to wear any jewellery for a particular sequence. She was all over the place at rehearsal and only got through the actual performance by sneaking a coin into her left bra cup.

So Marcia was about to select left, being normally a lady's privilege, when Bob took control and said, "Supposing I say straight on?"

"Well, we'd get to the north coast of Africa eventually," José informed him.

"What speed will we do?"

"For a comfortable ride, about 15 knots."

"OK, straight on for an hour, and then we'll start fishing."

José checked the charts. That was not such a bad choice, in fact. If he set a course slightly north of 'straight on', which would have been due south east, they'd get to a region of sandbanks which was likely to be reasonably laden with fish.

"Aye aye, sir," José acknowledged after due deliberation.

"So what about the ladies having a say?" Marcia interjected.

"What about Bob choosing the way out and the girls the way back?"

"Surely it's the same journey but in reverse," Marcia announced.

"Not with this navigator," José corrected.

"Then home into the sunset, if you can fix that" Marcia announced.

"Would that be okay with you, Maria?"

"It's fine with me. I've got good sunglasses. You'll need them if it's round about sunset."

José took out a marker pen and set out the course. Straight out, then a long unnoticeable 180-degree segment sweep, during which the girls could top up their tans, and then a steady course south in sight of the coastline, back to the marina on the second half of the voyage.

"OK, let's go," José challenged as they broke through the gap in the marina wall. He had radioed the pilot his proposed route, and obtained clearance. He stepped outside the wheelhouse and waved to the harbourmaster, who was having a morning cigarette outside the door to his cabin office and modest accommodation. Maria knew him well, too, so she added her friendly wave.

The harbourmaster recognised her. He'd been in the Rosas area when Paco had his accident. *The girl's done well,* he thought. *I would never have expected her to go to sea again after her experience. But then girls in these parts are of tough stock.*

There was a morning haze, indicating it would be hot, but the sea breeze would be their air conditioning.

"Bloody good coffee," Bob congratulated Maria. "Hope your gins and tonics are as good. About eleven o'clock would do."

"Bob, if you've got time to drink G&T then it means you're not the fisherman I expected you to be." Maria chided him. "I've told chef you'll want a barbecue of your catch tonight, so don't let's disappoint him."

They all breathed in the morning beauty for a while. There was no need for social conversation. Already José could sense Bob relaxing and that was rubbing off on Marcia, which in turn meant Maria's hostessing could be turned down at least a couple of notches.

José had the boat on automatic. "Bob, if you suddenly hear a loud bang and the boat starts veering all over the place, it'll mean we've hit some driftwood on the tide, or a wreck of some kind, just grab this wheel and try and get back on a straight course."

Bob said, "Are you serious?"

"No! Not at all. But if you could keep an eye on things – I need to go to the loo and secondly, I'd like to plot our intended course. I always like to know where I'm trying to be going."

Maria was now beyond associating all wrecks with Paco. It was hard at first but José, being cruel to be kind, had made a point of making no allowances; he would use everyday seafaring phraseology, however insensitive it might seem, and Maria would just have to accept it. He was right psychologically, of course, and Maria had now adapted.

The girls had taken themselves off to sit on the side banquettes facing the sun, which was showing signs of heating up the morning air. Neither chatted, they both appreciated the silence. Maria's thoughts were that she still had every usual sign of her 'date in the month', but she tried to put the confusion out of her mind. Marcia was wondering why her and Bob's normal days couldn't be this calm. Bob's diabetes sometimes made him irritable, some days he was tired and others irrational. He'd never taken Marcia inside his complex business world. He didn't want her to be worried by the volatility of the marketplace he was embroiled in, and when his worries showed through, he had got used to using his diabetes or the imbalance in his metabolism as excuses.

The irritability of the early days of his holiday were due to the fact that his company's housing stock of built property, ready for sale, was 45 per cent unreserved. He knew such figures could spell disaster. He was no rocket scientist and preferred the simple arithmetic approach to complicated reams of figures, which he only allowed to be produced because some pretend gurus at the bank head office needed volumes of information to fill their files and hence match the size of their lending.

Fifteen per cent intended profit with a 45 per cent downswing of sales indicated just one resultant figure, and a related question. It meant, in the simplest possible way, a 30 per cent loss. The outstanding question was: when? Bob knew that if things didn't change on his return, the proverbial shit was going to hit his fan and ricochet all over the faces of the smart bastards in their City pinstripes sitting in their ivory towers.

When the 45 per cent value of stock was £6 million, the prospect of a shortfall of £4 million was enough to make anybody irritable.

"So have you fished before, Bob?"

"Yes a couple of times, but only on the Solent on a day out with the boys and, to be perfectly honest, no-one was the slightest bit interested in catching anything other than a bloody great hangover. But I've got an idea of the principles. You get a hook, put a worm on it, chuck it in the water and some poor bastard of a fish grabs it... and then you pull in the line..."

"Fine! So you've got the rudiments. Why don't I try and keep you sober and we'll put a couple of lines out and see how you get on."

The rods were modern, strong and sophisticated, and borrowed from a very good mate. The lines were, apparently, strong enough to hold anything normally caught in these parts of the Mediterranean.

"Normally?" José had asked his friend.

"Well, for most fish apart from sharks and whales and the stray barracuda."

The hooks you wouldn't have wanted in your own mouth and there was a case, so José had thought, for saying they were cruel to the fish. "They're only cruel if the fish is daft enough to sheer through the line and escape," José's pal had explained. "Then he'd die slowly through inability to feed and digest. But if he hangs on to be landed, he'll be marginally better off." José was not convinced.

José left Bob on automatic pilot watch while he prepared the rods and lines. The girls looked on, Marcia in fascination, and Maria in pride. José was very neat and accurate in everything he did. He was economical where strength was required, not seemingly straining or making a fuss, and when it came to the final details of carefully knotting a line, he was gentle but determined.

The plan was to put out a couple of trailer lines to attract any fish in the locality and then, when by José's calculation they were over the sandbank, to cut the engines and invite a bite. If and when they had a fish on the line, they'd move off under power to play out the strength of any potential catch.

"You sure all this is necessary?" Bob enquired. "I'm happy to catch a John Dory or something small like a piece of cod or haddock."

"Cod and haddock are for pre-packed dinner packages. I expect you to pick up something in the range of ten to 20 kilos."

"Shit!" Bob exclaimed in his inimitable way. "It comes to something when your captain has one idea and the crew another. I booked an easy day out cruising, if you remember. The last animal I had to deal with at ten kilos was a turkey… and that came in a bag from the butcher at Christmas and was already dead and plucked."

"You'll be OK, Bob. The girls will give you a hand. Besides, you'll enjoy the power struggle, I'm sure." José finally sealed the deal.

He was ready now; he cast out the trailers and went up to take the wheel back. "Thanks, Bob. Well watched. Both rods are loaded. Give it about ten more minutes under power and we'll be over the sand. We'll go back down aft when we're there. Watch out for fish chasing us. They're the ones you'll have for supper with any luck."

Bob returned aft where the girls were watching the lines anxiously. Marcia turned to Maria and said jokingly, "Which one is ours?" nodding at the two rods carefully placed on the deck with the hooks protected.

Maria pointed to the one on the left. "Not ours. I've done this before. That's yours. This is your treat."

"You're joking!" Marcia said. "I'm not up to pulling anything today." They both giggled.

"Oh come on, Marcia, I'm sure you'll try." Again they screeched with laughter.

"You'll have to give me a hand. You've heard the expression, 'two on a rod', I suppose." Off they went again, down their route of double entendre as Bob reappeared in T-shirt, shorts, shoes without socks and a baseball cap.

For some inexplicable reason, Marcia found this funny. She thought it was because suddenly Bob had found something other than work that he was now announcing with a firm statement, through his uniform, that he would take seriously and, apparently, competitively.

"What are you girls finding so funny?" he asked seriously.

"I was just telling Marcia that she's on that line there," Maria informed him.

"Marcia hasn't been on any line since her bloody Bluebell ones. She'll never cope with something as big as ten to 20…"

Before he could spell out 'kilos', both girls broke into wild girlish laughter again. "She'll cope," Maria said, trying to choke back the laughter. "She says whatever she catches we'll eat together tonight."

Marcia burst into an uncontrollable, dirty guffaw of girlish fun. "I'm going to go and change into something more comfortable," she said, smothering her schoolgirl laugh.

Bob wasn't sure how much of the fun was poked at him. It seemed they found his get-up amusing. He countered defensively, "You'll need those fishnets you used to wear."

"Oh! You two," Maria sniggered.

"Come on, let's laugh the fish into the boat, Bob, I think José's cut the engines. That means you're meant to cast off."

"That's a new expression for it," Marcia said as a parting shot as she exited stage rear and went backstage to the stars' dressing rooms, from where her screeching laughter could still be heard until Bob moved across the deck and slid the saloon doors closed.

Bob didn't fully understand the sudden humour that had developed. He was sure he hadn't missed a round of drinks. Anyway, he'd best show willing to cast his line into the now calmer waters below him.

José arrived, having secured all necessary equipment in the wheelhouse, and dropped an anchor onto the sandbank. He methodically checked the reel and line on Bob's rod and then ensured that everything could run free if they attracted a bite. He demonstrated how gently to gear the brake on the reel into a fixed mode and then how to use the ratchet to haul in any potential catch. Bob then demonstrated his supposed battle with the target fish by leaning backwards and then forwards into the imaginary pull.

"No! No! No!" José shouted. "If you do that the fish will know that on every other motion, by you leaning in towards the fish, the hook tension in its mouth will be released and if the fish swims forward and opens its mouth, it'll be free."

"Christ! Am I dealing with a fish as intelligent as all that? It's how they do it in the films, anyway."

"That's for Hollywood. I promise you even the thickest fish will give you a run for your money. But we'll see. It's only a bit of fun after all. But if you were to pick up a tuna, you've got to know you'll be fighting a species that's been around in these waters since before Christ was teaching his disciples to fish, and if they've survived that long they must have got themselves off a hook or two to keep breeding."

José went down below and passed Marcia in the saloon. She'd changed into a pair of black hot pants and was wearing a loose fitting, long-sleeved Indian cotton peasant top which, although not close-fitting, still clung to her chest as she glided forward.

"Going to a disco?" José quipped.

"No. Goin' fishing. Or is it 'Gone fishing'?" And she burst into the chorus line of that song. She finished with a professional shuffle and a little bow to her single male audience.

"Well, take a bit of advice…" José said, giving the impression, she thought, like Peter, of not noticing she was a hot piece of female merchandise. "Keep well covered. The sun's getting high above. You can get carried away with the pressures and excitement of the hunt and not notice you're getting sunstroke…"

"You're right. Thanks, José, I've left my hat." She brushed in front of him and back into his son's quarters, reappearing moments later carrying a large black matador-style hat, moulded as a local raffia art passed down through the ages. It had a deep violet band around the brim.

"… and the other thing is… be careful if we get a male fish trawl, he might just fancy you more than the hook and take you under…"

"Are fish good lovers?"

"Well, let's put it this way, they're extremely fertile with mates of their own species. They leave their mates with whole sacks full of fertilised eggs. How they'd fare with young English ladies I don't know. But I don't think Bob would be too pleased about you experimenting."

"It wouldn't be up to him, would it?" she grinned. "I choose who to experiment with."

It suddenly seemed to José that he would choke on the perfume exuding from Marcia's body. He flushed, and knew he had. "Listen, I'm on a mission to get some bait."

"I hoped you just had," Marcia replied gently, cocking her left knee into her right and placing her right hand on its awaiting buttock. She burst into a little giggle and swung round, leaving her stage through the imaginary curtain of liquid oxygen, behind which was the aft deck where Bob was getting into fishing mode.

Perhaps this was the problem between them. He appeared not to notice she had changed, and her perfume was not powerful enough to counter the years of tobacco he'd surrounded himself with. All that was superficial, however. He'd made up his mind that she thrived on attention, and in his own, sometimes incorrect way, he decided to make it look as though he really hadn't noticed what he considered to be her attention-seeking ways. The labradors he'd kept over the years were the same, he'd reasoned, and when they realised he wasn't going to throw another stick or ball, or roll them over again and rub their stomachs, they would give up and snuggle up or curl around his feet, and reflect affection back to their master that way. This bitch hadn't yet learnt that art, so the natural adoration he felt for all the parades and mini-shows she put on for him would remain bottled up.

There was a slight indication, however, that she might be learning. When he didn't turn to acknowledge her grand entrance, she stood beside the deck chair in which he was sitting gazing into the mid-distance. She slipped an arm around his shoulder.

"Excited?" That single word itself excited him more than the forthcoming event. He moved a hand across his chest to take her own. He squeezed it.

"I'm only hoping José doesn't get disappointed. He seems pretty certain we'll catch something but somehow I think it might be just the cod or haddock I talked about."

"Bob. You and your knowledge from the local fish and chip shop! I don't think you get cod and haddock in the Med. The Admiral said the other night that he has caught big stuff out here."

"He'd be bound to exaggerate. You don't get many Frenchmen who don't think their willy is the biggest in the world so you can cut their stories about the size of the fish they've caught down by… well… most times 90 per cent."

"Ninety per cent!" Marcia screeched derisively. "Well, it's as well you haven't got any French blood in you as that would leave you with precious little."

"I never used to get complaints," Bob said defensively.

"Come on, Bob. Let's not scrap. Let's have a lovely day. If José thinks we're in for something big, give him the benefit until we get back with whatever catch, if any, we've bagged."

Below decks, José, still a little flustered, was expecting to find Maria in their cabin, probably changing. He knocked gently on the door. There being no reply, he called out her name. A response came from the loo. "I'm in here," she called out in a quiet voice.

"You alright?"

Well, she wasn't really. She was confused and worried. She now had little doubt she was entering her cycle. If Miguel was right, and he surely was, she was in danger of miscarrying. She'd just been contemplating that fact. After all, it was what she was planning anyway, with the help of Miguel's special potion. So wasn't this good news? Yes, maybe it was, but she really was scared of being hurt, and being on a boat with a boyfriend and two hotel guests would not be the best place to experience it.

"How long will you be?" José asked.

A girl doesn't want to be rushed on such occasions. "I'll be out on deck in a couple of minutes," she said curtly.

"Good. OK. Don't strip off too much. The sun's high. It's burning weather out there. Perhaps you'd keep an eye on Marcia. I've told her to cover up."

"Yes, I heard you," Maria let him know.

Oh no, he thought. At least she hadn't seen his face flush. Did Maria know Marcia had made a pass at him? But then, so what, he expected she made a pass at anything in trousers, or shorts in his case.

José went below into the engine hold and collected the two blue buckets. Re-secured the hatch doors and trundled back to the deck like a milkmaid with her daily wares.

Bob turned round, hearing José's approach. "Christ. They're big gins and tonics, aren't they?"

"Bob! You get your booze when we celebrate."

"Could be a dry day then," Bob laughed back. "What you got there, mate?"

"Bait."

"Why don't we just tip it into the sea and get a fishing net?"

"That's close to what we *are* going to do. We're going to tip the contents into the sea. I've chopped them up so that they'll disintegrate quickly, which will pick up the big boys' taste buds for up to a couple of miles' radius. They'll flock over and two of them will take a hook by mistake… and hey presto."

"If it's that easy why don't we get a net and just throw it over, then have our gin and tonic and haul it in later?"

"Actually, Bob, if we weren't out here to be doing some real sea hunting, and we were just involved in the commercial aspect of fishing, to provide food for the locals and tourists, we'd be setting traps."

"What are we after now then? Lobsters, crabs… ?"

"No. Big traps. More like cages."

"Are you serious?"

"Yes, of course."

"And what would you mostly be catching. The guys we're after?"

"Yes. Tuna."

"I thought that came in tins, anyway!"

"Yes, like cod and haddock come wrapped in newspaper in your country." José saw that Bob could be very controlling, and was determined to stay in the dominant role.

"What's been happening is that because tuna is a large fish, it generates big demand. In recent years, like a lot of other species, it's been over-fished and risks extinction. So hordes of scientists from all sorts of countries have been putting their heads together to control the level of fishing. Commercially, there's now a restriction on the smallest size of fish that can be caught and removed from the sea. By catching in traps, the fish sizes can be sorted out and the little ones thrown back to breed. So nothing below about 20 kilograms can be fished. Now the annual allowance in the western Med is something like 300,000 fish more than three years old that can be farmed."

"So do you seriously reckon we have half a chance of taking the level up to 300,002?"

"Let's see. You can't predict. But, here, give me a hand with one of these drums, would you."

José took the lid off the barrel of rotting fish.

"Christ," Bob said, "surely the bloody smell will put the big fish off coming near us!"

"Wait and see."

They poured the contents into the sea.

"What is it?"

"Sardines," José said, "and I spent all last night taking them out of their tins and getting rid of the bones!"

Bob well realised he was being mocked, but it was friendly banter and all part of the day out.

"What do we do now?" he requested.

Maria reappeared. "Drink this and get some of these inside you. It could be an hour or two before you get a free hand again."

Maria had prepared fresh fruit juice and some bite-sized tapas.

Half an hour passed, with José the whole time encouraging Bob to recast his line into where the patch of sardine bait was slowly drifting. Marcia had a bit of trouble with her casting and sought José's assistance, which she got in a somewhat close fishing encounter.

Maria was beginning to think she might have to throw a bucket of water over them both. She'd have a word with José when they could get a quiet moment alone. She didn't want him to make a fool of himself... or her.

Bob had noticed too.

"How's your rod doing, Bob?" Maria asked, actually quite innocently.

"He's all the better for your asking, darling. But you could give him a little hold to keep him interested if you like," Bob teased.

Maria flushed. All this imported double meaning was a hard part of the English language for her to master. Marcia had picked up on Bob's flirtatious chat with Maria, and that, unusually, was without a drink. She'd have a word about his familiarity when they got a private moment. Both men were close to being in trouble.

There was a long pause before the silence was broken by Bob. "Fuck!" he shrieked. All three looked out to where he was pointing.

"Shark, bloody shark! Christ! Two, three, six, eight of the blighters."

José laughed aloud. "They're your supper, silly! They're not sharks, they're blue-fins, blue-fin tuna."

"They've got that dorsal fin out of the water. You sure you know your bloody fish, mate?"

"Yes sure. They're what the locals call BFTs."

"That stands for bloody fierce teeth, I suppose."

"No, blue-fin tuna… and we want just two."

A dorsal fin broke away from the pack and set out on a wide sweep at high speed.

Bob shouted, "Look at the speed!"

"Could be 25-30 miles per hour," José informed him seemingly knowing he would relate to that. "Watch, he's going to sweep in on the sardines. Is your line free? Mind your fingers. Maria, watch Marcia."

José was well in command.

"I'm ready to leap up top. You'll hear the twin engines roar and prepare to be accelerated. That'll fix the hook in the tuna's mouth and then it's a matter of who tires first."

Bob put his hand up. "It's me. I've tired. Those things look like torpedoes. There's no way we'll hold onto them. Look, I'll buy you all dinner. Let's get back."

He seemed semi-serious, but nobody listened. Marcia was certainly up to the challenge. Maria was supportive because she had José's reputation and pride at stake.

Bob yelled, "Bite, fucking bite!" as he saw his float being rapidly pulled out to sea. He remembered to gear on the brake on the reel. Marcia nearly lost the rod completely. Her attention was taken up by Bob's excited shouts and she had not seen her own float dip deep below the water. Maria swung round and grabbed the rod with both hands. As she did so, it seemed the whole of her insides were twisted and ruptured. The five seconds of pain were excruciating. She tried to puff her breaths out and take in short gasps of the fresh salty air. The pain receded and her strength returned to allow her to give Marcia the added support she needed.

The float on Marcia's line was pulled downwards and Maria, who had seen this before, prayed quickly that the fish was not stupid enough to swim under the boat and surface with the line tangled in the propellers and rudders. "Come on, José!" she screamed. There was a mini explosion and clouds of condensation were released from the powerful engines. The boat accelerated forward, putting extra 'G' force strain on the backs of Marcia and Bob.

Maria yelled to Bob and Marcia, "Just hold steady!" They seemed to. "Just take the strain… don't try and pull." She was wedged firmly against the back rail of the boat, between the male and female controlled rods. She was like the conductor of a two-piece orchestra, signifying with her co-ordinated hands to strain or release, forte or 'wind in a little reel to teach the fish you're in control'.

The main thing was that they had achieved the upper hand. The fish, caught and under strain, was now battling against the hook in the roof of its mouth. This was some new, previously unexperienced venture, to which none of its ancestors had alerted it, presumably because, as in this case, the odds of it freeing itself to pass on the experience to others were remote.

Bob adjusted his sitting position and gingerly placed his feet on the solid upstand below the rails, which he hoped would give him additional leverage. He beckoned to Marcia to do the same. She managed to get her shapely legs into position, but to keep the pressure on she was having to lean too far back in her chair, which Bob now realised was bolted down through the deck, as was his own.

There was a lot of noise, but Bob was able to make a sign to Maria that one of the waterproof treated cushions from the banquette needed to be wedged behind Marcia's back.

José had got the boat up to speed and had very carefully checked the radar screen to pinpoint other vessels in the area and/or marker buoys. He made a final visual check, which he always did, given his trust in his own ability and his distrust of anything produced mechanically.

José thought he could leave the bridge for about five minutes, in which time he could play his part in the hunt. As he climbed down from the elevated bridge, he realised the aptness of the Hunts' name, which had not occurred to him before. He arrived between the two human combatants.

"So how's the Hunts' hunt?" he shouted.

"Oh, fucking marvellous, now that you're stringing the facts together." Bob always took exception to his surname being used in that way. He'd always given short shrift to girls enquiring in his younger days, "So tell me, Mr Hunt, do you still hunt? You know, by name and by nature..."

José could see that even this short span of strain was getting to Bob. He glanced across at Marcia, with Maria in close attendance. Surprisingly she was coping better than her husband. Her attitude seemed altogether different. She seemed content to let her body relax, her shoulders were rounded as if she was allowing her whole person to be pulled towards the fish tugging on the line.

Bob, on the other hand, was taut, his back muscles were rippling and his arms were under full strain, as were his thighs and knees as he pulled the fish along. Beads of perspiration were pouring off his forehead.

Neither appeared to have had time to put on their respective hats, though Maria was OK under her New York Yankee's baseball cap. José leant into the saloon and took Marcia's stylish headgear and Bob's cap from the table. He placed Marcia's on her head and then Bob's on his.

He beckoned to Bob to help him to get the rod into the anchoring device he had so proudly set up to support the base of the rod under just these conditions. They managed it together, with the aid of a bit of grunting from Bob.

José accomplished the same end result with Marcia's rod. While it did mean both rods were now almost vertical, under José's guidance the Hunts developed the confidence to take the strain on the rods in their left hands and arms, freeing their right hands to give a couple of turns on the geared reel to shorten the length of line between the boat and its prey.

Bob was clearly in great discomfort. Although he was sitting down, his ankles felt as though they were going to break. He felt unsupported by any muscular tissue, yet at the same time the muscles in his calves felt like they were about to burst. His knees were agony. He thought his kneecaps were about to explode. The fronts of his thighs were burning, and his hips were firmly locked, leading him to wonder whether he would ever walk again. He was well aware that his stomach muscles were suffering from lack of use, nowadays being used principally for holding in the booze. So each little area was being forcibly reminded it was there for an intended purpose and was now being put to test.

He had a crushing sensation in his chest and rib cage, his elbows hurt as well and his arms felt as though they might be pulled out of their sockets. The muscles in the back of his neck and in his shoulders had never worked, or needed to, as they were now expected to.

All in all, Bob was under strain.

Marcia glanced across at him. "Bob, you be careful!" she shouted above the screech of the engines and the noise of the sea.

Bob didn't look at her, but shouted back, "Be bloody careful! Too late for that, got a knife, I'll cut the bugger free... I'm off bloody fish."

That made both girls look across and, for some extremely perverse reason, they found it amusing seeing Bob under such strain. They started to laugh.

"Go for it Bob... reel it in!" Marcia shouted.

Maria turned away from her charge for a few seconds. Placing a comforting hand on Bob's burning thigh, she put an unsteady cheek close to his as the boat rose and fell between the light waves. She shouted, "You're doing really well, Bob! Keep going."

"I'd be better for a beer."

"OK, a beer, yes. Gin and tonic later."

She went into the saloon, holding onto anything she could – almost like being in a power cut at night without a candle. Taking a bottle from the fridge in the galley, she ripped off the cap and delivered it to Bob. He freed his right hand from the reel long enough to raise the nectar to his parching lips.

"What about you lighting me a cigar?"

"Bob, that's outrageous!" she shouted back. "No smoking on the boat… you know that…"

"I just thought… if I'm going to die I'd do it with either a fag or a smoke in my mouth…"

"Bob, you won't die… just hang on… the fish will tire first."

"I'm not so bloody sure! This bastard's not heading for any dinner plate at the moment."

José checked that all seemed well on the fishing front and climbed to the wheelhouse. The revs were as set and the autopilot was still auto. He checked the radar and all was clear. There was some heavy traffic, obviously in one of the Gibraltar-Marseilles shipping lanes, some five miles out and most likely some pleasure craft or yachts between their course and the coast. Sunday morning sailors, José supposed. He altered course to turn slightly north-east.

After panning all around, he took a fix on where he could see Bob's line entering the sea. Fifty to 60 yards, he thought. That would really cause Bob to suffer. Marcia was doing really well. Perhaps she had a smaller bite. Maybe she was stronger. They would see.

José reappeared on the aft deck. He shouted, "Everybody OK?" Bob turned and simply rolled his eyes, giving his rod a little pull and the reel a few revolutions. Each revolution, José thought, would pull in about six inches of the line. Six a yard or metre or so. At a rough guess, and at 50 yards, that would take 50 sessions if Bob achieved six spins a minute. They were there for the next hour. The hope was that the fish would give up after another 30 minutes or so and the remainder would be a steady pull.

José leant across to speak directly into Bob's ear. "Do you want a break, mate?"

"Not bloody likely, I've got to know this bastard. I'm not having it said I didn't do it single-handed. Could slaughter another beer, though."

"Coming up," José said encouragingly. He handed Bob the extra beer Maria had brought through, and crossed to where Marcia was still quite calmly reeling in her catch. José placed his hand on the rod and eased it back towards the saloon. He could feel the weight of the fish. It was pretty big, by his judgement.

"How are you doing?" he said to Marcia.

"She's doing really well," Maria replied.

"Doing my stomach muscles the power of good and burning up the little extra your chef has managed to put on my thighs," was Marcia's response.

José thought what a positive girl she was. In fact they both were. He only hoped another 30 minutes wouldn't daunt them. He'd give them a break, take the helm, where he'd feel safer and increase the speed. That should tire the catch and help the ailing anglers.

Nobody counted those 30 minutes. Bob thought either he was getting a second wind or the fish was giving up. He could now see his float only 15 yards or so from the back of the boat and he was able to reel in for a longer period each time before he felt his body was going to implode.

Marcia, if anything, was closer to the catch than he was. Probably got a little mackerel or something, he thought. Maria thrust another beer into Bob's hand and a coke for Marcia. She still looked as though she would do justice to a movie had the cameras been rolling. Not a bead of perspiration from her forehead, just a hint of sweat in the armpits of her blouse.

"Could you do me a favour?" Marcia said to Maria.

"Of course."

"My bloody bra strap has come down… no, not that one," she said. "If you're not quick, I'm going to fall out and the fish will have that bit of me for lunch. And lucky them, I have to say."

"You sure you wouldn't prefer José to do this for you?" Maria teased.

"Stop fooling around, Maria, I'm too busy to be groped, I'm fishing." Maria obliged.

"Bless you, my dear. Why is it girls are just happy to do as they're asked," she said, a little out of breath still. "If I'd asked Bob to do that simple little task he'd have taken it as an invitation to take the whole bra off. Would you reckon your Peter's inherited your deft touch?"

"No, he'd be like his father, I'd expect."

"How would that be?"

"Oh, he'd have your bra off by now too."

They roared with laughter. "What's the bloody joke?" Bob shouted over.

"Oh we're just comparing men with sharks… all teeth and thrash when they sense the bait."

"If I could hold my ribs," Marcia indicated to Maria, "I'd laugh with you, but have you seen how close the line is to the…" At that point the swell parted and a beautiful silver rocket leapt out of the sea and back in again.

"Christ!" Marcia shouted. "Did you see that? That's a baby dolphin. I'll have to let that go."

"No! Not a dolphin. It looks like a tuna. Let me get José."

Bob was slightly distracted and hadn't noticed that his float too was really quite near the rear of the boat. There was no sign of his prey leaping into the air with the joy of dying. Maria had beckoned for José to cut the engines and let the boat drift. The silence was amazing. They could speak and be heard.

José appeared with a grappling hook, and an air of calm control. "So let's decide," he said. "We can't land two together. Who's first?"

"The lady," Bob said.

Marcia was flattered. Usually, whenever Bob was feeling competitive, he would ignore any other being's presence. She had seen him on a golf course playing in a men's threesome and thought he was totally unaware that he was playing a social game with two other people. At his competitive best he was a loner, even ignoring the interests of his co-directors when he was in the fight for a contract, a sale or even, she thought at times, who should pay for the next round.

José did not see the significance of the decision. He shouted to Bob, "Don't relax, your bastard's probably playing a game with you. He's resting. He'll give you a hell of a pounding if you give him a break. Keep reeling him in. Don't let up. We'll land Marcia's and then get yours in."

Maria could now see the outline of a heavy silver object. She was right, she thought, a blue-fin tuna. There was little or no movement coming from the defeated prey.

José leant over the rail and hooked the line so that he too was pulling in the catch. "Quick!" he shouted to Maria. "Throw that other hook across!"

Maria obeyed, despite thinking a 'please' would not have gone amiss. It was better for everyone to be controlled, she thought.

José transferred the original hook into his left hand. "Can you hold this steady?" he said to Maria, who did as instructed. José caught sight of the magnificent body coming towards the back of the boat, to one side of the deadened engines. With one huge and accurate swing of the hook, he hit the apparent steel body encasing the fish, just behind the fin.

He took his eye off his target and looked to Marcia. "Now reel in the fish for all you're worth and don't stop till I tell you," he commanded. Shocked into action, she did as instructed.

José placed both hands on the long handle to the hook and heaved. "Up she comes!" he shouted.

Maria looked over the edge and saw the living torpedo, with ancestors going back thousands of years, suddenly explode. The sea turned scarlet with the sudden outsurge of blood. Maria felt for the pit of her stomach. She retched.

"Come on, darling. No time for emotion. We've almost got it in. Can you pull that sheet across," he called, indicating a plastic tarpaulin lying neatly to one side of the deck.

It took all José's strength, and Marcia's continuing winding, to land the fish. José guided it onto the deck and onto the tarpaulin. The one eye of the fish looked up at Marcia. There was a final attempt at a flap of the tail. Tears were rolling down Marcia's cheeks. "I've never killed anything before," she wailed.

"For fuck's sake, Marcia, cut the hysteria, come and give me a hand otherwise I'll be the second thing this bloody cruise has killed!" Bob shouted across.

José had almost forgotten about Bob. He turned round and said, "Christ! Your hand, Bob. What have you done?"

"Well I didn't do it wanking, you soppy bastard. I've been winding this bugger in while you've all been helping the lady. I have no problem with that except I caught my hand in the winder on the reel. It'll be alright once we've landed my matey on the line."

José looked over the rails down into the sea, which was still cloudy red from the culling of Marcia's catch. "Christ, he's a big one, Bob. I'd say 18 to 20 kilos."

"How big would you say Marcia's was?"

"Oh, about the same. Brother and sister, maybe."

"Shit! The way she was going on I thought she'd got a cod. Come on, mate. Give me a hand."

Lifting Bob's catch out of the sea was altogether a bit of an anti-climax. José threw a net into the water and the two men shared about ten kilos each to hoist it on board. The two large fish lay majestically beside each other like a couple of shiny metallic sculptures. The quartet looked on, Bob and Marcia with mixed surprise, José and Maria with satisfaction at a well laid plan.

José suddenly put his hand to his mouth. "I very nearly forgot."

"Forgot?" Bob said.

"Yes. You'll need a record of the catch. I'll get the camera." He shot off into the saloon and returned with a Kodak 35mm Instamatic. It was his latest pride and joy.

First he lined up Marcia to stand holding up her catch. She needed both hands, with barely room for a camera smile. "Hurry up," she screeched, "it's bloody heavy!"

Bob made less fuss, making a huge effort to hold his stomach in and beam at the camera.

Then José set the camera on the table and took a ten-second delayed shot of the four of them. They all laughed as he ran round from the back of the table just in time to be in the shot.

"OK. That's enough," Maria said.

She looked pale. "What was the heaving about over the fish?" Bob enquired.

"Oh, it was just so sudden, one minute there was a solid fish with an impenetrable armour and the next its dignity was burst out into the sea. It just caught a tender spot at that moment." Tender she was, and the pulling she had taken helping Marcia had not helped. Maybe she had done more pulling than she thought, but the tops of her thighs ached and her feet were as heavy as lead.

"Right," José said, ever the determined leader. "Let's get a bit of cleaning up done. I'll deal with the fish. Maria, if you could strap a bandage onto Bob's hand that'll stop him bleeding to death. Marcia. Now what job can we give you?"

Marcia thought that perhaps her job could be to go and have a shower and get out of her sweaty, salty clothes. Maybe to just throw on a bikini and recharge her body. She wouldn't admit to it but she was absolutely shattered. She'd always led a physical life, but even when she was auditioning hour after hour for a show, she'd never felt this bad.

"She can make good gins and tonics," Bob offered.

"Seems a good idea to me," José agreed.

"Are you on for bartender?"

"Yup, suits me, but I need a pee break. By the way, Bob, how did you hold on for so long?"

"Ah! Now there's a secret."

"What's that?"

"You give maximum concentration to something and the urge goes away. But now you've mentioned it, I need to go."

"Be quick. I'll just throw myself under the shower and then I'll use the loo after you."

As Bob came out of the toilet, Marcia stepped out through the shower door, not expecting him to be there. She reached for the towel she'd left on the hook.

"You're lovely, doll," Bob said, and leant forward and held her shoulders. He lifted the towel out of her hands and dabbed her shoulders, then her chest, stomach, thighs and legs.

"Come on, you," Marcia said firmly, "I've got to pee then do the gins and tonics."

"Come on, babe. It's me who wants the drink. I can wait a few minutes."

"You bloody can't for two reasons. Firstly we all need a drink and secondly you're slowly bleeding to death. Look at your hand. Look what you've done to the towel. So come on, give me back my towel. Oh look at it. You've put blood all over it."

Bob slinked back aft, feeling like a scolded boy who's been given his marching orders.

Marcia towelled herself down, remembering she had forgotten to bring her bikini into the shower room. Two strides across the passageway and she'd be in the berth they'd been allocated. She didn't want to wrap the entire towel around herself, as it was a bit bloody, so she held it to her body, opened the door and skipped across.

It had to be. "Nice body," came José's voice. Marcia stopped in her tracks and lowered the crunched up towel to cover her more private parts. It left her inadvertently topless.

"Now I knew I could have found you a special job," José said, standing in front of her holding an extremely heavy flat plastic storage tray packed with ice and supporting a still gleaming tuna.

Marcia actually blushed. Although as a show girl exposure was a normal part of a routine, somehow, on stage, the glare of the footlights set up a barrier between herself and the audience. There was not the closeness of this situation, nor the absence of anonymity. She lifted the towel as a compromise to nearly cover her breasts and her navel area.

"It's still a lovely body," José pronounced.

"Flattery won't get you a larger gin than anyone else and besides, Maria's is equally lovely."

"I'm not denying that," José offered. "But, as I always say, if I went to an art gallery and saw a painting I liked, I'd say so. As an art form you do have a very viewable body... but to take it home and hang it on the wall would be an entirely different matter... it's a simple statement of fact. Now I'll go dump this equally beautiful body of a fish and you hurry through with the drinks."

Despite his compliment, José had made her feel inadequate, and as she slipped into her white bikini, she kicked herself for not having been better prepared by taking it into in the shower. She liked Maria very much and didn't want José's attention to stray from her on her account. She would fuss Bob all day. He'd be surprised but that should give José the message. Besides, he wasn't her type. She liked a little less squeaky-clean-never-have-a-hair-out-of-place approach. Rogues went down well with her. Her father was a rogue.

When José returned to the deck, having stored the fish in the hold, he passed Marcia in the saloon mixing the drinks. He elected not to exchange any further dialogue. She might start taking him seriously and he didn't want an atmosphere with Bob and Maria on board.

Maria had got a bowl of hot water, which reeked of TCP, and some cotton wool pads and was bathing the cut on Bob's hand. "José, could you have a look at this? I think it needs a stitch."

José looked. She was probably right, but it was the fleshy part of his hand at the base of his thumb which he had caught.

"What I'd suggest is cut a couple of plasters into strips and put them diagonally across the cut to act as sutures. Then run a plaster down the length of the cut and over the top of the strips. You'd be effectively stitching the wound. Then a good protective bandage and, Bob, try not to use it for a while."

Meanwhile, Marcia had had second thoughts and put a matching white Romanesque robe over her bikini. She thought it might be more appropriate to stay covered up. She sensed the fishing had made the men particularly earthy.

"Fourer gins and tonics," she announced.

José was thrown. Although his English was now excellent – he spent an hour or so on the phone to the UK every day, and they certainly didn't ever speak a word of Spanish – he did not know the word 'fourer'.

"Fourer?" he enquired. He didn't feel so bad because Maria was looking pretty confused too.

"Oh, it's My Fair Lady English. Hasn't it reached you yet?"

"I don't think so," Maria said.

"It's a play. Well, a musical actually, based on a classic called Pygmalion. The girl who sells flowers and speaks in what's known as Cockney has trouble with her speech. She gets taken under the wing of a professor and he teaches her how to speak proper English. The classic line always introduces an 'er' into the pronunciation. Typically she says 'Wouldn't it be loverley', instead of just lovely. So I did a 'Pygmalion' on you. Anyway, to hell with it. There's one G&T each. Can you hold a gin and tonic with that bad hand of yours, darling?" she asked Bob.

"Listen, babe, if I'd lost both hands I'd still be able to pick up a G&T with my feet. Are we all charged up?" he said, looking towards José and Maria. The responses were in the affirmative. "Then here's to you two loverlies. It's been a smashing day so far. You've both been terrific. Haven't they, Marcia?"

"Terrific," she echoed.

"Santé," they all replied, and after much glass-chinking, they each gulped a swig of Marcia's concoction.

"You just cannot beat a G&T," Bob said.

Out of politeness, both José and Maria agreed. They both would have preferred a cool glass of wine but the hosts had to follow the whims of their guests on this occasion, particularly paying guests.

José had lifted both engines above the water and left the Maria de Rosas drifting. There was no tide out in the Med where they were and although he had to remain alert, they could all take some time out.

It seemed they had run out of conversation. They were all exhausted. They drifted for half an hour or so, then José announced, "We thought we'd head up the coast and find a beach. Maria is 'smashing' at picnics. Is smashing the right word? My colleagues in London are always saying that."

"That's great," Bob ruled.

"So why don't the three of you go up forward and get some sun and I'll do the driving. Let's say we'll beach in 45 minutes."

They beached on schedule and José off-loaded a couple of large beach umbrellas and staked them into the virgin sand, as if to mark a new territorial conquest.

Maria's picnic was certainly up to her usual standard. Smoked salmon, egg mayonnaise, salads. Cold beef and chicken. Apple tart. The food was complemented by a gentle French Chablis. They had lots of laughter. Bob particularly had them in stitches when he told them that at one stage he'd felt like chucking his rod overboard because it seemed an easier solution than pulling in the 'sodding tuna' for another half mile.

True to her plan, Marcia smothered Bob with affection and innuendo. "My heroic fisherman! My rod and your staff have always comforted me." Expressions that were lost on Maria and José.

The heat was going out of the day and it was a comfortable 20 degrees. José looked casually at his watch. "Hell," he said, "it's 4pm."

"Wow!" said Bob. "Where did that day go?"

"So what do you think? A swim and then head back and we'll bribe the chef to cook at least one of the fish," José suggested.

Maria cringed. Since lunch and a couple of generous glasses of Chablis, she'd had the odd vision of what lay in store for her. The next dose of Miguel's wonder killer medicine. She knew there was no alternative, but to go from the companionable high they had enjoyed as a foursome to the loneliness of that dark act was not something to look forward to.

Bob opined that a swim would not do his hand any good. Maria agreed, saying she shouldn't swim after the drinks she'd had. Marcia had to be careful. She too had probably downed the better part of a bottle of wine (they'd had three between them), although she would have loved to cast everything off and throw herself into the surf.

José was neutral. He'd swim if the others wanted to, not if the majority abstained. He waited for Marcia's vote. She was a good liar at times. "If I swam now," she said seriously, "I'd be embarrassing. Apart from peeing in the water, which I seriously do need to do, I'd probably then sink… is alcohol heavier than salt water? I don't know."

"So I think the vote seems to be three negatives," Maria announced. "José?"

"Not for me then," he ruled. "I'm happy to head back slowly into Marcia's sun."

"Oh. I'd forgotten," Marcia said. "Are we really going into sunset cruise mode?"

"It was the lady's wish," José announced. "Then, as I see it, I think it's the girls on the front sun deck propped up and watching the sun settle, and the boys can go in the wheelhouse and tell tales of catches lost and mermaids won."

Bob turned to José. "You seem to know all about fish. Do you actually know how to do it with a mermaid?"

"Let's take the girls' advice and move on, but I'll tell you on the way back."

They took the dinghy back to the boat, which José had anchored about 100 metres out. The girls certainly settled on their respective lilos on the foredeck. The guys talked in the wheelhouse – not, alas, about mermaids, but more about 'how the hell do you learn to drive one of these things?' and 'how the hell do you know where we are?', and other questions from a novice sailor to a more experienced one.

Bob suddenly clutched José's arm. They had worked out many minutes before that the girls were asleep. "José, do you know where we are?"

"Broadly, yes."

"Over there," Bob said, pointing to a beach about a mile to the west.

"Yes," José responded. "There's a farmhouse and fields of sunflowers."

"Where's that?" Bob asked somewhat urgently.

"Don't exactly know. There are a few bays like that along the coast."

"That... that, José, is a magnificent bay though. I'd never realised it was sheltered by the hills behind it. Look. All the land either side is falling into shadow, but there must be... what?... about a mile of sunflowers still lifting their heads to say goodnight to the sinking sun."

"What's the great interest, Bob?"

"The great interest, amigo, is that Peter reckons he's bought the whole sodding bay."

"Peter? What, Maria's Peter, Pedro?"

"Yes. That's right."

"Really? I hadn't heard that. What, for the sunflower seed oil?"

"No, you soppy bugger. To develop."

"Develop?"

"That's right."

"How's he afford to buy that?"

"I've got no idea. But I'll say two things about Peter. Both complimentary. He's the only young man who hasn't made himself look a prat by making a pass at my wife."

"Prat... what's a prat?"

"Oh, suffice it to say a young man who makes a pass at my wife!"

"And the second... ?"

"Mark my words. If ever I've seen a young man who knows where he's going, it's Peter Martinez. If he has bought that, and I don't think he'd lie, then there, if I'm any judge at all, is a very valuable piece of real estate… you don't buy 12 hours of sun that often. I'm sure that's the bay, I'm sure I'm right. José, can you mark it on your charts. We'll check it tomorrow."

"Sure," José confirmed.

There was now a distinct chill in the air. The girls had stirred. The sky was beginning to fade from the deep blue of the hot day to paler shades with a hint of pink and a sunset to come. Bob seemed still to be mesmerised and was looking back at the bay. "José, mate. You're a sailor. Look at the formation of the bay when it hits the hill coming down into the sea. Isn't that a natural harbour, if ever you've seen one?"

"I'd say so, yes. If the Romans hadn't seen Ampurias first, I think it would have been an equally natural landing point. Then it would have already been developed."

"So for harbour read 'marina'. It wouldn't take a lot to build a sea wall using the rock, which is bound to be excavated to bring in the road where the track is now. Dig it, dump it. It would be so economic. I hope that boy realises what he might be on to."

"I'm sure he does," José said, almost defensively of Peter. He thought maybe he should have a word, but then who was he to interfere?

The girls were now silhouetted by the sun setting ahead of them. Their background was that softening red hue, beckoning the ball of fire to hit the sea and fall below the horizon. A clump of evening clouds sailed past, causing the sun's rays to act as a series of spotlights on the calm sea.

Marcia was first to sit up on her haunches. She stretched both arms high to the sky and eased each vertebra, down to the base of her spine. Her stomach muscles ached. She couldn't remember such a work-out before. Maria must have felt the movement. She was slower to rise into a sitting position. She'd been sound asleep; her eyes blinked into the sun's rays. It was a sudden awakening. Her body felt numb, and she felt a stabbing pain in the pit of her stomach.

José was looking ahead. He picked up a strange whirlpool on the sea's surface some 300 metres from the port side of the boat. You sometimes got these where the sea bed below had a faulty seam and, given the right set of currents, such as there were in this part of the Med, a swirl would set in and manifest itself as a spinning hollow on the surface of the sea.

Maria picked up on it too, but as she did the hollow changed from its black-blue shimmering colour to a rosé hue, and as the shadows of the whirlpool changed to deep red, she held her breath. "Not again!" she shouted, but her words didn't come out. Her head started to spin, she clenched her teeth and through slit eyes she just made out the form rising from the depths. It was large. It was human... anguish overcame her... there in the pool of blood... Paco... she tried to speak but her eyes slammed shut. Her head fell forward.

"Christ!" Marcia shouted out. José picked up on what was happening. Bob said, "What's up?"

Maria's back arched forward and she fell slightly sideways, partially forward onto the deck. Marcia threw herself across to stop Maria sliding to the unprotected side of the upper deck. Maria was groaning and blowing saliva through her lips.

José cut the engines and said to Bob, "Here, hold this," indicating the wheel. He leapt round the wheelhouse onto the bathing deck, and was on his knees in a flash. His initial thought was that she had fainted.

Maria began to groan. Seconds had been an eternity. Her eyes rolled slowly open, gazing into the calm friendly face of José.

"Paco," she said. José knew what she meant.

She pulled her knees up towards her chest. "Pain, José, such pain. José... say goodbye."

"Oh, come on, darling. You're fine. You're fine. There are no goodbyes."

"José..." she now whispered. "Say goodbye, goodbye to our child."

José was stunned to silence. He looked down towards Maria's stomach, now realising what was happening. She was miscarrying. The signs were there. Her black slacks were drenched around her upper legs. He held her in his arms. Marcia looked like death. Bob couldn't work out what was going on.

José looked across at Marcia. "Miscarriage, I think."

"Looks like it," Marcia replied. "Here, this is girls' stuff. Can you go and get some water and some towels? Here, Maria, I'm with you now," she said as she took hold of Maria's trembling body.

As José rushed below, Maria looked up into Marcia's face. "Friend," she said, her own face betrayed the agony she was going through. The pain reached a sudden peak, which led to an easing and a lower clammy body warmth. Perspiration broke out on her brow.

"I'd say that was it," Marcia said quietly. Maria was now calmer. The colour was returning to her cheeks, or was it the reflection of the setting sun?

Maria was able to sit up. She looked across to her left. "Cheers, Paco," she said in a happy tone.

"What's that mean?" Marcia enquired.

"Oh, some people have expressions. When something traumatic happens to me I say 'cheers, Paco'. It's just a habit. Wow. Thanks, Marcia, that was tough."

José arrived with towels and water. "Here, darling," he said as she turned to him.

"You go and get this show on the road again back to Llanfranc. I'll sort myself out, I'm fine now. Totally embarrassed but fine."

"If you're sure, I think it's best if we get you home." He squeezed her hand, but hovered slightly awkwardly.

Marcia had slipped back into the saloon. The excitement and fear of it all had sent her scurrying off to the loo.

"I had no idea," José said quietly in their furtive shared moments alone.

"I couldn't tell you."

"You should have done. It's something to share."

It made Maria remember the day she'd told Paco she was pregnant. He'd shown excitement, that's true, but after that it was very much her province to deal with the trials and tribulations of pregnancy. How different José was, and yet this was a lost cause.

"How long's it been?" José asked tenderly.

"I'd say seven or eight weeks. You're a man. You do the counting. When was the hotel opening?"

"Not in the changing room, on the lilo? You can't mean then!"

"I'd say it was."

"Oh, I'm so sorry. That was totally my fault. The last thing I thought I'd need at the opening of a hotel was a condom. I really am sorry."

"Don't be. I've had a wonderful couple of months knowing you've been inside me."

"There'll be another time," José said. "When everything's right. Maybe the Gods are saying it wasn't the right time."

Maria thought, *Paco didn't think it was the right time either,* but she kept such thoughts to herself.

Marcia returned. She had brought a pair of ladies' jeans she'd found in the cabin. "Are these yours?" she said to Maria.

"Well, if they weren't, I tell you, José would have some answering to do!"

Marcia had a bundle of other bits and pieces José couldn't identify. "Look, José, this is girl territory. I'll get Maria fixed up. I'll trade you that for you fixing my tough hero an evening gin and tonic. He's gone totally to pieces. He said he thought Maria was about to die. He just doesn't appreciate how tough we girls have to be. And when I did say that, bless the darling, he looked down at his bandaged hand and said 'It's alright for you. You haven't got a great gash in your hand. It hurts like stink', bless him."

José asked Maria if she was sure she was OK now.

"I'm fine. Just a mess I'd rather you not get involved with."

"I'll get this tub back to base then." He leant across and kissed her lips, then went back to the wheelhouse. "How long has all that taken?" he asked Bob.

"It's 6.10 and when I took the wheel, for some reason I noticed it was exactly six. There was something creepy about that."

José took a pocket calculator out of a drawer and did some frantic calculations. He pronounced, "Two and a half miles, due north-east," speaking a language Bob just did not understand.

José rummaged in a lower plan drawer and pulled out a chart with a series of red biro lines criss-crossing what even Bob recognised as being the sea. He took a couple of fixes from the navigating equipment he'd had installed and made some markings on the map. He then took out what Bob recognised from his own surveying days as a scale rule, and plotted new lines on the map. He seemed to double check, then stood back. He turned, took a deep breath and said, "Shit."

Bob looked worried. "What's wrong?" he said.

"Nothing," José replied. "Absolutely, as you say, bloody nothing… listen, mate, would you like a G&T?"

"Wouldn't I, captain! But could you do a left-handed one? My right hand's throbbing like fury. It's the gash, you know."

They made good time back and were into the harbour by seven. Maria was OK to walk and was stronger. Nurse Marcia loaned her a shoulder to lean on and a blanket. Maria said she was cold. *Probably shock,* José thought. Bob actually fetched José's car for him while the captain made a makeshift attempt at quickly putting the essential parts of the boat to bed.

They were all on the jetty, with Maria bundled up in the back of the car. José was ready to drive back to the hotel. He sat behind the wheel. He suddenly unleashed the expletive he'd picked up too readily from Bob.

"Shit!" he said.

Bob said, "What?"

Marcia said, "What now?"

And Maria said, "José, your language! What now?"

"The bloody fish!" José said in despair. "I'll have to get them. They'll rot overnight." He scurried off back into the boat, unlocking the rear doors into the saloon. About ten minutes later the double catch was in the boot, a little riper in smell than when freshly caught.

José got back behind the wheel.

"She's asleep," Marcia said.

"That's probably a good thing. How do we cope with getting her into the cottage if Peter's there?"

"We'll say she got tight and needs to sleep it off. I'll go in with her and pretend to be tipsy too. Who knows… it's Sunday evening, he might be round playing with Meribel."

"Doubt that," José said.

"Really?"

"Yes, Maria says they're finished."

"Go on! I'd say they were almost bound to make it into a future together. He seemed very keen."

"Oh, I don't think you know Peter that well. He's got ideals. He won't rush into anything permanent except his university career. No, he and Meribel I'm sure got on, but as you English would say, 'That's it, it's over'."

Marcia's mind was ticking. *I'd love to know what happened there. So what's he going to do now for his oats?*

Eventually she pronounced, "That's sad, isn't it, Bob?"

"Bob's asleep too," José said.

"So it's back to you and me to make polite conversation."

"Seems so."

Peter was out when they arrived back. Marcia and José helped Maria from the car, down the path and into the cottage. By the time they got to the door, Maria was able to support herself, brushing off any assistance.

Once Marcia was satisfied her friend was OK, she said she'd leave them to their own devices, but made Maria promise that if she needed something in the night, she would phone Marcia's room and she'd be over like a shot. Maria assured José she'd be best left to have a bath and go to bed.

"I'll leave you with your privacy on condition you swear you're OK. I'll give the fish to chef and he'll store it overnight. Then I'll come back, tuck you up and ring you in the morning."

"I'm fine. Yes, OK about the fish. I'd love you to tuck me in, but what about if Pedro comes back?"

"So if he does, he does, I'm not leaving till I know you're safe and sound."

He left later when she was clearly OK, against a promise that she would ring in the night if she needed anything. Maria felt secure and very, very tired. She dozed but remembered to pray, as she did almost every night without fail. It was a standard pattern for God to bless Paco wherever he was, and for her to say sorry to him. To ask God to bless Pedro and keep him safe and strong and determined, to bless José, darling José (but not to let Paco know). To bless her parents, long gone, and Marco and Virginia, for them to be happy with each other… oh, and to thank Marcia for being a true friend, and Bob, and bless the baby she had lost.

Some nights she'd fall asleep mid-prayer and wake not knowing whom she had missed. Occasionally she'd finish her prayer by asking God to help her. Tonight she thought that would be too selfish…

CHAPTER 20

The Sunday of the boat trip, Natasha Cook was casually watching Peter as he came off the court on his way for a break as the midday sun was high above them. As he got to the end of the pool at the foot of the steps up to the hotel, her heart fluttered a little as Philippe came into view.

Philippe was dressed in tennis gear in anticipation of the needle match between him and Georgio Jnr, and Peter and Dr Guibaud. The game had been hyped up by the men for almost a week, certainly because the four of them were the best players in the hotel at the time. Georgio had amazing flashes of brilliance, but was temperamental. One fluffed shot seemed to take him a couple of games to outgrow. Philippe (in Tasha's eyes anyway) was the strongest and marginally the fittest, although their nightly assignations once her parents had hit the sack were beginning to show.

Peter was actually the best tennis player. He had the most skill and imagination and could just about carry the lesser abilities of the very steady French doctor. For Tasha, seeing Peter and Philippe together was a bit of a turn on. Although she would never dream of showing it, she quite fancied Peter, probably because he didn't seem to be available while Philippe, from the outset, had shown that he was.

Hell, she thought, if she lay here watching too intently, Mum and Dad would notice like they had the day before and tell her she should really be studying for her upcoming A-level in English Lit. If only they knew about her nights out, they'd go berserk.

"So it's the big game at two?" Philippe challenged Peter.

"Fine with me. Are the others OK? I haven't seen Georgio for a while."

"No, he's playing golf these days with the young Englishman, you know, Andrew, the third captain at the Olympics. He's apparently only just taken the sport up, but he's very good already."

"I saw the French doctor last night. He's up for it. So yes, 2pm it will be. Pistols at two."

Peter continued up to the hotel. Being at the forefront of the hotel's daily activities as the tennis coach certainly made him aware of many a young lady's glance. He'd noticed Natasha following his every step as she lay back on her sunbed, trying to give the impression of staring straight ahead. The give-away was when he smiled at her, and she mirrored it immediately.

The glimpse of her now in her bikini set his juices going. It had only been a day or so but if he was not missing Meribel for herself, he was certainly missing Meribel, the ready supplier of most things a young man needed. He'd thought about a couple of hundred pesetas tucked into Tania's bra, but resolved to stick to his rule that he would never pay for favours.

The reception was quiet. Most guests were either at the beach or pool and on a Sunday, the restaurants wouldn't be too busy either. It was really too hot to eat. Peter wondered how his mother was getting on aboard the boat, and Marcia, of course. He bet she'd have her clothes off by now. Now that was some thought… maybe he'd best go and find Tania after all.

Sñr Martin was at the desk.

"Hi!" Peter greeted him.

"Buenos dias, Sñr Peter. Cómo estás hoy?"

"Cada día mejor," Peter replied chirpily.

As Peter turned towards the kitchen to scrounge a salad or something light, Sñr Martin called after him. "Sñr Peter, by the way, there's a message for you, Meribel rang. Could you give her a call before 1pm? I was going to send the message down to the court, but I thought you'd come up for a break as usual, and you have."

"Thanks, Sñr Martin."

Now what did she want? Maybe she needed a bit of fulfilment herself and thought he wouldn't mind her asking him. Well, he'd have to see. He wouldn't hurry to call. He'd have his snack and then call her.

When he made himself get round to it, the phone rang for a while. It was answered by her mother. That's all he wanted. She'd be frosty once she knew it was him.

"Good morning… could I speak to Meribel please?"

Knowing full well it was Peter, she nevertheless went through the, "Who's that please?"

"Peter."

"Oh! I'll get her for you." No small talk this time.

"Hi!" came Meribel's voice. It was soft and calm. "How are you?" she asked.

"Good, thank you. And you?"

"Fine," she said. "Thanks for ringing back."

Was he about to hear that she'd changed her outlook and had decided to start actually screwing, and she wanted him to be the first to know and, in fact, the first to sample her new delights?

"There's a letter here for you."

"Sorry?" Peter replied.

"There's a letter here for you."

So this was not a news-breaking change in philosophy after all. He almost pinched himself back to reality.

"Oh, a letter." He had sometimes used Meribel's address if he didn't want his correspondence to be scrutinised by his mother before he got to open it. It was not that Maria was intrusive; like all mothers, she just wanted to be interested and if there was a letter from England she'd be keen to find out what it was about.

"Can you see the postmark?"

"Yes, it's from England."

"Oh, that's interesting. Can we meet and I'll pick it up?"

"I expect you'd like it today?"

"If I could."

"Well, I tell you what…" She seemed to suddenly cool. "… I'll be out but if you want to call round, Mother's in all afternoon and evening, you could collect it. And I left a couple of bits in the locker at the hotel – a jacket and a pair of shoes. I'm not sure what else, but do you think you could clear whatever there is and drop it round when you come?"

"Sure." There was no need for him to clarify the point that she would not be coming back.

"Do you have any idea what time you'll call in?"

"Possibly sixish. But tell your mother not to hang around for me. If she wants to leave the letter on your front verandah, maybe wedged up against the little window, I can collect and leave your stuff without bothering her." He thought that might be best anyway, he'd rather not face some sort of confrontation about how he'd had her daughter's best years and had now done something so terribly wrong that she didn't want to know him anymore.

"Is that OK with you then?"

"Yes, fine," Meribel replied cheerily.

"Off to anywhere nice?" Peter went on to enquire, partly just out of general curiosity because he knew Meribel didn't usually go out on Sunday nights (which had often been a bone of contention between them), and partly because he was intrigued that she had got a social life in place so soon after their split.

"Yes. I think so, anyway. It's certainly set to be a calm evening with no silly rows."

That stung him. But he wouldn't rise to the bait. "Right then. I'll collect the post. Thanks for that, and I'll drop your clothes in… shall I hold back any

329

you've borrowed?"

She slammed the phone down.

Peter smiled to himself. *She's lost her sense of humour,* he thought. *Women!*

He was intrigued by the prospect of the letter. When he'd had his final interview at Madrid, he'd got through all the academic appraisals with flying colours. The professorial staff had been amazed by his determination to do architecture. Most student applicants had a few ifs and buts about whether architecture would become their career, or whether it was a stepping stone to another vocation: archaeology, interior design; some even believed they might finish up in theatre or film design. Peter, however, was almost blinkered. He had few illusions about redesigning the centre of Paris, or finishing the Sagrada Familia cathedral for the late, somewhat eccentric Gaudi.

His motivation seemed squarely to hinge on commercial functional design. He appeared to have a natural bent for the living environment and the environment for the living, as he phrased it, to the bewilderment of most of the interviewing staff, who had never come across such a notion as 'both environments'.

The first confused urban design lecturer had had the courage to ask, "Peter, you say 'both environments', what do you mean by both? Isn't there just the one?"

"Oh no! Certainly not. There's the environment, or more precisely an environment, which for some economic or cultural reason needs developing. Now the 20th century logical approach has been to clear what's there and totally rebuild." He supposed the war might have had an influence on that insofar as the bombs over Europe had indeed done the demolition and there was only flattened space then to be built upon, at speed, for socio-economic reasons.

"What I'm advocating," he continued eagerly, "is taking the environment that's ready and ripe for whatever need of development. In my mind, I'd leave, say, half exactly as it is. Let that element of the environment continue to live. I'll call that the living environment. So if you've got ten acres of olive trees, use five acres, exactly as they exist, to become part of the overall design plan. In housing, start the residents off with a garden full of olive trees. Why not? The trees have the right to be there, it's their home after all. The nouveau cultivated back gardens in Europe or the USA don't need to be imported to our native surroundings. So let the established environment live.

"Then there's the driving force for the development in the first place – the need to create places to live or, in commercial locations, manufacturing space, then the buildings for office users. Those are the environments for 'living in'. There you have the two. If it's houses you're designing, then arrange the windows to look out on the olive trees in the structured design, not to emphasise the view to some distant horizon that's only now visible because swathes of trees have been removed to make way for the construction."

That first lecturer was surprised by the forthrightness of Peter's thinking. Peter was right, most new developments did look out onto cultivated back gardens, and looking out over the roads leading in was not a pretty sight. Rarely had he interviewed a candidate who held his attention so thoroughly all the way through the interview.

He told one of his colleagues, "This chap you'll meet after the coffee break is already there. He's into his career. I doubt we'll teach him anything about design, or change his thinking. OK, colour and textural influence maybe. All he really needs to be here for is to learn construction so that his designs are practical and buildable. Then, as far as I see it, he's there."

The colleague responded, somewhat sarcastically, "… and I suppose this young man's name is Corbusier Jnr, and all he's doing is practising what his old man has said right through his life."

"No, I went through that. I said that I supposed his father was an architect and he was just preaching the paternal influence. 'No, not at all', he had said and went on to explain his father was a fisherman…"

"What, one of the disciples?"

"Come on, Juan. You're being a bit jaundiced. I'm trying to tell you about a keen young man who's going to go a long way."

"He just sounds glib to me. Surely we need people with brains that are clean slates. Then we can influence them the way it should be…"

"If you'd taken that view with Brunel, Wren, Michelangelo and some of the other greats, you'd have had very little from them. They had design in their blood. I'm telling you, Peter Martinez has."

"OK, I'll make my own mind up about the lad. But I bet he drops out before the end of the course."

Joseph Brand was the University of Madrid's senior administrator, and he had been listening to the conversation from the adjoining table. He had heard condemnation of student enthusiasm before, and hated hearing it. He imagined they were talking about Peter Martinez, whom he had already met and whom he too had found fascinating. He decided to make a point of having another discussion with him, which came about in the last session of Peter's interview.

Joseph had received all the feedback about which applicants would be offered definite places. Peter was one. Out of the others, the staff were disappointed that they had one applicant too many for the remaining available places.

When Joseph saw Peter for his final round-up, he was able to confirm the offer of a place. Peter was delighted. Joseph, a straight-talking man, told Peter he hoped he would not be offended by what he was about to say, coupled as it was with the offer.

"Of course not," Peter said, wondering what on earth this pleasant, obviously clear-thinking administrator was going to say.

"I don't want you to take this the wrong way. We'd welcome you. But…" Peter hated that word. *But…* he would have to listen on to determine if he was about to be let down.

"But… my personal perception of you is that, in the most literal sense of the word, I don't see you as being 'an academic'. You're academic, of course, you can pass exams. The knowledge you gain I believe you're likely to put to practical good use and, who knows, the ultimate combination of academia and practical ability might eventually set a new standard for others to follow. Madrid, I'd say, isn't ready yet to be turned in that direction. The course here is academic. The theory is brilliant but allowing you in your university time to put it to practical interpretation would not be an option.

"Now there are places in Europe where you can learn theory and finish up with a degree, which on paper would look the same. The difference is the course there would allow you to feel a brick, or see it being made, so that your postgraduate design ability allows you to interpret the practical as well as the theoretical. The places in the UK are called polytechnics. I'm just wondering if you've considered that approach. We have a sort of trading pact with a few. We can swap students for all or part of their course. The other thing I'd have to say is that you'd be studying in English, which would be commercially very valuable for you.

"There's no doubt, in my mind that, as Europe grows, and it will, then English will also grow. In your case, as I'm sure you'll finish up in a successful commercial position, the combination of improved English and a practical degree should suit you very well. I'm inclined to recommend, which I shouldn't really, that you say you'll take our place, but that you also apply to perhaps the Regent Street Polytechnic, as it's known – it's actually the Polytechnic of Westminster. It's in central London and has an excellent reputation. Anyway, think it over for a couple of days and then phone me. I could make out an application and you could see how you get along."

Peter had discussed the idea with Meribel. They took an interest in each other's study plans, and she felt it was well worth applying. "Nothing lost," she had said.

"What do you think my mother might say?"

"Well, sooner or later, you're going to move away. So now might be as good a time as any. You'd be back for the holidays. I think she'd encourage you if she knew."

"I'll wait till I've heard whether there's a place before telling her, I think."

"She'll see the letters, they're bound to expect a lot of answers." Meribel thought on. "Tell you what though, if you wanted to, you could use my parents' address as a post box. Then your mother would be none the wiser."

Peter had jumped at that opportunity. Now he could only imagine the letter would contain the final answer about that place in London. He was almost counting on it.

By six that evening he'd know. As he came out of his mother's office, where he'd made the call to Meribel, he passed the doors to the staff changing rooms, an etched female figure on the one door and the head and hat of a matador on the other. He suddenly remembered Meribel's request for him to empty her locker. *What a pain,* he thought to himself, because he'd got nobody to ask to retrieve her gear at 1pm on a Sunday. All the staff would have gone by then, except for one waitress and a couple of kitchen hands. So he decided to get that task out of the way by emptying the locker himself.

He went to reception, took the master locker key and went back to the girls' changing room. He walked straight in, determined on his mission.

It was as if Peter had walked through an alarmed door and broken the beam to set off a piercing siren.

The scream was so sudden and loud, it acted just like a brick wall, stopping Peter in his tracks. The girl was clad in only black pants, holding a matching bra, so her naked breasts were fully exposed. She screamed again as she grabbed a pink candy striped overall to cover herself.

Peter froze.

Tania's head appeared round the corner of the end locker in the middle row. She too was half-naked and she joined the other girl with an equally piercing scream.

Tania stopped and drew breath. "You bastard voyeur pervert!" she yelled.

Peter put up his hand, as though to suggest she should hold back her comments until he had explained.

The other girl was by now crying and quite hysterical as she pulled a towel around herself and rushed towards Peter. In a crazed panic, she started hitting him on the chest with her clenched fists. Peter took the second of the two instant options he sensed he had. Rather than combat her punches, which was hardly a sensible prospect, he pulled her into a bear hug to stifle the wild charge, then he stepped back, holding his left arm at full stretch and, ensuring he did not touch any part of her body, he was able to put her flailing arms out of range. The towel dropped to the floor.

Tania, who had by now also grabbed a towel and made an attempt to cover herself, also threw herself across the changing room at Peter.

"Don't you dare touch my little sister!" she screamed and, in what appeared to be a family trait, started to pummel him on the chest. The elder by two years, she was altogether stronger than her sister, and the strength developed from her couple of years of chambermaiding made her more of a threat.

Peter released Beth and reached out for Tania, pulling her towards him to stifle her blows. Instinctively she screamed and Beth, now re-clad in her towel, joined the chorus. Peter tried to shout over the frenetic screeching.

As Tania raised her knee, aiming for Peter's groin, he shouted, "Tania, for Christ's sake, I'm here to go to Meribel's locker!"

It was as though she heard but didn't want to hear. She kept trying to break free of his hold, but he tightened it until she could barely breathe. She weakened and her screams turned to tears, which were smothered by her great gasps as she tried to recover her breath.

She was suddenly a woman again. The animal that had first been aroused seemed tamed.

The door opened behind Peter, which was in her full view, and she screamed again. Beth joined the chorus once more, until Marco's voice took over.

Peter turned his head, to be met by the sight of his flustered uncle.

"What the hell's going on?" Now it was his turn to shout. Behind him in the doorway, clasping a copper-bottomed omelette pan, was the second chef.

Peter released Tania as he turned to acknowledge Marco. She ran straight to Marco and threw one arm round his neck as she sobbed against his chest.

Marco looked embarrassed by such familiarity from a member of staff, more so as Beth, the newcomer, joined Tania to get her share of protection from the patron, as she knew him to be.

The atmosphere in the changing room now shifted from being that of a fighting arena to a much calmer courtroom, where soon the jury of patron and chef would judge the explanations for such a furore.

Marco had heard the screams as he walked through reception a good few metres away. The chef, who had been in the midst of beating eggs for a Spanish omelette for table six, had rushed towards the screams, pan in hand, leaving ingredients all over his work surface.

Peter spoke first to Marco. "Thank God! Am I pleased to see you."

Marco was stern. "On first glance I'd say you shouldn't have been..."

"Look. Let's straighten things out. Firstly, it's my fault, but if these two young ladies had listened to what I had to say rather than screaming the place down, we wouldn't be in this state.

"What happened, if we're all now going to remain calm, is that I'd just had a phone conversation with Meribel. She's not coming back to work and she asked me to get a couple of things, personal things, she'd left in her locker."

As he said that, Peter had the presence of mind to show them the key he had taken from reception, dangling it between his thumb and forefinger.

"I was in a hurry and I forgot it was Sunday. My mother's not around, otherwise I would have asked her to collect the stuff for me. I just didn't think anyone would be in the changing room at this time, but I now realise there was a chance that whoever was on duty would be finishing and might be in there. But let me ask you, Marco, would you have ever thought that the staff would be almost naked in there? That they'd be changing their underclothes as well before going home?"

Marco looked a little unsettled. He knew damn well that they did. He would sometimes climb the old mill tower across the courtyard at about 4pm and watch the girls stripping down as they prepared to go home. He knew very well there was one set of underwear for work and one for play, in the case of most of the female staff. Particularly in Tania's.

"No! I'd agree," he said gingerly.

Tania shot him a disbelieving glance. "If you want your little bonuses you'll need to wear black," he had insisted, once he had broken the ice and established that a little play could earn a compliant chambermaid some extra pin-money. In fact he knew bloody well, Tania thought, because he'd paid for the first lot of underwear because she didn't have any money. She couldn't, of course, inform those listening of that fact.

Peter continued. "So, my mistake – for which I totally apologise – was to come in without knocking, or not to have got a lady to come in for me. I could never have imagined it would be like a dressing room at the Moulin Rouge. By the way..." he added, intending to lighten the atmosphere, "either of you could get a job there, and in the Folies Bergère!"

That did it. Tania was clever.

"So you see," she turned to Marco, and then to Juan the chef. "You both heard that. I think Mr Peter is using that story about the key as a cover-up to sneak in and look at us in our undies. I was bare up-top, and Beth was too. Look at her. She's young. She's probably never had her naked breasts seen before by a male, let alone scrutinised to see if they'd fit into the chorus line of the Folies. He came in for a peepshow. The key's just an excuse."

Marco looked sternly at Tania. "Now come on, young lady. It's not the first time you've been naked, I'm sure. I bet you even break your vows with your church by sunbathing without a top on." (He knew she did because there were never any strap marks on the top of the body he paid to see.) "As for young sister Beth, she's got nothing to have a hang-up over. It was an honest mistake, that's all, and we can all forget it."

Everything had calmed down now, everyone was more rational.

Marco turned to Juan. "OK, Juan, thanks for getting here quickly. It could well have been that some stalker had got into the locker room. You'd better finish what you were doing in the kitchen. Perhaps you girls would like to thank him too." Marco had taken control, it seemed.

"Thank you, Juan," both girls said in unison.

Tania still had that wild gypsy look about her quick, darting eyes, behind which was an equally quick mind.

Juan left.

"So what about us, Mr Marco?" Tania pouted. We've had a very nasty shock. Look! I'm still trembling, so is she."

"Firstly, I'd suggest you put some more clothes on. It's not fair on Mr Peter or myself to have to continue to sort this little misunderstanding out when you're both in this state of undress. Not that we'd complain. But you ought to get dressed. Bang on the door, we'll be outside. Then we'll come back in and finally sort it out."

Peter and Marco went outside. Marco turned to Peter with a broad smile. "Now there's another one of life's rich experiences for you. Pretty little things, aren't they?"

Peter was now the serious one. "Oh, come on, Marco, you didn't see them when they were like animals! I don't understand it. OK, they've stripped off, the door opens and they see a man walk in. If there's one of them there alone it could have been quite frightening for her, I admit. With two it's unlikely, besides, it's a well-lit area and Tania must have recognised me straight away. They can't have thought I was there to perform some wildly perverted act on them, or in front of them. I tell you, I think their reaction was put on. Tania led it. That little lady has money signs coming out of her backside, where others of a more pleasant nature have the rays of the sun."

Marco laughed. "So you got that close to her to have a good look at her, did you?"

"Come on, Marco!"

"Right, what I suggest happens is we go back in… that's only when invited. You get the stuff from Meribel's locker and show Tania that the reason for you being there was genuine. Then we'll apologise again, give them a few pesetas extra pocket money and tell them to go home and forget about it. You OK with that?"

"Anything never to be attacked by a couple of wild chambermaids again. Yes, fine."

They waited a couple more minutes and the door opened. Tania was certainly dressed. She had a short red mini-skirt on, with blending blouse with long puffed sleeves. She seemed taller but it was height gained from her black strappy sandals. Beth looked pretty, dressed in a black mini-skirt with a black off-the-shoulder crocheted top. She had a black choker round her neck which, Peter thought, made her look at least four or five years more sexually mature. He must resist finding a 16-year-old attractive. He was in enough trouble.

The two men went back into the female domain. Marco broke the ice. "So are we all friends again?"

Tania now had an impish attitude. "We were never not friends. We just didn't like being peeped at. At least, Mr Peter, that's how it looked. The other day and all that too. I was frightened."

"The other day?" Marco questioned.

"Same thing, now you mention it," said Peter. "So I suppose I understand a bit more. I rushed into the laundry room to get some clean towels for the tennis court and found Tania up a ladder getting something down... what were they... ?" He tested Tania's loyalty.

"Pillow cases," she replied.

"That's right, they were. Anyway, I made her jump then. I suppose I've got a habit of surprising her. Anyway," he continued taking the key out of his pocket, "why doesn't Tania help me sort out Meribel's locker. She can tell me if some of the stuff belongs to the hotel."

"I'm happy to help," Tania said.

Marco and Beth stayed by the door as Peter and Tania made a joint performance of putting the key in the lock and almost turning it in unison, as if to display a new-found togetherness. Peter, though, knew those gypsy eyes. His father used to point them out in the fish market. "See that one. Don't sell to him. He's from the hills. He won't deal straight. They're gypsy. Be careful, those eyes spell danger."

It was Peter alone who opened back the full-length locker door. There were bits and pieces of clothing, all in a mess. Peter had always known Meribel to be a tidy person, but he supposed you never did know the truth about somebody until you looked in their linen basket, or in their drawers. Now that was a thought... Marcia Hunt, he knew, was tidy through and through. Meribel and Tania had witnessed that too.

"Here," Tania said, "use this laundry bag,"

He found it hard to come to terms with the fact that only 15 minutes earlier, this lively little vixen had been beating him about the chest and screaming as if he was raping her. He still couldn't follow quite why. The main thing now was to accomplish his mission and get back to the tennis court for the planned 'big match'. Yet here she was, offering him help of an unexpected nature.

"Hers?" he asked, pulling out a blouse and a shirt, a few bits and pieces, a couple of fashion magazines.

"Si!" Tania replied.

There was a short silence as they stared inside the locker. Tania broke it as she gazed at Peter with her piercing black eyes. Paco was surely right when he said not to trust them.

"I suppose you're going to tell me you've never been to this locker before," she murmured coolly.

"Never."

"Then you have a problem," she whispered.

"A problem?" he repeated in an equally low voice.

"I've already offered to help you with it."

"What problem?" Peter asked, with a degree of trepidation.

"Come on, you two. We've all either got work to do, or to go home. Just shovel it in," Marco ruled from the doorway, not hearing their discussion.

"Those," Tania said, pointing at a pair of used white knickers.

Peter didn't recognise them, but then he'd not seen every item of Meribel's underclothing. She'd have some not such good stuff she'd wear to work, he was sure.

"Meribel's, I presume…" he half-stated, half-enquired.

"No! Mine! You've put them there," Tania said behind a wicked smile.

"I've done what?" Peter replied, finding it difficult not to raise his voice.

"I'm telling you, Mr Peter, you've got the master key in your hand, you've obviously taken them from my locker and put them here, you thought, for safe-keeping. Look. No problem. No fuss. I won't say anything. Here, give them back to me, then nobody will know. But I've told you, if you want help, all you've got to do is ask. I'll keep quiet about these, though."

Peter had never been near any locker in the room before. He had no interest, or so he tried to believe, in Tania's knickers, and certainly had never opened Meribel's locker before in his life.

He felt very uncomfortable. He sensed he was being meticulously and professionally set up. Tania must have reached into the locker with the underwear screwed up in her hand. *Why?* he thought.

Now Peter shovelled the rest of the stuff into the laundry bag. Tania turned to Marco and her sister. "There, that's done," she said. "I guess we can go home now."

Marco slightly pushed Beth ahead of him back into the room and took a couple of steps towards Tania.

"Look, it's been an unfortunate end to your working day. I think you'll agree Peter was here on a mission, and thanks for helping him with that. It was a misunderstanding and Mr Peter has agreed he should have knocked. Thank God it was him, though, and not a kitchen hand or a gardener. There would have been a graphic description of both your pretty young figures throughout the hotel by now. So all's well that ends well."

Marco had heard there was a fiesta in the village a few kilometres away, close to the Barcelona Road. "Are you going to the fiesta tonight?" Tania said they probably were. "OK, look, we'd like to treat you to a bottle of wine and maybe some barbecue."

Marco stepped forward and placed a 1000-peseta note in each of their hands. He'd normally get to grope Tania for about that if the circumstances were right. Not now, though. Peter realised they had been bought off and although he was less than happy about being set up over Tania's knickers, as he was sure he had been, the event was now over, he hoped.

He looked at his watch. "Gosh, I'm due on the court in a minute. I must go. I'm sorry again to have upset you both."

"… and us you," Tania said, her black devious eyes glittering. Peter left them all in the lobby and hurried off towards the court.

The girls were leaving by the staff entrance/exit when Marco called Tania back. She readily obeyed.

"The bonus…" he said. "Shall we say it's on account?"

She knew exactly what that meant. He was not one to be too generous, so he expected her now to owe him some pleasure time for free.

"We both got a bonus. Both Beth and me. If I'd known we were on account, I'd have suggested you took Beth and I'd have your hunky nephew for a change."

Marco pointed his right forefinger into Tania's face.

"Now listen! Don't start getting cocky with me. What I've got on you would put you out of circulation for as long as your body will be able to offer sex to the highest bidder. So just don't get clever! Your sister's not a part of our deal. She got her bonus for crying when you told her to. Mr Peter is not available to you. He has girls falling after him all over the place. He won't need your favours. Is that clear? That's on account, and for me… in advance, OK?"

"Yes, patron… and I'll make out I enjoy it as much as being paid, too."

"You do that, young lady."

The words were firm. The conditions were harsh, but on an ordinary day, as most were, that suited them both. She didn't agree, though, that Peter wasn't interested. She'd see about that.

The tennis was hard-fought and close. Georgio Jnr, for him, had an average day, which evened things out. He'd been disturbed by his mother's constant bickering about why his father was putting the problem with the aircraft manufacturing at home before his family holiday.

The men played five sets in the heat, through to the cool of the early evening. Peter worked out he would not be at Meribel's before seven, unless he skipped a shower. He didn't want to do that; he wanted to look fresh and honed. You never knew, she might be there after all and there was something about putting on the style to allow for all potential outcomes.

As he showered, he reflected back on his lunch-time drama. There was a danger and an excitement about Tania. Her mischievous rant had been designed to arouse him, and he had to accept that the duo's little frolic had indeed aroused him, although he felt sure he hadn't shown it.

Their duet in Marcia and Bob Hunt's suite had had the same effect. He must make sure never to be alone with her, he told himself. She must have been descended from a witch. Maybe she had the advantage of a gypsy family of fortune tellers who had marked her cards on his account. Whatever the case, Tania spelt both danger and attraction with what she was openly offering to him. He was annoyed with himself to realise that here he was, alone and about to get out of the shower, without any physical contact, yet he was erect just at the thought of her.

His rush to get on his way soon took his mind off that. He was off to collect a letter that would decide which academic path he would take. If it was an offer to attend the Westminster Polytechnic in London, it would shape his life forever, and for others too.

He dressed in his carefully selected outfit: white jeans and a dark blue short-sleeved shirt, and blue and white leather shoes that looked like something out of the 1930s. They might well have been, because he'd bought them off a stall in Palafrugell market which tended to harbour weird memorabilia, and sometimes produce of dubious origin ferried in from North Africa and across the Pyrenees from central Europe.

He remembered he had told his mother that he wouldn't need her car, as he hadn't originally been planning to go out. Fortunately the car was there and the keys were in their usual place. She'd get a lift back after her boat trip with the Hunts, he felt sure, but he would leave a note to say that he had changed his plans.

It was about 7.15pm when he pulled up outside Meribel's parents' house. Maybe he had imagined it, but he thought he saw a shadow of a figure move behind the almost totally closed shutters of Meribel's room.

He doubted if any other member of the family dared go in there. She had established that her room was her domain. She would clean it, make the bed and keep it in good order. Living with parents is rarely a private affair, but she wanted her own space.

He walked up the path, ensuring he had a half-smile on his face in case she was watching. At the doorbell, he realised he had left the laundry bag in the car. He had emptied it out when he got back to the cottage and gone through all pockets of the garments, just in case the mischievous Tania had planted something. He had then folded things neatly.

He retraced his steps back to the car, feeling eyes burning into the back of his head. He was sure Meribel was there, not out on some new and exciting date, as she'd made out. He rang the bell and Meribel's mother answered the door. She seemed pleased to see him, which surprised him. They exchanged questions as to each other's health and how was the hotel doing. She was fine, and her husband too.

"… and Meribel?" Peter enquired.

"She's fine, dear, absolutely fine. Don't you worry your head about her. She's out and about all over the place, catching up with friends she hasn't seen for ages. She'll be off to university soon, of course, so that won't give her a moment to spare."

"Is she in?" Peter enquired.

Meribel's mother hesitated, looked up to the ceiling for a moment, then seemed to remember her rehearsed response.

"Oh no, she's out with a friend. She won't be back till late…"

"I know that's what she said to me. I really didn't know she liked bullfights and Barcelona's some way to go, but Cordobés is there tonight. I thought she wouldn't want to miss that for anything. Only what made me ask was that there was somebody in her room as I arrived and I know how protective she is about that domain… her space… so I just wondered if she'd developed a migraine or something and had to cancel. If she was here I'd just like to say hi."

Meribel's mother seemed a little thrown. "Oh no, no change of plans…" She thought for a little. "Yes, we were surprised about the bullfight, but there you are."

"Anyway, I'd best leave these." Peter presented her with the laundry bag. "Now I gather there's a letter for me."

"Yes," she said, "it looks exciting, it's from England."

"I thought it would be."

"Let me just get it for you. I won't ask you in because I expect you're rushing off somewhere yourself."

"Oh, I understand."

She slipped into the house and reappeared with a large foolscap envelope.

"Thank you very much for taking my mail in for me."

"That's a pleasure, dear"

"Right. Adiós."

"Adiós."

She leant forward and kissed him on the cheek.

"I hope the fight wasn't too gory for Meribel. You know what she's like about saving lives."

He moved backwards off the step and continued for about five or six paces so that he was facing Meribel's mother as she waved. It also gave him the chance to peep at a distance through the crack in the double garage doors. The parents' car was parked in the road outside, he noticed. He could just about make out the bonnet of a white car in the garage. *That's Meribel's,* he thought to himself. Impulsively, he looked up at her bedroom window. She was there. He knew it. Her eyes were piercing his skin through the slats in the shutters.

It didn't matter a jot really. It was rather nice for a mother to play along with a daughter's cover-up. But surely they could still meet, correspond, be friends. It seemed silly to plunge from the heights of intimacy to absolutely nothing. Time would tell. In any case, he bet Meribel would be wild with her mother if she'd heard as much of their conversation as he believed she had.

Indeed, that night the air in the Meribel household was blue. Meribel screamed abuse at her mother when she told her daughter that she hadn't known what to say when Peter mentioned the bullfight.

"You should have just said 'Bullfight? I don't know anything about her going to a bullfight, she didn't tell me where she was going...' because, dear mother, that's how it's going to be once I'm at university. I'll lead my own life. You won't need to tell my friends where I am."

Peter was busting a gut to read the contents of the envelope. He would have to drive away before he could open it, though. He drove a couple of miles towards Palafrugell before stopping in a lay-by. It was just light enough for him to read.

It was on smart headed notepaper. *"Dear Sñr Peter Martinez,"* it began. *"It is with pleasure that we confirm we can offer you a place..."* His brain blurred. He read it again. In fact about four times. He then slowly scanned the remainder. Some words he did not readily understand, but the gist was there.

It was a three-year course for about 30 weeks of the year.

He had not cried now for probably the best part of... well, it didn't matter how long. It was the day Paco didn't come home. Now tears again rolled down his cheeks. This would mean he would be leaving his mother and Marco and Virginia, and the entire environment he knew and understood.

But he'd be back, he consoled himself, for 20-odd weeks and could still help out in the hotel in the summer. He wondered if he would see the Hunts in London while he was there. The letter informed him that they had no halls of residence, but that there were many flats not too far from the 'poly', where students rented and the graduating ones passed down their tenancies to the younger blood as they moved out into the working world beyond.

He and Meribel had debated the hypothetical pros and cons in case the opportunity arose. They had always, on balance, come to the view that Peter must take up the offer if it were to be offered. So he would take it up. He was happy, but he would wait until exactly the right moment to tell his mother. He would have to get his skates on now in doing the preliminary further studies on the 'Girasol' development.

He had to take control of his excitement and drive back home slowly. Hell! He hoped his mother wouldn't still be up. He'd find it hard not to tell her. He was always honest and straight with her. But it was relatively early so there was a strong chance his news would come out during the inevitable inquisition about how Meribel was and why he had gone to see her.

As he approached the outskirts of Palafrugell, the sun had set and there was now a strange light hanging hauntingly over the town square. It reminded him that on the way to Meribel's he had noticed there was a fair in town and it was, of course, 'Feria de Agosto', the week-long town fiesta coming to its final-day crescendo.

The streets looked as though they were buzzing. On impulse, Peter decided to stop for a beer. He might meet some old friends. There were bound to be some young men and women from his school there. They had all now broken up to go their separate ways, but they'd agreed to keep in touch and have a beer every now and again. Perhaps this would turn out to be the first natural occasion.

He parked the car in a disused town garden that had become an unofficial car park. As he alighted, his heart jumped. It always did when he heard an orchestra playing Sardana music. It never failed to remind him of the last time he saw his father, and again and again the haunting memory. Paco and Maria had been so happy that night in Rosas. They'd danced Sardanas and included Pedro. He would always be touched by the happiness and unhappiness the music portrayed before it reached its crescendo, always encouraging the rings of dancers to swirl gracefully at pace.

He saw an empty table for two at the corner café bar. There were tables free because the majority of revellers were dancing and swigging sangria from the many jugs that had been spread out along the communal tables in the middle of the adjoining streets. He sat down in one of the unused chairs, from where he could see the dancers.

The waiter swung through the outside area of the bar in time with the music. Everybody found the traditional Catalan rhythms infectious. They had been brought up on the chords, and their blood, not just their feet, had learnt to tap in time with the music. That blood pulsed to the beat of an ancient drum.

"Señor."

"Una cerveza."

"Sólo uno, señor? No hay una señorita?"

No, there was no señorita and yes, it was just the one beer. Surely the world could contain single people as well as couples, or clubs and clans.

His chilled beer arrived. He said, "Santé," to himself, then, "Well done on the London result."

The beer tasted good at the end of a long hard day.

He watched the jumping, twirling circle of people. Singles were rare, he thought. Mainly they formed up in the lines as couples. It was unlikely, in the traditional format of the Sardana, that there would be someone in the gyrating circle who needed an unknown partner to take their hand. Women danced and stepped in unison with other women – maybe sisters, mothers and daughters. Men together looked like fathers with sons, perhaps widowers whose sons were supporting them in their loneliness. That brought a lump to Peter's throat.

Peter spied a splash of red interwoven with the blacks and other neutral colours worn by traditionalists who were not quite sure whether to celebrate the anniversary of a saint's death, or mourn it. It was more of a Spanish tradition to follow the mourning route rather than the celebratory one, so the flash of red really stood out. Quite refreshing, in fact, and the way it moved showed it to be happy, uninhibited, dynamic: a Ferrari amidst the three circles of the otherwise Seat and Citroen models that had formed.

Between the moving dancers, Peter picked up the red again. Below the red, which he discerned now to be a short skirt, were slim, well-formed legs.

Christ, he thought, *that's got to be Tania.*

He could still only see the young lady's rear. It would have been too much of a coincidence for two people, in whatsoever circumstances, to come into his life on the same day wearing identical shades of red. A couple of spaces around the ring was a younger girl in black, throwing her head back with abandoned, drink-fuelled laughter.

The lady in red was much more composed. Her spine was rigid yet her shoulders were relaxed. Her legs were strong and economical in their every move. The black sandals seemed to be part of her body, whereas other girls and their mothers in the Sardana ring had abandoned their shoes.

It was Tania. Her black glossy hair was now loose and dancing its own formations. There were signs of perspiration under her arms. Peter had heard that was unlikely in northern Europe now, as the girls shaved more of their bodies than some men did. Meribel had, of course, started doing that too. "It's more hygienic," was her excuse. Peter was yet to be convinced as to whether it was more sexy too.

Tania, had she followed tradition, would have had her partner to her right, in which case she'd have linked with a man who could have been her brother. Certainly, even at a distance, he and she had the same black, darting gypsy eyes.

The music was reaching its crescendo. Peter downed his beer and left the money on a plate with the bill. His plan was to move across the square, find Tania and even pull her leg about his mistake that day, and how she looked better dressed than not... but then that would have been such a huge lie.

As he got closer to her, he realised she was with Beth, her sister. Neither had seen him. The Sardana circles had broken up and the dancers were spilling back onto the pavements where trestle tables were the meeting, greeting and drinking points. The two girls were partaking of the sangria, Beth freely for her age and inexperience, Tania sipping more sedately.

The Catalan flautist played the opening bars of the next intended Sardana in the traditional way. At first each other musician appeared to play off-key, as they do. The crowd started pairing up, some ladies with ladies, boys with girlfriends, families inter-mixed.

There was a moment where Peter the opportunist saw a lull in the proceedings in which Tania was involved. He moved forward from behind her, covering the few metres' gap he had strategically placed between them. He had the advantage. She was unaware who the owner was of the strong left hand that was now controlling her movements. He took her right hand into his left and raised it as if to indicate they would form their own circle, which the rest of the Palafrugell population would join. She took the available hand quite naturally.

She then turned to find herself looking up into his strong face. If captured on a screen, it would have been scripted as a double take. "Do you want to be friends again?" he enquired.

Her eyes darted all around. They had a look of fear in them.

"Look," she said, "we shouldn't."

"Give me a good reason. I'm passing through. I fancied one Sardana set, then I'm off home. I saw you and thought we could put a seal on a bad day."

She looked like a hunted animal riveted to the spot.

The music started. Within seconds, as if in a trance, Tania moved on impulse, replicating Peter's long and short steps. They were off on the magic of their swirling roundabout.

At the kerbside, three pairs of black piercing eyes were fixed on Tania and the interloper. One pair were turned to focus on Beth, Tania's sister, who was standing out this next round of Sardanas, preferring yet another sangria on top of the few too many before.

"Who's that?" came the young man's question. He was the one who had been dancing next to Tania in the previous set.

Beth slurred, "*That* is one of the bosses who burst in, yes, really burst in on Tania and me at lunchtime when we were quietly changing in the women's changing room, because he wanted to see our bodies." There was a hint of a giggle in her voice.

"What?" The young man sounded angry.

"Yes, really."

"And did he see them?"

"See them! I'm surprised he didn't eat them, he was so interested."

"Did he touch you?"

"Yes. Well… yes but then he punched me away from him."

"… and Tania?"

"Oh, I don't know," Beth said, now holding her head as though to stop it bursting.

The young man leant forward and whispered, "Tell me if he touched Tania and I won't hurt you. You don't want to be hurt, do you?"

Beth started to cry.

"Tell me!" the young gypsy demanded.

"Yes he did. He put his arms around her so that she couldn't move."

"Was she dressed?"

"No."

"So what stopped it?"

"Mr Marco did."

"Who's he?"

"Oh, he's the patron. He's the big boss."

"So who's this chap?"

"He's the boss's nephew. He's quite lovely, isn't he?"

"Too lovely for me."

The guys behind the other two sets of black eyes had been listening to young Beth's tale. They could see Tania, now perfectly relaxed in the company of a man not of their kind. No man should interfere in their society. That was a matter of culture… and honour.

Peter and Tania laughed their way to the crescendo, encouraging each other to leap higher than each previous step.

The music stopped and the reality of the situation began to strike, like

Cinderella's midnight warning. Tania looked up at Peter and said, "I'll explain another day. Please leave now."

"Look, I said I was just here to dance one Sardana set. That I've done. Let me get you back to your friends and then I'm off home."

"No. That's the worst thing you could do."

"Oh come on. Which ark have you all come out of?"

"One that hasn't changed since the original floods. Look! Just go. It was fun. That's the way it stays. What the hell! Don't you know the meaning of suicide?"

"I just wanted you to know that one day... you never know... I may take you up on your offer."

She could see the fun in that, and a little madness more akin to her unsophisticated culture than his own.

"Mr Peter, you're mad. Now you must go. You really must." She squeezed his hand and slipped back into the crowd around the tables with the jugs of sangria.

Peter took his bearings. Shrugged and walked back to the car. He recognised the makeshift car park and turned into it. He could feel the key in his pocket, but by some quirk of instinct he thought it best to leave it there until he was nearer the car.

He had a feeling of unease. There had been an air of panic in Tania's voice.

He was about to understand why. Suddenly the back of his head felt as though it would explode. Initially, he had the strength to turn around. Pairs of staring wild eyes surrounded him. He focused away from the faces and at the bodies. One was carrying a thick branch from a fallen tree, the size of a baseball bat.

"Asi que quieres mirando chica lo hace," he heard from one of the twisted mouths. The eyes were now circling in front of him, and as he half-turned his body there was a second impact to the back of his head.

Peter felt a heavy fist in the pit of his stomach. He fell to his knees. He grimaced as he saw the branch hurtling through the air, this time towards the side of his head. The blow was horrendous. He collapsed to the ground. He summoned up the strength to open one eye. That was enough through which to see a heavy leather boot flying through the air to kick the front of his head, as though it was a football on a penalty spot, waiting for one final match-winning thrust.

He never did know how long he'd been unconscious. All he could tell was that period of time took him into a blessed oblivion, respite from feeling the terrible pain that had been inflicted upon him.

Tania had pushed her way back to where she'd left her sister and friends. Her sister was crying. "What's wrong?" Tania said.

"I've told them."

"Told them what?"

"About Mr Peter coming to look at our boobs."

"You what!"

Beth kept on crying.

Tania was horrified. "They'll kill him!"

"They said they'd hurt me if I didn't say what happened."

"Oh hell. Come on, I'll get you home. There's trouble about."

Peter moved the toes on one foot. He could hardly tell which foot. Then the other. He rolled onto his back and pulled both legs up to his stomach, which exacerbated the pain in his pelvis. He tried one arm, and then the other. As his senses started coming back to life, so did the extreme pain. He put his hand to the back of his head. God, it hurt, but his hair was dry so he presumed there was no blood. He tried sitting up, which he was able to do, but with clenched teeth.

He was perspiring heavily, so he brushed the back of his right hand across his brow. It felt sticky and in the half-light he could see it was dark-coloured. He put the back of his hand under his nose. Blood. He'd know that smell anywhere from his hunting days with his father. His teeth seemed OK.

He tried lifting himself with the aid of one hand. With the help of the other grabbing onto the handle of the car, he was able to stand up. His head was swimming at first and his legs had little strength. His eyesight had now focused in the limited amount of light. The car he was leaning against was not Maria's, yet he was sure he was in the right parking lot.

Now he could just make out the outline of his mother's car, which he stumbled towards. He instinctively felt for the car keys. They were still in his right trouser pocket. Could he drive? Well, there was only one way to find out. He unlocked the door and slid painfully into the driver's seat. Fumbled the key into the dashboard lock and it slid in. He turned it to the right and the engine fired. He could control his feet and his hands, after a fashion.

Although everything was aching, his body was becoming controllable, probably stimulated by the adrenaline rush at the prospect of getting away from the battlefield into which he had stumbled.

He selected reverse and backed into the road using all mirrors. He couldn't readily turn his head.

A small tributary of blood trickled into his left eye. He felt for his handkerchief and sat for a minute or so pressing the cotton compress hard over the wound. He removed his hand and the pad stayed in place, sticking to the congealing blood. He moved the shift into first gear and gingerly drove away.

"So where are you two going?" the lips below the wildest pair of black eyes enquired.

"We didn't know where you'd gone so we thought you'd ditched us and so we decided to go home."

"Ditched you, oh no. We don't ditch naughty girls."

"Naughty girls?" Tania asked defensively.

"Oh yes. Showing tits to the 'other' people is naughty girls."

Tania knew what her sister had told them must have been distorted by the confusion of alcohol. This was bad news. The guys were into holding kangaroo courts for those they termed 'naughty', and were known for meting out their own special brand of punishment.

"Showing…! We didn't. We got peeked at. We couldn't do anything about it. But it was all an accident and got sorted out."

"It has been now. Your peeping Tom. He's had a real accident now." Tania's heart sank and her stomach churned. *Peter. An accident.* She knew all about their structured 'accidents'. He'd be really hurt.

"You shouldn't have done that, he's my boss. Beth and I will both lose our jobs."

"So you should for letting him look at you. That's why you're naughty girls and that's why you've got to say sorry."

She knew what saying sorry meant. That was usually painful too. She'd suffered the hurt and indignity of punishment before.

"Please don't make us do that again. We'll say sorry, but it was all a big mistake. But don't make us say sorry the way you want us to. Not my sister. Please!"

The leading pair of piercing eyes took Tania by the arm. The other two each held one of Beth's arms. Piercing eyes number one was a gypsy second cousin to Tania named Toni. He spoke menacingly again. "I'll show you where you're going to be sorry."

The three cousins hustled the two petrified girls through the crowd and back to the car park. In some perverted way Toni had rather hoped that Peter would still be there, now sufficiently conscious to witness the girls being punished.

"Now you can get hurt or be nice. What's it to be?" Toni threatened Tania.

"I'll be nice."

"Then lie down there."

There was really no point in not. She knew from experience she'd get really hurt if she didn't co-operate.

"Here," she said, fumbling in her bag, "you'll need this," and handed him a condom.

"OK. It makes it nice for me," he said. "I'll do it for me. You'll understand it's not for you." She'd sold him that idea once or twice before and now he saw it as his pleasure enhancer, not having a clue as to its intended purpose. He performed… well, technically it was not rape, because she'd consented, albeit for her own good, and didn't put up any resistance. Neither did she put any feeling into the obscene act, or attempt to extract a single second of pleasure.

Toni lifted himself from the ground and stood over her. He removed the condom and threw it across the car park.

Beth had had to watch and was trembling with fear, sobbing.

Tania didn't move. "Hey, you guys want to have a good time with a big girl rather than a scrawny little schoolgirl?"

One of them looked at Toni, then the second.

"Go on. Have her on me. She shouldn't have been so naughty." Toni gave them the answer they wanted.

Then the third. He hesitated, still holding Beth firmly by her right elbow.

Petrified, young Beth cried all the way through the second performance, knowing Tania had sacrificed her own dignity to save her sister's.

Tania sensed the third of the cousins probably wanted to be the pioneer among them. The way he was holding Beth indicated she was to be his conquest.

Tania rolled on to her side and looked up at him. "Hey, big boy, come down here and show me if you can outperform your big cousins. That scrawny little sister of mine won't know if you're any good or not." He rose to the bait and unfortunately, aroused by the challenge, proved the most physically demanding of the trio.

When it was over, Toni held his hand out and helped Tania to her feet. For a moment, she thought he had some feelings after all. It seemed he felt that element of emotion too, but could not accept the risk of showing even the hint of a chink in his armour.

He released her hand and then, as though executing a Peter-coached forehand drive, but without a racket, he hit her hard across her left cheek.

Her head dropped under the shock of the stinging pain and instinctively she put her own open palm over her rapidly bruising cheek.

"That's for showing your tits to someone not of our kind. You won't be doing that again. Will you!"

She shook her head, choking back a tear.

As Peter summoned the energy to drive home, he pondered three things. Should he call in at the hospital and check if he needed a stitch or two? His handkerchief seemed pretty sodden. He thought he would.

Secondly, why hadn't he listened to what he was now sure were Tania's warnings? She obviously knew that her boyfriend, or whatever relationship she had with the lead gypsy, became manic with jealousy when confronted with somebody approaching his girl. He should have listened.

Thirdly, how would London be? He'd had a bit of a stressful time of it in the last couple of weeks. While others were on holiday to relax and recharge their batteries, he seemed to have been the battering ram for various people and their need to release tension.

Michelle…

Marcia…

Meribel…

… and now Tania. All were well tangled up in his life.

After some reflection, he decided that he should get to the hospital quickly and check the need for stitches. Then steer well clear of Tania and her young sister and get to London, and a new beginning.

CHAPTER 21

When Maria woke on the Monday morning, although she was conscious of the tenderness in her stomach, there was no continuing pain. It seemed a little heavier than her usual cycle but she could bear that, compared with the prospect of a clinical abortion.

She hadn't heard Peter come home, though she could see her car on the drive. Remembering the note, she realised he too was not rising at his normal hour. Perhaps he'd had a date she didn't know about.

In the adjoining room, Peter was, however, stirring. "Shit!" he winced. His stomach didn't belong to him. The back of his head had had a melon implanted into it, he thought. The plaster the nurse had put over the two stitches in his eyebrow felt taut. "Are you worried about not being beautiful any longer?" she had asked.

"It doesn't concern me," Peter had replied.

"Oh, come on. We get some pretty rare sights in here, and not many beautiful ones. You're rare... and the good news is that, although I had to shave your eyebrow, I've managed to put two stitches where the hair should grow and cover the scar."

Peter heard his mother get out of bed and go into the toilet. He fully expected then to hear the shower, which would signify she was in 'going to work' mode, which would mean ordinarily he would then follow her and get ready for whatever the working day had in store for him.

So it was unusual that she went back into the bedroom. *What's she forgotten?* he thought, and smiled to think that even she was human and could forget the odd thing or two these days. Maybe he dozed. He wasn't sure, but it must have been some ten minutes or so later that he realised Maria was not in the shower.

"You alright?" he called out. They often spoke between rooms like brothers with elder sisters.

There was no instant reply. That in itself was unusual.

He called out again.

"Oh! Yes, fine," came a hurried reply.

"Didn't you hear me the first time?"

"I must have gone back to sleep."

"If you're 'fine', why aren't you getting ready for work?"

She dreaded inquisitions. "I'm having a lie-in. I overdid it on the boat yesterday."

As she said that, the phone rang in the living area. It seemed she was in no hurry to answer it.

"I'll get it, shall I?" Peter called out.

"Would you?" Maria replied.

That again was unusual. She normally took all the calls at home and if it was one of Peter's girlfriends, or female acquaintances, she would often field the call for him.

Peter grunted as he put his feet to the ground. God, he hurt. He moved slowly to the phone.

"You alright?" his mother called out. "You sound as though you're moving like an old man."

"Hello," Peter answered into the mouthpiece. Phones always seemed heavy to hold but today it was extra leaden.

"Peter? Hi, it's José."

"Hi," Peter replied.

"How's things?"

"What, at this time in the morning? Never the best," Peter responded.

"Is your mother around?" José couldn't waste time on any more pleasantries.

"Well! I don't really know. Technically not. She's having a lie-in. Says she overdid the boat yesterday, but you'd know about that, I suppose."

"Yes, she wasn't 100 per cent at the end of the day."

"Let me see if she'll come to the phone or call you back. Can you hold?"

He didn't give him the option as he laid the phone down on the dresser unit.

Peter went into the doorway in his mother's room. "It's José, would you like to speak or shall I say you'll call him back?"

Maria raised herself onto her elbows. "Could you... Christ! On the life of the Virgin Mary, what on earth have you done?"

"Done?" Peter echoed. He hadn't yet looked at himself in the mirror.

"Have you been in a fight or something?"

Peter moved into the room and peered into Maria's dressing table mirror. Even he agreed that he looked a mess. His forehead was blue, verging towards a yellowish green outer ring about the size and texture of an orange above his left eye. He had a large plaster covering the whole eyebrow and there was a hint of congealed blood around his eyelid.

Thank God she can't see the rest of my body.

"I walked into a tree. Now, what d'you want me to say to José?"

"Say I'll ring him back within 30 minutes."

Peter was back a moment later. "So, are you OK?" he enquired. "Yes, fine."

"Look, you're not. I've never known you be in bed on a work day. Tomorrow's your day off. So come on. Level with me and I'll level with you."

"OK. I helped Marcia reel in a huge tuna. I was standing at a bit of an angle and, without wishing to go into the finer detail, I think I temporarily ruptured something and I've got a small problem."

"How 'small' is small?"

"Oh, Peter, you've had girlfriends with periods, surely. Well that's me. Just a bit heavier than normal."

Peter looked embarrassed. He often thought he could tell when the lunar influences were around; it was not difficult to pick up the mood swings. But he had never wanted to be privy to it.

He had yet to find a girlfriend who was prepared to complete his practical biological education. He presumed that would have to wait until marriage lifted all the barriers.

"Well, if you say you're fine then you must expect me to accept that. So I'm relying on you, OK!" He walked across and kissed her on the cheek.

"Thank you, Pedro. I love you." She paused so as not to spoil the moment. "Now you. How the hell did you do that on a tree?"

Peter was stymied for a while. "You won't believe this."

"Let me be the judge of that."

"Well, I'd been round to Meribel's."

"She did it! Little bitch."

"No. I went round to take the stuff she'd left in the locker. Oh, and by the way, Marco and I had a bit of a to-do with Tania and her sister around about lunch-time yesterday… all a great misunderstanding… but that can come later.

"Anyway, I was driving back and…" He was thinking on his feet. "… I was driving along the road between the hedges and a young deer, well I think it was, jumped the hedge and landed in front of the car. I thought I'd hit it because it fell to the ground just near the passenger wing. But by the time I'd braked and walked back, it had gone. There was a farm gate open so I ran in to see if the deer needed any help, and blow me down I ran into this tree. I actually think I was knocked out. When I came round I realised I'd hurt myself and so I took myself off to the hospital and… well… this is it."

"It looks more like you've been hit by a baseball bat. You're OK, though?"

"Yes. Like you, fine, and you can rely on that, as I rely on you."

"I'd best ring José. Why don't you shower and I'll cook you breakfast?"

"Wow, that would be a treat."

Peter returned to his room, got some clothes and went into the toilet. His routine was a regular one. Maria knew she had about five minutes before he would then go to the shower and after ten minutes or so would be back out, shaved and ready for the fray.

She phoned José, who said he was about to go into a meeting, which was good news, because she didn't really feel ready for a great post-mortem yet. She promised she was fine.

José said, "About the baby!"

That stunned Maria.

"Well, just to say that God will give us our time again, I'm sure. Next time he'll approve and he'll provide us with a beautiful little daughter." Tears welled up in her eyes. "I do love you, José."

"Listen, if you don't get back to bed you'll love an out-of-work insurance executive. So off you go. I love you too. Now take care. Rest. You looked as ill as I've ever seen you look yesterday."

"Oh thanks! You know how to make a girl feel good."

"No, seriously. I was worried about you."

"I'm fine. Speak to you soon."

"Tomorrow. I'll ring to see if you're better."

They blew each other kisses and hung up.

Maria glanced into Peter's room as she went by and saw an envelope lying on the floor. He didn't get much post. She'd missed the Sunday delivery because she had gone to the boat early and wondered if it was a letter intended for her. She bent to pick it up. She felt dizzy as she stood back up. *Stupid,* she thought. Change in blood pressure, she should have done that more slowly.

The letter slid out of the envelope into her hand.

She read the heading. *The Westminster Polytechnic.* Dear Sir... she read the first six important lines. Her mind blurred. Her eyes clouded and she swayed slightly. She replaced the letter into the envelope and put it back on the floor. This time she rose slowly, went back into her bedroom and closed the door. She knelt at her dressing table, in front of the wedding photograph of her and Paco. "Oh Father," she whispered in her mind. "Please forgive me for invading Pedro's privacy. Please tell me what I read was all something in a bad dream. Please help me to not lose my lovely son."

It occurred to her that this was not a prayer, more a selfish expression of self-pity. "Forgive me for my selfishness. Please guide Pedro on a course that's right for him and will bring pride to his father and me. Help me to encourage him on his way and provide him with enough love to save him from homesickness, and make him want to come home often."

She crossed herself as she had since she was a child and stood up slowly as she experienced a dragging pain in her groin. She put on her housecoat and the rehearsed morning routine of living and abluting around each other enabled their paths to cross like some highly planned motorcycle display at a county fair.

Passing Peter in the hallway and seeing him in a better light, she said, "God, you look awful!"

"Well, it's just as well you look good. At least one of us in the family has a bit of colour back in their cheeks." Little did he know it was where she had hurriedly rubbed her tears away.

Over breakfast he told her all about the Tania locker room scene, and Marco's involvement, but no mention of London. He'd tell her soon enough, she was sure. He said he wasn't going to play tennis today and would try and find Michelle to take over his coaching.

He was just about to leave when the phone rang. Peter looked at his mother. She indicated for him to get it.

"Hello."

"Peter?"

"Hi, José. So you can't leave my mother alone. Eh!"

"Hi, it's not José. It's Miguel Mendes."

"Shit. Sorry Miguel. Look, excuse me, I'm just leaving. I'll put my mother on. See you soon. Oh! By the way, have you got Michelle under control?"

"Peter, no man on this planet can get Michelle under control. She exudes life itself. But if was asked, how's the treatment going, I'd say she's doing fine and I'm bearing up under the strain."

"Are you serious?" Peter enquired. "I thought it was just down to you prescribing a few herbs and some acupuncture and then it was down to her."

"It is normally. But we get to the end of the session and she's all set to go out into the world under her own steam. The first time was typical, I asked what she would get up to and she said she was going to go down to the beach and look out for two or three young tourists, enquire if they'd trade weed for sex and get herself high on both."

"Does that surprise you?"

"No, not at all. It's quite common."

"So what then?"

"I said 'Please don't do that' and she asked what I'd do to prevent her doing it.

"I had no idea. So I asked her. The answer on Saturday was to take her on a picnic. Sunday was to take her to a bullfight…"

"… and today?" Peter enquired.

"Well, I really do have to work so she's agreed to stay at the hotel till about four, and then she's going to some boutique to do some modelling... or so she thinks... so I get some work done."

"I'm sorry if she's becoming a nuisance."

"Becoming a nuisance? She's terrific. I'm enjoying it. Now, where's your mother?"

Maria kissed Peter adiós and waited for the door to close as he left the cottage.

"Hi, Miguel."

"Hi, Maria. How are you?"

She explained what had happened. Miguel was delighted. "That's a combination of God and his nature performing where man is a mere imitator. Great! Now, just rest normally today. Promise!"

"Promise, Miguel. You alright with Michelle?"

"Alright? Ecstatic!"

"See you."

"Adiós."

"Oh, by the way, Michelle is modelling for Mercedes this evening."

"Good for her. Do you know what she's wearing?"

"Extremely little, she tells me. Are you going?"

"Good God, no. I've got the business to run and at the moment, if she carried on being as demanding as she has been recently, I'll go broke. Incidentally, don't throw the medicines I gave you away. I can re-store them. They're a standard prescription."

Peter walked into reception. "Buenos días," he addressed Sñr Martin. "Buenos días," he replied, without at first looking up. Then: "Sacré coeur! Have you been in a fight?"

"No! It's a long story. I saved a young deer's life and, in the process, had an argument with a tree."

"Looks more like a clout from a girlfriend who's just found out you've been two-timing her."

"I find trees more reliable," Peter said, and walked on.

He didn't need breakfast, but he thought a shot of espresso would sort him out, so he headed for the kitchen. As he walked in Juan, who was on duty, approached with a smile.

"Wow! Yesterday was a day..." and then, "... Christ, Mr Peter, who hit you?"

Peter perceived this was bound to go on all day. He'd go back into the office after his coffee and write a sign and put it round his neck. It would be fun anyway. He just hoped he didn't see Tania, because he'd have a word or two to say to her.

Juan was waiting for a reply. "It's a long story, but I ran into a tree."

"Wow, boss. Some tree! I haven't seen your mother yet. Is she around?"

"No. I don't think she's planning to work today."

"Don't tell me she ran into a tree too!"

"No. She had a sail out yesterday and I think a combination of the sun and some heavy fishing got to her. She's resting up a bit."

"Well, if she had anything to do with the tuna that's been dumped in the kitchen, at least her arms would ache. That's what I need to talk to somebody about."

Peter went back into the office, took a menu card out of the filing drawer and a marker pen from Maria's desk tidy. He wrote in large capital letters:

"I RAN INTO A TREE, YES I'M FINE, THANKS FOR LOOKING."

He found some string, punched a hole in each top corner and threaded it through, knotting it at just a sufficient length for it to be put round his neck and for the sign to balance on his chest.

He left the office and walked through the breakfast area. Marcia called across from their table, having read the sign.

"Who'd believe that! It's got the imprint of either an angry or disappointed young lady, more like."

And so the day continued. Word would get round but it would finally die a natural death.

Tania always washed through the kitchen floor as her first job of the day. Maria had worked out there was a lot of time wasted waiting for people to get up in the mornings and vacate their rooms, and that the chambermaids made the most of that by having an easy time. So she had extended their remit to deal with the kitchen area and not just bedrooms.

Juan was busy getting the tuna sorted but on his way to the stockroom had to step around Tania's precise mopping.

"Buenos días," he said. "Have you got over your traumatic experience yesterday?"

"Oh yes. I think so."

Thank God he was only talking about the changing room debacle and not the aftermath of the fiesta. The fact that she had difficulty walking was neither here nor there. Three young gypsy studs who believed the more they hurt, the more they satisfied their sexual prey were bound to have made her bruised and sore. Her satisfaction came from the certainty that the Virgin Mary would help her to get her own back. She knew who each of them was. She'd been brought up with them. But she was sure God's intention with Adam and Eve had been to provide more love and satisfaction than she had yet to experience in her life.

Tania knew very well the performance with Mr Peter in the locker room had been designed both to get his attention, and to enhance her take-home pay.

Juan interrupted her thoughts.

"He'd not need to come and peep at you," Juan advised. "He's, by all accounts, got plenty of others to feast his eyes upon, and that's no doubt with their consent. I came in halfway through, I know, but I'd say you misjudged the situation."

"Maybe we did," she said. "It was the two of us though."

"Yes, OK. Anyway. Is that all forgotten?"

"Oh yes! Mr Marco put that right," she said with a giggle.

"Have you seen Mr Peter this morning?"

"No. Why, is he around?" Her mind raced. She wondered what he might say, as this would be the first opportunity to pursue the issue he was bound to have with her having planted her knickers in the locker.

"Around. Only just. He's got a huge shiner."

"Shiner?"

"Yes. Black eye. I'd have said one of his girlfriends beat him about the head with more than a hairdryer, myself. Anyway, must get on. Got a couple of tuna to sort out." And Juan wandered off into the cold-store.

You can't get a lot of inspiration, or so you'd think, from looking down at a quarry tile floor and slopping a mop over its surface. What you do get is thinking time, and Tania's brain was racing. Toni and his two cousins made it clear they had it in for Mr Peter who, as they had interpreted Beth's story, had given them just cause. Their style would be to 'teach him a lesson' in the same way they had dealt with Tania and her sister. Toni had spoken of an 'accident'. She'd thought then, as she knew now, what he meant.

She added some more bleach to the water. The other side to this was Mr Peter's version. If he had been involved in one of Toni's 'accidents', why was he not going to the police or, at least, saying to people he had been mugged by an unidentified mob? Possibly to protect her. But why would he do that when she had made an attempt to stitch him up the day before?

The non-communicative reflection looking back at her from the glistening floor didn't help her work it out.

She put her mops and lower level tools back into the cleaning cupboard and made her way up the service staircase to start her daily chores, room by room. Ordinarily, the only stimulant would be what clothes of the female guests she could have a peep at, and which of them had indulged in their holiday sexual treats the night before. Today she had interest in neither pursuit. Other people's clothes could be looked at any time. The thought of sexual activity made her feel sick. Her sole concern was whether Peter could ever forgive her for being the cause of his grief.

From the room next to the Hunts' suite, she could see Mr Peter down by the court. He shouldn't spend so much time with the French girl, she thought. In fact he shouldn't spend any time with any other girl when she herself could give him what every young man wanted. She knew he was up for it, just like Toni and the others, except he would use his brain and heart, not just the appendage with which they were all endowed, and which God had obviously added as an afterthought, as her mother had always explained.

Her father should have shown her that side of himself. He might not have had a huge brain like Mr Peter but, as her father, he should have shown her his heart and not his body alone. She hated those nights when her mother went out to work and left her husband in charge. He'd say, "Let's put little Beth to bed, and then you can make up for Mummy not being here."

Once, in fact the only occasion, when her juvenile brain had discerned for her what was good and bad, she had said she didn't want to play the game of Mummy not being there. "We'll see about that," her father had said as he took the leather belt from his trousers. Thereafter, she'd never let it get to the point of him striking her. She'd always agree to play before that happened, although never out of desire.

Tania was short on being loved.

So why couldn't she get through to Mr Peter that she was available to exchange some real love? Her suggestion that it would only cost a few pesetas was just something she had said, thinking he might then think any involvement with her was 'safe' and without commitment. But she'd be happy with no money, and to have instead this thing called love, which she'd heard so much about.

He was probably the only male to whom she had ever wanted to communicate her availability. Although Marco was kind to her, and gave her pocket money, Peter, being more her age, should surely jump at her offers. He might even treat her nicely in return.

Peter glanced over Michelle's shoulder as they talked about the coaching she was covering for him that morning.

He was sure that was Tania on the balcony, cleaning the outsides of the windows. *That girl,* he thought, *that wild gypsy girl... with the cruel manic friends... at least she won't be anywhere near London.*

Maria phoned Marco on the internal network. It was now about 11.30am.

She'd had another couple of hours' sleep and she really felt fine. It had been sensible to rest. It had done her the power of good.

"Hi Marco, Maria."

"Sure. I can actually recognise your voice now," he said sarcastically. "What are Virginia and your plans for dinners this week?"

"You're not going to fix me up with that bloody Admiral bore again, are you?"

"Marco! He's a valuable guest. But no. I'm looking to fix a family dinner. The four of us. Call it supper, it would make it more relaxed."

"What's the agenda?"

"I'm guessing, but I think Pedro might be wanting to say something to the family." The line went quiet. Marco was wondering which way this one might go. Either Pedro had rumbled his association with Tania, and wanted to tell, or he was going to confess that he'd had devious intentions when he burst into the changing room.

"How's Wednesday?"

"I'll check with Pedro. Pencil it in. I'll barbecue here at the cottage, if you like."

"That seems a nice idea. As long as you don't finish up with all the guests queuing up because your food's better than the kitchen serves!"

By the Wednesday Maria was fine, back to normal almost. She had told José about what she thought Pedro might be planning. He said to wait and see but to be philosophical, as he knew the benefit of being more where the action is. Everything important happened in his company back in the UK, so if Peter started there it would be an enormous help in his career. The barbecue went well. Marco, as always, found a couple of bottles of Pouilly Fumé, which were just right. These days he didn't even seem to have to look at his watch. He knew exactly when 'pledge time', as he called it, was and had stuck to it.

Maria seemed shocked, as Peter had fully expected her to be when he capitalised on the family occasion to announce he'd got an opportunity to study architecture in the UK. Marco, too, was stunned. Virginia was quite congratulatory. A few moments of chilled silence hung in the air until Maria spoke.

"Well," she said. "Don't keep us in suspense. What have you decided?"

Marco looked surprised. "Well he can't go... can he?"

"Why not?" Maria asked.

"Well, who'll look after you?"

"Good God, Marco! We're talking about Peter's life. His career. I'll look after me, but I'll ensure, at a distance, he'll look after himself first and not ever forget where his roots are. Back to the question. Don't keep us in suspense. When are you going?"

Maria thought a tear came into Pedro's good eye. "Mother, if anybody's made all the decisions in my life so far really easy, it's been you. The things is, the further education I'll get in England is unquestionably better than in Spain. It would be broader and more international and more fully European. The other factor is that it would be an education in English, so linguistically I'd be better off too. Of course I know where my roots are and always will. I'd be away about 30 weeks of the year and home here for the rest, probably. I'd have not only the family to pull me back but the development too."

"So that's that," Maria said chirpily. "That's decided. We all agree, and besides I'll be able to come and see you and buy all sorts of new clothes. Here, I haven't congratulated you. Winning the place is an enormous feat. Papa would be so proud of you." She got up and kissed his forehead.

"Well, Pedro, I'm pleased for you too," Marco said, "but you be sure to get your head down over there and concentrate on your degree. There's a lot of English girls over there who, I'm sure, would be happy to get a virile Spaniard in between the sheets and never let them get out to study."

"Marco," Virginia reprimand him, "if *you'd* even been in England as a student, that might have been *your* aim, but our nephew will drink in all the culture of England and won't be giving sheets, other than his own, another thought. Won't you, darling?"

"If you say so, Virginia."

Laughter returned to the table, and the buzz of chatter as they took in this new dimension in their ever-changing family drama.

One solitary pair of black eyes glowed from behind the bushes near the hotel. They were focused on Maria's patio and the four bodies featured in the candlelight. *How could they be laughing?* she thought, almost aloud. Tania had wanted to see Peter to speak to all day. She realised that it wasn't unusual not to see him for a few days. His was an outside job and hers was inside. She wanted to say sorry for all the trouble she had caused him, first in the locker room and then after the Sardanas. She wanted to see how badly they'd damaged him so that she knew how much revenge to take on Toni and the cousins. They'd pay for that, and for reviling her. Just Toni was OK. It meant nothing. It was a sort of expected clan thing. Like with her father.

But to invite the other two to enjoy themselves at her expense was not reasonable. Her mother had said boys could give girls diseases, so she must be careful, not least to make sure she didn't get pregnant and to make whoever was with her use a condom. She'd also explained how you could steal them from machines in the toilets and cloakrooms of hotels or clubs where she might be doing the cleaning, and to store them up for the future.

Tania couldn't understand why Marco bothered with his wife. She didn't give him sex, of that Tania felt sure. So how could Mr Marco take his pleasures with her and go straight back to his tired wife and finish up in the same bed? Supposing she told Marco she would only do his favours if he moved in with her. She wondered what he'd say.

It looked as though the party was breaking up and Mr Marco and his lady were saying goodnight. Would Mr Peter go inside, or go out for a night walk? She'd watch and if he did walk out, she'd be there to speak to him. To say sorry. Even to kiss his bruises and make him feel good.

Her worst fears were compounded. They carried the dishes and plates indoors.

Maria. She was a force to be reckoned with. If she found out about Marco and Peter with Tania, she'd sack Tania and her sister. And Tania had nothing on her. But she did on Marco, and now in connection with Peter with Mrs Hunt's knickers.

Maria blew out the candles and went inside. Tania watched as the shutters were drawn. She wouldn't get to see her Mr Peter tonight, wouldn't be able to say sorry.

Maybe tomorrow. She'd cycle home now.

Indoors, Peter and Maria were talking like an old married couple. "Are you really happy about me going, or are you just putting on a brave face?"

"Look, Pedro, sooner or later you'll spread your wings. Even if you were in Madrid I'd still probably only see you for 20 weeks of the year. One day it may be only 20 minutes a week, and then you could be just a couple of miles away with a family of your own."

"You really want to be a grandmother, don't you?"

"No. Not yet. One day I want there to be someone who loves you as much as your father and I do, and to give you an heir. You know that you're the last of the Martinez line? It's down to you to keep it going with a son."

"I've never really thought about that. So, I've got a very good reason to start trying to put that right." Of course, it was said with a smile, and it had the expected effect on Maria.

"Listen, my darling Pedro, Marco and I would only be interested in legitimate heirs so that's no excuse to sleep with every girl at the polytechnic."

That brought a reciprocating smile to Peter's face.

"Mother, do you mind if I ask you a question?"

"No. But I haven't said I'll answer it."

"Why didn't you and father have more than one child?"

"I said I didn't mind if you asked a question. You, my son, need to learn. Try, 'Do you mind if I ask you to answer a question?' Then I'd be obliged to answer it. But that question, I don't have an answer to. It just never happened that we 'clicked' a second time."

There was a pause.

"You'll come and see me, won't you?" Peter said.

"I really will. And I'll so look forward to it. You'll have to clear the girlfriends out while I'm there though…"

They laughed.

Maria carried the dishes into the kitchen.

Peter said, "How about one more glass of wine?"

"That's one I can answer."

"Is there another one you can answer?"

"Oh, Pedro, it's late. What are you going to ask me this time?"

"Is there somebody, in answer to Marco's very real question, who would, or will, look after you?"

Maria drew breath.

"So it's a night for revelations… you know José… well."

She poured out most of the facts about their relationship. Peter listened intently for the best part of an hour. She missed out the miscarriage, but told him most of the other facts.

"I think I knew," Peter said eventually. "José and I have always seemed to have something in common. I've never known we were sharing the same woman… and what about his son?"

"We've met a couple of times. He's quite a quiet lad. He's a bit shy. José says he's a super golfer… could have a bright future. But there's never been any pressure for us to accept each other. José isn't ready for permanency. His career's blossoming, and doesn't need restrictions. Time will tell… Pedro, my dear sweet little boy, you look dreadful. Done in. The tree didn't do you any good whatsoever. Bed!"

"You too, Mother."

They kissed. "Lavate bien."

"Oh, Mother! Won't you ever give up?"

"Careful, or I'll 'chiquito' you. I wonder if you'll play football in England?"

"Sure, I expect I'll play for Chelsea."

Maria laughed.

That night, Maria kept her prayer a lot shorter than usual.

"Dear Father. Please ensure bon voyage for our little boy…" And then her eyes closed.

They both slept like logs.

Maria had never quite realised how their lives actually ran together. Broadly speaking, they woke at the same time. Then they fitted in to their ablution routines like gloves, enjoyed the same breakfast and normally left the cottage at the same time, just like a married couple.

That next morning was no different. Maria was feeling a lot better and had almost put her Sunday experience behind her.

Peter's body was less riddled with pain and the mound on his forehead was receding. It was at the yellow phase of bruising, still enough for an onlooker to say, "Ouch!" Maria prepared coffee and called Pedro.

"How about you taking a week off?" he suggested to his mother.

"Goodness, how could I do that… and why would I need to?"

"I need someone to hold the other end of a tape."

"What do you mean by that?"

"Well, I need to get on with preparing some ideas for the layout at Girasol. The first thing to do is to prepare a pretty accurate survey. When, or if, I get permission, I'd have enough incentive to go to a firm of topographical engineers to prepare a dimensional land survey and details of levels. Initially I need to just measure the area and, quite simply, I need someone to hold the other end of the tape."

"Does it need any skill?"

"None at all."

"So! Is that why you asked me?"

"Oh! Come on. I walked into that. No. It needs someone who would understand my signs and, well… just do what I want them to do."

"I've been talking to Marco. Have you considered Tania?"

"What! Are you mad? I wouldn't let her get within the 20-metre length of the tape if we were alone."

"Marco says she's got the hots for you."

"Well, she can keep them. That girl is trouble all the way with a capital 'T'."

Maria thought. That reaction was good. A lot of young men, especially on the rebound, would jump at the sort of open invitation Tania's Romany blood instinctively taught her to send out. *So he's going to keep some standards,* Maria thought, and was relieved.

"Why don't you speak to Carlos the gardener?" she said suddenly.

"Surely he's far too busy to take time out."

"No. Not to borrow Carlos. He's got a son, Jaimé, about 12 or 13. I'm sure he could hold a tape and he'd only cost a few pesetas."

"Good idea. Michelle can do the tennis, she's been doing it very well in the last few days, and I'll get the survey sorted. I'll speak to Carlos."

"Great. By the way, you ought to know Jaimé's deaf and dumb."

"Oh shit! Mother! Why do you do these things to me?"

"Because it's pointless you going and getting a degree before you've had as much exposure as you possibly can in the University of Life."

"Well, I know that. But I've no experience of spending time with somebody who can't hear what I'm saying, and can't argue back."

"Precisely. That's what I'm saying."

Carlos was duly asked. Jaimé was available.

"You know he can't hear or speak, Mr Peter, don't you?"

"Well, so I understand. As long as he can get used to my sign language we'll get on well."

"You know, Mr Peter, you're very kind. You get that from your mother. God will reward you one day, I'm sure."

"Carlos. Let me let you into a secret. God has already rewarded me. I'm still paying off the account."

Both men laughed off the embarrassment of the situation. Coming from the father of a handicapped child, an older man at that, it pleased Peter to get such a compliment, particularly, somehow, from someone with an artisan background.

The deal having been fixed, Peter went to the hotel to sort out the tennis reservation book, then rang Michelle's room to make sure she was up. After that, he borrowed his mother's typewriter in order to write to the poly and accept the position, which he'd have to do in English, he thought. He went into the hotel kitchen first, to grab another cup of coffee to inspire his writing.

"Sod it!" he muttered as he nearly fell over the 'piso mojado' sign. Not because he almost tripped, but because it meant Tania was about. He wasn't quite ready for such an encounter.

He was still annoyed with himself. He was usually of stronger resolve but Tania, across the square with her black hair flowing and the red of her skirt spelling the danger within, and the clinging top, had fired his male juices. No, he told himself, it was not Tania who had done that, it was the call of the Sardana music, and the rush of blood the flutes and the oboe always caused.

He reflected on the physical connection of joined hands and her vibrant, twirling body. His surprise that the hands he so often saw scrubbing had been creamed into soft silk, to be held socially, and their unexpected smoothness matched the lovely arms and shoulders.

He didn't want to admit that he felt a certain excitement in the way Tania had developed the Catalan national dance into a teasing flamenco spirit, more suited to a campfire in the plains around Madrid and Seville. Her hot body oozed the smell of hotel soap in the warm night.

The reality was, however, that a few moments' sensuous thrill had been paid for with the beating of all beatings, with a scar and bruising to show for it. So he had no wish to see Tania and had managed to avoid her since the event.

Not now. She was there in front of him on her hands and knees, scrubbing the quarry tiles. Even doing that, her body moved as teenage girls' bodies had been designed to move. She lifted her head, having heard the scuffling of sliding feet and Peter's expletives. Her hair, normally scraped back off her face when she was working, had strayed from the bone-carved comb that held it in place. She wore a gold crucifix on a delicate gold chain, which swung as gently as a pendulum to the steady, firm scrubbing movement practised over most of the years of her life, at first as a treat for her mother, then for pocket money from her grandmother. Now it was done for a living, supplemented by the pocket money from Marco, and the joy she had lately developed from her newly discovered love for Mr Peter.

He stopped in stunned silence.

She stood up, taking an imaginary camera image from a number of angles of the bruising and scarring she'd heard them talking about in the staff eating quarters. Peter had removed the plaster over his eyebrow, exposing a cut about 25mm long with a couple of neat stitches dividing the healing wound into thirds.

Tania slipped off her right rubber glove, exposing the soft silk of her hand, which explained to Peter the reason for the lack of roughness. She put her hand to his cheek, still not saying a word. She then moved it tenderly and slowly towards the yellow blue bruising. She smelt warm again. The perfume, he was sure, was Chanel. It was the only one he knew other than the one his mother wore. The light smell of rubber from the latex glove made him think of a condom. This witch had aroused him yet again.

Tania spoke first. "I'm so very, very sorry," she said as her hand strayed beyond the damaged areas and into his hairline. Right then, he could have kissed her gypsy lips and laid her on the damp floor and accepted her offerings, now with a greater need.

He held his breath. Kept telling himself that he had willpower.

"I walked into a tree," he said, getting back in control of himself.

"So everybody tells me, Mr Peter. You and I know that's not true. You're a gentleman anyway, but you're a gentleman for not telling the truth. I am so sorry I'm such bad news to you. I took some punishment too."

Peter seemed shocked. He looked closely at her face, but there were no signs. Her arms were clear of bruising and, from what he could see, standing back and appraising her body, clad in the pink and white housekeeping smock, she might have been kidding. She took his hands and held them on her outer thighs. "Here, they're almost black."

He had to concentrate, he mustn't be a slave to her sensuality.

"You mean they beat you?"

She laughed bravely. "No, they raped me."

Peter's legs went weak. "Raped! You must tell the police. The guys are maniacs! They must be put away."

Tania laughed again. "Mr Peter," she said seriously, "you really don't understand our culture. Why we've survived through the centuries is because we're banded together by blood and tradition. We interbreed, cousins with cousins, some fathers with daughters, and it's a sin to the entire Romany family to cast our eyes beyond the barbed wire around the great cultural circle.

"In the cousins' eyes, there was something between us that was spiritually not acceptable. In teaching you not to interfere with our traditions, they've also shown me why I mustn't allow you to enter their domain. To tell the police would be to sign myself a death warrant, and probably yours too."

"What about Mr Marco? A beating of this nature," Peter said, pointing to his own head and ribs and other aching areas, "could kill him."

"Mr Marco's alright. There's nothing spiritual. They'd accept it was prostitution and as long as I treat them to drinks and an occasional snort, they wouldn't see that as an intrusion into the family unit."

"So you could have saved me a lot of pain if you'd told them there's nothing spiritual between us, and I'd given you a few hundred pesetas for favours received."

Peter was hardening up to the facts and the risks. "… and another thing… they might well be asking, and so do I, whether the perfume you're wearing is stolen from a guest's room."

Tania looked hurt and shocked. "It wasn't me who told them anything about you and me, it was Beth, and as to the perfume… Mr Peter, I couldn't do that. Mrs Hunt gave me a little sampler she said they gave her on the boat. We don't steal. We'd lose our jobs if we did."

She stepped back. "If you want me to get out of your life, I don't need a few hundred pesetas to go away. But for us to both stay alive, separate lives is the only solution, and that's how it'll be, Mr Peter. But you must just know, where some girls would do anything for Elvis Presley, or Steve McQueen or Cordobes, I'd do anything for you."

Peter received that with mixed sentiments, and was about to respond with the news that he'd be the one going away when Juan appeared.

"Morning, Mr Peter," the chef greeted him as he came on duty. Then, seeing Tania: "Morning Tania." He stopped and peered into Peter's face. "You'll watch out for trees next time, won't you. But the damage is healing up well."

As he said that, Tania cleared her bucket and replaced her glove. "You'll have to excuse me, Mr Peter, I've got loads of work to do." And she vanished into the outer corridor.

Bloody girl, Peter thought. *Loads of trouble.* He'd have to have a word with Marcia about fraternising with their staff. *Well,* he thought, *at least when I'm in London I'll put all this drama behind me.*

Now the letter. He must get the letter written. It was quite short and to the point. Yes, he'd accept the position offered. Yes, he'd start in October. Yes, he'd like to be put on a communal list to flat share.

… and thank you for the confidence shown in my ability. I hope I can add something to the course myself.

He had typed the letter but signed it in ink with Maria's fountain pen.

He put it in an envelope and left it unsealed, with an idea in his head. He went out to reception and looked out on to the breakfast terrace. He could see Marcia but not Bob. He made his way across. "Where's your man?"

"He's just walked into vision."

Peter turned round to look for Bob. He couldn't see him.

"Where?"

"*You* are my man, standing right over me checking my summer cleavage."

"Funny," Peter said, with some embarrassment. "So how are you?"

"Great. I've run hard the last couple of mornings to work the tuna out of my system, but poor Bob reckons he's put on so much weight that he finds it hard to move out of bed. So I've left him to diet in peace. Why don't you join me for coffee?"

"I've just had another one too many, thank you. I'm busy."

"Do sit down. We haven't talked for ages."

"Well, five minutes, or I'll get shot."

"How's your mother?"

"Oh, she's fine now. I gather you helped to sort her out on Sunday on the boat."

"Oh, not really. She was pretty well contained by herself. I gave her a few words of female comfort, that's all. Now tell me. I've heard you'd split up with Meribel, does that give me a way in?"

"We've as near as damn it split, yes."

"What about my question then: do I get a way in?"

"Marcia. You always play with me. There's not much I can give you to match up to Bob."

Marcia looked at him with piercing, mischievous eyes. "Now who's making fun of whom?"

"Let's change the subject," Peter interjected. "Could you do me a favour?"

"Are we back to what you can offer that Bob can't?"

"No. Look, I'm being serious. I've had to write a letter in English. I'd love you to check it for me to see if I've dropped any howlers."

"I'm not going to read it if it's to some English girl you've fallen in love with and it's one of those luvvy duvvy 'missing you' type letters. I'd be too jealous."

"It's not like that. I've been offered a place at Westminster Polytechnic."

"What, Regent Street? London?"

"Yes."

"Peter, that's terrific! Is it still to do architecture?"

"Yes."

"Oh, that's fantastic! Look, you must speak to Bob."

"Would you read my letter?"

"Sure, but speak to Bob. I think either he or one of the architectural practices he uses has an intake link with Regent Street."

"Intake link? Sorry, I don't know what that is."

"Oh, you know. Vacation work experience, practical years out. Things like that."

"That sounds interesting."

"There's another thing too."

"What's that?"

"I'll get to see you all year round, not just when we come out to Spain."

Peter hadn't reckoned on that but inwardly he wasn't sorry at the prospect. He had a feeling that London might be a big, lonely place.

"Where's your house from Regent Street?"

"Dulwich. I'm not much good at distances, but I'd say about 30 minutes by car. That's the way I drive."

"Do you drive? I've never ever thought of you driving, other than the Bentley. What do you drive?"

"I've got a California soft top… and… don't suggest that's anything to do with the degree of tan I have or me wanting to attract attention to myself with the hood down, which all the other blokes tease me about. It's a Hillman car. I love it. All the blokes on the top deck of London buses do seem to pay me a lot of attention though." She threw her head back, laughing at her own situation comedy.

"Where's the letter?"

She gave it 95 per cent and said that the errors were natural ones any recipient would make allowance for. They'd also know the letter hadn't been cribbed for a perfect impression.

"Cribbed? There are so many words I don't know. It's not going to be easy."

"All you need to do is ring me. I'll translate. Cribbed means cheated, written by someone else on your behalf."

Peter was buzzing now. The bonus of it all would be contact with Marcia.

"Look, I'm really going to have to get on. I'm doing a survey of Girasol... so that I can get started on the layout design. I've got to get some things together."

"You really are serious about that development, aren't you?"

"Yes, I am! You were there at the beginning. You'll have to follow it through."

"Can I, Peter? I'd love that. I know a bit about such things. I'm sure I could help."

"Do you help Bob?"

"Heavens, no! He says my ideas are useless, then I find some months down the road that he either slips them in, in his own name, or feeds them to somebody else to. He's very jealous of other people's original thinking. Unless he's paying for it. He's beside himself you pressed ahead with The Sunflower Bay, or whatever. He reckons you stole his idea, but don't worry, I've clearly marked his card. I was there. I saw it all unveil, I'm sure the final design will be all your original idea. Hey, can I come back to see it again? Just you and me, before we go back?"

"Marcia, my beautiful friend, how do you get that time off?"

"You fix the day with Bob and I'll fix the rest."

"Marcia, I don't think it's right. The idea's good, but I'll need a promise."

"Promise coming up then. What is it?"

"Please, if we do that, please don't flirt with me. It has to be a pact, it's strictly a business trip so that you can come up with ideas."

"If it's really that important to you that I don't try to get you out of this great shell of yours where I'm concerned, then I'll have to agree to that deal. I'll try my hardest, but don't go walking into any more trees, otherwise I'll want to nurse you even more than I want to now."

"Marcia, you must be the wildest woman I'm ever likely to encounter."

"You've only tipped the surface so far, iceberg man!"

"I'm off. I can't take you anymore. Oh, by the way, can I have a serious word?"

"Oh, don't spoil the fun again!"

"Seriously. I don't think you should be so generous to the staff with access to your perfume."

"Peter. What do you mean?"

"You wear a very distinctive beautiful perfume. You apparently told Meribel to use it when she needed cheering up, and you gave a sample phial to Tania, the chambermaid. So I'm having it thrust down my nostrils by girls who don't have the charisma or style or right to try and imitate what's yours by right."

Marcia nearly split her sides with laughter.

"What's so funny?" Peter said.

"Funny? No, not funny. I'm laughing in total delight!"

"I'm lost," he said, with a wave of his hands and a roll of his good eye.

"Peter, my darling. I've wanted you to notice me so much. I'm stooping to the lowest level of cheating. They're merely my emissaries, sending messages out to your senses. Fortunately, you're finding there's no substitute for the real thing."

As she got to that part in her script, she pushed back on the arms of her chair, placed her breakfast napkin on the yet to be cleared table and walked to a position immediately to the right of where Peter was sitting. She bent down, picking a pink rather than yellow or blue region on his forehead, leant down in full view of anyone still breakfasting – even Bob, who had now emerged onto the balcony – and kissed his brow…

"There, take a deep breath of the real thing."

Imaginary cameras rolled, background music played, the camera team panned away. "Now leave fixing Bob to me. One thing more. If you're off to this Girasol of yours, would you stop off and say hi to those beautiful sunflower friends of mine? Ask them to shake some pollen your way. That might do the trick as well as the Chanel." And she threw her head back, shrieking with laughter at her own humour.

CHAPTER 22

Peter picked Jaimé up from the hotel as planned. Carlos, his father, explained in a mixture of widely-mouthed words and extensive gesticulations that he should be good, do what he was told, not get too excited and learn from the day's experience.

Peter knew the journey well by now. Jaimé sat in the front alongside him and if Peter saw something of interest, a hawk or a special tree or a new model of a car (not that they saw any Hillman California soft tops), he pointed it out and they had a silent conversation about it. Peter found he actually understood what Jaimé was saying. As an example, when Peter pointed out an eagle up in the hills, Jaimé graphically explained what the bird's beak was like, and how it could rip its prey apart, and swoop on a running rabbit.

Peter was carefully watching the road. It had now become that bumpy stretch indicating the proximity of the Girasol beach. He realised what a double handicap Jaimé had. Not only could he not speak, but he wouldn't have heard the rattling of the bits and pieces Peter had packed into the boot of the car or on the back seat.

Peter's gathering of essentials for the survey was typical of his organisational side. He'd put together six bamboo canes to be used as ranging rods, a 20-metre tape, a hammer and an old, fairly blunt hand scythe. He found a couple of rolls of white lining paper left over from the building contract in one of the hotel store rooms and purloined pens and pencils from the hotel's stationery cupboard. Marco had loaned Peter his prized binoculars, against a solemn promise that they would not be damaged or, at worst, lost. There were a couple of large bottles of Perrier water and one of the patio umbrellas and, as an afterthought, a couple of rolls of toilet paper. Jaimé suddenly became very animated and was pointing past Peter towards the fields on the left hand side of the road. Peter braked and slowed, looked to see what had caught the boy's attention.

Of course, the late summer girasols. Peter pulled the car over to a halt. Jaimé pointed at his own chest, then at the fields of flowers. He made a running movement. Peter understood. He wanted to go and see the plants (which, now at their final annual height, were bound to dwarf him), and he'd be quick.

Why not? Peter thought. He nodded. The boy turned round and looked out of the rear window. He'd obviously been trained to check for traffic. Nothing was coming so he opened the passenger door, jumped out, slammed the door and, at enormous pace, ran round in front of the car and was gone, like a dog let off the lead. He disappeared among the girasols.

He'll come back, Peter thought optimistically.

Peter remembered Marcia's request. He was really too much of a realist to put his heart into trying to remember the exact message she had asked him to pass on. He decided to walk down one of the heavier trodden avenues in between the majestic flora that lead to the vast areas of gently sloping views.

Surprisingly, he actually felt like Franco, or in a more contemporary sense, the King of Spain, inspecting the troops on one of their anniversary parade days. The sunflowers wore no medals depicting their history but he felt comfortable that he was walking amidst friends. He understood why his female companions had felt they could converse with the large, open faces before them.

The avenue here was less defined. There appeared to be a natural cluster at the end of the pathway, with no warning sign that it was the end of a cul-de-sac, developed as a freak of nature by the light breeze that sometimes blew inland and, in this case, had carried with it seeds that had fallen in a random way.

Peter had now gone far enough in this unexpected diversion. He stopped and half-turned to go back to the car. Something told him not to, to explore further.

The sunflowers blocking his way were quite close together and were joined together at about two-thirds of their height by the branches carrying just leaves which, through the summer and without disturbance, had intertwined.

He ducked under the bridging foliage and found himself in a natural clearing encircled by the sunflowers.

A shiver ran up his spine. *No, it's not possible.*

But it was. He had ducked his way under two partners in a Sardana circle.

He turned and looked back. The plant on the left as he looked out of the circle was the height, or thereabouts, that his childhood memories indicated would have been his father's. To the right as he looked from the inside of the circle was his mother, on her left it was Marco, then Virginia. Carlos the mayor was proudly holding his wife's hand high, could it be Miguel and Michelle next? And then there were five or six completing the circle who were not identifiable.

Were they images from the past? He realised that their heads were slightly turned outwards, looking towards the upper slopes of the fields and over the hill.

"Good God!" He actually spoke out loud. The future. Of course. This was no historic family Sardana circle, it was an indication of the family chain yet to come.

He turned about and impetuously approached Paco. He lifted his right hand and gently brushed the sunflower's face. He turned his open palm to bring it into his own field of vision.

It was what Marcia had suggested. His palm was a deep ochre colour.

"The family's pollen."

Peter nearly jumped out of his skin. Something was pulling hard on his shirt-tail, which had come untucked as he entered the circle. It was the silence attaching to that which made him start. He turned, expecting to see some wild animal about to take its revenge on him for being a party to so many killings on hunts gone by.

If Jaimé could have spoken, he would have shown his agitation with Peter. "Come on," he might have said. "I've been looking all over. I thought we had a job to do."

Whether it was relief or being so suddenly returned to reality, Peter didn't know, but it made him laugh.

"Señoras y señores es hora de que me vaya." He made his excuses to leave. All that remained was to say a final adiós to his father. The others were still within reach.

He kissed the palm of his pollinated right hand and patted his father on the top of his head.

"Come on, Jaimé. Let's go and get the future sorted out."

Jaimé looked confused. Peter held out his left hand and the youngster instinctively placed his right one into it. He didn't need to duck out of the circle. He politely allowed Peter to lead the way. Neither looked back. Both were going into the future along the open path, which Peter retraced with ease. The way to the car and, Peter suspected, the future too, was laid open.

ABOUT THE AUTHOR

He said he couldn't bring himself to say it, which is out of character. But I suppose one is bound to be coy when you are unsure as to whether a storyline you have thoroughly enjoyed putting down on paper may appeal equally to others too. Certainly his first enforced attempt at recording a sort of biographic history about him and some friends in early life, *Blokes, Jokes and Forty Stags*, turned out to be quite an epic effort. Principally, it was written for a limited readership of the twenty blokes who were the subject of the book, which was hailed a success by them.

Their message seems to have been that he should go further and so he got round to his first novel *Last Sardana*, its sequel *Sardana Encore*, and it becomes a completed trilogy with its addition of *Sardana Renaissance*.

Personally, I have been gratified by being alongside my husband's very successful business career founded upon his expertise as a Chartered Surveyor. I've loved being able to read books by established authors, taken from the shelves of WHSmith, Waterstones, and the like, and now on my Kindle, in the exotic places dotted around the world where the excuse has been that he writes better on holiday, and in the sun. That's in fact where Last Sardana began. On the Costa Brava, in the 1970s, with him turning to me and saying "What do you think that chap does?" indicating a fellow hotel guest the other side of the pool. It was a few years later we were there to find a sunflower crop to photograph, on which the book covers were to be founded.

His thoughts and inventiveness have, as always, escalated to the now six Sardana novels, and it's not untypical that, because his writing is a hobby, if the books sell, it is intended to commit part of the income to the charities in which we have interest.

Hope you enjoy.

Dean Harwood